Three billiona
royal ancestry
magnificent d
are as untame

THE

PRINCES

The story begins with:

"*The Sheikh's English Bride*, by Sharon
Kendrick, delivers a fiercely sensual love
story…from hot love scenes to exotic
locales to a happy ending, this book will
satisfy readers until the last page."
—*Romantic Times BOOKReviews*

THE

Desert

PRINCES

SHARON KENDRICK

DID YOU PURCHASE THIS BOOK WITHOUT A COVER?

If you did, you should be aware it is **stolen property** as it was
reported *unsold and destroyed* by a retailer. Neither the author nor the
publisher has received any payment for this book.

All the characters in this book have no existence outside the imagination
of the author, and have no relation whatsoever to anyone bearing the
same name or names. They are not even distantly inspired by any
individual known or unknown to the author, and all the incidents are
pure invention.

All Rights Reserved including the right of reproduction in whole or
in part in any form. This edition is published by arrangement with
Harlequin Enterprises II B.V./S.à.r.l. The text of this publication or any
part thereof may not be reproduced or transmitted in any form or by any
means, electronic or mechanical, including photocopying, recording,
storage in an information retrieval system, or otherwise, without the
written permission of the publisher.

This book is sold subject to the condition that it shall not, by way of
trade or otherwise, be lent, resold, hired out or otherwise circulated
without the prior consent of the publisher in any form of binding or
cover other than that in which it is published and without a similar
condition including this condition being imposed on the subsequent
purchaser.

M&B™ and M&B™ with the Rose Device
are trademarks of the publisher.
Harlequin Mills & Boon Limited, Eton House,
18-24 Paradise Road, Richmond, Surrey TW9 1SR

THE DESERT PRINCES © Harlequin Enterprises II B.V./S.à.r.l. 2010

These novels have been published in separate, single volumes in the
UK as follows:

The Sheikh's English Bride © Sharon Kendrick 2007
The Sheikh's Unwilling Wife © Sharon Kendrick 2007
The Desert King's Virgin Bride © Sharon Kendrick 2007

ISBN: 978 0 263 87728 1

012-0610

Harlequin Mills & Boon policy is to use papers that are
natural, renewable and recyclable products and made from
wood grown in sustainable forests. The logging and
manufacturing processes conform to the legal environmental
regulations of the country of origin.

Printed and bound in Spain
by Litografia Rosés S.A., Barcelona

The Sheikh's English Bride

SHARON KENDRICK

Sharon Kendrick started story-telling at the age of eleven and has never really stopped. She likes to write fast-paced, feel-good romances, with heroes who are so sexy they'll make your toes curl! Born in west London, she now lives in the beautiful city of Winchester – where she can see the cathedral from her window (but only if she stands on tiptoe). She has two children, Celia and Patrick, and her passions include music, books, cooking and eating – and drifting off into wonderful daydreams while she works out new plots!

Look out for Sharon Kendrick's latest exciting novel, *The Royal Baby Revelation*, available in June 2010 from Mills & Boon® Modern™.

To Fiona (passenger) Hartley –
inspirational walking companion and general
bonne amie

CHAPTER ONE

XAVIER dangled the skimpy pair of panties from an out-stretched finger and raised a quizzical black brow at the pouting blonde.

'Aren't you forgetting something, *cherie?*' he murmured, in the outrageously sexy accent which sometimes caused people to ask whether he did radio voice-overs in his spare time. The answer, of course, was no—Xavier de Maistre did not need to dabble in the media to supplement his already vast income.

Only once had he exploited his sensually beautiful dark face and muscularly hard body—when he had been talent-spotted as a teenager, walking down the Champs Elysées. He had been paid a fortune to advertise an aftershave, but had astonished the world by turning down the many lucrative offers which had followed the campaign's massive success. Instead, he had taken the money and used it to found his property empire, which was now one of the biggest in the world.

The blonde parted her lips. 'Don't you want to play that game any more?' she questioned huskily.

Xavier's cool expression did not waver. Did she imagine that nothing had changed since their affair had ended last year, and that he would have stayed the same instead of moving on? That he was turned on by the fact that she had arrived—supposedly for coffee and a 'catch up'—and then left the most intimate item of her underwear in an exquisite heap on the polished floor of his Parisian apartment?

His mouth curved in derision. Ex-lovers could be so *boring*. Could anything be less of a turn-on than the thought of having sex with a woman you had tired of?

Yet, when she had telephoned him yesterday, he had readily agreed to a meeting. A year had elapsed, and so he had assumed they'd be able to have the civilised drink she'd suggested. But from the moment he had seen her—the expression in her eyes and the oh-so-obvious way she had sat squirming and drinking coffee—he had guessed what she wanted. He sighed. Some women just never let up

'I think we exhausted all the possibilities of that game a long time ago, don't you?' he replied evenly, his black eyes glinting. 'Nice try, *cherie*—but maybe you should replay it with a man who can appreciate you— as you should be appreciated.'

'Xavier—'

But he stayed her with a slight shake of the head. 'Didn't you say you had a plane to catch?'

Xavier could read the momentary indecision which flitted across her lovely face. She was wondering whether he was really turning down the opportunity to have sex. But she was also an intelligent woman, and maybe she recognised that there was no point. That some things were best left unsaid, and at least that way you left with your dignity intact.

So she shrugged and took the panties from him, and began to wriggle them on underneath her pure silk skirt—and at that moment Xavier's resolve wavered and he almost changed his mind.

It would have been ridiculously easy. There was a bedroom located at the far end of the corridor, with a large bed with crisp Egyptian cotton sheets and views right down to the River Seine.

Xavier owned the entire building, and it housed the offices of his empire—but he maintained a luxury apartment in the penthouse, hence the bedroom. The excuse he used was that sometimes his business deals went on through the night—he needed to have a place to sleep and he wasn't crazy about hotels.

It was well known in the city that he entertained his women there, and its presence only added to Xavier's legendary status as lover-extraordinaire. He was a man with a huge appetite for all the good things in life—and he had worked hard to get to just this place.

He turned to look out of the window, where the vast stretch of the river glittered and glimmered in the afternoon light.

From here he could see the boats which glided through the sleek waters, filled with awestruck tourists as they overdosed on the beautiful monuments which lined the river. But Paris had that effect on people. It was a city that infused his blood, his heart and his soul—a place which engaged him more than any woman ever could. He frowned, realising that he couldn't remember the last time he had made love.

So why turn down this opportunity? mocked a voice in his head.

Maybe because it *was* too easy. Xavier had never liked anything which came too easily—probably because nothing ever had.

'I don't suppose I'm ever going to see you again, am I, Xavier?'

The blonde's voice broke into his thoughts and his black eyes narrowed as he slowly turned around, acknowledging that her particular appeal had faded for ever and knowing that he shouldn't be surprised. It always happened. No matter how beautiful or accomplished his lovers, his appetite always grew jaded. Was it that once he had conquered them there seemed nothing left worth staying around for? A challenge, always a challenge—and, once conquered, there was always another just waiting...

'Who knows, *cherie*?' he murmured, with a lazy shrug of his shoulders. 'Sometimes I am lucky enough to travel to New York. Maybe we could have dinner next time I'm in town?'

They stared at one another, both knowing that this would be the last time they would meet. But what did she expect? She bit her lip. 'Sure. You're a bastard—do you know that?' she said softly.

'Am I?' he queried. Then the phone began to ring and he turned his back on her to answer it.

'*Oui?*'

He frowned as he listened to what his assistant was saying.

'I have someone down here who would like to see you, Xavier.'

Without an appointment? Xavier stilled, for he had an instinctive distrust of being taken by surprise. And what the hell did Security think they were playing at?

'Not another damned journalist?' he snapped—for the building had been practically under seige for a couple of weeks after France's biggest-selling weekly *Bonjour!* had published some snatched balcony photos. The pictures of Xavier sleepily buttoning up a pair of faded old jeans seemed to have found their way into the national consciousness, and women were downloading the images off the internet. Given the country's fierce privacy laws, the matter was currently in the hands of his lawyers.

'No, it's no one from the Press,' said his assistant.

'Well, who is it, and what does he want?' he snapped.

'It's a she, and she won't say. She says she wants to speak to you personally.'

'Oh, does she?' Xavier lowered his voice. 'Do I know her?'

'She says not.'

'I see.' Just the fact that his assistant had not kicked the unexpected stranger out spoke volumes. Xavier only employed people whose instincts he trusted, and he was always prepared to listen to them.

His gaze flickered over to the blonde, who was still staring at him with a sulky expression, and he wondered how the hell he was going to get rid of her. Maybe this unknown woman was a blessing in disguise—presenting him with a legitimate reason to seamlessly extricate himself from this awkward situation.

'Tell her to wait,' he said smoothly. 'I'll be down in a little while, when I have finished here.' He put the phone down.

The blonde turned on him and nodded her head slowly. 'You've got someone else. Of course you have. How stupid of me.' She gave a hollow laugh. 'Did I somehow imagine that you'd still be available a year later, maybe pining for me, and hoping we could pick up where we left off?'

A shadow passed over his dark face. 'I never promised you anything, Nancy. I didn't realise that there was going to be some kind of *problem*.'

'That's just the trouble,' she said softly. 'You create the problem because you're so damned *good*. Goodbye, Xavier—and thanks for the memory.' And she walked out of the room with her head held high.

Xavier's eyes narrowed into ebony slivers as he heard the elevator whirring into action to take her downstairs.

Had he acted dishonourably? No, he had not—to have been dishonourable he would have availed himself of her body today and then sent her on her way. He felt the ache of sexual frustration and knew that other men would think him a fool.

But Xavier was careful. He was fastidious in his choice of lovers, and he had only two rules when it came to making that choice: that they must be very beautiful and that there must be no deep emotional attachment or commitment. He made it clear very early on that he was neither interested in love nor marriage, for he had scant experience of the former and no wish to try the latter—and woe betide the woman who attempted to change his mind.

Raking his hands back through his hair, he felt the welcome subsidence of desire. The memory of her would soon be forgotten. He would have his assistant bring him coffee and he would listen to what this unannounced woman wished to say to him.

And then he would go home and take a long, hot shower before going out for dinner. Xavier gave a brief, hard smile at his reflection in the mirror.

Wasn't freedom the most delicious thing?

Perched on the edge of a scarlet sofa which clashed with the expensive suit she was wearing, which she still wasn't quite used to, Laura glanced around.

Over the past few weeks she had had a crash-course in expensive luxury, which had culminated in a stay in an ancient palace in a wildly dramatic country. She had thought that such opulence couldn't be topped—but the offices of Xavier de Maistre came pretty close.

The huge room resembled a luxurious home, rather than the nerve-centre of the successful corporation it undoubtedly was—with cream walls and sumptuous fittings. The chandelier which glistened and danced from the high ceiling looked priceless, and the rather old-fashioned oil paintings of horses and riverbanks gave the place a very traditional and masculine feel.

Carefully, Laura smoothed her fingertips down over her new silk skirt, still getting used to the feel of it. Touching the sensuous material made her shiver—but then these expensive new fabrics felt so different against her skin.

She was scared—or maybe nervous would be a better way to describe it—but she was confident that she was well prepared. Preparation was the number one lesson of being a good lawyer, and although she might not be a great success in other areas of her life Laura had worked very hard to become a good lawyer.

Her mind skated over what she already knew about Xavier de Maistre—international businessman and playboy, and France's reluctant sex-symbol.

A powerful man, with a powerful reputation. He held a vast property portfolio in Paris—as well as in London and New York—and recently the papers had been speculating that he was soon to start a low-cost airline, operating out of Orly airport.

Which meant, of course, that he might not be impressed by what she was about to tell him—and the money which might soon be his. Money—certainly in Laura's experience—only really mattered if you didn't have very much of it.

She heard the lift doors slide open and sat up expectantly, but it was not Xavier de Maistre who emerged but a beautiful blonde woman, who gave Laura a look which was halfway between sympathy and envy.

'Take a tip from me, honey,' she drawled. 'He's great in the sack—but men like de Maistre are *bad news*!'

'I'll bear that in mind,' said Laura politely, though her heart had started hammering, adding to her already nervous state.

Xavier's cool-looking assistant had scrambled to her feet—as if she was about to rugby-tackle the blonde—but the woman was already flying out of the revolving glass doors, so the assistant gave Laura a *can-you-believe-it?* shrug and sat down again.

Laura blinked—because to be honest she didn't usually inhabit the kind of world where women flounced out of sleek offices, giving opinions on the sexual prowess of the man in charge of them!

'Is this an inconvenient time?' she questioned awkwardly.

'But surely you do not care whether it is inconvenient or not?' challenged a soft, silken voice from behind her. 'Since you walk in off the street, demanding to see me— as though I am as accessible to you as turning on a tap.'

Laura rose to her feet and turned around, her mouth

opening to voice her rehearsed little apology—but the words froze on her lips. Of course legendary playboys were always going to be mouthwateringly good-looking, and his reputation had already preceded him—but the reality of seeing Xavier de Maistre in the flesh for the very first time hit her hard. Harder than she had expected. Laura blinked at him foolishly, like a woman who had never seen a man before. But in truth didn't it feel a little like that, because she had never seen anyone quite like *him*?

Legs slightly parted, hands splayed rather arrogantly on narrow hips, he stood like a man with all the confidence in the world—his whole stance one of sexual appeal and authority.

She had seen photographs of Xavier de Maistre—a whole glossy black-and-white set of them—and remembered dispassionately noting a curved beak of a nose and a mouth which was both sensual and cruel. She had known that his skin was darker than most of his race, and now she knew why. But what she had not been expecting was that his physical presence should be so…so…

A peculiar feeling washed over her.

So *overwhelming*.

His deep olive colouring contrasted against the pale and exquisitely cut suit he wore, which was set off by a silk shirt and silk tie. Yet, although he carried the outfit off with the kind of sensual panache the world automatically expected of a Frenchman, his hard and lean body seemed almost too *rugged* to be constrained by the expensive clothes. As if he should be wearing something much rougher, and more basic, or…or…

Or he should be wearing nothing at all!

Now, what on earth had made her think *that*? Laura didn't do the sudden lust thing—and hadn't that been thrown in her face as both her strength and her weakness? Her eyes widened. She was shocked at the progression of her thoughts, but unable to tear her eyes away from him.

He seemed to dominate the room with his compelling charisma, but it was his eyes which drew her in the most— brilliant black eyes that had her fixed firmly in their sight, the coldest and cruellest eyes she had ever seen.

'You do not answer me,' he observed. 'I should have thought that someone who had the temerity to walk in off the streets expecting to see Xavier de Maistre would have had a million smooth remarks to make.' *But your eyes are too busy devouring me,* he thought, without surprise.

With an effort, Laura dragged her mind back to the real reason she was here. 'I know this is an unconventional approach,' she conceded.

So she was English. 'Such understatement is typical of your country,' he observed smoothly. 'Are you selling something?'

She stared at him, shocked. Did she look like a saleswoman in this outfit, which had cost as much as she normally earned in a month? 'No.'

He was staring at her quizzically, but inside he was racking his brains. Had he met her? *Non.* He would have remembered. His eyes ran over her in swift assessment—yet he was having difficulty categorising her, and he was perplexed as to what made her seem so... He frowned. So *different*.

Was it her hair? A deep, dark mass which was lit with red, making her skin look almost snow-white against its intensity? Or was it her eyes—surely the most beautiful eyes he had ever seen? Large and wide, and as green as the most expensive emeralds which were for sale in the jewellery shops in the Avenue Georges V, just along the road.

Her figure was slim, but unfashionably feminine—with rounded breasts and a tiny waist which made the most of the curve of her hips. Clearly she had dressed to suit her shape, for she was wearing a suit—but a suit made of claret-coloured silk, which took the edge off its functional nature. With it she wore a wicked pair of shoes, made of the softest and sexiest suede he had ever seen. Their high heels accentuated the curve of her narrow ankles, and Xavier suddenly got a vivid and erotic image of what it might be like if those ankles were wrapped around his naked back...

He swallowed, and cursed himself for not having satisfied his sexual hunger earlier, when he had had the chance. But he had always prided himself in being able to quell desire at will, and he did it now.

'Haven't you heard of the telephone?' he questioned sarcastically, in an accent as smooth as honey, underpinned with steel. 'Didn't it occur to you to try the normal channels to set up a meeting with me?'

And risk him questioning her about just *why* she wanted to see him? He might have accused her of being mad—and wasn't there a part of her which wouldn't have blamed him?

'Of course it did,' she answered carefully. 'But I had my reasons for this somewhat unusual approach.'

'Did you? How very intriguing.' His eyes narrowed, for there was something about her attitude towards him that he wasn't used to, and he couldn't quite put his finger on it. Because she was not quite as adoring as women usually were? Or maybe because she was not displaying quite the right amount of deference? 'Who are you?' he questioned softly.

His black gaze seemed to scorch over her skin, and suddenly Laura wasn't sure. The mind which had been trained to sift information and compartmentalise it suddenly became a jumble as her thoughts trickled through it like a sieve.

All she was aware of was the magnetic quality of his stare, and the coiled power of his hard body, and the way that it seemed to make her want to…to…

It made her want to despair—because this was business; strictly business.

Or was it?

Because if she looked beyond the professional to the personal for once she could recognise the impact of what she was about to do. And somehow this didn't *feel* quite like business.

Didn't the information she was going to give to

Xavier de Maistre have the potential to change his life—
or certainly the way he thought about life? Laura knew
that she must play this very carefully—she *must*—
because she was in possession of emotional dynamite,
and she did not want it exploding in her face.

Extending her hand towards him, she gave her most
brisk smile, which she hoped masked her sudden lurch
of misgiving and the effect he was having on her.

'My name is Laura Cottingham,' she said.

'Laura,' he repeated, rolling the 'r' around his
tongue and somehow making her Christian name
sound unbelievably sexy. Black brows arched in
question as he caught her slim fingers within his grasp
to shake her hand, allowing his thumb to slide over her
narrow wrist, where he could feel the rapid beating of
her pulse. She was as slim as a young tree, he
thought—and probably just as supple. 'Do I know you?
Your face is unfamiliar to me, and I never forget a
beautiful face.'

Beautiful—her? Expert cosseting expressly for this
unusual job had brought out the best in her, but Laura
would never have described herself as beautiful. How
could she when all her life she'd been chasing her tail,
trying to make something of herself? Only to fall
straight into an unsuitable relationship with someone
who'd made her feel positively *ugly* inside.

Her throat constricted as she felt the warmth of his
skin, the subtle caress of his fingertips, and she pulled her
hand away. 'No,' she said breathlessly. 'We've never met.'

'So why are you here?' he questioned, as his black gaze seared over her like a spotlight. 'Why do you even now hesitate to tell me your business when most would have babbled it for fear that I would kick them out onto the *boulevard*?' he said softly. 'I am intrigued, Mademoiselle Cottingham, and intrigue is such a tantalisingly rare sensation for a man like me.'

A man like me. He was arrogance personified, and yet he had the looks and the charisma to be able to get away with it. How much would he be forgiven, she wondered, simply because his eyes were like dark fire and his face was that of a fallen angel?

Laura shot a look at his assistant, who was watching and listening to the proceedings with rapt attention— even if she was pretending not to. Concentrate on the job, Laura told herself.

'I'd prefer it if we spoke alone,' she said.

Now, why would that be? Xavier's eyes narrowed. Did she think that her beauty allowed her to simply name her terms? And then he stilled as another, darker possibility dawned on him—one which had been tried and had failed on many occasions.

'You're trying to tell me it's a paternity claim?' he demanded softly, and saw her recoil in something like shock. 'You are here on behalf of a girlfriend?'

'No, no. Nothing like that.' Laura shook her head, but then realised with a sudden sense of confusion that unwittingly Xavier de Maistre had put his finger on *exactly* what it was. Just not in quite the same way as he thought. 'I simply think it's better if we have this conversation in private.'

His eyes fixed on her assessingly, as if he were trying to look deep into her mind and read her thoughts—so that by the time he dragged his gaze away Laura felt as if she had been stripped bare.

'*Eh, bien.* We will go into my office, *cherie*,' he agreed softly. 'But it had better be worth it—for I do not like having my time wasted.'

He turned and began to walk towards a door at the far end of the large room, and—her heart beating with nerves at the thought of what she was to do—Laura picked up her briefcase and followed him into an inner sanctum.

'Shut the door,' he said, turning round to watch her wiggle her way in. Had she deliberately worn a close-fitting skirt and high heels, knowing that they would make her walk in a certain way that all red-blooded men would find irresistible?

Laura pushed the door to and faced him, suddenly feeling daunted by the fact that she really *was* alone with him. He hadn't asked her to sit down, so she stood in the middle of the vast room, holding her briefcase and feeling like a traveller who had just missed her train.

'It's kind of you to see me so promptly, Monsieur de Maistre,' she said softly.

'I can assure you that it was not *kindness* which motivated me—it was convenience. You see, you did me a kind of favour, Mademoiselle Cottingham. You provided me with an escape route from a situation which had become rather…tedious.' Black brows were raised imperiously as he waited for her to pry, as women inevitably did—particularly when they were scoring points off one another. But, to his surprise, she did not pursue it. Just gave him a cool, almost glacial smile, which was not the way that women usually looked at him at all.

Laura knew that it was not her place to comment on his arrogance—or to pull him up on his cruel hint about getting rid of the blonde. Yet she suddenly felt an overwhelming pang of sympathy for the woman who had flounced out of the office. He was an easy man to desire, she suspected—and a hard man to leave if he rejected you.

'I would have made another appointment if today had been inconvenient,' she said quietly, as she began to open her case. 'But my brief was to make sure that I spoke with you face to face.'

Something in her tone and her words aroused Xavier's survival instincts, and he suddenly realised his first impression had been right—there was something in her demeanour which did not add up.

People usually came to him because they wanted something. When a man was as powerful and as wealthy as he was, there were few things in life which came without a price.

Laura Cottingham's manner was pleasant, but brisk, efficient and matter-of-fact—the manner of someone who was doing the giving, not taking, and suddenly he was intrigued. *My brief*, she had said.

'Your brief?' he shot out.

'Yes.'

'You are a lawyer?'

'Yes.'

He paused very deliberately. 'I don't trust lawyers unless they're working for me,' he said softly.

'That's probably a very healthy instinct.'

She obviously expected him to laugh, but he did not. His laughter was rare, and usually controlled—for laughter made you vulnerable and he was never that. 'Why did you not contact my own lawyers if it is a legal matter?' he questioned silkily.

'Because…' Laura hesitated. 'Because this a delicate matter for nobody's ears other than your own.'

Her words were tantalising—deliberately so, he suspected.

'How intriguing,' he murmured. 'Tell me, do you like to tease and play games? Are you like this in bed? Or are you going to stop being coy and tell me more?'

Laura flushed deeply at his sexual taunt, but she was in no position to flounce out—and the best way to deal with such behaviour was to ignore it.

'Certainly, Monsieur de Maistre,' she said crisply. 'I'm actually here on behalf of someone else. As a representative of Sheikh Zahir of Kharastan.'

Xavier stilled. He was rarely surprised by anything, but this woman had succeeded in doing just that, and—

inexplicably—his heart missed a beat. A sheikh? Yet he had no business interests in that part of the world. 'I do not understand,' he said softly.

'I don't expect you to. But I will attempt to explain.' Laura took a deep breath, remembering her plan for how best to broach this. 'You have heard of Kharastan, perhaps?'

'I have heard of most countries.' He stared at her unhelpfully.

'You know that it's an extremely wealthy mountain state, which borders on the ancient country of Maraban?'

She was met with an obdurate expression of pure steel.

'I do not need a geography lesson from you,' he said, in a voice which was soft with menace. 'And neither do I need you preparing the ground to cushion the effect of what it is you are about to say. You have been granted access to me and my time is precious! So, either you tell me why you are here, or you get out.'

Laura had been intending to lead into the subject gradually—but she could see the impatience sizzling from him, the irritation which was burning from his black eyes, and she knew that there was no time for any groundwork.

'I'm here to talk about your father,' she said quietly.

Xavier froze as if she had turned him to stone, but beneath the stone his heart gave a strange and painful lurch as she strayed into forbidden territory. He took a step closer to her, lowering his voice so that it was an accusatory whisper.

'How dare you bring up a matter as personal as my parentage?' he questioned menacingly. 'You, who are nothing more than a stranger to me. How *dare* you?'

Laura didn't flinch beneath the accusation which burned from his eyes, telling herself that he had the right to be angry, that anyone would have been angry in similar circumstances.

'I am merely carrying out orders,' she answered, and prayed that she wouldn't stumble over these precious and important words. She was aware of the burden of responsibility which lay so heavily on her shoulders, and suddenly realised that her boss had been economical with the truth. There was no such thing as 'easy money'.

He took a step towards her—the silent menacing step of a predator. 'Whose orders? *Dites-moi*,' he hissed. 'Tell me what you know.'

Laura drew a deep breath, realising that there was no way to prepare for this, or cushion against its impact. He needed to hear the facts in all their stark and compelling simplicity.

'I'm here on a mission because of who you are—or who we think you are. You see, there is reason to believe that you are the son of the Sheikh of Kharastan,' she said quietly.

CHAPTER TWO

XAVIER felt a strange sensation as Laura spoke to him. He could hear a muffled roaring in his ears, and yet he felt curiously detached from his own body. It was as if he had floated up to the summit of the room and was looking down on the scene, in the way people sometimes described a near-death experience.

He was a man who had—necessarily and ruthlessly—subdued anything which came close to emotion. Had that not been the way he had been taught to survive? Yet now he was experiencing feelings which were unsettling him and threatening his equilibrium—and her words seem to echo round and round in his head.

'There is reason to believe you are the son of the Sheikh...'

All he could see was the woman who had come out with such a shocking announcement, with her pale face and her thick dark red hair.

'You lie!' he breathed.

'No! Why would I lie about something like that?'

Logic and reason told him that her statement was nothing but far-fetched fantasy, and yet in the back of Xavier's mind was a nagging doubt which stubbornly refused to be silenced.

For hadn't he always felt that he was different?

He had grown up in poverty in the Marais, in a time before it had become one of the most fashionable places in Paris. During Xavier's youth there had simply been lots of old and dirty houses where artisans would live and work—surrounded by small restaurants, narrow streets and few shops. He and his mother had lived in a tiny garret originally meant for servants—but amid the squalour his mother had worked every hour to provide a good home for her only child.

The exterior of the house in which they'd lived might have been crumbling and depressing, but inside it had been a haven. The walls clean and bright, the curtains crisp and perfectly pressed. There had always been soup or a *pot au feu* bubbling away on the stove—a jug of fresh flowers on the table.

And if his mother had been bitter—so what?—it had been easy to escape from the occasional tense atmosphere at home. If you walked south a block or two you would get to l'Île de la Cité, with the dizzy, imposing height of Notre Dame and the lavish, stained glass splendour of La Sainte-Chapelle.

Sometimes Xavier would go there after school and look at the soaring monuments, and vow that one day he would break free from his poverty stricken world and live surrounded by beauty and space.

His mother had forced books upon her clever son—'For only in education lies an escape from poverty', she'd used to tell him—and she had discouraged him from loitering around the streets with other boys his age.

But Xavier had not cared for the company of his peers, and they had always viewed him with a certain degree of suspicion—his lofty, ambitious attitude and his outstanding looks marking him out. The mane of raven hair, the dark, luminous skin and jewel-black eyes had branded him as someone different from the rest of them.

'Qui est ton père?' the other kids had used to mock him—but Xavier had never answered, for he had not known his father's identity.

Ground vividly into his childhood memory was his mother's tight-lipped fear whenever he had ventured to ask a question about him. Her reluctance to talk.

'He is a powerful and dangerous man who will try to take you away from me. Forget him, Xavier!' was all she would say.

Xavier had been afraid of no one—yet what choice had he had other than to accede to her wishes?

How could he have gone against the woman who had given him life, who had given up all her own ambitions in order to fend for him? Perhaps a part of him had thought she might mellow with age, but his mother had died five years ago—leaving behind nothing but a faded piece of pink ribbon and a gold and ruby ring—and in a way Xavier had felt that he was honouring her memory by letting her secrets die with her.

After that, he had convinced himself that some things were better left alone—that it freed him from burden and complications not to have known the man who was his biological father.

And now this English woman had come here today and was claiming that she knew his identity!

Suddenly Xavier felt anger rising in him, and without warning he reached out and caught hold of her, his fingers gripping into the soft silk which covered her arms. He hauled her up close—close enough to smell the faint scent of lilac she wore, and to see the pulse which beat convulsively against the paper-thin skin at her temple.

'How can my father be a sheikh when I am a Frenchman to every fibre of my being?' he hissed. 'What fairytales do you concoct?'

Laura froze in his grip as his dark features swam in front of her, his breath hot on her face. His eyes were flashing black fire, and she could detect the raw scent of animal passion which clung to his skin. She felt dizzy with his proximity and shook her head, which felt heavy as lead—as if her slender neck did not have the strength to bear the weight of it.

'It isn't a fairytale,' she breathed. 'I swear it isn't!'

'Your word means nothing to me—why should I believe you?' Yet the cold and logical side of his character was already assessing the possibility of the redhead's bizarre declaration being true. *No.* He brought her even closer. 'Who sent you?' he demanded.

His dark-skinned face was so close that her senses were swimming, and Laura could barely get the words out. 'I am acting on the Sheikh's wishes—though he made them known through another.'

'Through another?' he repeated, as if she were speaking in a language he could not understand.

Laura nodded, wishing that her usual crystal-sharp thought processes hadn't deserted her—but how could she concentrate when this man's powerful masculinity seemed to be seeping into her very pores?

'Yes. The Sheikh is old and frail, and thus I dealt mainly through one of his aides.' Laura hesitated. 'His ill-health is one of the reasons he wished to make contact.'

Xavier scowled. The Sheikh's constitution was of no interest to him, but he could not stop the unfamiliar word she had used from stabbing at his heart. *Father.* It was as likely as looking up into the night sky and discovering that the moon had been made of blue cheese all along. As his take on reality shifted and changed irrevocably, he tightened his grip. 'Liar! This man is not my father—how can he be?'

She felt his fingers biting into her flesh. 'It's true, I tell you—it's true. Please. Let me go.'

'Not yet.' He loosened his grip slightly, but he did not set her free. He could see the tremble of her lips and the rush of emotions which her outrageous claim had released were such that he was tempted to drown them all in the sweet oblivion of a punishing kiss.

He could feel the hard, angry nudge of an erection, and for one brief second he wondered how long it would take him to enter her. How quickly could he make her wet with desire and rock against her, relieving these sharp, painful questions with the sweet oblivion of sex?

But as the primitive and powerful animal reaction overwhelmed him, he used his steely will to banish the desire. For now. Because sex would weaken him, would briefly have him in her thrall—and he would not risk that happening until he was acquainted with all the facts.

'Tell me what you know,' he grated.

Laura knew that she had to assert herself before this went any further. That his proximity was too distracting to allow herself any more of it—and it was with a shock like a slap to the face that she recognised that the danger she felt was in part sexual. That she was guilty of desire in a professional setting—and that she was jeapordising all that she had worked for. Oh, Laura—*stop* it, she told herself.

She lifted her chin and her green eyes burned into him. 'Only if you take your hands off me.'

He stared at her for a long, considering moment, his angry black gaze clashing with the emerald fire of hers. 'As you wish,' he ground out.

He dropped his hands so suddenly that Laura was almost caught of balance. Her breath, she realized, was coming in short and unsteady gasps, as if she had come to the end of some long race—but the race, she knew, was only just beginning.

'Now begin!' he ordered, but already rogue thoughts had begun to swim into his mind. Would this woman's statement make some sense of the many questions which had dogged his early years? And yet, in a way, wasn't it almost better if those questions remained unasked?

At the moment Xavier's life was perfectly ordered and exactly as he liked it. He called the shots and had all the control—but now this Englishwoman threatened to lay before him a nest of vipers which one by one would reveal their slithering bodies...

Laura bit her lip. 'Your father is—'

'No!' His voice rang out like a lash of steel. 'You will refer to no one as *my father*. Not when you are recounting this story to me. I do not have a father and I never have had! Do you understand?'

Laura nodded, because this was something she was well-equipped to deal with. Denial. People did it all the time—they buried their heads in the sand and pretended that something wasn't happening because the thought that it was hurt too much.

Hadn't she done it herself with her cheating ex-boyfriend, when the writing had been all over the wall in letters twenty feet high that he no longer wanted her? That he had got what he wanted and after that she was expendable. And hadn't she—like a fool—made excuses for the fact that he had been slowly edging her

out of his life and making her into a laughing stock into
the bargain? Oh, yes, Laura knew all about denial.

'Very well,' she said calmly. 'How would you like me
to tell the story?'

For a moment his black eyes narrowed with suspicion. Was she mocking him? But as he searched her pale
face Xavier detected a glimpse of empathy in the shimmering depths of her green eyes and he tensed, for he
was not a subject in need of pity.

'You will simply answer my questions. For now.'
Drawing his broad shoulders back, he shot her an imperious look. 'Who are you working for?'

Laura nodded. What had Malik said to her? *Bring
the Frenchman back to Kharastan with you, no matter
what it takes.*

'I work for Sheikh Zahir of Kharastan.'

His mouth hardened into a slash of censure, his fists
clenching by the shafts of his powerful thighs—and
suddenly it became easier to channel his frustration and
rage outwards, rather than turn it in on himself.

'And just how do *you* come to be in a position to know
all this?' Xavier demanded. 'Are you a hanger-on to this
family of sheikhs? One of those women who are turned
on by the strong, dark, silent type—perhaps secretly
hoping that one of them will whisk you away to his desert
tent and ravish you? Is that what turns you on, *cherie*?'

It was clearly intended to be insulting, and it
worked—but unfortunately she found his words erotic
as well as a slur.

Had she thought this would be easy?

Yes, she had.

Armed with the knowledge that she was about to en-lighten Xavier de Maistre and tell him that he was the son of a man so fabulously wealthy that it made your average billionaire look like a pauper, she had imagined that he would want to be on the first plane to Kharastan to rove his eyes greedily over his prospective inheritance.

How wrong could she have been?

He had failed to grab at the carrot she had dangled before him. Maybe a man as successful as Xavier could not be bought or even tempted by the lure of a possible inheritance.

'You say nothing,' he taunted softly. 'And you have told me nothing of your own place in this unusual desert hierarchy.'

'I have no place in it,' she answered. 'I'm working for the royal family of Kharastan; it's as simple as that. I'm a temporary employee with no agenda of my own.'

'No?' His eyes seared into her. 'Everyone has an agenda, *cherie*.' Especially when a man was as rich and as powerful as Xavier was. He had never met anyone who didn't want *something* from him. 'Tell me, are you being employed for your legal capabilities—or because you have beautiful breasts and come-to-bed eyes?'

Laura stared at him. He was making her sound like some sort of *hooker*. 'I don't have to stand here and be insulted like that!' she said, in a low, shaking voice.

'You think that it is an insult to be admired for your

very obvious attributes?' he mocked. 'But you are right—you do not have to stay and submit yourself to anything which offends you.' He flared his nostrils like an aristocratic racehorse as he gazed at her with haughty contempt. 'You do not like what I say to you? Then leave—and leave now—for I am not stopping you!'

He was calling her bluff—he knew it and she knew it. But she did not dare leave for fear that she might not get another chance to return and state her case.

What Xavier de Maistre thought of her and said to her was irrelevant—she was here to do a job, that was all, and this was strictly business, not personal.

So *stick* to business, Laura told herself. If he only came up to her knee and had spots all over his face would she be melting in some kind of pathetic pool on the Persian carpet? Of course she wouldn't.

She forced a glossy smile. 'Do you have a photograph of your father here in the office?'

'What do you think?' His gaze flicked over her, icy-black and unfriendly. 'Do *you* keep photos of your parents in your office?'

'I'll take that as a no,' she said quietly, ignoring the sarcasm. 'Would you like to see a photo that I've been given?'

What he would like would be to walk away from the potential dynamite of this situation, but it was already too late. Like being witness to a crime. You couldn't rewind the clock and wish you hadn't seen it because of the complications which would follow in its wake.

'I suspect that you are about to produce one from your bag,' he observed caustically. 'Like a magician performing a trick at a children's party.'

Her fingers were trembling as she unclipped her briefcase and withdrew the card-backed envelope which contained the portrait. She held it out towards him.

Xavier took it from her without a word and sucked in a long, low breath as he stared hard at the photograph.

It was a professional studio portrait, and the man in it had been captured in his most virile prime. Glimpsed beneath a white flowing headdress, held in place with a circlet of knotted gold, his hair was as raven-dark as Xavier's, and the cruel beak of a nose and sensual lips were instantly recognisable.

Xavier felt his throat tighten, for the resemblance was undeniable. 'Okay, so he looks a little like me,' he grated.

A *little*? But Laura said nothing.

'We both have black eyes and hair,' he said with a shrug, and then, when still she said nothing, he lifted his head to stare at her. Without a word, he put the photo down on his desk, then strode over to where Laura had since sat down.

Something in his expression both alarmed and excited her, and she sprang up to face him, trying not to flinch beneath the fierce onslaught of conflicting expressions which had suddenly turned his rugged face into the face of an adversary.

'Where did you get this?' he demanded.

'I told you,' said Laura, her tongue flicking out to

moisten her parched lips as she saw something in his eyes far more threatening than anger or contempt. Something which looked uncomfortably like desire. 'From the man....' She picked the phrase with care, remembering his admonition. 'The man who claims to be your father.'

He made a low, growling sound at the back of his throat, and then, reaching out, he caught hold of her and brought her right up against his hot, hard body—registering with satisfaction but no surprise that her pupils dilated in automatic response and that the tips of her breasts were pushing against the sensually soft material of her suit.

'What do you want from me?' he demanded, but his hand had snaked around her waist and had begun to caress its narrow indentation.

Breathlessly, Laura stared up at him as he began to stroke her, feeling tension coiling at the pit of her stomach, the hot prickling of her breasts, and a kind of dazed incredulity at the situation in which she found herself. This was outrageous! Yet his proximity was nothing short of destabilising—his touch as irresistible as freedom to the caged animal. And, just like an animal, she gave a tiny whimper of disbelief.

Her throat felt so tight that she could barely get the words out. Because this was desire given a whole new meaning. 'I can't think straight when you're...'

'When I am stroking you?' he purred, and he bent his head down to whisper into her ear. She could feel the warm caress of his breath, and his words were the most irresistible sounds she had ever heard. 'But you like me stroking you. You would like me to be stroking you far more intimately, I think….'

With my fingers parting your thighs and touching you where you are like a molten blazing furnace. Touching you until you shudder beneath me and cry out my name, then kissing the sound into silence.

'Stop it,' she said breathlessly, because she could sense his desire—taste and smell it, almost hear it—as if it were thrumming in the air around them. She felt like a piece of wax left in front of the fire, dissolving beneath the warmth of his touch. 'Stop it right now.'

He dropped his hands like a man who had been playing a game he had become bored with, enjoying the sight of her darkened eyes, the way she was trying to gulp air into her lungs and the faint flush which had shaded her pale skin. He would have her—of course he would—*mais pas encore*.

Not yet.

'You still haven't told me what it is you want,' he said tonelessly.

Laura gave herself time to compose herself—to rid herself of the erotic pictures which were playing in slow motion in her protesting brain, and the sensations which were dancing dangerously over her sensitised skin. 'I have orders to bring you back to Kharastan,' she said slowly.

He flexed his long olive fingers and then curled them down into the palms of his hands, so that they resem-

bled the claws of some predatory bird, fixing her in the
ebony sight of his gaze as if she were some helpless prey.

'Orders?'

'I'm sorry—that was an inadvisable choice of word.'

'Damned right it was!' he gritted out. 'But the word
is not nearly as inadvisable as the sentiment.'

He leaned forward, his eyes spitting fire, so that Laura
got some idea of what the coals of hell might look like.

'Do you really think that a man like Xavier de
Maistre can be *summoned*?' he demanded. 'Taken to
some God-forsaken country to meet a man whom I do
not even believe *is* my father?'

Freed from the seduction of his touch, Laura felt
reason began to return—but she knew she could not
allow herself the luxury of answering him back. Just
stay with it for a little while longer, she urged herself.
All she had to do was get him on that plane, and then
she would have earned her bonus and need never set
eyes on his dangerous, sexy face again.

Once again, Malik's words came back to her.

*'Bring the Frenchman back to Kharastan with you,
no matter what it takes.'*

What would it take? Laura looked around at the
costly furnishings. Not a bribe, that was for sure. Nor
vague promises that might never been fulfilled.

What would a powerful man like this treasure
above all else?

The truth, perhaps?

For what else did she have to offer him?

'I think you may regret it if you do not agree to accompany me,' she said boldly.

Her words did not seem to be what he was expecting. *'Regret?'* he echoed incredulously. 'I can assure you, *cherie*, that regret is not a part of my nature.'

No, she could imagine that with those cold eyes he would move restlessly ever forward, like a shark—never looking back or experiencing that wistful ache that maybe something should have been done differently.

'I think this may be the exception which proves the rule,' she said, and sighed, her green eyes troubled as she looked at him. Because this had now become much more than a job to be successfully completed. She didn't really know Xavier—and what she did know of him she didn't particularly like. Yet deep down he was a man who risked throwing away an opportunity which might never come again—and so she spoke to him from the heart.

'The Sheikh is old and frail,' Laura said softly. 'You might be right—this whole incident might be the result of a series of misunderstandings. Perhaps you aren't his son. But unless you go, you'll never find out. Once you have the truth, you can reject it if you please—but how would you feel if he *was* your father and you missed this opportunity? If you want a chance to meet your father, then I advise you to act now, before it is too late.' Laura lifted her chin and met his gaze. 'Because old men can die at any time, Xavier.'

CHAPTER THREE

THE atmosphere in the sumptuous room changed, became electric—as if the mention of death had somehow charged it with life.

Xavier stared at the woman with the dark red hair and felt the slow, powerful beat of his heart—followed by an odd, inexplicable twist of pain which he quashed as ruthlessly as he would a fly.

Drawing himself up to his full impressive height, Xavier subjected Laura to a stare of insolent question. 'Is there anything else you want to tell me, *cherie*?' he drawled, his rich accent edged with sarcasm. 'Mmm?'

Laura shook her head uncertainly. Hadn't she already said enough?

'No? Not about to disclose that you are working for some cable TV reality show and are carrying a secret camera to film me in the sanctity of my office?'

Laura was about to ask him why he was being so sus-picious—until she remember the snatched photos in

Bonjour! magazine. No wonder the black eyes were glittering with such hostility.

'Get out,' he said quietly.

This wasn't how the meeting was supposed to end, and Laura stared at him in disbelief. 'But surely you want to—'

'Do not try to second-guess me!' he interrupted furiously. 'Just go—and go *now*! *Maintenant!*'

Laura looked into his face and read something implacable there, and she knew that further words would be wasted. She nodded and picked up her bag, taking from it one of her business cards which she laid down on the desk. 'That's my mobile number,' she said. 'I'm staying at the Paradis if you want to contact me.'

She went to pick up the photo, but his voice rang out across the office.

'Leave it here,' he ordered. 'If it is—as you say—a photo of my father, then I can lay a greater claim to it than you.'

'But—'

'I said leave it!' he said icily. 'And go.'

Aware of his dark eyes burning into her, Laura made her way across the vast room and somehow managed to walk out of the door with her head held high—but by the time she had re-emerged on the pavement in the fashionable eighth arrondisement her hands were trembling.

Her hotel wasn't that far away—but her fancy new suede shoes were most definitely *not* designed for walking. So she hailed a cab, which crawled through the affluent streets before dropping her at the Paradis.

Was it possible that she had failed in her mission at the first hurdle?

The lift zoomed her up to the vast suite which the Sheikh's aide had insisted on providing for her. Just as he had insisted on supplying a stylist, who had taken her on a comprehensive shopping tour once she had arrived in the city. Because it seemed that although Laura had the brains, the discretion and the qualifications needed for this very unusual job, she did not have the wardrobe to carry her comfortably into the highest echelons of society.

And, whilst her well-pressed navy blue suit and cream blouses were ideal for life as a small-town lawyer, she was infinitely grateful for the couture clothes she was wearing today. Clothes could protect you, she realised. They could make you look the part you were playing—even if inside you felt as insecure as a little child left alone at a party where she didn't know anyone.

Once safely inside the suite, she kicked off her shoes and lay back on the sumptuous hotel bed, staring at the ceiling, wondering what on earth she should do next. Hang around like a puppy dog, waiting to see if Xavier would take the bait and call?

And if he didn't, then what?

Then she would have wasted a perfect opportunity to explore a city she'd never visited before. Time would hang heavily if she just waited, and she would find out soon enough whether or not she would be banking the huge sum of money she had been promised *if* she succeeded in her mission to return with Xavier.

Carefully, Laura took off the new suit and hung it in the wardrobe, enjoying the luxury of choice before pulling on a russet-coloured cashmere dress which should have clashed with her hair but somehow didn't. A gold chain belt and flat brown boots completed the look, and she set off to sightsee. Yes, it would be easy to get used to being a wealthy woman, she decided ruefully.

'Are there any messages for me?' she asked the chic young woman at the reception desk.

'Non, madesmoiselle,' the girl replied, with an apologetic shrug.

The major attractions were all within walking distance, but Laura felt as if she was only half there. To the outside world she was aware that she must look like a woman awestruck by the sights of the city, bewitched by the majestic Eiffel Tower which straddled the Trocadero like a giant steel croquet hoop, enchanted with the Sainte-Chapelle, whose glowing stained-glass interior was like being inside a jewelled casket.

But beneath Laura's pleasure ticked the worries which had arisen as the result of her meeting with Xavier, and *her* automatic questions about whether she could have handled it any better.

It had all seemed so simple when her boss had called her into his office to ask whether she would like to take a short sabbatical and earn enough money to substantially reduce her debts by working for the royal house of Kharastan.

Laura had still been reeling from the huge hole in her finances—if not quite her heart—left by her boyfriend Josh's departure, and she had blinked at her boss, wondering if she'd misheard him.

'Working for a royal family?' she had verified.

'That's right.'

'You mean I'd have to fly out to Kharastan?' she asked.

'I certainly do,' replied her boss, smiling. 'All expenses paid. Private jets. Designer clothes—the lot!'

'Don't! It sounds too good to be true,' Laura protested.

'Well, it's not. It's legit.' Her boss smiled. 'I've been approached by a friend of a friend—that's how these things work. They want a lawyer who's young, enthusiastic, discreet and…female.'

'Why female?' she asked.

Her boss gave her a wry look. 'Women bring a different dimension to matters which have the potential to be emotionally explosive—which this one does.'

'But it's…safe?'

He burst out laughing. 'Hell, yes! You're a single woman, and you'd be under the protection of the Sheikh himself in a notoriously strict and old-fashioned country—you'll be as safe as houses!'

It had sounded so easy. Too easy, she now realised—or perhaps she hadn't actually taken into account how the illegitimate son would react to such a piece of news.

Yet maybe she should have done. She should have

had the sense to realise that reactions to events weren't straightforward. You could never predict the outcome to a situation, because people weren't predictable.

Laura walked slowly back to the Paradis, wondering just what to do next. Should she ring the Sheikh and tell him about Xavier's initial reaction? Or give the Frenchman time to mull it over?

She was so deep in thought as she walked into the foyer that she barely registered the man who sat in the shadows, observing her with eyes that gleamed like jet.

Who then rose noiselessly to his feet to follow her, his grim gaze never leaving the provocative sway of her bottom.

Laura had just walked into her suite, and was preparing to close the door when it was levered open. Her automatic open-mouthed fear was not banished when she saw that it was Xavier.

'What the hell are you doing?' she cried, as he shut the door behind him as if he had some inalienable right to do so.

'What does it look like ? You wanted to talk, didn't you?' His voice dipped into a caress of pure silk. 'Well, here I am, *cherie*…all yours.'

Had he intended to make that remark sound tinged with sexual promise? And did he know that it had worked? 'I would have liked a little notice,' she said breathlessly, her fingers flying to her bare throat. 'Being jumped on like that isn't my idea of fun.'

A nerve flickered at his cheek and an added tension

crept into his body. 'No? Then you have not lived. And anyway—I thought you liked the element of surprise,' he drawled softly, enjoying the soft creep of colour into her cheeks which followed his sexual taunt. 'Wasn't that precisely how you ambushed me?'

Laura attempted a smile, but it wasn't easy—not when he was looking at her that way. Did he look at all women as if he could melt their clothes off their body with that sizzling black stare? And did some treacherous side of them always want him to? Assert yourself. Sound professional. Pretend he's just walked into your office. 'Would you like to sit down?'

He glanced around the room, his gaze coming to rest on the vast four-poster bed. 'And where should we sit…over there? Wouldn't that provide something of a distraction? I don't know about you—but I would find it very difficult not to get horizontal if I was on a bed with a woman as beautiful as you.'

Laura's heart hammered. 'Don't be disgusting.'

'Disgusting? All I'm doing is telling the truth. I wonder, are you always so uptight, *cherie*?' Her body belied her words, he noted with satisfaction, as he saw the tips of her breasts harden in response to his words, outlined with disturbing detail through the fine material of her dress.

Ruthlessly he dragged his thoughts away from the physical—there would be time enough for that. 'But let us forget about the bed and all its delightful possibilities and concentrate on the matter in hand.' His eyes glittered. 'I want some answers.'

Laura nodded. Answers she could deal with. 'That's what I'm here for. Ask away,' she said.

'You think that—even if I had the desire—I could just drop everything and travel east with you?'

'Of course. You're the boss—a powerful man who can do as he pleases.'

'You flatter me.'

'I wasn't intending to.'

'Weren't you? Don't you know that all men love to be flattered?'

'It isn't something I've made a special study of,' she said archly, something in his taunting tone making her forget her vow to keep this on a strictly business level. 'And perhaps some men have had a little too much of it all their lives. I suspect you might be in that category, Monsieur de Maistre.'

Xavier gave the kind of smile a wolf might give to a helpless lamb before he devoured it. With her defiance, she had sealed her fate—for no conquest was more exciting than that of a woman who was trying very hard not to be interested.

Why had she been chosen for this job? he wondered. Was she bait, designed to bring him back to the Sheikh— chosen for her particular type of beauty to ensnare him as women had ensnared men since the beginning of time?

Should he test her out? Kiss her now? Quell his anger and frustration at her revelation by losing himself in the softness of her lips? But lovemaking would distract him from this curious dilemma he found himself in.

Ever since he had ordered her out of his office his thoughts had been in turmoil, and it was not a state he usually experienced. He despised being at the mercy of such feelings—but it was as if a silent and very necessary battle was taking place inside him.

The cold, calculating side of his character was telling him that there was no point discovering a father at this stage in his life—even if her bizarre claim *should* turn out to be true, which he doubted. He didn't need a father.

He had made a success of his life and he had done it on his own terms—it was not in his character to yearn for some kind of reunion. More importantly, he foresaw a million complications—both practical and emotional—should he choose to pursue this line of action.

Yet her astounding revelation had awoken a curiosity inside him, and he knew that to leave the possibility unexplored would be to leave him with a lasting sense of regret. And—as he had already said—he didn't *do* regret.

And wasn't there an added enticement which would make the trip worthwhile? The thought of bedding the delectable Laura Cottingham, who was doing her best to pretend she wasn't interested! Xavier gave a slow, steady smile of anticipation.

'You are right,' he said slowly. 'I can do as I please—within reason. I have never in my life received such an intriguing invitation issued by such an irresistible woman—how could any man refuse it? So you can lose the look of anxiety which is tightening those pretty lips and relax, *cherie*—for I will return to Kharastan with you.'

For a moment Laura could hardly believe what she was hearing—she had been so convinced that he would do the opposite.

'I'm very…pleased,' she said, aware that it was a ridiculous word to use—but her relief was tempered by a prickly awareness that she was dealing with a man who spelt danger, and that was sending her thoughts haywire.

'I expect you are,' he said coolly, because he needed to maintain control in this extraordinary situation—and in order to do that he needed to keep her guessing. She must be in *his* power. She would be his to control and his to command. 'But I am not there yet, so I suggest you contain your excitement until then.'

Laura nodded. 'A car will pick you up at nine-thirty tomorrow morning and take you to the airfield, if that suits?'

'It doesn't.'

'It *doesn't*?'

Xavier allowed himself a smile—a devilish curve of his lips which hinted at a wicked kind of pleasure. His peers at La Bourse—Paris's famous stock exchange, built by Napoleon himself—would have trembled if they had seen that smile.

'*Non.* I do not think you understand how I operate, *cherie*. You will not dictate a time nor a place nor a method of travelling,' he demurred silkily. 'You will fit in with *me*.'

'I'm not quite sure I…understand,' said Laura unsteadily.

'It is quite simple. I intend to arrange my own transport to Kharastan.'

Laura stared at him. 'But that's crazy!' she protested. 'The Sheikh has a luxury aircraft ready and waiting to fly you there at a moment's notice.'

'You think I am tempted by a *luxury aircraft*?'

'No, of course not. I didn't—'

'I will not be beholden to the Sheikh,' interjected Xavier. 'These are my terms, and either you accept them or you return empty-handed—for I will not compromise and neither will I change my mind.'

The steely glint of determination in his eyes told Laura that he meant it, and there was a pause as she looked at him speechlessly. Because what *could* she say? He had her over a barrel, and he knew it.

'But there's no direct flight to Kharastan,' she pointed out. 'It could take ages to pick up connections.'

His eyes mocked her. 'You think I fly on scheduled airlines? I will use the charter company that I always use. At least I can entrust them with my life.'

'And what's that supposed to mean?'

'Think about it. If I am, as you say, the son of the Sheikh—then surely it is in the interests of more than one member of his family to wish me harm.'

She wanted to tell him that people didn't think or act like that—until she remembered the dizzying array of events which had led her to this bizarre moment, and suddenly anything seemed possible.

But it was not the imagined threat of physical danger

which had set Laura's senses tingling with fear—but the real and present risk of being in this man's presence. Of this terrible, almost aching awareness of his powerful sensuality.

Xavier's eyes narrowed as they raked over her face. So pure, he thought. So white. So...wary. He felt his loins tighten. 'What is the matter, *cherie*?' he mocked softly. 'You look nervous.'

'Why on earth would I be nervous, Monsieur de Maistre?'

'I think we both know the answer to that.' His eyes flashed. 'And perhaps you had better start calling me Xavier from now on.'

He was only telling her to use his Christian name— yet with that rich, French accent which flowed over her skin like silk it sounded as if he was suggesting a breath-taking intimacy.

Laura looked into the mocking depths of those eyes, and suddenly she was scared.

CHAPTER FOUR

'WE WILL be landing in just under an hour, *monsieur.*'

Xavier glanced up from the sheaf of papers he had been studying and into the doe-like eyes of the beautiful stewardess.

'Merci bien,' he said, and turned his gaze to Laura, who was sitting opposite him, reading, in the opulent cabin of the aircraft, which had been created to resemble a rather smart salon.

She had surprised him during the flight for he had expected her to babble, to make conversation just for the sake of it, as women inevitably did—never seeming to realise that silence could sometimes be the most alluring quality of all. But instead she had picked up a rather serious-looking novel and proceeded to read it.

It was ironic that for once he could have used some inane chatter in order to distract him from the troubling nature of his thoughts.

Last night his sleep had been haunted with strange, disturbing dreams, and he had woken with a start. He had sat up in the bed of his Parisian apartment, his body naked amid the rumpled sheets, and stared into the black mantle of the night—aware that the Englishwoman had forced him to address an area of his life which had always been a mystery. Even if her claim were true he was unsure whether he wanted that mystery revealed— and yet somehow he felt compelled to commence this voyage of discovery by something he hadn't known was within him.

For a man used to being in control, it had unsettled him. But Xavier had done what he did best—compartmentalized, shutting out the disquieting feelings and the *what ifs* with a steely determination. What was the point in trying to imagine what he might find when they landed in Kharastan when they would be there soon enough?

So he had brought work with him for the journey and attacked it with his usual thoroughness. But now he had finished he was left alone with thoughts he would have preferred not to have. And the glossy redhead was not paying him the deference he would normally have expected—which of course made him want her all the more. Desire was something he could deal with—far less disturbing than the subject of his identity. Desire had a beginning and a conclusion, and once he had this Laura Cottingham under his spell he would tire of her.

'You would like something more to eat?' he queried softly. 'Or to drink?'

Laura looked up from her book and wondered if he had noticed her reading and re-reading words which had been stubbornly refusing to make any sense. He was a difficult man to concentrate around.

'No, thanks. I'm not hungry.'

'But you barely touched your lunch,' he observed.

This was true. The perfectly poached piece of fish and green vegetables had failed to appeal—and even a chocolate extravagance of a pudding which would have normally had her drooling back home in England on a night out with the girls had made her feel very slightly queasy.

She could blame her lack of appetite on the flight— but that would have been a lie. The plane journey had been smooth and noiseless—with only the slightest turbulence when they were flying over the mountainous terrain of Dashabhi.

No, her lack of appetite and extraordinary feelings of self-consciousness could be attributed to one cause and one cause only—and it was sitting staring at her now.

'Women don't eat as much as men,' she answered stoutly.

The black gaze changed direction, lingering appreciatively on the outline of her legs, which were stretched out in front of her. 'English women never eat properly,' he observed caustically. 'They skip breakfast and eat crisps for lunch.'

'Well, actually I never eat crisps—I wouldn't be able to deal with clients all afternoon if I existed on junk food. And, as well as being an outrageous generalization, I really don't think my dietary habits are a suitable subject for discussion, do you?'

'*Au contraire,*' he demurred, because flirting was a lot easier to deal with than thinking about what might lie ahead. And her lawyer's tongue was sharp enough to make him want to pit his wits against her. 'If you do not want a man to remark on your sensational body, *cherie*, then you should not show it off in quite such a way.'

Laura looked down at herself as if her outfit had been replaced while she had been reading without her noticing—as if she might suddenly find herself sitting there in a skimpy little bikini. But of course her new wardrobe was still taking a bit of getting used to.

The stylist had chosen clothes for Paris and clothes for Kharastan—and the two were vastly different. Paris was cling and Kharastan was camouflage, and today she had dressed accordingly—in a manner befitting an employee of the Sheikh soon to arrive in a land where women's clothes were expected to be modest.

From neck to ankle she was covered in a long-sleeved dress of pure silk in a pale buttermilk colour. A fairly demure split went only as far as the knee—and that was to facilitate movement rather than to show off any leg. Gold sandals shimmered on her bare feet, and the only real extravagance was a pair of heavy and intricate dangling earrings set with beautiful deep green stones.

'But I am not dressed provocatively!' she defended.

'No?' He raised a dark brow. 'Surely that dress was designed to emphasise the very feminine shape beneath? One of those cleverly cut shapes which is supposed to be modest and yet looks anything but—particularly to a member of the opposite sex. Sometimes concealment can be unbearably exciting, as I am sure you know. I commend your taste, *cherie*.'

He was making her sound like some kind of temptress who had deliberately set out to seduce him! Should she tell him that this was a million miles from what she would normally have worn? That she had been guided by the expert eye of a stylist employed to dress her by Sheikh Zahir? But why tell him more than he needed to know? That sort of information would probably result in him interrogating her as to what she usually *did* wear, and then no doubt those intelligent black eyes would narrow and that sexy voice would start asking her even more personal questions.

And she didn't want to get personal with him, for that way lay danger—instinct told her so. In the past, she had been guilty of ignoring her gut feelings—of doing what she believed was the right thing to *do* instead of what she knew in her heart to be right for *her*. But not any more. From now on she stayed true to herself—and a cool, professional distance was exactly what was required.

Laura looked at him. After telephoning the Sheikh's disbelieving and angry aide last evening to tell him that Xavier had stubbornly insisted on arranging his own transport, she had done a lot of thinking.

It seemed to be a given that Xavier was going to flirt outrageously with her. He was good-looking and he was French—and even if he was only half-French weren't they a race of men who prided themselves on being superlative lovers? And if the rest of his blood really *was* that of a royal sheikh—sheikhs also being renowned for their sexual prowess—then *of course* he was going to behave in a way Laura wasn't used to. A totally inappropriate way—or was that just her lack of experience?

There weren't many men who looked like *him* strutting around the small town of Dolchester. If there had been then she might have gained a little practice in dealing with them and been better equipped at coping with Xavier de Maistre.

No, a man of this calibre was outside her experience—and just because she had been employed to accompany him back to Kharastan that did not mean that she had to put up with his blatantly sexual scrutiny or provocative remarks. Hadn't she decided after the Josh debacle that never again would she let a man take advantage of her?

The pilot's voice informed them that they were cruising at a steady altitude and would shortly be beginning their descent. Soon she would step out onto the tarmac at Kumush Ay—the capital city of Kharastan—and her job would be completed. It was no longer essential for her to maintain the effort of trying to placate him—she could stop walking on eggshells.

That did not mean that she was about to start being rude to him, of course—simply that she might open his eyes to the way that most women liked to be treated. It might do him good.

'Monsieur de Maistre,' she sighed.

'I keep telling you to call me Xavier,' he inter-jected silkily, aware that her reluctance to do so had intrigued him.

'Xavier,' Laura agreed, and then hesitated. How could his name be so…so…*enticing*? Because it was so foreign to her lips—lingering there like the juice of a fruit she had never tasted before? Or because it was im-possible to say it without first softening your voice? She swallowed. 'I really don't think it's appropriate for you to make comments about my figure, or my choice of apparel.'

He laughed softly. 'Apparel?' he echoed. Was this the stiff, starchy attitude so beloved of generations of Englishmen—because they wanted their women to sound like their nannies? 'But you are a woman—do you not care to be admired?'

Laura sat up straight and looked at him reprovingly. 'Obviously, if I find myself in a situation where such a reaction might be more relevant.'

'Such as?'

'Well, at a party. Or a social function.' Laura shrugged. 'Something like that.'

'You think that men and women only play with one another when they meet *socially*?' he demanded incredulously.

Play with one another. Unwanted images swam into Laura's mind as she recalled the way her blood had pounded when he had gripped her arms, the melting way he had made her feel inside. Now he was threatening to do the same again if she let him—just by the outrageous taunts he was making and the way he was looking at her.

'Why do you twist my words round?' she demanded. 'Can't you get it into your head that not every woman with a pulse wants to leap into bed with you?'

There was a pause, and when he spoke his eyes were glittering.

'Whoever said anything about leaping into bed, Laura?' he questioned softly, enjoying her answering rise of colour.

'Oh!' Laura glared at him. This was madness. She *had* to get a grip of herself before they landed. Malik had hinted that other work might be available to her once this job was over, but he was hardly going to be impressed if she was in emotional tatters by the time she arrived. 'I think I *would* like that drink, if it's all the same to you,' she said.

'Me, too,' he said, pressing a button by his seat to summon the stewardess. He spoke rapidly in his native tongue and the girl disappeared into the galley.

Laura met his eyes. He was staring at her as if he would like to jump on her and eat her up, and she wished he would do up the top button of his shirt. That crisp, dark hair peeping out was *very* distracting. 'This may be the last proper drink you get for a while,' she said. 'I suppose you're aware that alcohol is frowned on in Kharastan?'

'How kind of you to alert me to local custom,' he

observed sarcastically. 'And there I was thinking that it would be one long booze-fest from dawn to dusk!'

Laura bit back a smile, because surely to admit that she found him amusing would be another admission of weakness—and hadn't she demonstrated enough of that already?

'Your English is pretty amazing,' she observed instead. 'Did you learn it as a little boy?'

The shutters came down. 'But surely you know everything there is to know about my early life?' he questioned softly. 'Hasn't your Sheikh had a report made on me?'

Stupidly, Laura felt herself blushing. 'Well, yes—he did, actually,' she said awkwardly.

'Let me see it.'

For a second Laura hesitated—but only for a second. What was the point in trying to refuse him when his look of unyielding determination told her it would be pointless? Pulling out the report from her briefcase, she handed it to him, meeting the question in his eyes with a shrug.

'I was only doing my job,' she said.

He noted her defensive tone with a grim kind of pleasure. How it would have pleased him to have taken the moral high-ground with her—to scorn her for invading his personal space—and yet hadn't he done similar, or worse? In the past, hadn't he been called unscrupulous in his business dealings—been both lauded and feared for his cold-hearted determination to succeed?

Yet you don't like it when it is done to you, do you?

His eyes scanned the notes, which were gratifyingly

brief—simply stating that his home had been in the Marais. There was his school record, naturally, and a list of his mother's patchy employment history—it had suited her and her employers for her to be paid cash-in-hand, so that her name appeared as infrequently as possible on national records.

He saw now why the newspapers had always come up with a blank whenever they had tried to investigate his past. Apart from a few non-starter articles by a couple of ex-schoolfriends—who had provided the unsurprising facts that as a youth he had been a bit of a loner and popular with the girls—there had been nothing. 'Not very much,' he observed.

'Surprisingly little,' agreed Laura.

So his mother's wish had been granted, he thought, in a rare moment of reflection. She had strived for and achieved a private life which had bordered on the secretive. Had that contributed to his cool detachment—his almost icy indifference to relationships which women had always complained about?

He stared at Laura. 'Does he have sons of his own?' he questioned suddenly. 'I mean legitimate sons?'

'No,' she answered slowly. 'He has no legitimate sons.'

'So maybe he's clutching at straws—desperate to find someone he can call his own. What exactly is the purpose of this trip?' Xavier questioned.

Laura saw the way his mouth hardened. 'Isn't it obvious?'

'Is it? A reunion inspired by sentiment or practicality, I wonder?' he queried, his voice brittle with sarcasm. 'Does a powerful man ache to see his seed made flesh before he passes from this world into the next? Or is he planning to allocate his riches to a man who grew up in relative poverty?' His black eyes glittered. 'Do you think I am about to inherit a vast fortune, *cherie*?'

'That's a very mercenary attitude,' she said.

'You think so?' He shook his dark head. '*Non*. I am merely being practical. Or would you think it more appropriate if I affected wide-eyed surprise if such an offer was made to me?'

'That's what most people would do,' she said, thinking about the readings of wills she'd had to deal with during the course of her career, and the baser instincts it brought out in people.

'Well, I don't need or want his damned money!' continued Xavier, as if she hadn't spoken. 'Even sheikhs must learn that loyalty and affection cannot just be bought at the end of a lifetime.'

It seemed a curiously *moral* attitude for a notorious playboy to have, and was an insight into a character Laura suspected was far more complex than it first seemed.

The stewardess chose that moment to arrive with the wine, and Laura was glad to have the distraction of dark burgundy being poured into crystal glasses. She took a large mouthful.

'Is that better?' he questioned softly.

'Much better. It's delicious.'

Xavier sipped his own wine as he watched her, aware that the balance of information was tipped heavily in her favour. What did he know of her, after all? Wasn't it perhaps time he started to even things up? 'So, tell me about your connection with the royal family of Kharastan.'

It was more a command than a question. 'I have been in the employ of the Ak Atyn family for a month.'

'Only a month?' Xavier's eyes narrowed. 'So short a time to be entrusted with such a *personal* matter.'

'I was employed by Sheikh Zahir specifically for this purpose,' she said softly.

'To bring me to him?'

'That's right. I'm an expert on family law—and all Kharastani legal documents are drawn up in English, too.'

'So how come a nice girl like you ends up running errands for a sheikh?'

'Thank you for your supposition that I'm nice.'

'Don't you have a boyfriend who minds you going on missions to ensnare strange Frenchmen?'

Laura raised her eyebrows. 'Why would he mind? Are you one of those men who thinks a woman needs permission to breathe?'

'So you *do* have a boyfriend?'

'Actually, I don't.' Now, why had she told him *that*? 'And is my personal life really relevant?'

Xavier made a small sound of exasperation. '*Alors!* Why do lawyers never answer questions directly?'

'Perhaps because we are paid to ask them, not to

answer them. I'm the Sheikh's international legal advisor. That's all you need to know.'

'I'll be the judge of that, *cherie*,' he contradicted softly.

Laura met the formidable glint in his black eyes and suddenly some of her composure left her. 'We'll…we'll be landing soon.' And she couldn't wait. Being cooped up in here with him, with the tension growing by the second, was her idea of a nightmare.

Laura unsnapped her seat-belt and stood up, wanting to get away from the mesmerising spotlight of his stare and his increasingly probing questions.

Acutely aware of his eyes following her every move, she went over to one of the round porthole windows and stared down at where mountaintops were capped with snow which looked like thick white daubs of paint. Oh, please let's just get there, she thought.

'So what was the particular *talent* which made you the successful candidate for this job?' he murmured. 'Or can I guess?'

'I told you. I'm a lawyer—there are papers I need to witness.' She turned round to see that Xavier had also risen to his feet, and that his eyes were gleaming with something which was fast approaching menace.

'Don't play disingenuous,' he drawled. 'It doesn't suit you. There are a million lawyers out there who could have done the job, but none that look as good as you. Were you chosen for your beauty and your sex-appeal, do you think?'

Sex-appeal? Laura knew that the stylist had worked

an almost complete transformation on her physical appearance—but it was hard to change your own view of yourself. Because the mirror *could* lie—every woman knew that. How you looked had little to do with how you felt on the inside—particularly for someone who had fought insecurity all her life.

She had been the hand-to-mouth daughter of a hard-up mother and then the diligent law student. And latterly—with Josh—she had been frigid and uptight Laura, the cash-cow who had been laughably easy to milk and then send on her way. Yes, she was wearing a fortune in clothes—but sexy? Her? Never in a million years. Not according to Josh, anyway.

'Of course I wasn't!' she defended. 'I may have been chosen because women have different qualities to men, but my sex-appeal is not only irrelevant but inappropriate to a country like Kharastan.'

Was she really naïve enough to believe that? he wondered. He walked over to the window to stand beside her and looked down into her face, his eyes narrowing in perplexity as he saw that her green eyes were huge and dark in her white face.

Women did not usually shrink from him like this, and it was turning him on—deep down he wanted something or someone to lash out at for the unusual situation he unwillingly found himself in. And why should it not be her? Don't shoot the messenger, urged a voice inside his head, and Xavier's mouth tightened. *Ah, non*—he wasn't intending to *shoot* the messenger.

'So you reckon it's just some kind of coincidence that they should have appointed a nubile young woman to do the job?' he questioned, his voice edgy with desire.

'I don't know,' she whispered, as if she had suddenly come to realise the trap she found herself in. Backed up against the wall, ostensibily alone on a powerful jet with a powerful man whose whole large and muscular frame emanated a raw kind of sexuality. It shimmered from his skin in a hot, almost tangible radiance—so that despite knowing she should be distancing herself, or calling for the stewardess, Laura found herself curiously debilitated, unable to move, or to think, or to…

'Don't you?' he whispered back, and touched the tip of his finger to her chin, tilting it upwards and forcing her to meet the piercing black gaze. 'I think you do. Just as I think that someone told the Sheikh's entourage about those rosebud lips and knew that I would want to do this…'

He was lowering his face towards hers, and Laura felt like one of those women in a sci-fi film—zapped into compete immobility by some alien's ray-gun. Except it was nothing remotely alien which was freezing her to the spot—it was a feeling as old and human as creation itself, even though it had never hit her quite like this before. Xavier lowered his mouth down onto her trembling lips.

Perhaps if it had been a hard and blatant kiss—a demonstration of his superior power and experience— then Laura might have had the strength or the desire to push him away. But it wasn't. It was the cleverest kiss in the world, for it coaxed and hinted and tantalised and made her yearn for more. So that it was *her* mouth which parted slightly, and *her* tongue which gave a little flick towards his.

And *his* low laugh of triumph and anticipation as he placed his hands on her waist and then slid them down to cup her buttocks and draw her towards him, as he deepened the kiss with an instinctive display of sensuality and mastery.

'Mmm,' he murmured against her lips.

'Xavier!' she gasped.

'You like that?'

'Y…yes! Oh, *yes!*'

Xavier laughed again, tempted to cup her breasts, or to slide the long filmy dress up her long legs and explore her most secret treasures. But a hasty mental calculation told him that there was no time to enjoy any kind of sexual game. Starting something might mean that they were both left high and dry—or, worse, that they might be interrupted by the stewardess telling them that they were coming in to land.

No, there was no time for sex—but plenty of time for sexual promise. And it sure beat worrying about what lay ahead in Kharastan. Xavier knew how much value women placed on a kiss—how they played it over again and again in their minds, like a much-loved piece of music. Well, then, let her have the long, sweet kiss of all her romantic fantasies.

Using his mouth like an instrument, he continued to

explore her lips in soft and provocative caresses until, with a little cry, Laura reached up to cling onto his broad shoulders and began to sway slightly as the kiss became harder now, and deeper.

His lips tasted sweet, the sweetest thing she had ever tasted. Laura had been kissed before—of course she had—but never like this. Oh, never like this. She could feel the sticky rush of desire, the debilitating sense of wonder which made her want him to…to…

With a soft smile Xavier drew back from her, hearing her tiny moan of protest. He stared down into eyes which looked almost black, so dilated were her pupils, and her mouth was darkened too by his kiss. There was a faint flush accentuating her cheekbones—and he knew with arrogant certainty that if the flight had been just a little longer he would be having sex with her, right now.

'Alas, *non*,' he murmured regretfully, for he was so hard that he felt he might burst. 'There is no time for love, *cherie*.'

Was it his totally inappropriate use of the word 'love' which brought Laura crashing back to reality? Like someone who had been thrown from the confusing blackness of a cave into blinking light?

She took a tottering step back in complete and utter horror, her hand flying to her throat. 'Wh…what are you *doing*?' she breathed unsteadily, and then shook her head in disbelief. 'Or rather, what am *I* doing?'

He laughed. 'You want a biology lesson?'

'I want….I want…. Oh! How could I have been

so…*stupid*?' To let him kiss her like that—to open her body and her mouth up to him, telling him in no uncertain terms that for that brief moment she had wanted him in the most complete sense. How could she possibly play the cool lawyer *now*?

Xavier gave a lazy smile. 'Do not beat yourself up, *cherie*—it is no crime to want me. Most women do.' He shrugged. 'And what better way to pass the time during the long nights ahead in the desert?' To use sex as an escape from thought—ah, yes, it had many uses other than pleasure and procreation. 'We will make love just as soon as we get an opportunity to do so.'

Common sense splashed over Laura's senses like a cold shower at his arrogant sexual boast. Her hands flew up to her hair and she knew she must straighten it before they came into land—and, more importantly, that she must make it clear that there would be no repeat of what had just happened. None. No matter how provocatively he kissed her. *And you aren't going to let him do it again!*

'I don't think so. That was a very serious error of judgement on my part,' she said, her voice steadier now. 'One which will not be repeated—for once I have effected an introduction between you and the Sheikh then my dealings with you will be over, and I will bid you farewell.'

Xavier resisted the desire to contradict her. How little she knew! How naïve and foolish if she thought that he would allow such a scenario to take place. She would bid him farewell only when *he* had tired of her, and that would be not be until he had had her.

He felt a pulse beat deep within his groin.

Oh, yes—she would be his for the taking.

But sexual hunger was replaced with a different kind of tension as the sound of the jet engines changed and the plane began its descent into Kharastan.

CHAPTER FIVE

JUST a month earlier and Laura had made this very same landing, onto a runway fringed by huge and distant snow-topped mountains, and it had made her gasp aloud in wonder. But then she had been hopeful as well as nervous—filled with the kind of excitement you got when you were stepping outside of the confines of your normal world.

She had been slightly terrified of meeting the Sheikh's representative—but equally she had been feeling strong. The hurt and the subsequent fall-out she had experienced from the break-up of her relationship with Josh had somehow transformed itself into a brand-new attitude of resilience and defiance.

Most importantly, she had done everything in her power to extricate herself from the situation with something more than pride. She had seen her mother suffer financially at the hands of men, and she was determined not to repeat her mistakes. Yes, this time a month ago, life had looked hopeful.

And now?

Now she just felt the terror and none of the strength. It seemed to have been sapped by the sexy man who had kissed her with such unbearably sweet and restrained passion on the plane and left her aching and uncomfortable. And how unprofessional was *that*?

Laura shot him a glance as they stood at the top of the aircraft steps, watched his reaction as he breathed in his first breath of the warm Kharastan air which seemed to envelop her body like a warm caress. But she didn't want to think of being caressed, because that would take her mind to pointless places.

She wanted to feel something other than this prickly state of ebbing desire, and tried to concentrate on his high-handed arrogance instead. But somehow she couldn't seem to do it. His black eyes had narrowed as they took in his surroundings, and for a moment there seemed to be an almost unguarded air about him. Stupidly, it made her think about a little boy searching for his father and his roots—instead of a calculating playboy who knew how to kiss a woman in order to guarantee seduction— and, even more stupidly, she felt her heart turn over.

'Ready?' she questioned softly.

'Wait,' he said, his deep voice as soft as hers.

Xavier looked around him, as if excessive sound might disturb the natural quiet beauty of this place, and a peculiar sensation shivered over his skin as he stared out at a stunningly unfamiliar landscape.

The sun was beginning its slow descent in a clear sky

of intense cobalt, and it seemed a much bigger sun than the one he was used to—a gigantic, fiery ball of coppery red which was turning the snow on top of the distant mountains into pink cream.

He saw the dark shape of a huge bird swooping by him, and noticed the dust and the dry air and the heat which seemed to seep straight into his pores—and for a moment he felt utterly mesmerised by this strange new world.

He had grown up in a city, had lived and breathed an urban life since birth, and he loved Paris with a passion because it was impossible not to. Yes, he had travelled, but always more west than east, and his trips to the latter had been infrequent working trips to the highly populated finance capitals of the world. But this place looked wild and almost desolate, and it struck some deep, warm chord—made his heart lurch in a strange and unexpected way.

'Mais c'est magnifique,' he whispered.

'Yes,' said Laura slowly, and she stopped and caught the moment and just drank in the beauty. Magnificent indeed. And, under the guise of reaquainting herself with the landscape, she couldn't resist snatching another look at that strong and rugged profile—etched like a stark and beautiful portrait painting against the deep blue backdrop of the sky behind him. As if he was meant to be here. As if he belonged here. I wonder if he feels that too? she thought suddenly. Or whether it's just fanciful imagining on my part?

Xavier's gaze swept from the panoramic view to the

airport itself, where there were gleaming, state-of-the-art buildings and high-tech radar—as well as the control towers. But when his eyes had adjusted to the clear light he could see armed soldiers on the edge of the airfield, along with convoy of dark and gleaming vehicles and a number of motorcycle outriders.

'Here they come,' he observed softly, as a handful of people—all men—proceeded towards them, their silken robes and headdresses shimmering in the dying light of the sun.

Can this be for real? Xavier wondered. Or had he wandered onto a film set—where fantasy was cleverly designed to mimic reality? Yet had his whole world not been turned upside down within the space of a couple of short days?

'Which one is the Sheikh's special aide?' he questioned tersely.

Laura's eyes were raking over the granite-faced group. 'The tallest of them,' she said slowly. 'The man in the white robe. Malik.'

'And you say they are related?'

'Only very distantly, I believe—but he is definitely the Sheikh's confidante. He tells him everything.'

Xavier's eyes gleamed with satisfaction. And had she not answered as *his* confidante? He had been right—as usual—a taste of his sublime lovemaking had been enough to guarantee that all her loyalty would soon lie with *him*. It was time for him to take control. 'Come,' he ordered. 'Let us go and greet them.'

Laura blinked as he preceded her down the aeroplane steps, wondering whether Xavier had decided that he was going to start *acting* like a royal—for wasn't there something suddenly imperious in his manner?

And did she imagine the merest flicker of hostility in the eyes of Malik as he approached them, bowing deeply from the waist?

'Good evening,' he said formally. 'I, Malik—on behalf of His Most Eminent Highness Zahir of Kharastan—bid you welcome.'

A nerve flickered at Xavier's cheek. There was a part of him, a primitive part, that wanted to demand answers to a few incisive questions—to demand some kind of proof of the outrageous claim which had led to him being here on foreign soil. Something more than a damned black-and-white shot which could have been mocked up by any half-decent photographer! But it was not Malik's story to tell.

Instead, he nodded his jet-dark head in response. 'I thank you for your extravagant welcome,' he answered silkily.

'You must be tired, and thirsty after your journey,' said Malik. 'The car awaits to take us to the Palace.' He turned to Laura. 'You will take the first car, where you will find Sidonia, your maidservant, awaits you,' he instructed. 'Monsieur de Maistre and I will follow in the other.'

His voice was definitely cool, and Laura suddenly felt as if the men were closing ranks and excluding her. She had achieved what they had asked her to do—did that mean she was now superfluous to requirements?

I don't *want* to travel in a separate car with a servant, she thought—flicked away as you would an irritating fly on a hot summer's day. She turned to look at Xavier, but his eyes were stony and his face unmoving—the man who had kissed her so passionately on the plane now seemed like a distant dream. Would he object to this sudden segregation of the sexes? she wondered. Would his obvious desire for her go as far as wanting her companionship on the journey to the Palace?

Xavier met her eyes. He knew that she wanted to stay with him—and, in truth, would he not have preferred her beside him? Familiar and beautiful. But her beauty was distracting—and not just to him. He wanted to keep all his wits about him—and, like a small animal locked outside in the cold and rain—her gratitude would know no bounds when he took her back into the warmth of his arms once more. Let her have a taste of what it was like to be rejected by Xavier de Maistre, and in future she would acquiesce to his every desire!

Besides, Laura and Malik both had the potential to be his enemy, and was it not best to divide your enemies? So that if necessary you could play one off against the other…?

'Run along now, *cherie*,' he murmured. 'As you see—everyone is ready to leave.'

Laura didn't react—even though his patronising dismissal felt like a slap to the face. Yet she had travelled out here before under her own steam and managed admirably—because she had been playing her professional role instead of allowing a passionate kiss to knock her guard down. So start playing it again! You are here as an employee, she reminded herself, and nothing more.

She nodded and gave a serene smile. 'Yes, of course. You men will have plenty to talk about. I'll see you at the Palace.' And she turned and walked towards the car without another word, knowing that they watched her.

For a moment both men were silent as a guard sprang to attention and opened the door of the armoured car for her.

'She is beautiful, is she not?' asked Malik reflectively.

Xavier turned his head back to look at the Sheikh's aide, acknowledging the glint in the other's eyes with a stony response. Had this man already been intimate with the luscious redhead? he wondered. And a dart of sexual jealousy lanced right through him. 'Laura?'

'Of course,' said Malik, and then paused. 'She is your lover?' he questioned deliberately.

A furrow appeared between Xavier's black eyebrows. 'Is it the custom in Kharastan to speak of women in such a way?' he demanded.

Malik acknowledged the barb with a slight shrug. 'You come from the West—where attitudes towards sex are liberal, and where your own reputation with women is that of a legendary stud.'

'And where only schoolboys boast to each other of sexual conquests,' returned Xavier.

'I was not asking you to boast—I was merely trying

to find out whether Miss Cottingham has yet joined the long list of your lovers.'

'My *reputed* lovers,' drawled Xavier. 'If I had bedded all the women who have offered themselves to me then there would be little time for anything else.'

'So is that a yes or a no?' persisted Malik.

Xavier's eyes narrowed. Was it just masculine pride which made him reluctant to admit that Laura had not yet been his, since the Sheikh's aide was clearly obsessed with her? Or was it a niggling doubt that perhaps she actually might do the unthinkable and resist him? Never! There was not a woman born who was foolish enough to deny herself *that*.

Think about the way she responded to you on the flight over, he told himself, offering a tantalising foretaste of the abundant pleasures to come. 'You display a curiosity on the subject which borders on the distasteful,' he gritted.

Malik shrugged. 'Perhaps I am thinking of sleeping arrangements.'

'Or perhaps you want her for yourself?' Xavier challenged. 'Tell me—is it necessary for you to employ a woman to be able to take her to your bed?'

There was a moment of disbelieving silence. 'Your comments could be construed as insults, Monsieur de Maistre,' observed Malik coldly. 'Is that wise, do you think?'

But Xavier refused to be cowed by the menace which had suddenly crept into the other man's voice. I don't *have* to like this man, or respect or pay homage to him, he thought. 'If I were being wise, then I probably wouldn't have agreed to come on this damned journey in the first place!'

'Then why did you?'

Xavier's lips curved into a glacial smile. 'I will talk to the Sheikh,' he said carelessly. 'And not to one of his henchmen.'

He saw that his incautious words had made Malik clench his fists in the folds of his silken robes in ill-disguised fury—and suddenly Xavier felt almost *reckless*. As if he had just been given a draught of cool refreshment after being parched and dry for longer than he cared to remember. Before him lay a gilded path to the unknown, and suddenly that excited him—because for all his freedom and his many glittering successes hadn't his life become just a little *predictable*?

After all, there were only so many fine wines you could drink, exquisite meals you could eat and beautiful women you could bed. When you wore nothing but silk or cashmere or Irish linen next to your skin, when every whim and wish was granted—did you not lose something of the fierce hunter which lay at the deepest core of every man?

A luxurious palate could grow jaded, but for the first time in as long as he could remember Xavier's blood began to fizz with an elemental excitement as the car drove down a wide avenue, where rows of guards saluted as they passed.

He sighted an ornate set of metal gates—turned blood-red by the dying embers of the sun. Through them he could see a glimpse of water, spraying up in a white plume from a huge fountain, and unknown trees throwing down dark and dappled shadows onto immaculate paths.

As they approached the compound he could see a domed building covered in exquisite mosaic and the glint of gold. Alongside the gold was blue of every shade imaginable—from summer sky to ocean deep.

And, despite his unfamiliar heightened state of emotion, Xavier suddenly felt a strange and powerful sense of destiny—as if it was his place to be here, now.

'We are here,' he observed slowly, and saw Malik had been quietly watching him, an unfathomable look in black eyes so like his own.

'Indeed we are,' said the Kharastan man softly. 'The Blue Palace is very beautiful, yes? And it is here that Zahir the Great awaits you.'

Zahir the Great. *The man who claims to be my...father,* Xavier thought, and then a strange sense of isolation crept over him. What if none of it were true? What if this strange, almost dream-like state turned out to be exactly that?

Because—for all his money and his power and connections—Zahir might have made a fundamental mistake: the kind all men were capable of. It might turn out to be some random error—and then what?

Xavier must be very careful indeed not to allow his

customary cool composure to slip. To remain as indifferent as he always did—because he would be watched closely for his reactions, and an unguarded moment could be interpreted as weakness. And that he would *never* allow.

'When will I see him?' he questioned suddenly.

There was a pause. 'It has not yet been decided,' said Malik.

Xavier could sense the other man's authority reasserting itself, and he knew that he must demonstrate his own power.

Because they want you here far more than you want to be here, he reminded himself.

'I have travelled out here at considerable inconvenience—and I will not be left dangling like a puppet on a string,' he asserted fiercely. 'If Sheikh Zahir wishes to see me, then so be it—but it must be accomplished as quickly as possible. I am a busy man who does not play to another's whims.'

Malik's eyes became stony. 'It is not a game that we play with you, Frenchman,' he grated. 'Zahir is old and frail and the time of your meeting will be governed by the state of his health—by that, and that alone.'

Xavier's heard the raw note which had distorted Malik's voice, and his eyes narrowed. Was he genuinely fond of his master, in the way that sometimes happened with a subordinate? he wondered. Or was he just projecting into a future without the Sheikh and worrying about his own livelihood?

But he looked into the other man's eyes and saw genuine grief there, and it smote at Xavier's conscience. 'I did not intend to cause you pain,' he grated.

Malik inclined his head in thanks and appeared to regain his composure. 'Obviously, the meeting will be arranged as soon as possible.'

There were a million questions teeming in Xavier's mind—but now was not the time to ask them.

Malik's voice broke into his thoughts.

'Dinner will be at nine, after you and Miss Cottingham have had a chance to refresh yourselves. I hope that will meet with your approval?'

And suddenly Xavier knew that he wanted—needed—to assert himself in other ways, too. To follow up on the promise of his kiss with the beautiful Englishwoman. Because what else was he going to do with the idle hours while he waited for the Sheikh to see him? 'What *will* meet with my approval is if the sleeping arrangements are to my satisfaction,' he said, with soft, smooth emphasis.

Malik stiffened. 'That depends on what you mean by *satisfaction.*'

'I think we both know what I mean,' said Xavier softly.

There was a moment's silence. 'Obviously it would greatly offend Kharastan sensibilities if two unmarried people were openly put in the same room, but…' Malik shrugged his shoulders and a knowing look passed between the two men. 'I am certain that something can be arranged to your satisfaction.'

'I'm glad we understand each other,' said Xavier.

CHAPTER SIX

'I THINK there must have been some kind of mistake!' declared Laura, as she looked around the room with a mixture of anger, fear and unquestionable excitement.

'Mistake?' echoed Xavier innocently as two servants put down the last of their bags. 'And what kind of mistake would that be, *cherie*?'

'Sharing a suite!' she declared. 'With *you*!'

She was glaring at him as if he was devil himself, and Xavier allowed a feeling of brief contentment to wash over him. How much easier to allow his thoughts to be dominated by the familiar frission of sexual tension rather than wondering about the wisdom of having come here on such a strange quest.

'Well, it isn't exactly *sharing*, is it, *cherie*? We have one sitting room in common—surely you can deal with that for a few nights?' He raised his black brows in mocking query. 'Did you never share with members of the opposite sex when you were a law student?'

'That's *different*!'

'How is it different, Laura?'

'Playing the innocent doesn't suit you, Xavier,' she said. 'Are you behind this?'

'Behind what?'

'The fact that we're going to be virtually living on top of one another!'

His dark, sensual face now assumed an expression of faint perplexity. 'You think that the possibility of my being the Sheikh's illegitimate son means that I have been able to wield control, perhaps even from France? What did you imagine, Laura—that I somehow managed to acquire a direct line to Zahir and demand that he put us in close proximity?'

'So you *didn't* have anything to do with it? Was that a yes or a no?'

Ah, *oui*—she was clever; he would give her that. Or maybe it was her lawyer's training, seeing straight through his elaborately bluffed response and realising that he hadn't actually answered her question.

'Is it such a bad arrangement?' he questioned, gesturing around the cool, shaded room, with its stone floors and priceless silk rugs in faded jewel colours. There was a glorious bureau, inlaid with many different gleaming woods, and on it stood a vase of sweetly scented roses. 'It is a beautiful room—in fact, it is so large that it could easily be divided into three rooms. And what is there to complain about when we have been given separate bedrooms?'

'Except that there aren't any keys in the locks, are

there?' she pointed out. And he still hadn't answered her question.

'Really? I hadn't got around to checking that.' He raised his dark brows and gave an arrogant laugh. 'Do you think that a locked door would keep me out if I really wanted to get into your bedroom?'

Laura's heart missed a beat. 'You don't mean you'd *break the door down*?' she questioned in a faint voice.

'Why? Is that one of your abiding fantasies?'

'No!'

'What I meant,' he murmured, noting the automatic way her pupils had dilated and feeling an answering stir of desire, 'was that if I wished it, then you would turn the key and let me in.'

'Are you crazy?' She stared at him. 'Do you live in the kind of world where women just fall in with your every whim?'

Their eyes met. 'Pretty much.'

Laura shook her head. 'You treat women like sexual objects,' she complained.

'Which they are.'

'I can't believe you said that!'

'Because it is true,' he mused, enjoying the verbal sparring for its rarity value as much as for a distraction. 'Your objection is in the wording—and all the associations which have grown up around it. When a man looks at a beautiful woman he thinks of sex—but it works both ways. Women think the same way about men—if only they would have the courage to admit it.' He slanted her a shamelessly provocative look from beneath his thick black lashes. 'You were thinking about just that on the plane today.'

For once Laura was momentarily speechless. The trouble was that she couldn't fault his logic, his clever-ness with words. He would have made a good lawyer himself, she thought reluctantly. 'Well, maybe I'll ask Malik to change my room.'

'You could try,' he said softly. 'But perhaps it might be a waste of your time—and time is so precious, is it not?'

Their eyes met, and in that moment Laura under-stood. 'Oh, I see,' she said. 'So I was right—you *were* behind it. It's a *fait accompli.*'

'How perfect your French accent it,' he murmured. He let his gaze drift over her. And how perfect *she* looked, he thought—that creamy silk providing a glo-riously neutral backdrop against which to appreciate her natural beauty.

Her dark red hair had been drawn back from the perfect oval of her face and woven into an intricate kind of plait, which began at the top of her head. Yet its almost severe style contrasted with the luscious hint of curves beneath the soft silk, and he welcomed the familiar leap of sexual hunger which silenced all the cla-mouring questions in his mind.

How many men had known that exquisite body? he wondered jealously, remembering Malik's casual ques-tioning in the car. *Then have her,* mocked a voice in his head. *Have her and then you can forget all about her.*

'Do you never wear your hair down?' he questioned softly.

It wasn't what Laura had been expecting. She had seen the hungry way his eyes had been devouring her, and she had anticipated some sensual little taunt, steeling herself against the seduction of his words. But his sensual question made her feel just that. Her fingertips touched the carefully crafted style, skating over the slippery silken surface of the thick dark red locks.

'Sometimes I do,' she said.

'In bed?'

Don't let him get to you. Don't give him any inkling that you keep remembering the sweetness of his kiss... She saw the hectic glimmer in his black eyes and realised that he was remembering it, too. And that the greatest victory would be not to get herself moved from the temptations of an interjoining room—but to resist temptation altogether.

'Of course I let my hair down in bed,' she said briskly. 'But you won't ever get to see it, Xavier.'

He gave her a hard, swift smile. 'Don't you know that a red-blooded man can never resist a challenge?' he murmured, flicking a quick glance at his watch. 'And— while you look utterly delectable as you are—you might wish to change before dinner.'

He walked into his bedroom and shut the door with an exaggerated sense of care, leaving Laura staring after him with a growing sense of frustration which was more than sexual. As if he had just got the better of her and she wasn't quite sure why.

Outside, the stars hung bright and brilliant in the indigo velvet of the sky—as big as if a child had painted them on with large brushstrokes. And drifting into the room was warm, soft air—heavily scented with the fragrance of roses and jasmine and sandalwood.

She walked slowly into her own bedroom and closed the door. She should have been bouncing around with satisfaction, feeling *good* about herself, and yet she was all churned up. Was that because Xavier was managing to unsettle her? Or because she was terrified of the way he was making her feel, and even more terrified of the way she suspected he *could* make her feel?

Laura sighed. Just make the most of this opportunity, she told herself. Banish the Frenchman from your mind and enjoy the experience of staying as a guest in a real-life palace. Not many Western women get this kind of chance. She thought of how her mother would marvel if she could see her little girl now—her sweet mother, who seemed to attract chaos and never had a penny in her purse without wanting to spend it.

Within the hour, Laura felt like a different person. The palace might have dated back to the fourteenth century, but the bathrooms were most definitely rooted in the twenty-first—with powerful showerheads as big as dinner plates and a stand-alone bath you could practically swim in.

She applied the minimum of make-up and slithered into a fitted dress in deepest jade silk, which skimmed her ankles and brought out the deep green of her eyes. Then she pulled her hair back into a chignon to give her finished image a rather defiant look.

Drawing in a deep breath, she opened the interconnecting door to find Xavier standing looking out at a huge crescent moon. He turned round when he heard her, and for one immeasurable moment they both stood staring at each other, like two people who had stumbled over each other by mistake.

Xavier stilled, feeling the sudden deep pounding of his heart. She had no flesh on show, save for her face, and yet he had never seen anyone look more sexy in his life. How did she do that touch/don't-touch thing so beautifully? he wondered. He had been aching when he had gone to take his shower and had been tempted to pleasure himself…and now he wished he had.

'You look beautiful.'

Stupidly, she felt her lips tremble. 'Xavier, please don't.'

'Don't what?'

'Don't *say* those things.' *Don't look at me that way!*

'All men say those things.'

'No, they don't.' *Not like you do.*

'You want me to lie, is that it? Because I will not. And you are. Very beautiful.'

Laura felt a glow suffusing her skin as his words whispered over her—because when he looked at her in that lazily appreciative way he made her *feel* beautiful. But it wasn't right to conduct a flirtation with him—under any circumstances, and especially under ones such as these.

Even though Xavier seemed unconvinced that the Sheikh was his father, Laura was pretty sure he was. And very soon he was going to meet him. Already their worlds were miles apart—he was a wealthy playboy and Laura was a small-town lawyer from another country—but add a royal connection into the equation and he would be completely out of her reach. So keep resisting him, she told herself fiercely. Keep yourself safe from his Gallic charm and his dark, sexy looks.

In the distance, a sonorous bell was rung, its chime sweet and low and long, just as someone tapped on the door and an unknown male servant in plain white robes bowed and indicated that they should follow him.

Instinctively, Laura glanced up at Xavier.

'Are you…nervous?' she ventured.

Usually he would have deflected her observation with a cold indignation that she should dare suggest that Xavier de Maistre should be nervous of anything! But tonight he did not. Maybe it was the scent of sandalwood on the air, or the crescent moon in the sky, but tonight he did not feel like the Xavier of old.

'Not at all,' he murmured, as they passed tall marble pillars and intricate fretwork lamps which hung down from a jewelled ceiling. 'I feel a little as if I am surrendering to the inevitable—but to something which is nothing to do with me.'

'I don't think I understand.'

'None of this matters,' he said slowly, as if he was making sense of it to himself as well as to her. 'If—which I question—the Sheikh *does* happen to be my father, then it is merely an accident of birth. Nature's random lottery. It is not part of my life. It never has been and it never will be, nor can be.'

'Are you sure?'

But her question went unanswered, for by now they were approaching a vast set of ornately carved double doors which were thrown open upon first sight of them.

Inside, he could see torches of fire set out at intervals around a vast room with an ornate table at its centre, on which glittered precious crystal and silver with tall, ivory candles amid fruit and flowers. *'Mon dieu,'* he murmured. 'Look at this.'

Xavier glanced down at Laura but she was not looking at the lavishly set banqueting hall. Instead her face was turned to up his in question, the green eyes clear but curious—as soothing as a smooth green lake—and he found himself wanting to dive in and lose himself.

'Did your mother ever talk about your father?' she asked suddenly.

Had the enchantment of an Eastern night worked some of its magic on him? Was that why he didn't shoot her down in flames for her impertinance? 'You have no right to ask me something like that, Laura.'

'Don't I?' she retorted softly. 'Considering we're sharing living space, I'd say that gives me a few rights.'

She was tenacious, he would say that for her—and brave too, to pursue a subject which he found uncomfortable. And if she had the courage to ask him, then surely he had the courage to answer? Yet it was strange to give voice to thoughts he had always repressed— partly because there had never been anyone in whom to confide before. But Laura knew most of the story—so why not answer her?

'My mother said next to nothing about my father,' Xavier answered, his black eyes as hard and impenetrable as jet. 'His identity was the secret she carried closest to her heart. All I knew was that he was rich and powerful and potentially acquisitive. But he had no part in our lives, not even in anecdotes...' He clicked his fingers, like a sorcerer demonstrating someone disappearing in a puff of smoke. 'It was as though he was dead to her—as though he never existed.'

As though he never existed.

It was a damning and terrible testimony passed down from mother to child, and neither of them spoke for a moment—as if his stark words had robbed them both of the power of speech.

'Maybe you'll hate him,' said Laura suddenly. *And then what?* Had Malik—or Xavier—or even the Sheikh himself—thought about the possible consequences of that happening?

The scent of jasmine wafted through the air as they walked towards the entrance to the hall. 'Maybe I will,' agreed Xavier in an odd kind of voice.

CHAPTER SEVEN

'YOU will perhaps eat a little more dessert?' asked Malik softly.

Laura shook her head as an ornate golden dish, gleaming black and scarlet with grapes and pomegranates, was presented to her by one of the many silent servers at the meal.

She sat back in her chair. This was the only official Kharastan function she had attended, yet the evening was proving far less of an ordeal than she might have imagined, given that she was seated next to the flinty-faced Malik, with Xavier on the opposite side of the table.

'Thank you, but, no—I couldn't eat another thing.'

'You enjoyed it? I think perhaps it was a little plain for your sophisticated Western palate.'

'Are you kidding?' asked Laura. 'A night out where I live usually involves a trip to the cinema followed by a curry. But this was different—and I loved everything about it. The dancers were incredible. Obviously I couldn't understand a word of the poetry, but it had

such a wonderful rhythm that it didn't seem to matter—
and the music which accompanied it was beautiful.'

'Yes,' said Malik, looking pleased. 'All good poetry
transcends language. And the flute you so admired—the
sound it produces sounds exactly like the wind blowing
across the desert, does it not? Ah, I see you frowning!
Have you ever been in the desert, Miss Cottingham?'

'No, I haven't,' said Laura, her eyes drifting across
and down the table, to where Xavier was sitting talking
to a beautiful Kharastani woman garbed in lavishly embroidered robes, with filigree earrings of sapphire and
gold hanging from her ears. Did he find the woman
attractive? she found herself wondering jealously.

He chose just that moment to look up—or had he
sensed her staring at him? His lips curved into a mocking
half-smile and his eyes flashed with promise as they
lazily ran over her face. Laura felt her throat tighten. She
folded her fingers in the soft jade silk at her lap, aware
that they were trembling and wondering how the hell she
was going to cope later. When they were alone.

Malik's eyes followed her gaze. 'The guests here
tonight are old and trusted confidantes of the royal
household, and Fallalah is married to one of the Sheikh's
many godsons,' he said obliquely as small teacups were
placed before them. 'Just in case her chatter with the
Frenchman should give you any cause for concern.'

Laura blinked as she dragged her gaze away from
Xavier. 'Concern?' she said, clearing her throat. 'Why
should there be?'

'Forgive me,' said Malik slickly. 'But I thought perhaps that you and he were…' He shrugged and let his voice trail off, the pause giving rise to a hundred silent questions.

It was a clever way of eliciting information, Laura acknowledged—but she was damned if she was going to start discussing her relationship with Xavier. She smiled to herself. And what relationship would that be? A man who made no pretence about wanting sex with her, and a woman who told herself that it would be wrong, no matter how much her body tried to persuade her otherwise. Not much of a relationship!

'You're speaking in riddles, Malik.'

'Am I? Forgive me.'

Laura nodded, but said nothing in response.

'So you are discreet,' Malik observed. 'And loyal.'

'Wasn't that why you employed me—for those very qualities?' Laura folded her napkin and, placing it neatly on the table, looked up at him. 'Maybe it's time we talked about that. I know you want me to witness the signing of some documents, and I can do that first thing.' Her gaze was steady, hopeful. 'After I've done that can I assume that my job is completed, as I will have accomplished everything you asked me to do?'

The Kharastani nobleman took a white grape from the dish and turned it in his olive fingers reflectively. 'As I recall, when you were interviewed you were told that more work could be available on completion of this assignment and depending on its outcome.'

Laura shifted in her seat. What tricks the light could play, she thought. Tonight, in the guttering light from the candles, she thought how much Malik's jet-black eyes seemed to resemble Xavier's. Or was her perception simply being warped by the travel and the upheaval and the sheer mind-blowing beauty of the Blue Palace and this heady evening?

'Well, the work *is* nearly completed,' Laura said softly.

'No,' he demurred. 'It is completed when the Sheikh instructs that it is so.'

'And when will that be? Days? Weeks?' With the two of them thrown together in the most bizarre and intimate circumstances in the meantime. As Laura looked into Malik's eyes she realised that he was as ruthless as Xavier. What he wanted, he got—and behind the outward courtesy she had been shown tonight she could read the implacable determination in his eyes. She was here to stay until she was given leave to go, as simple as that.

At that moment Malik turned his head and looked towards the door, just as a slim young woman entered the room. She wore a light-blue gown and was veiled, but Laura couldn't help noticing the gleam of pure blonde hair beneath it, and her pale, clear skin. Her overall appearance was positively medieval, and Laura watched as her blue eyes sought out Malik, giving him one brief but definite nod of her head, before quietly slipping out of the same door she'd entered by.

'Who is that?' Laura asked.

There was a pause. 'Her name is Sorrel.'

'She doesn't look like a Kharistani.'

'No. She is English, and she is my ward.'

'Your *ward*?'

'You sound surprised, Miss Cottingham.'

'A little. It's an old-fashioned term which doesn't get used very much in England these days.' But it seemed to match the girl's old-world appearance—redolent of a time when women needed to be placed under the care of a guardian.

'We are an old-fashioned country,' said Malik carefully. 'And we protect our women. Sorrel's parents are dead, but her family has for many years had ties with Kharastan. And she is very close to the Sheikh,' said Malik. 'In fact, I understand that his Supreme Highness is now ready to receive the Frenchman.'

Malik was rising to his feet and summoning one of the servants to his side. He bent his head and uttered something in his native tongue, and Laura watched the servant go round to speak to Xavier.

'You will excuse me?' questioned Malik. 'Someone will show you back to your quarters.'

'Thank you.'

He bent his dark head and spoke in a low voice, so that Laura had to strain her ears to hear him. 'In case it interests you, there is a key which fits your door, should you require it. You will find it in the small box made from mulberry in your dressing room. You will also find alcoholic beverages in the large bureau in the sitting

room. You see, we cater for honoured Western guests
even if many of us do not share their tastes. I will bid
you goodnight, Miss Cottingham,' he added mockingly.

'Goodnight,' said Laura faintly, looking in surprise
at his retreating figure. Had Malik just offered her the
modern-day equivalent of protecting her honour? *We
protect our women*, he had said earlier.

She saw Xavier rise to his feet, his face as unmoving
as if it had been carved from a piece of granite, his
mouth hard and his eyes cold, yet her heart went out to
him, despite his forbidding look. Because surely deep
down he *was* a little apprehensive? He might be a billionaire playboy but he was still only human—and how
would anyone feel if they were on their way to find out
if an ancient and powerful ruler was really their father?

She watched him and Malik leave the room together,
as if they were compatriots of old, with none of the
visible tension which had existed between them earlier.

So was it protectiveness which had made Malik tell
her about the key—or was he just determined to make
it as difficult as possible for the Frenchman to take a
lover while he was here?

She bit her lip as Xavier's mocking boast came
back to her:

Do you think that a locked door would keep me out?

Back in her room, she washed and undressed by the
light of an ornate lamp which threw delicate shadows
onto the silken rugs. Then she took out all the pins con-

straining her thick hair and, once it had fallen free, pulled on a soft silk nightgown.

But Laura could not sleep, even though the low divan with its crisp linen sheets was cool and inviting. She kept thinking about Xavier and wondering what was happening with him and Zahir. Eventually she admitted defeat, getting up to open the shutters of her window which looked out onto the Palace gardens—and the view she beheld was simply breathtaking.

Washed silver-white by moonlight, a wide path led down to a lake which was lined with perfectly trimmed shrubs. From here she could make out the scent of unknown flowers and feel the faint breeze which shimmered the leaves and her hair. This could have been Versailles or Hampton Court—or any of the famous palace gardens which had been designed on a lavish scale. Only the dark, gliding shape of the occasional bird of prey overhead reminded Laura that—although man could control his environment to some extent—this was a much wilder land than the one she was used to.

Minutes ticked by as she sat there, and eventually she heard the sound of an outer door being opened, and then closed again. Laura held her breath as if she was waiting—but waiting for what? To see if Xavier would knock, perhaps?

But there was no knock. She heard careful movements of shutters being pushed open, as if someone was trying very hard not to make a noise, and then nothing but silence—and yet more silence.

Xavier had clearly gone to bed, and she ought to think about doing the same—but her throat was parched dry by the air-conditioning. She would slip next door and fetch herself a cool drink—maybe that would help.

Pulling on a silk-satin robe which matched the negligee beneath, and knotting it tightly at the waist, Laura walked through into the sitting room. At first she didn't notice the dark figure silhouetted against the spangled sky, silent and unmoving as a statue—at least not until it moved, like a character on stage coming to life. Laura gave a little cry of alarm.

Xavier turned round, but his face was so shadowed that it was impossible to read what was there. But even if the sun had been overhead would Laura have known what was going on his mind? Or would his features be as tightly shuttered as they had been when he had walked out of the lavish banqueting hall with Malik earlier?

The sight of a half-naked woman following straight on from his meeting with the Sheikh was one stimulation too many, and the reality of her luscious breasts pushing against the silk of her robe set Xavier's pulse hammering and his already confused thoughts into overdrive.

'What the hell are you doing in here?' he demanded.

'I couldn't sleep.'

He stepped away from the windows into the room, and the light from the lamp showed a cold, hard look in his eyes.

'Well, try,' he instructed harshly. 'Because you certainly won't manage it standing up, looking at me.'

Looking like that. Like the answer to every man's aching dream. 'What are you doing here?' he snapped. 'After all the damned fuss you made earlier about sharing did you then decide you would like to tantalise me by drifting in here during the dead of night, dressed in next to nothing?'

'It's not next to nothing and I didn't know you were still awake!' she retorted. 'I wanted a drink of water, that's all!'

'So get one!' he bit back.

This was a different Xavier. Laura could see the sharp tension which was tightening his rugged features—even if she hadn't heard it distorting his voice. The skin seemed to be stretched tightly over his face, and she could see a muscle working frantically in his cheek. All that pressure building up inside him—wouldn't he explode if he didn't let it out?

Stupidly, Laura found herself wanting to stroke the tangled softness of his black hair as his taciturn attitude made her heart soften. To hear him lashing out defensively like that surely meant that on some level he had been affected by what he had heard tonight. Because— for all his wealth and his influence and the women who adored him—Laura suddenly recognised that tonight the powerful playboy was completely alone in the world.

And why should you care?

'Would you like a drink?' she questioned, ignoring the mocking question in her head and telling herself it was only because no one could fail to be affected by the bleak expression in his eyes.

'Not water, and no more of those damned melon cocktails I had to endure during dinner. I could do with a real drink, if you must know.' His eyes narrowed as he watched her move like a dream across the room towards a polished cabinet made of walnut and apricot wood. 'What are you doing?'

'Getting you a drink.'

'I just told you—I don't *want* a soft drink.'

'That's not what I meant—there's some alcohol here. Malik told me.' Laura pulled open the door of the cabinet to reveal an assortment of bottles and different sizes of glass. 'I feel a little bit like the fairy godmother waving her wand,' she said. Surely you mean Cinderella? mocked the voice in her head. She looked up at him. 'What would you like? Wine? Beer? Champagne?'

'Not champagne,' he said flatly.

So we're not celebrating a paternal reunion, thought Laura. She pulled out a bottle of Kharastani wine and held it up. 'Shall we try this?'

'Why not?' He took the bottle from her without a word and poured the almost black liquid into two crystal glasses, glad to have the distraction of action. 'God knows what we're drinking,' he observed wryly. 'Kharastani wines aren't exactly a must-have for every good cellar.'

Laura accepted a glass from him and sipped it. It was thick, sweet and quite strong—and maybe that's just what he needs, she thought. Maybe just what *I* need. 'Gosh! That's strong.'

'You like it?'

'I can taste liquorice and something sweet.' Laura stared at him. 'But we've said everything there is to say about the wine—are you going to tell me what the Sheikh said to you?' *Whether he really is who he says he is and whether you have accepted that?*

Xavier took a mouthful of the liqueur-like drink and winced, then ran his tongue over lips suddenly grown dry. 'I guess that if I were in your situation I'd be curious, too.'

Very curious, thought Laura. She sat on one of the divans and looked up at him expectantly. 'What's he like?'

There was a pause. 'He's *old*,' he said flatly, and then shrugged. He looked up to see that her face was completely calm, as if someone had wiped every emotion away other than genuine concern.

'You wanted him to be strong and virile—a man in his prime—a man you could relate to?' she hazarded.

He shook his dark head. 'Of course I didn't. On an intellectual level I knew he'd be old—just not quite *that* old. I'm thirty-three and he's over eighty. He was nearly thirty years older than my mother!'

'Is that such a big deal? In Hollywood terms, it's nothing.'

'In France it is nothing either,' he lanced back, aware that he was not thinking rationally. 'But perhaps such a gap hits you hardest when you see the reality for the first time in old age.' Had it made him aware of his own life—and how quickly the years were passing?

She heard the edge to his voice. 'You're angry,' she observed.

'Yes, I am angry,' he agreed hotly. 'So what?'

'You ought to decide what it is you're angry about.'

His mouth twisted. 'Since when did lawyers start specialising in amateur psychology?'

'Have people spent their whole lives agreeing with you, Xavier?' she demanded. 'Or is it just that you can't bear to think someone else might have a different opinion which might just be right?'

He was taken aback by her straightforwardness, and more affected than he wanted to be by the compassion in her emerald eyes. Xavier had thought that he had grown a careful immunity to feelings, yet it was now clear that he had not. Was it a crime to concede that the whole experience had shaken him more than he would have thought possible? Or would anyone else have felt the same in the circumstances?

'Maybe,' he conceded, and met the question in her eyes. 'It's a story as old as time itself,' he said slowly. 'My mother was a young actress in Paris when the Sheikh first laid eyes on her. Zahir said that she had fire and passion and ambition in her heart.' His voice hardened. 'Which presumably is one of the things which drew him to her.'

'And presumably she was very beautiful?'

'Oh, she was beautiful,' he said flatly. 'She was exquisite.'

'So what happened?' asked Laura.

'They had an affair.'

'Secret?'

'*Mais, bien sûr.* Of course. He was a married man. And a high-profile one.'

'And...then what?'

Uncharacteristically, Xavier hesitated. The look in the Sheikh's eyes had spoken of regret—but was that the ruefulness of a man coming to the end of his life who looked back with wistfulness as he remembered the long-past pleasures of the flesh? Or was it genuine regret that he had abandoned a woman who was in love with him, without ever thinking that there might have been consequences to their ill-fated affair?

'Zahir came back to Kharastan,' he said slowly. 'And never saw her nor spoke to her again.'

'So he wouldn't acknowledge you as his son?'

Xavier looked at her, an odd note stealing into his voice. 'That's the strangest thing of all. He never knew about me—or so he claims,' he said. 'He only discovered my existence a couple of years ago, when he was trying to put his affairs in order. My photo had been seen by his aide in one of the French newspapers,' he said wryly. 'And the resemblance between us was pointed out to him. How ironic that he was prepared to be convinced by the evidence of a photo while I was not.'

'So what was it that finally convinced you that he *is* your father?' asked Laura quietly.

He could tell her that it was something he'd felt, something in his gut which was bone-deep and primitive, but that would be an admission too far for a man who rejected instinct—who relied on the infinitely safer world of fact and evidence.

Putting his hand into the pocket of his trousers, he withdrew a small object and placed it in the palm of his hand, where it gleamed in the moonlight. 'I brought it with me from Paris,' he said. 'It was all my mother left me—apart from a faded piece of ribbon.'

'What is it?' she whispered.

Xavier walked over to the divan and held his hand out, and Laura took it with trembling fingers. It was a ring of gold, with a stone she thought might be a ruby, though it was difficult to tell in the moonlight, and it was set like a star.

'Zahir has one exactly the same,' he said. 'It is very precious, and the gift of this ring is rarely made.'

'Which means your mother must really have meant something to him—do you think she knew that?'

He shrugged. 'Who knows?' He doubted it. She had been too busy struggling to survive and trying to hide her son from a man who could have helped her. Had he inherited his mistrust of others from her example? he suddenly found himself wondering.

'Maybe it was easier for her that way,' he said slowly. 'Because if you think someone cares it's all too easy to keep a dream alive—no matter how hopeless it is.'

Laura put her glass down. 'She never tried to tell him?'

Xavier shook his head, knowing that it would have been easy to shift the blame to his mother, for having denied him a father and having inculcated him with fear. But with the benefit of age and experience he could see now why she had acted as she had.

'He had no legitimate heir of his own in a land where male supremacy is unquestioned,' he said. 'Perhaps she was frightened that if he learned of my existence he might exercise his vast power to try to take me away from her. Presumably that was why she kept her own family in the dark, too—for fear that someone else might be persuaded to tell him. That was why she simply "disappeared", and we lived our strange life in the shadows, poor as church mice.'

'Poor?' asked Laura. surprised.

Xavier gave the ghost of a laugh. '*Oui, cherie,* poor—I was not born wealthy, you know. But we lived well—with food on the table and a fire at the grate.' Yet he recognised now the lasting legacy of his upbringing. Had the struggle and the secrecy of their lives been the driving force behind his need to acquire enough personal wealth for a million lifetimes, without acquiring any emotional baggage along the way?

'So why did he want to see you? And why now?'

'Because his wife died last year and that gave him the freedom to act—to tie up all the loose ends in his life. He felt that as long as the Sheikha was alive, it would be distressing to confront her with an illegitimate child.' His mouth twisted into an odd kind of smile. 'It seems that he is capable of respect, if not fidelity.'

'Is he…going to make you his heir?'

'He said something rather strange about that,' answered Xavier, recalling the way the Sheikh had brought it into the conversation almost absently—like a man reciting from a poem. 'That a crown could never be chosen, only inherited.'

'What does *that* mean?'

Xavier's eyes narrowed. He had already told her far too much—and now it seemed that she was getting turned on by the fact that one day he might rule a country like this. Would that make her more accessible to his bed? he wondered. Wasn't it about time he found out?

A pulse beat deep in his groin. Was he going crazy? Alone in a darkened room with a beautiful woman and what was he doing? *Telling* her stuff. Giving her access to his innermost thoughts. Instead of losing himself in the sweet sanctuary of her body.

He could feel the pulsing of his blood intensify as he stared at her. 'You have let your hair down,' he said suddenly.

Laura felt something in the atmosphere shift, alter. Something in his eyes had changed, too. Their blackness now seemed a beguiling contradiction—like a kaleidescope which could change from moment to moment, from hard and glittering to soft with promise.

'You have let your hair down,' he repeated huskily. 'Running like a blood-red waterfall down your back.'

It was an erotic image and her mouth dried to dust, all her earlier fluency dissolved by the sensual caress of his words.

Slowly and deliberately he hooked a finger in the air to beckon to her.

'*Viens,*' he whispered. 'Come here.'

It should have been easy to say no—and if he had said the same thing earlier, in a different mood and at a different time, then Laura might have done.

But his disclosures had changed something—had smashed through her defences to leave her vulnerable to the longing which was now flooding into her unguarded body. He had reached out to her in a way she could never have imagined, and his confidences had humbled her and made her feel connected to him in a way that somehow went beyond the physical attraction she had felt for him from the word go. She wanted more than sex from this black-eyed Frenchman. She wanted to hold him and to comfort him, to draw him to her breast and stroke his ruffled black hair—but did she dare? Did she dare give in to those desires?

He raised his eyebrows. Had he ever had to ask a woman more than once? Never! 'Yet you hesitate?'

Laura drank in his dark beauty while a fierce battle raged within her. Would it be so wrong? He had paved the way for intimacy with all the things he had just told her—surely that must mean he also respected her?

And wouldn't this be a kind of balm to her spirit—to help erase the memories of her disastrous time with Josh with a man who seemed to be everything a woman could ever want?

And then what? What if you give your heart to him—

because this man is in a different league from Josh, and he could easily smash it into a million pieces?

She wouldn't.

Men could just enjoy sex for what it was—so why couldn't a woman? Lots of her friends did.

And, silencing the doubts which began to bubble to the surface of her mind, Laura gave in to her heart's desire. She stood up and walked straight into his waiting arms.

CHAPTER EIGHT

UNSEEN in the half-light, Xavier's lips curved into a hard smile—his desire briefly dominated by triumph as he took Laura's soft body into his arms. Yet even as he thrilled at the very touch of her was he not aware of a faint trace of disappointment?

It had been as easy as it always was! Ah, if only she knew how much her uncertainty had turned him on—how the short wait had tantalised him—then might not she have made him wait a little longer?

His thumb skated down over her peaking breast and he felt her shudder. 'Do you know how long I have wanted to touch your breasts like this?' he questioned idily.

Laura closed her eyes with pleasure. 'No.'

'Well, you should. From the moment you walked into my office I wanted to take your clothes off.'

'Do you…do you think like that about all women?' she asked shakily, aware that this line of questioning might take her into dangerous waters.

'All women? *Non*. But a woman as beautiful as you—ah, *oui*—then it is certain!'

Laura stiffened. *So don't ask him stuff if you can't bear to hear the answer!*

'Relax, *cherie*,' he urged softly. 'Don't think about the others—for it is you who are here with me now.' And then he bent his head close to her ear, so that she could feel his breath warm on her neck. 'Do you know that I could continue to touch you like this until the end of time? Do you?'

Tracing a soft line over her nipple, his thumb circled a featherlight path of pleasure so intense that it was easy to let the troublesome thoughts just slip away. Laura closed her eyes in a delirious mixture of shock and pleasure. This was supposed to be just sex, so why did it feel like getting on a fast train to paradise? *Already!*

'Xavier,' she breathed in disbelief.

He moved his hand to cup the other. How completely she capitulated. And what a contradiction—the buttoned-up lawyer with the soft siren beneath. He bent his head to brush his lips against the sensitised mound, his tongue teasing her nipple so that his voice was muffled. 'I could take it into my mouth and lick you there until you cried out your pleasure. Has a man ever made you come from sucking your breast alone, *cherie*?'

Something in the erotic boast unnerved her—despite Laura's vow to just enjoy this for what it was without reading anything else into it. Xavier must have known some of the greatest lovers in the world—so how could she possibly compete?

'Have they?' he prompted silkily.

Suddenly, she was scared. The man whose dark head was bent over her breast was intent on pleasure but what if she couldn't pleasure him back? What if he thought she was some racy, experienced type? How would he react when he discovered the truth of her relative inexperience?

'Kiss me, Xavier,' she whispered nervously, as she clutched his shoulders with her trembling hands. 'Just kiss me!'

Her unsophisicated little plea startled him, and he straightened up to look down into her face, lifting her chin with the tip of his finger. Her green eyes were like two huge, glittering emeralds in her pale, heart-shaped face, with her glorious red hair tumbling free.

How wild and beautiful she looked, he thought, as he drove his mouth hungrily down on hers. But something in the breathless wonder of that first touch affected him, and the kiss became something other than what he had been expecting. Hard and hungry became soft and caressing, and then a sweet melding, and then—like the most glorious intimacy—the meeting and exploration of two mouths.

On and on the kiss went, as her arms reached up to entwine themselves around him like delicate vines, and Xavier felt weak with the intensity of it—forcing himself to concentrate on the hot, urgent shaft of his erection. But he felt he was fighting on so many fronts. His startling paternity. The way she made him feel. Himself.

'Laura,' he groaned.

He spoke the word into her open mouth and Laura trembled. 'What is it?' she whispered.

He wanted to say *Don't kiss me like that.* He wanted her to act dirty—*that* was how he liked his women to behave in the bedroom. Not like…like…

With ruthless erotic efficiency he began to stroke her. 'How can I play with you when you make me want to rip this exquisite nightgown from your body, push you up against the wall and take you like I was a teenage boy?' he demanded unsteadily. 'Tell me, is that how you like it? Hot and fast? Or slow and sweet?'

'I don't know,' she whispered, wondering what a man of the world would like best.

At another time and in another place her submissive reply might have been one of the most erotic things anyone had ever said to him. But coming on top of the emotional impact of the evening and his subsequent unburdening to her, Xavier felt exposed—as if the dry, gritty sand of the desert was being buffeted against his naked body.

'You don't know?' he repeated sarcastically.

She was going to mess up; she knew it. Josh had been right. 'Show me.'

Show her? He tensed as the unbelievable flew into his head. *'Mon Dieu,'* he breathed. 'You're not a virgin?'

Was that how she appeared—as fumbling and inexperienced as if she had no knowledge of men? 'Of course not.'

What the hell was he thinking of—asking a question which risked making a fool of him? Since he had been transported to this exotic and unknown land he had started inventing fairytales—was that it? As if a woman of her age who looked like she did would be a virgin!

Oh, yes—he would show her, all right. He began to slide the slippery silk up her leg, splaying his hands and stroking his fingertips along the soft surface of her inner thigh until she gasped.

'Unbutton my shirt,' he instructed unevenly.

Laura complied, silently willing her fingers not to fumble, but she was so eaten up with nerves and excitement that it wasn't easy. Please make this everything I think it could be and want it to be. Or was that asking too much? 'My hands are trembling,' she admitted.

'So I see,' he said drily.

'Xavier!' she gasped, just as his mouth dipped to kiss the curve between neck and shoulder, just as his hand slipped down between her legs to where the heat was most intense.

'Shall I make you come first with my finger?' he mused. 'And then my tongue? And then with…this?'

He guided her hand down to where he was exquisitely hard. Just let go, she told herself. If this is the only night you have with him, then why not give in to your every fantasy? 'No,' she whispered as she touched the rocky ridge of him. 'I want to feel you inside me.'

'Mon Dieu!' he moaned. 'You drive me crazy! You touch me and you talk to me like…' Like what? Not like a virgin, no. But with some quality which made it feel special, different. As if she was speaking from the heart.

He was used to worldly lovers who used polished and erotic skills to *pleasure* him—but there was something so *unaffected* about the way Laura reacted to him. As if it really *mattered*. Xavier tensed. And it didn't matter.

Who cared if she was unworldly? She was a woman he had been foolish enough to confide in—but that was done now, and this was the perfect opportunity to wipe that memory away and replace it with something else.

In that second, something in Xavier's resolve changed, and he felt it in the almost imperceptible hardening of his body. It was time to demonstrate his finesse, to make love to her in such a way that every man who followed would provide just a pale imitation of the pleasure she had known with him.

Without warning, he lifted her up into his arms.

'What are you doing?'

'What do you think? I am taking you to bed because I want to enjoy you in comfort,' he ground out, as he began to carry her towards his bedroom.

Enjoy you in comfort.

She couldn't work out whether that was sexy or insulting. But her craven body told her that it was too late to back out now, and she just leaned back against his hard chest as he carried her into his bedroom.

Her first thought was that this room was on a much

more lavish scale than hers, but then he was laying her down on the bed and towering over her like a dark statue—his black eyes gleaming as they swept over her in sensual assessment.

'I think that I am wearing a little too much, don't you?' he observed, as he peeled his shirt off and tossed it aside.

Laura swallowed. His torso was rock-hard and honed with muscle, and the sprinkling of dark hair on his chest arrowed enticingly down to where he began to unbuckle his belt.

He saw her emerald eyes widen as he began to slide the zip down, and he smiled, because this was how he liked it.

This was Xavier in control. Xavier about to pleasure a woman and then walk away, as he always did. Maybe not today, or even tomorrow—but walk he would eventually, without a backward glance or a single doubt.

'Xavier,' Laura whispered, because as he slid his trousers off she became suddenly daunted by the sheer magnificence of his body. Those tensile thighs, like iron itself, and narrow hips, and…Laura closed her eyes.

'Open your eyes,' he said softly, as he moved onto the bed and pulled her into his arms, a frown creasing his brow. 'Why do you shiver so? You are frightened? Because I am so big?'

'Daunted.'

He gave a cool laugh. 'You have the lawyer's precision with words—but this is no time for them, and you are wearing far too many clothes. *Viens ici.*'

He slid her negligee off, and the matching night-gown—until she was as naked as he was. He groaned as he looked at the lush breasts and the enticing triangle of dark red hair between her thighs.

'Later I shall feast my eyes on you,' he murmured. 'But first we shall feast on each other, because my hunger is too great to wait any longer.' Xavier bent his dark head to take the puckered rosy tip of her nipple into his mouth, his tongue flicking around it, his teeth gently grazing.

A shaft of desire shot through her. 'Oh!' gasped Laura, her head falling back against the pillow. 'Oh, Xavier!'

Xavier lifted his head and murmured his appreciation as the dark red hair tumbled into a fiery waterfall down her back. He let his tongue move between her breasts, roving to the dip of her navel, then continuing on an inexorable path downwards. Laura caught hold of his shoulders.

'No!' she cried. 'Xavier, please.'

He heard the raw appeal in her voice and something touched him through the slow burn of desire. He lifted his head again, ebony eyes narrowed. 'You don't like that?'

She wasn't really sure, because Josh had never been a big fan—and it suddenly seemed just too matter-of-fact to discuss their erotic preferences like this. Like going shopping in some sort of sexual supermarket, and she didn't want it to be like that.

Laura had convinced herself that this was never going to be anything more than great sex—but she was only human, and wasn't there also the very romantic side which no woman could ever quite suppress? That dreamed of hearts and flowers and happy-ever-after when she was intimate with a man? And even if they didn't mean it, *then* surely they could *pretend*?

'What is it that you want, *cherie*?' he questioned, sensing her doubts.

'I want you. Properly.' She didn't want him to perform a million of his clever little variations on a theme, for she was terrified that she wouldn't know how to respond to half of them, terrified that he might compare her to other women he had known who did.

'Tell me,' he murmured, and put his face very close to hers.

'I want you to fill me. I want…I want…'

'Want what, Little Miss Lawyer?' he teased, even though he was aching in a way he had never ached before. 'Don't tell me that a word has escaped you.'

'I want to feel you,' she said boldly. 'Inside me.'

Xavier could not see her blush, but he could feel it in the warmth of her cheek against his, and suddenly he felt more than a little overwhelmed. Was it because a blush was something a woman couldn't fake? Because it was a true glimpse into the way she was feeling—and Laura was feeling *shy* about making a request that had sounded so *delightful* to his ears.

'Then feel me you will,' he said starkly. 'Right… *now.*'

He moved over her, bending his head to kiss her as he thrust into her and set about making love to her as if it was a masterclass. He loved to take women to the edge over and over again, until they were begging him to put an end to their sweet torment. But Laura was different.

She kissed him a lot. She touched his face a lot. She ruffled his hair with her fingers and traced light little patterns across his skin with her fingertips until he shuddered—and he couldn't work out why. But she made love as if it was important—and even though it wasn't it didn't seem to affect his response to her.

So that for once it was Xavier who was lost—swept away on a wave of something so...so delicious that it defied description.

Afterwards he lay looking up at the moon-dappled ceiling, telling himself that it was just an incredible orgasm. But Laura's head was leaning against the crook of his arm and her hair was spread all over his chest, and he fell asleep with a much deeper feeling of contentment than usual.

CHAPTER NINE

MOLTEN gold morning sun flooded over her bare skin and Laura blinked as her eyes accustomed themselves to the light. Someone must have opened the shutters. She yawned, still disorientated in the aftermath of a fitful night spent…

Her eyes snapped open as she turned her head to see the empty rumpled space beside her.

A night spent making love with Xavier de Maistre!

'Good morning,' came a soft voice from the other side of the room. And there was Xavier. He was naked, except for a tiny towel wrapped around his hips, and his hair was still damp from the shower. And he was watching her as a wary biologist might observe a newly discovered species.

'Did you sleep well?'

'I…' She met his eyes. He had woken her three times in the night to make love to her. It had been the best night of her life, and at one point she thought she might have told him so. Had he forgotten all that—or did things you said while you were having sex simply not count? Was this the language of sophisticated lovers—that next morning you acted as if nothing had happened? Or was he using a subtle code to warn her not to make it into something it wasn't—not to come out with gushing words of praise for his undeniable sexual prowess or—worse— to tell him how easy it would be to fall in love with him?

Well, she would take her cue from him. They were both adults—she wasn't going to play coy or cringing or regretful or anything else negative. She had enjoyed every second of it—and so, presumably, had he.

'No, I feel great this morning,' she murmured back.

He walked over to the bed and kissed her hair. 'You smell great, too.'

'So…so do you.'

Their eyes met as he slipped his hand between her legs, and suddenly Laura felt shy without the concealment of darkness and kind shadows cloaking expressions and hiding any tell-tale signs of vulnerability or insecurity.

'Xavier.'

'Mmm?'

'I think I ought to be getting up.'

'Shh, that's my job. Take the towel off,' he instructed on a sultry whisper.

Had she thought she needed darkness to feel liberated? Well, that just went to prove how wrong she could be—because with him touching her in that light, teasing way Laura was suddenly overwhelmed with desire, and she pulled the towel from him and tossed it away.

'Like that?'

'*D'accord*. Just like that!' He shuddered and closed his eyes as she encircled him. 'Mmm—that is so good, *cherie*.'

'Is it?' Made bold by his murmured praise, Laura rubbed her hand up and down him in a wanton way which seemed both alien to her and yet utterly right. Or was that just the Xavier effect? Making a relatively inexperienced woman suddenly feel as if she would like to work her way through the entire *Kama Sutra*? 'How good?'

'Too good,' he groaned, and, snatching her hand away, lifted her up and slowly lowered her onto him instead, placing his hands on either side of her hips and moving her up and down on his body, while he pierced her honeyed sweetness with his thick shaft. It was unbearably erotic to see the contrast of her pale skin with the thick curtain of dark red hair which spilled down over her rose-tipped breasts. But her eyes were closed. 'Look at me,' he urged. 'Laura, look at me.'

Laura did—feeling suddenly shy. For it seemed the most intimate act of all for their eyes to meet and hold while he thrust into her. She felt her pleasure suddenly escalating out of control—her heart contracting along with her body as a great whooshing wave of emotion began to carry her away.

'I can't wait,' she cried out as spasms of profound pleasure began to pull her under.

Xavier's felt her tighten around him. 'Then don't,' he urged, helpless himself when, minutes later, he let go and was sent shooting into orbit by another orgasm of such intensity that his heart seemed to stop for a brief moment. And when the waves of pleasure had died away he was shaken as that feeling stole over him again—the lazy contentment which made minutes drift into hours, so that he must have slept.

When he awoke it was to find Laura lying watching him—and as he stretched luxuriously he wondered if they could get away with spending the whole day in bed.

'Hello, again,' he said, and stretched lazily.

Laura knew she had to pull herself together. She had been lying there watching him while he was sleeping— the two thick black arcs of his lashes feathering the dark olive skin. Mainly, she'd been feeling a kind of dazed bliss.

In sleep he looked softer—almost vulnerable. Yet hadn't there been traces of that same vulnerability when he had been telling her about his reaction upon meeting the man who had sired him? Or was that just Laura projecting what Laura wanted to see?

'Hello,' she said, and then, employing her usual sharp thinking instead of some love-hungry little-girl yearning, she forced herself to confront the reality of the situation.

Fact: they had just had sex.

Fact: Xavier was here to spend time with his father, not to be in bed with his father's lawyer.

So what would any other woman do in this situation? She would give him a cool thanks-for-the-memory kind of smile and she would get out early, with her dignity and her pride and her heart still intact.

'I'd better go,' she whispered, and even managed to lean over to plant a kiss on his nose.

Xavier shook his head. 'Let's ring for coffee,' he yawned.

'I'd rather not—I don't want anyone to know I'm in bed with you.'

'Why not? Malik didn't make you sign a vow of celibacy before you arrived, did he?'

'Of course not,' said Laura. 'I just don't particularly want to broadcast what we've been doing, if it's all the same with you.'

'Oh, come on.' He gave a slow, cynical smile. 'You would have to be *very* naïve if you believed that anything which goes on within the walls of this Palace isn't already known by Malik and his spies.' He tilted her chin with his finger. 'And I am sure that this bewitching lawyer is far from naïve.'

There was something in his tone she didn't like—something which was making her regret what had happened.

Determined not to make a big deal of it, Laura slid off the bed and began to pull on her clothes as unselfconsciously as possible—which wasn't easy with those eyes following her every move.

It wasn't until she had dressed and composed her face into the kind of even-though-we've-just-had-sex-I'm-not-going-to-come-over-all-heavy-on-you expression she knew was expected, that she dared to look at him again. And despaired that her heart melted at just the sight of him.

'So what are you going to do now?' she asked.

She had clammed up, he thought suddenly. Retreated from him in a way he was unused to. His eyes narrowed. Now, why was that? 'I presume you aren't talking breakfast?'

'No.' Her cool expression was starting to slip, and Laura was torn between wanting to be spirited out of there and wanting to climb back into bed and into his arms. 'I meant how long are you planning to stay here, in Kharastan?'

Xavier stretched his arms above his head, not bothering to hide his nakedness or the fact that watching her slipping on her underwear had been enough to make his body stir once more. He ached. He wanted her again—but he was damned if he was going to beg her to get back into bed with him. Women did not usually leave his bed unless he asked or ordered them to. *He* was the one who left it first!

Frustration bubbled over into anger, but he sublimated it with a cool look.

'Are you interested from a professional or a personal point of view?' he questioned.

Laura's heart missed a beat. There was something in his voice she didn't like. Was he worried that she was going to start getting all clingy and possessive? And warning her not to?

'Professional, of course,' she said crisply.

'I haven't decided what I'm going to do yet,' he said slowly.

His troubled face in the dead of the night came back to haunt her. It had torn at her heart then and it tore at it now. 'Why not stay?' asked Laura gently. Because— no matter what the outcome of their intimacy—she felt that he owed it to himself to explore his roots. 'And get to know your father.'

'You think I should?'

Did that mean he valued her opinion? Laura felt as if she'd been given some kind of moral reprieve and nodded her head. 'Definitely!'

Xavier's black eyes narrowed suspiciously as everything suddenly began to click into place. How completely she had switched from cool to passionate, then back to cool again. Her seemingly inexplicable appearance in his room last night, wearing clothes designed to seduce—as indeed all her clothes were.

During the journey from the Sheikh's apartments back to his room, had Malik somehow got word to her that Xavier's mood was dark and unpredictable? Had she been told to pacify him in the most elemental way known to women?

'How very persuasive you are, *cherie*,' he murmured. 'Tell me, is that also part of your brief—to convince me to stay?'

Something in his tone sent another whisper of alarm along her spine and the meaning behind his question became clear. Laura stared into eyes suddenly grown cold and thought how little she really knew of him. How could you connect with a man on a physical level, which at moments last night had seemed almost spiritual, and yet when you came back down to earth all that was left was emptiness and suspicion?

'I told you,' she said stiffly. 'My job was simply to bring you here.'

'And sleeping with me?' he drawled. 'Would you define that as a perk—or a condition?'

Laura froze, for a moment thinking that he couldn't possibly have meant it. But one look at the icy set of his features told her that he had. 'If I were the hysterical type I might just slap your face for that remark—but as I'm not I'll treat it with the contempt it deserves.'

'But you enjoyed it,' he challenged softly. 'In fact I'd go so far as to say you absolutely *loved* it—so I'd say it definitely fell into the category of perk, wouldn't you?'

Something about the way he said it reminded Laura of how eagerly she had writhed beneath him. The way she had wrapped her thighs around his back and the way her body had arched ecstatically beneath his. How she would have loved to tell him no—that as a lover he was a dead loss—that she had endured what had happened with gritted teeth. But he knew and she knew that would be the biggest lie of all.

'Oh, you're right. I did love it—the sex was great,' she said. 'But then I expect it always is—men don't get reputations as super-lovers without it being backed up by fact.'

'Why, thank you, *cherie*,' he drawled.

'It wasn't supposed to be a compliment!' she snapped. 'If you want to know, I think that going around seducing everything that moves is a pretty sad and empty way to live.'

'Whereas dressing to seduce and luring men back for wealthy Middle-Eastern potentates *isn't* sad and empty, I suppose?' he snapped.

Laura opened her mouth to tell him that the silk-satin clothes she wore were a million miles away from the way she usually dressed—but surely to do that would only bring substance to his argument? If she admitted that her wardrobe had been commissioned by the Palace—and at great cost—he might reasonably ask why her clothes had been of such importance. And, in a way, she wasn't completely blameless, was she? When she had been told to acquire the expensive garments she had readily agreed, hadn't she?

Because she had wanted the job, that was why—and because she had been willing to play the part she had been complicit in their schemes. But if she had allowed herself to be decorated like a cake—then she couldn't really complain if Xavier had wanted to take a slice of her for himself, could she?

Because you didn't have to let him!

She lifted her chin, telling herself that his last memory of her would be as a strong, proud woman, and not one who was crumbling inside and wishing it could be different.

'You know what?' she said. 'A constant stream of different women throughout your life means that you can cleverly avoid any intimacy and commitment, and that's okay—that's your choice. There will always be willing and available women for a man like you, Xavier.' She leaned forward, banishing self-interest and regret from her agenda, her green eyes on fire. 'But you've only got one father—remember that—though maybe the one you *have* got doesn't fit in with your particular image.'

Xavier stared at her. 'What are you talking about?'

'Maybe it will suit you to have a rich father you never knew. Maybe it makes you feel better—knowing you were denied access and forced to spend your early life in poverty. Though, ironically, that's probably the main factor in your success.' She studied him as dispassionately as was possible. 'Maybe you're one of those people who likes going through life with a reason to be angry— thinking it makes their unreasonable behaviour in some way acceptable. Well, it doesn't—not in my book.'

'How dare you speak to me like this?'

'Isn't it time that someone had the courage to?'

'Get out!' he flared furiously.

Laura suddenly felt the most delicious and heady sensation of power. 'I think you're forgetting yourself, Xavier. I don't work for *you* and therefore I don't take orders from you—and besides, I was leaving anyway, remember? I've got some paperwork to do, and after that I'm going to ask Malik to get me on the next flight out of here!'

Feeling his eyes burning into her back, Laura stalked out. It was possibly the most stylish exit she had ever made, but the satisfaction of knowing that did nothing to hide the pain she felt inside.

CHAPTER TEN

'Do you have *any* idea how much longer Malik will be?' questioned Laura, trying like mad to hold onto her temper, which was becoming more frayed by the second.

'You will be informed just as soon as he becomes available,' said his secretary smoothly, and Laura stared mutinously at his back as he disappeared through the door of Malik's office.

She had been kept waiting outside the office of the Sheikh's aide for almost forty minutes—growing angrier by the minute. She couldn't even go back to her suite—because Xavier was there and, having stormed out of his bedroom, she would look and feel a fool if she had to go crawling back again.

Yet neither could she just pack her bags and leave. She had flown here by private jet, she was the Sheikh's special guest, and as such it was going to be difficult to make her own travel arrangements and get back again. She wasn't even sure if there *were* any scheduled flights back to the UK—they almost certainly wouldn't be direct.

And they were bound to be expensive. Having gone to all this trouble earn herself enough money to get herself out of a financial fix, wouldn't it be a bit stupid if she then blew a large chunk of it on a ticket because her pride had been hurt and she felt used?

The sensible thing to do would be to wait and speak to Malik and gently remind him—if it came to it—that he was contractually obliged to pay her and send her home.

The door to Malik's large suite of offices opened and another of the male secretaries appeared, and bowed.

'Miss Cottingham,' he said, in the now familiar Kharastani accent. 'Malik Al-Ahal asks that you meet with him in the Perfumed Garden—will you please follow me?'

Laura frowned. Had Malik exited from his offices by a different entrance, or had she been misled into thinking that he had been there all along? Not that she would bother asking his secretary, she thought, as she stepped out into the brilliant Kharastan day. His undoubted loyalty to his boss told her it would be a waste of time.

Instead, Laura forced herself to concentrate on the beauty of the Palace gardens and try to erase the beauty of Xavier's face and body from her mind. Because a man could not be said to be beautiful or handsome—not if he had a black soul and a suspicious mind, and would pluck a woman up as if she were a flower to then be crushed underfoot.

But he could only do that if a woman let him.

The torment of her thoughts was momentarily

soothed by the sweet scent of the flowers which drifted out from the Perfumed Garden. It was intoxicating and evocative, and Laura breathed in deeply as she followed the secretary through an arched arbour, where honeysuckle grew in wild profusion.

And there was Malik—standing with his back to her as he snipped a perfect white rose from its bush.

He must have heard her footstep, for he turned when he heard her and said something rapidly in his native tongue to his secretary, who bowed deeply, then left.

Malik held the rose out towards her. 'You will accept this flower?'

Laura's face was grave. 'Only if I can be certain it comes without obligation.'

Malik raised his eyebrows. 'Perhaps you will tell me why you insisted on this meeting?'

'Because I want to finish up whatever work is left and go home—to England.'

'I'm afraid that may not be possible.'

Laura's blood ran cold. It was worse than her worst fantasies. 'What do you mean—not possible? My boss knows I'm out here, and he'll get worried if he doesn't hear—he's expecting me back at work,' she breathed. 'So you can't keep me here against my will!'

Malik gave a short laugh. 'My dear Miss Cottingham! We do much trade with England, and I do not think that the government of your country would look kindly on us if we started keeping its young women prisoners!'

Laura stared at him suspiciously. 'Then why won't you let me go home?'

'It might be a little more…' Malik hesitated '…*convenient* if you stayed. Just for a couple more days, you understand?'

But it was a velvet-cloaked order, not a polite request, and realisation slowly began to dawn on her. 'This is Xavier's doing, isn't it? He has demanded this?'

Malik didn't react.

'*Isn't* it?' questioned Laura.

Malik shrugged. 'You cannot blame the man for wanting you to remain here as his…companion—not in view of what has happened.'

Did Laura imagine the faint note of censure in his voice, or was she just feeling vulnerable and raw? 'I'm not with you,' she said. But then she saw the way he lowered his eyes, and suddenly she knew exactly what he meant.

He *did* know that she'd slept with Xavier—had Xavier told him, or had one of the servants gossiped? Laura was aware of the sting of colour to her cheeks, knowing that to try to defend herself would be a doomed enterprise certain to lead to even more embarrassment.

What excuse or reason could she give to condone her behaviour in a country where a woman's honour was as highly prized as rubies? She could not even offer up deep emotion as a contributing factor—who would believe her when she had known Xavier for such a short time?

Yet it was not as it must have looked to an outsider. Deep emotion *had* been there—well, certainly on

Laura's part. She had wanted to comfort him as well as to be made love to. She had wanted to touch him in ways which were more than physical—the sad thing was that she had ever believed she *could*. Something strong and powerful had reached out to her—something so rare that she had felt nothing remotely like it in all her twenty-six years.

But now?

Laura bit her lip, wondering if she had been completely stupid. Whether what had happened had been all about her writing the script for what she *wanted* it to be—rather than the reality of what it was.

But if Xavier thought that she was going to continue with the intimacy, then he was badly mistaken. What was done was done—she couldn't blame him for taking what she had so freely offered—but now it was time to look after herself.

'This is intolerable, Malik,' she said in a low voice, but the Kharastani man was shaking his head.

'Only if you make it so,' he demurred.

'But we have interconnecting rooms,' she pointed out.

'And you have a key,' he said sharply.

He didn't say *And maybe you should have used it before*—but he didn't have to. It was all there, written on his face, and Laura flinched.

'And I suppose that if I make a fuss then my salary will suffer? You'll withhold it—or use complicated international machinery to delay payment for so long that by the time I get it I'll no longer need it?' she challenged.

Malik's eyes widened fractionally, as if matters as vulgar as money were not talked about within the rarefied surroundings of the Palace, but Laura didn't care. She was not—like him—cushioned by the untold wealth of a royal family and its courtiers. She was a working girl.

'I must ensure that everyone is kept happy,' he said.

'Everyone except me, that is,' returned Laura as she recognised her predicament. She had no choice other than to stay, but at least she could word it to sound as if it had been *her* decision—her wounded pride demanded that much. 'Well, I'll stay for as long as it is necessary, but no longer. I'm not prepared to sacrifice my livelihood simply because I made a poor personal judgement.'

'I think it will not be as bad as you anticipate. For all its antiquity the Blue Palace has many facilities for you to enjoy,' countered Malik. 'There is an Olympic-sized pool, a gym—and our cinema houses the most up-to-the-minute films. And I have assigned Sidonia to cater for your every need.'

Laura raised her eyebrows. 'A gilded cage, you mean?'

'There are many ways of looking at a situation,' he said softly. 'You could always try to enjoy it.'

Laura met his eyes. 'If you say so.' But it wasn't as easy as that. If Xavier hadn't been part of the deal, then it might have been—but how could she enjoy what sounded like a state-of-the-art holiday camp if she was worrying about fighting him off? Or, worse, fighting off her own attraction to him?

She turned on her heel, not knowing or caring

whether she was supposed to wait for the Kharastani nobleman to leave first. If they were breaking the rules of her employment then she would damned well break a few of her own in return!

Emerging from the direction of the palace, Laura saw Sidonia walking towards her, and suddenly she was pleased to see the friendly and welcoming face of the servant.

'Good morning, Sidonia,' she said.

'Good morning.' Sidonia folded her hands together, the tips of her fingers beneath her chin, and gave the elegant bow of the traditional Kharistani greeting. 'You wish perhaps to take breakfast now?'

Laura shook her head. 'Not just yet. What I would really like is some exercise. Is there any way you could get hold of a swimsuit for me?'

Sidonia nodded, then spoke in her sweetly accented English. 'But of course. The pool is equipped with everything you could possibly require.'

'Just for me?' Laura wondered aloud as they walked towards the complex.

'For all our guests. The Sheikh often has visiting dignitaries who expect things to be primitive—it gives him great pleasure to show them how much a part of the modern world we are here at the Palace.'

Laura shot the servant a curious look as they walked past exquisite flowerbeds, each symmetrically planted with a different colour theme—scarlets, golds and blues. Her pride in her Palace and her Ruler were touching.

'From the air, the flowers in this part of the garden resemble our Kharastan flag,' said Sidonia. 'You see the shape of the falcon's head?'

'Yes, I do.' Laura smiled. 'Your English is so good.'

Sidonia nodded. 'I am pleased with my progress—but the credit for that must go to Sorrel.'

The name rang a bell, and Laura remembered the young blonde woman who had appeared at the banquet, summoning Xavier to the Sheikh, and nodded. 'Is that Malik's ward?' she questioned, and Sidonia nodded. 'How did that happen?'

'Her parents were the British representatives here in Kharastan—both great Middle Eastern scholars,' said Sidonia. 'They died in an aircrash over the mountains of Maraban and everyone thought that Sorrel would go straight home. But she had grown up here and loved it—she considered Kharastan to be her home and was reluctant to leave. She attended the university here—very few English women are fluent in the Kharastan language. One day she will go back to England, but she will not do so until the Sheikh dies.'

Laura wondered how much Sorrel—and indeed Sidonia—knew about Xavier. Were they aware that he was the Sheikh's son—perhaps with a legitimate claim on his kingdom? And what if Xavier made no claim, or did not meet with the Sheikh's approval? Who would rule Kharastan then?

For some reason Malik's face swam into Laura's mind, but they had reached the poolhouses now, and she was dazzled by the sheer opulent splendour of the pool. It was a vast rectangle of perfectly clear water, and it was lined with beautiful golden and blue mosaics which depicted scenes of Kharastan life. The poolhouses themselves were the very last word in luxury—with a steamroom and sauna making it look like a lavish and very exclusive health club.

'You will find everything you need here,' said Sidonia.

'Thank you,' said Laura, as she gazed round in delight. 'And I wonder if you could bring me some day clothes from my room? Perhaps trousers might be suitable?'

'Certainly.'

After Sidonia had gone, Laura selected a plain black costume and dived into the water, emerging like a seal mid-way down the pool and beginning to swim. She had been good at swimming as a child—with free baths close to their home. Often—if her mother had been working in the evenings—Laura would go there straight from school, swimming length after length in a steady crawl.

It had always invigorated her rather than tired her out, and it did the same now—so that by time she had finished her swim she felt ready to face anything.

Afterwards, Laura showered and changed into the linen trousers and silk shirt Sidonia had brought—tying her damp hair back with a green ribbon which echoed the colour of the jade and silver beads she slung round her neck. Narrow sandals were slipped onto her bare feet and she felt in control.

She looked just right—cool, sophisticated and sleek.

Now Laura could see that the Sheikh's insistence that she wear designer clothes from top to toe had been about much more than dressing to lure Xavier back here—as he had accused her. It meant that she didn't look out of place in these august surroundings. That she looked as if she fitted in. And that was rather a nice feeling.

'I'd like breakfast now, Sidonia. Is it possible to eat outside?' she asked the maidservant.

'But of course!'

A table was set for her beneath the dappled canopy of some exotic large-leafed tree, and she was just spooning mulberry jam onto her plate when a shadow fell over her. She looked up, her heart beginning to pound in her chest when she saw who it was.

'Xavier!'

She was the first woman who had ever run from him, and yet here she was—looking cool and amazing in linen and silk, with the sun shining on her glossy red hair and some stunning beads emphasising the intense emerald of her eyes.

'You are hiding from me?' he asked silkily.

'Does it look like it? Hiding would imply fear, and even though it seems I am virtually a prisoner here the last thing I am is frightened!' she returned. 'Especially of you!'

Xavier smiled. Her feisty form was like a breath of fresh air after the tumult of the previous night. His meeting with the Sheikh had affected him more than he had anticipated. He had thought that sex with Laura would wipe it all away—his troubled feelings as well as his lust for her—but he had felt none of the expected sense of closure this morning.

So he had come looking for Laura, expecting... what? To find her tearstained or regretful—not sitting in the sunshine eating her breakfast!

'Then why did you run away?' he probed.

'Because your remarks to me were insulting.'

'So you weren't asked to seduce me to entice me to stay?' In the bright, clear air of the morning the accusation sounded ridiculous as soon as it fell from his lips.

'I'm a lawyer, Xavier—not a professional siren! Tell me, are the women you usually deal with unscrupulous enough to do something like that?'

He shrugged. 'Sometimes.'

'Then you've been mixing with the wrong kind of woman.'

Their eyes met in a long moment. 'Maybe I have,' he said slowly.

Laura saw the cat-like dilation of his black eyes and felt the tiptoe of awareness shivering its way down her spine. 'And that wasn't supposed to be a come-on!'

'Maybe I want it to be.'

But Laura shook her head, praying for the strength and resolve she needed. 'No, Xavier. And it's no good looking at me like that—I mean it.'

'No?' he echoed, in disbelief.

His arrogance was staggering! He thought he could say whatever he wanted to her and she would just lie back and let him make love to her!

'You are something else,' she breathed. 'But—just so that there's no misunderstanding—let me make myself clear. Sex with you was utterly fantastic, as I'm sure you know—but sex for women, *most* women, involves a lot more than that. Respect and self-worth play a pretty important part in the equation. If you really think me capable of going around and sleeping with different men on the Sheikh's say-so then you have only yourself to blame when I insist on keeping you at arm's length—no matter how good a lover you are.'

'You cannot mean this, Laura,' he objected. 'You have voiced your anger towards me, and I accept it. Perhaps I even deserved it. I apologise for the things I said to you. I take them back.' A smile curved the edges of his lips. 'There.'

Shaking her head, she pushed her chair back and stood up. 'You just don't get it, do you, Xavier? It can't just be made better with a grudging apology accompanied by a sexy smile.'

He could smell her newly washed hair and the faint drift of scent on her skin, and something about its innocent freshness made him want to groan aloud with frustration. 'But I want you, Laura—I want you *now*!'

'Read my lips,' she said, savouring the heady sensation of having taken back control. 'Which part of the word no don't you understand? There will be no intimacy. But that doesn't mean we can't be friends.'

'Friends?'

'There's no need to make it sound as if I've suggested something obscene—you do *have* friends, I suppose, Xavier?'

Of course he had friends—but no real close women-friends. And never lovers who *became* friends, because they always wanted to continue the intimate side of their relationship. And would Laura be any different, despite her vowed intentions?

Xavier's face was like stone, but beneath its unmoving exterior he felt the heavy pulsing of his blood as he stared down at her parted lips and her determined expression. The light of battle suddenly flared in his eyes.

No intimacy?

Like hell there wouldn't be!

CHAPTER ELEVEN

'YOUR resolve is admirably strong,' breathed Xavier in reluctant admiration. 'But I think that the strain of resisting what you really want is beginning to get to you—don't you, Laura? Your face is pale, despite the sun, and see how you tremble whenever I am near. And you really shouldn't lose any more weight—your body is quite perfect as it is.'

Never had Laura been so glad of the canopy of her wide-brimmed hat—which not only protected her pale skin from the scorching heat of the desert sun but also hid her face from Xavier's piercing black stare. Because if he had the opportunity to look closely he would discover that he was right—she *was* finding it difficult to withstand his relentless, sexy appeal.

Since their—she supposed you might call it showdown, they had spent nine days and nights in close confines within the walls of the Blue Palace, where she had learnt a surprising yet uncomfortable fact.

Naïvely, Laura had supposed that women didn't feel

sexual frustration in the same way as men did. She had
certainly never been afflicted by it before. Her split with
Josh had had rather terrifying financial repercussions,
but she'd been greatly relieved at no longer having to
endure his acrobatic but ultimately unsatisfactory style
of lovemaking.

But this was different.

Lying in bed at night—knowing that the magnificent
olive-skinned body of Xavier de Maistre was lying
naked on the other side of the door she now insisted on
locking...well. It would be enough to make any woman
ache, surely—especially if she'd already tasted his
sensual skills?

She considered his accusation now, as she slid two
fingers easily inside the waistband of her trousers—
had she lost weight? 'Everyone loses weight in hot
weather,' she defended.

'But not everyone watches the object of her desire
with hungry eyes instead of giving in to that desire.
How stubborn you are, Laura.'

But Laura was less stubborn than concerned that her
clever plan might have completely backfired on her.
She had kept Xavier at arm's length and told him she
wanted to be friends without realising that friendship
broke down barriers in the same way that sex did.

If you lived very closely with a man and he wasn't
kissing you the chances were he would have to talk to
you, and you to him. And, as two foreigners in a strange
land, they'd had plenty to talk about.

Laura had already decided that it would be easier if they liked each other—what she hadn't realised was how *easy* it would be to like him. Nor had she expected the look of admiration in his black eyes when she stuck to her guns and would not be swayed by his occasional flirtatious comments. It was as if he had been waiting for *her* resolve to crumble, and when it hadn't he had been forced to look at the situation—and her—in a completely different way.

Gradually, his expression of wry frustration had become replaced with a growing *respect,* and that made Laura feel good. It gave her back her *self*-respect, which meant she relaxed, and the more she relaxed the more he did—and, *oh*, that made her feel vulnerable all over again!

In her attempt to protect herself she had made herself susceptible to his careless charm, which was almost as devastating as his kiss.

She wiped the glow of sweat from her face as they stood on the summit overlooking the wide, sweeping plain of Kharastan's flat and rolling desert. The stark and dramatic country was becoming a little more familiar to her day by day—since every day something different had been laid on for the benefit of the Sheikh's honoured guests.

They had been to visit the bustling bazaars in the capital of Kumush Ay, and had been mesmerised by the sights and sounds and wonderful smells and bright colours of the busy marketplace. They had been taken to the formal riding school and witnessed a magnificent display by a troop of Akhal-Teke horses. And this morning they had come to watch Malik and a group of other Kharastani noblemen engage in the ancient sport of falconry.

Laura stood a little way back as she watched, aware of Xavier's rapt air of concentration and the realisation that this was very much a male bonding thing.

'Today we still practise this noble art as a mark of respect to the survival of our forefathers in the desert,' said Malik, as a terrifying-looking bird with cruel eyes perched on his leather-covered arm.

Xavier had revelled in his stay in the country—aware that he and Laura were being shown a variety of Kharastan life and recognising how rich and diverse it was. But through all the banquets, the shows and the lavish displays, he had remained somewhat on the sidelines. A spectator rather than a participant—until today. Under this beating desert sun, in this harsh and unforgiving terrain, something had happened to him.

Xavier had been captivated by the powerful raptor as it flew low across the coarse desert. Bobbing and veering like a drunk teetering home late at night, it shot high into the air as the lure was thrown. It was primitive and elemental, and in a moment of clarity he could suddenly see the point of the sport. But it was more than that.

It was like the click of understanding when you reached fluency in a foreign language. For the first time he allowed himself to feel the connection between himself and his forebears, to acknowledge his birthright.

His ancestors must have stood on this hot and harsh terrain, he thought, as tiny grains of sand whispered against his skin. When survival in the desert was a daily battle and falconry was not an elegant sport but a means of obtaining food. And at that moment he seemed a long long way from his elegant Parisian apartments.

It seemed that he was not who he had thought he was—instead he had discovered a man who was almost a stranger to himself. And he knew in that moment that he had changed, and that he could never go back to being the person he had been before. How could he? He was half-Kharastani!

The thought shook him—and, just like his early ancestors must have done, he sought refuge from his troubled thoughts in the calm balm of a woman's soothing presence.

He turned to look at Laura, who was standing watching the display with a mixture of fear and fascination, and he recognised that it had been her determination to push him away which had allowed him to focus his mind and his thoughts, like an athlete preparing for a big race. The absence of sex had filled him with a new and inner sense of purpose and—yes—of identity. But now he ached for her in a way he could never remember aching for a woman before.

Now, in the bright desert light, he narrowed his eyes to see if he could see the dark blot on the horizon which would herald the return of the strong, graceful bird they called the Saker Falcon. The skies remained clear, but inside Xavier was still troubled.

He thought of the local name for the Saker—hurr, meaning noble, or free. Malik had told him about it when they had come from Zahir's room last night, after one of their regular evening meetings with the Sheikh.

'How is Zahir?' Laura asked, her soft voice breaking into his thoughts.

Xavier looked at her, a picture of loveliness in the wide-brimmed hat which shielded her fair skin from the fierce Kharastani sun. He wanted to pull the ribbon from her hair and shake it loose, lose himself in its thick, scented satin. To feel rather than think—about *anything*—and yet she seemed determined to torment him, one way or another.

'He's about the same.' He shrugged.

'So what do you and he talk about, night after night?'

'*Sacre bleu*, but you stretch my patience, *cherie*!' Xavier laughed in spite of himself, for at that moment they saw the Saker contrasted against the bright sky, and there was whoop of joy from all the men. He turned to Laura, his face animated and alive with pleasure at the ancient ritual he had just witnessed. 'You keep me at arm's length, Laura—and yet you pry into my soul!'

Laura shook her head. 'I don't mean to pry, Xavier,' she said truthfully. 'I just wonder if it's good for you to keep everything bottled up—not to talk about this huge thing in your life that has happened. Unless you discuss it with Malik, of course?'

Xavier shook his head. The Sheikh's aide seemed to

have a curiously ambivalent attitude towards him. At times they were at ease together, yet at others there was tension and once—just once—Xavier had looked up and been surprised to see a look almost of *jealousy* there. Did he resent another man's growing closeness with the Sheikh? he wondered. After years of being his sole and trusted aide?

'No, I don't talk to Malik,' he said flatly.

'Then why not talk to me?' asked Laura, as she climbed into the back of their four-wheel drive and Xavier got in beside her, before the car moved away in a cloud of desert dust.

'Why should I do that?'

'Well, I'm a good listener. I'm impartial—and I'm honest enough to tell you what I think rather than what you want to hear—which in your case is no bad thing.'

'Are you quite possibly perfect in every way?' he asked, in a voice which was silkily sardonic.

When they'd first arrived here Laura might have viewed this question as making fun of her. But she had altered—was altering—she could feel it happening even now. She had stood firm in her resolve not to be a compliant bedfellow that he would soon tire of, and had regained her self-respect by managing to resist his breathtaking allure.

Friendship you had to work harder at than sexual chemistry—but she felt they were getting there.

But it was much bigger than just what *she* had got out of the experience. Laura had been looking outwards,

as well as inwards. She could see the chase of conflicting emotions in Xavier's eyes, and suddenly found that
she wanted to help him come to terms with what was
happening to *him*.

'Quite possibly completely perfect,' she agreed, half
turning in her seat to look at him. 'Tell me if you want.
Don't if you don't.'

Her neck was like a graceful arc, down which the
rope of dark red hair fell like plaited silk. What did he
have to lose? 'In the absence of much more distracting
pursuits I can see no alternative to talking,' he said. 'Yet
are you bound by professional confidence, Laura—or
will you be contracting my story to the highest-bidding
journalist on our return to the West?'

She shook her head and sighed in mock despair. 'You
have such a low view of other people.'

'It is based on experience,' he observed. 'Women
selling stories about my prowess as a lover! Business
rivals describing me as unscrupulous.'

'You probably *are* a bit unscrupulous, though,
aren't you?'

He stared at her for a long moment, and then unexpectedly began to laugh. 'Ah, but you are outrageous,
cherie,' he murmured admiringly.

The compliment warmed her more than it should
have done—and Laura forced a prim smile. 'If you
don't want women to sell their story, you should get to
know them properly before you have sex with them!'

He slanted her a look. 'Like I did with you, you mean?'

Laura blushed. 'That was cheap.'

He nodded. 'Yes, it was,' he agreed—because what he had shared with Laura felt anything but cheap.

The colour began to fade from her cheeks. 'If you're worried about confidentiality—I would never break the confidence of a friend.'

Was it because of her job that he found himself wanting to talk to her? Yet he had dated lawyers before without feeling the need to bare his soul, hadn't he? *But you have never found yourself in a situation quite like this one.* And hadn't talking been the precursor to that incredible night he had spent with her?

He felt free with her. Free to be able to put his thoughts into words and not have them stored in an emotional bank to be used against him. It was like allowing yourself to swim naked in the sea after years of being restricted by a tight rubber wetsuit.

'It's weird,' he said thoughtfully. 'It's just the little things that make you realise. The Sheikh is left-handed, and so am I. He never watches television but he devours non-fiction, and so do I. He is shrunken now by age, but his eyes…'

He had seen a photo of the Sheikh in his glorious youth—strong and indominitable—taken long before he had met his mother. But seeing the man in the flesh, even shrivelled flesh, was profoundly different—for in that virile face Xavier had caught a glimpse of himself, a merging of past and present which was a whole new and slightly shattering experience.

'His eyes are the same as yours?' guessed Laura.

'Yes,' he said simply. 'Exactly the same.

Laura suspected that on one level Xavier knew that traits such as left-handedness and eye-colour were inherited—but some things went beyond mere science. It was the human connection which was the important one here—the missing link in his life which had now been joined up.

'Do you think this discovery will change how you live your life from now on?' she asked quietly.

It was a perfectly reasonable question, he supposed—and yet he reacted badly to it, like someone allergic to strawberries being exposed to the refreshment tent at Wimbledon.

'You are suggesting there is something wrong with the way in which I live my life?'

Laura shrugged.

'Aren't you?' he persisted softly. 'I want to know, Laura.'

What did she have to lose? They were hardly going to be bumping into each other on opposite sides of the Channel after this trip. Once she might have been tempted to tell him in order to deflate some of his arrogance—but now she wanted to tell him for a very different reason. Because she was a friend, and she cared.

'Okay, then, I'll tell you,' she said. 'Yours seems a rich life only in the most superficial of ways. Like you're being carried along on a wave of luxury and not really connecting properly with people. Like money matters and nothing else.' Her voice tailed off and she gave a little shrug. 'That's all.'

'That's *all*? You demolish my very existence and say *that's all*? You think your own life is so great, do you, Laura?'

'Of course I don't!' she burst out frustratedly. 'I *knew* this would happen. I'm not here to sit in judgement on you, Xavier—but you did ask.'

Yes, he had—and she had told him, with breathtaking honesty. He could not think of a single other person in the world who would have had the courage to do that. Was some of what she said right? he wondered.

'Why did you take this job?' he asked suddenly.

Laura stared hard at her fingers, which had acquired a faint tan from the Kharastan sun. How much more of her honesty did he want—and how much of her story did she want to tell? But friendship—true friendship—wasn't one-sided.

'Oh, the usual. A man. Josh.'

'And you were in love with this *Josh*?' he said, scarcely believing that *he* should ask such a question. He was sounding like one of those men he had always despised. Like one of those jealous fools who were bothered by other men.

'I *thought* I was in love with him,' Laura answered. 'But that may just have been my own justification for sleeping with him.'

In one sentence she had exposed her relative innocence, and Xavier wondered if she was aware that her

faint shudder had told him everything he needed to know
about her physical relationship with this other man.

Was that what made him suddenly feel so guilty—
the fact that he had judged her so harshly and made
those false allegations against her?

'But, no, on reflection—it wasn't love,' she said,
after a bit more thought. 'He dazzled me—but he turned
out to be shallow. He just seemed so *exciting*. I'd worked
hard to get my law degree—taken so many jobs during
the holidays because money was tight—that I'd never
really stopped to have fun.' She gave a rueful smile.
'And while Josh had the worst CV I've ever seen—he
certainly knew how to have fun.'

'What happened?'

Laura shrugged. 'We bought a house in joint names,
but our contribution to its upkeep was—how shall I put
this?—unequal. Josh still wasn't working, and I was
putting in more and more hours just to pay the bills.
When he started playing around I knew I wanted him
out of my life—but I wasn't prepared to lose the home
I'd worked so hard for. I'd spent my childhood in a
series of rented flats, and I couldn't bear to go back to
that way of life. And so when my boss suggested that
the royal household of Kharastan needed a discreet
lawyer urgently—well, it seemed like the answer to all
my prayers. I'd be able to buy Josh out and be free.'

'Free?' he said thoughtfully.

'That's right.'

There was silence while Xavier thought about what

she had told him. He wanted to reach out to touch her, to run his hands over the slippery red satin of her hair. But he had no right to do that.

For, while his lips might curve with disdain at the antics of her ex-boyfriend, in a way, wasn't he, Xavier, just as guilty of using her, of trying to impose *his* wishes on her as Josh had been?

He had spoken to Malik and asked—no, *demanded* that Laura stay here. But that had been when he'd imagined she would change her mind about sleeping with him again. Because it was inconceivable that any women could not be seduced, or bent to his will.

But her quiet resolve had been firm, and suddenly Xavier was appalled at his own behaviour. His determination to succeed—or rather to have exactly what it was he wanted—had spilled over from his professional into his personal life. And he didn't like it.

They were almost back at the Blue Palace—he could see the wide sweep of road which led to the main gates and the pluming fountains beyond. He knew what he needed to do.

'I won't hold you here any longer against your will, Laura,' he said heavily. 'I should never have done so in the first place. You are free to leave at any time. You can go home.'

Laura had been staring out of the window at a bird with orange plumage, nestling in among the flowers on some beautiful unknown tree, and his words hit her like a bucket of cold water on a hot day. Carefully, she composed her face into some sort of smile, hoping against hope that it masked her dismay.

'Home?' she questioned, as if it was a word in Kharastani that she was hoping to learn before they arrived back at the Palace.

He nodded. 'Just as soon as you like. I'll speak to Malik.'

Here was the freedom she had convinced herself she wanted. Yet wasn't it ironic that you could tell yourself you wanted something over and over again and yet, when it finally came, it left you feeling as if someone had blasted a great hole in the centre of your heart?

CHAPTER TWELVE

'THE Sheikh wishes to see you.'

Laura looked up from her case—which, to Sidonia's horror, she had insisted on packing herself—to see Xavier standing framed in the doorway of her bedroom. His black eyes were watchful as she folded an exquisite silk-satin evening gown, and she wondered if she'd ever get the chance to wear it again. But at least focussing on practical considerations like that stopped her from thinking how much she was going to miss the Frenchman.

'He wants to see me? What for?'

'Mind-reading has never been a particular skill of mine,' he drawled 'Why don't you ask him yourself? I'm to take you there.'

'Not Malik?'

'Apparently not.'

Their eyes met. Laura wanted to tell him that she was going to miss him, that she wished now she'd opted for one more taste of the joy she'd found in his arms. She wanted to tell him that she longed to stay here, in this enchanted paradise—with him. But he was letting her go, and she must do just that. Laura was headed home. Alone.

But I *am* going to miss you, she thought sadly as she stared into the soft ebony blaze of his eyes.

Her hand flew up to brush away a stray strand of hair from her cheek before she met the Sheikh. 'Do I look okay?'

He knew that this was not the disingenuous snaring of a compliment. He knew that the boyfriend who had tried to rip her off had destroyed a lot of her confidence. But in her simple linen dress, with her red hair tied back in a ribbon, she looked good enough to... He felt a nerve work in his cheek. 'You look beautiful.'

Laura supposed it would be churlish to tell him that she wanted his approval, but not with such a high rating—because when he used words like *beautiful* it made her start wanting what she had told herself she couldn't have. And she could *never* have Xavier in the way she would most like him—as a proper boyfriend she could do normal relationship stuff with.

She had thought that friendship was the answer, but in that it seemed she had been wrong—because friendship was almost as perilous as sex in making you feel close to a man. Well, maybe more so. The sex she'd had with Xavier had been the best sex of her life, and even though she had laughably little to compare it with she knew deep down that she would never have another lover like him.

But their friendship felt special. Different. As she suspected it was. He was letting her come closer than he would normally let *anyone* come—because of the bizarre circumstances of their being literally thrown together.

Well, today it was coming to an end, and while Laura was trying to tell herself that it was a job well done, inside her heart was heavy. But as she slipped out into the wide marbled corridor she thought that she hid it rather well.

'I wonder what he wants?' she mused, as Xavier fell into step beside her. 'You know—it's actually the first time that I'll have met him. I've always dealt with Malik before.'

'Presumably he wants to say goodbye.'

'I hate goodbyes,' said Laura fiercely.

Usually Xavier didn't. Usually he relished closure—the chance to cut ties, to move on and start anew. But today didn't feel anything like that. Laura was leaving, and he was not experiencing his habitual release.

'Have you…decided how long you're going to stay?' asked Laura.

'No.' He gave a short laugh. 'For the first time in my life I'm not certain of anything. I'm lucky enough to have the choice—many men are locked into jobs they cannot take leave from.'

'You *are* lucky,' she echoed.

'Yes, I am,' he agreed quietly. But when had he last *counted* his blessings? Got off the speeding train which was his life in order to enjoy some of the benefits he'd worked so hard for? Look at the way Laura's face had lit up when she'd spoken about buying Josh out and getting her own house and independence. Had prosperity made this former Paris urchin spoilt and unappreciative?

'Maybe he'll make you his heir,' said Laura. 'What then?'

'I doubt it,' said Xavier, with a frown. 'And don't you know that you should never plan for the future?'

Laura didn't want to think about the future, so she concentrated on looking at some of the ancient paintings of Kharastan which lined the high walls.

Their echoing footsteps took them along more wide marble corridors, and Laura thought about the strange contradiction of the Palace. How exquisite and beautiful it was—while outside lay the wild and unremitting desert, like a hungry beast just waiting to reclaim the land.

Did the Sheikh think of things like that as he grew ever older? she wondered. Was it a cultural imperative for him to hand the reins over to his kith and kin—and was he now about to pass on such a weighty responsibility to Xavier? Because if he didn't make his son his heir, then what would happen to Kharastan, and who would rule it?

She stole a look at his hard, set profile and he looked down at her, his eyes momentarily softening in a way they rarely did.

'You look sad,' she observed.

He sighed. She was so perceptive. And you're going to miss *that*, aren't you? taunted a voice inside his head.

'I am—a little. It feels strange that, having found him,

I shall soon go back to my own life in Paris. Life is so un-predictable that this might be the last time I ever see him.'

'It might,' she agreed. 'But at least you've had this heaven-sent opportunity to get to know him.'

They were outside the Sheikh's apartments now, and the ornate doors opened and Malik appeared, his eyes black-chipped and hard.

'He will see you both now,' he said curtly.

The light in the Sheikh's glorious golden room was muted and soft, and the air was cooled by some unseen fan and scented with the faint perfume of fresh flowers.

Aware of Malik behind her and Xavier by her side, Laura suddenly felt like an outsider. Why did Kharastan's ruler want to see her? she wondered.

'Approach,' came the soft command from a divan, and Laura suddenly forgot all her misgivings as she realised what a great honour was being afforded to her. As she drew close to the old man she sank instinctively into a deep curtsey—without having been aware that she even knew how to perform such a graceful gesture of homage. There she stayed, her eyes downcast, until she felt his hand on the top of her head.

'Arise,' he husked. 'Thank you for bringing my son to me, Miss Cottingham.'

'It was my…pleasure,' said Laura, her heart beating fast with nerves.

Xavier had moved forward, too—and Malik was indi-cating that she should sit on a low stool beside the Sheikh.

Laura didn't know what she had been expecting.

Golden robes denoted his privileged position, and the Sheikh was old, yes—but he carried with him the indefinable aura of power. And Xavier was right—his eyes were as memorably black as his son's. He sat up—as if the sight of the three of them had in some magical way revitalised him. A male servant appeared, to offer him a drink from a goblet inlaid with precious stones, but the Sheikh waved him away.

'Xavier, you are my son,' said the Sheikh. 'And I am granting you the freedom of Kharastan. Designated lands and great wealth will be made available to you in this, your country.'

'I thank you, but I have no need of your gift,' said Xavier proudly. 'And that is not the reason I came.'

The Sheikh nodded approvingly. 'I know and understand that—for you have made your own wealth in life. You have succeeded as I would have expected. These gifts are not made because of their financial worth—but because they are yours by birthright. The past can never be rewritten, my son—only the future is ours to forge, and yours lies ahead of you. You must go where destiny takes you—but you will always have a place and a home here, as one of the Sheikh's sons,' he finished quietly.

There was silence for a moment, and Laura was so awestruck that she wasn't really listening with her usual sharp and analytical lawyer's ear.

But Xavier was. And his eyes narrowed as one phrase leapt into his mind and fastened itself there, like a leech.

'*One* of the Sheikh's sons?' he repeated.

Laura saw the look which passed between Malik and the Sheikh.

'There is another son?' Xavier demanded hoarsely. 'I have a...*brother*?'

'You have a half-brother,' said the Sheikh carefully. 'Unlike you, he is Italian, and lives in the land of his birth.'

Xavier stared at the Sheikh. *'Why?'* he whispered.

It was a question which could have been interpreted in many ways, Laura thought—though the Sheikh seemed to know exactly what it was that Xavier demanded to know with that single word.

The Sheikh glanced around the room, nodding to dismiss the servants so that only he, Xavier and Malik remained. And Laura of course—who was half expecting them to ask her to leave as well. But they did not.

'Because I made a great dynastic marriage at a time of civil unrest in Kharastan, and my people dearly loved my wife. As did I,' he added softly. 'It was a successful marriage on many levels except on one—I never had a child with her.'

'You just went round procreating throughout Europe, did you?' accused Xavier hotly.

Laura saw Malik scowl and half rise, but the Sheikh stayed him by lifting his hand.

'You have a right to express your anger, Xavier—but, as I have already told you, we cannot rewrite the past, and we prepare for our future only by how we behave now, in the present.'

For a moment there was silence, and then eventually

Xavier spoke, but even to his own ears his voice sounded strange and disconnected. He had a *brother*! 'And what of this half-brother of mine?'

The Sheikh stared at him. 'Would you like to meet him? We could send Miss Cottingham to Naples, to persuade him to come to Kharastan.'

Xavier's fingers curled into two tight fists and his face darkened as he looked at Malik and Laura.

'Leave us!' he commanded them all. 'Please leave me alone with the Sheikh, my father.'

It was, Laura noted, the first time Xavier had acknowledged the relationship aloud. She also noted Malik's questioning glance at the Sheikh, but the old man nodded, so he rose to his feet and so did Laura, before she followed him out.

As she went back to her room, she *did* feel like an outsider, and strangely overcome—by all that she had seen and learnt, by the sense that an opportunity lay ahead for her to go on another great adventure to bring back son number two. But the feeling which most overwhelmed her was one of immense sadness.

Because you have to say goodbye to the man who has ensnared your heart? Is that why you'll even *consider* going to Italy, to deal with the half-brother, knowing that it will somehow keep you in Xavier's life? Is that what you want?

She had finished packing and was standing by the window, watching one of the guards on horseback as he clip-clopped his way around the grounds, when she

heard footsteps behind her. She turned round to see
Xavier standing there.

His face was like stone—cold and unyielding. Yet his
eyes glittered suspiciously bright, and Laura was more
surprised by that than by anything. Had Xavier actually
shed *tears*?

'What did you say to him?' she questioned huskily.

He looked at her and his eyes cleared—as if he were
just emerging from a forest into a bright open space, but
as if the shadows of that dark place he had visited would
never quite leave him.

'We said things which shall forever remain between
father and son,' he said gravely.

She saw the pain in his eyes and heard the dignity in
his voice, and in that single moment her heart turned
over and she knew that she loved him. She knew too that
it was a non-starter—but as long as she could hold onto
that fact then she'd be okay. Because what had Xavier
once said to her? Regret wasn't part of his agenda?
Well, it wouldn't be part of hers, either.

Let him go, she told herself. Don't be like the blonde
who flounced out of his office the first time you met
him. There are streams of women like her in his past,
and no doubt streams of them waiting in his future. So
replicate *his* dignity as you say goodbye.

'You'll stay here?' she asked.

'For a while. Laura—'

Her head jerked up, her eyes wide. 'What?' she questioned breathlessly.

'You won't take the job of going to find Giovanni, will you?'

The hope in her heart sank like a stone in a muddy pond, gone without trace. 'Is that a request or an order, Xavier?'

There was a heartbeat of a pause. 'It can be either,' he said steadily.

'You're *forbidding* it—even though the Sheikh himself asked me?'

'I can override that request if it does not please me,' he said stubbornly.

'If it does not please me?' she choked. 'What's the matter, Xavier? Do you think I'll end up in bed with your half-brother?'

'Stop it!' he snapped, as unwanted erotic images swam darkly into his mind. That kind of turmoil was the last thing he needed at the moment. 'Very well! Take the damned job if you wish to!'

'Thank you—I will!'

'You will?'

'I'll give it some thought.'

He scowled. 'Have you finished packing? Because I'm going to take you to the airport.'

And witness her breaking down into tears? His angry words washed over her and brought Laura to her senses. What of her hard-won self-respect and the dignity with which she wished to be remembered?

'Thanks, but no thanks, Xavier,' she said quietly. 'I'd

prefer it if one of the drivers took me. And now, if you wouldn't mind leaving, I have a plane to catch and I need to change first.'

CHAPTER THIRTEEN

LAURA arrived home in Dolchester and couldn't quite shake off a feeling of disorientation which didn't feel like jet-lag.

It wasn't just the fact that it was raining—a soft summer rain which washed all the dust off the flowers—because the rain felt quite soothing after the heat of the desert. Or the fact that the boiler had stopped working and she had no water for a bath.

It was...

Xavier.

Of course it was Xavier.

But, in a funny way, being back in the little market town helped. Just looking around at it and contrasting it with what she had left behind in Kharastan was enough to help her try to see things clearly. What was the point of shedding tears for something so unobtainable as the Sheikh's son?

Even if he hadn't been half-royal he was still totally wrong for her. And as the familiar surroundings re-established themselves on Laura's consciousness they made a mockery of her heart's desire.

Could she ever really imagine Xavier here? Stooping his tall body to get in the front door, knocking his dark head on one of the beams which hung so low in the sitting room? Or perhaps going down to the local pub with her and ordering a pint of lager? Maybe even braving the local shops, where you had to be prepared to divulge your life history if you wanted to purchase so much as a bunch of bananas?

Of course she could switch it around the other way. Laura in Paris! Laura sticking out like a sore thumb as she marched up the smart Avenue Georges V, or dined in the top-rate restaurants which Xavier no doubt frequented all the time. Laura with her schoolgirl French, trying to make herself understood in the *boulangerie*.

She had put all her Kharastan clothes in a wardrobe in the spare bedroom, because they seemed all wrong here. Until some enterprising soul opened one of those Middle-Eastern restaurants which were taking London by storm she could hardly wear them—could hardly walk into the local bank with embroidered jade-green silk brushing the floor, could she?

On the plus side, she had bought Josh out with her generous settlement from Kharastan, and Laura wouldn't have been human if that hadn't given her satisfaction. He had boasted of sleeping with one of the barmaids at the Black Dog pub, but as soon as Laura had shown a bit of financial clout he'd seemed to find *her* desirable.

'Get *off*, Josh!' she had said, when he'd made an un-expected lunge at her just after he had signed the papers transferring the cottage into her name. 'I'm just not interested any more.'

'What's got into you?' he'd sneered.

Laura had resisted the urge to tell him that a real man had made her realise just what she'd been missing for so long, because she was more mature than that. Xavier was her own special secret.

And you know that Josh will mock you if he finds out that it's over!

But she'd blocked that thought and closed the door behind Josh once and for all. She wasn't going to think negatively. Seeing Zahir nearing the end of his life had made her realise how precious time was, and she was going to treasure every second of it. She couldn't have Xavier, no—but that did not mean she was going to waste her life crying pointless tears about him. She would treasure the memories—put them in the back of her mind to be brought out on rainy days and Sundays.

It was night-times she found most difficult—that was when the stupid yearnings became hardest to push away. Like wishing she had been his lover for the whole time they'd been there—because what had she gained by resisting him, other than pride and an aching sense of what she had missed? And pride made a lonely bedfellow.

Laura told herself that it was natural to cry, and cathartic, too—even if some nights she had to bury her face in the pillow so that she wouldn't have to listen to the sound of her own broken sobs echoing round the room.

She had been back a month, and had just about accepted that she wasn't going to hear any more from Kharastan after writing to Malik declining the offer to go to Naples, saying that she really could not take any more time off work. It was a sunny Saturday morning, and she paused in the act of ladling strawberry jam onto a slice of toast as she heard a loud knock at the door.

The postman? she wondered as she opened it—and froze when she saw the man on her doorstep, dark and golden, glowing and vibrant, and looking just too good to be true against the backdrop of her tiny front garden.

Laura clutched the door-handle and stared at him, as if he might be a figment of her aching imagination and might suddenly just disappear. Yet after their last fraught meeting surely she should have felt anger, or indignation? So why was she experiencing a wild, fluttering kind of joy—tempered only by uncertainty?

'Xavier!' She almost put her hand out—as if to see if it was an apparition. 'Is it really you?' she whispered.

'You think I have a double?'

God, no. They'd broken the mould when they made *him*. 'What…?' She swallowed. For heaven's sake, Laura—just pull yourself together. 'What are you doing here?'

His lips curved into a quizzical smile. 'English hospitality leaves much to be desired,' he murmured. 'Aren't you going to ask me in?'

'Yes. Of course. Come in. Mind your— Oh, Xavier! Have you hurt your head?'

'Non,' he murmured, rubbing it with a grimace and wondering if England had once been populated by a race of pygmies.

Laura smoothed her hands down over her hair, which was hanging loose to her waist, and wished that someone could wave a magic wand and transform her. She wore a pair of old jeans, a T-shirt she'd had since college which said *Lawyers Do It In Briefs!*, and not a scrap of make-up on her face.

'Why didn't you tell me you were coming?' she demanded. 'At least I could have dressed up.'

'I didn't want you to dress up. I like the way you look,' he said slowly, as his eyes drank her in. 'You look…different.'

He looked different, too—Laura realised. In black jeans which emphasised the long, muscular thrust of his thighs and a dark leather jacket. And he was taking the jacket off without being asked, she thought, as a wave of dizziness washed over her. Did that mean he was staying? Well, he hadn't come all the way from Kharastan—or even Paris—just to turn around and go back again! But staying for how long? And did she have the guts to ask him what he was here for?

'Would you like coffee?' she babbled frantically. 'It's

not real coffee, because I only buy that when I'm having a dinner party.'

'Not *real* coffee?' he asked, genuinely perplexed for a moment. 'You mean it's...pretend?'

'It's instant.' Now he would see for himself how the real Laura Cottingham was—nothing but an unsophisticated small-town lawyer, who wore unsophisticated small-town clothes and drank instant coffee from a jar most of the time!

Xavier shook his head slightly. This wasn't going as he had planned, and for the first time in his life he felt the shimmer of doubt.

The air was very still for a moment as he looked at her.

'You didn't take the job?'

She shrugged. Had she really entertained the notion for more than a nano-second that she would track down Xavier's half-brother? 'No, I decided it wasn't really such a good idea.'

In that they were in perfect accord. Xavier expelled a long breath of relief, but he was still no closer to obtaining his heart's desire.

'Would you like to come to Paris instead?'

Laura's heart missed another beat. 'Paris?' she repeated cautiously. 'What for?'

Their eyes met.

'What do you think?'

'I don't know,' she whispered. *Ask him.* 'Why are you here, Xavier?'

'Because something has happened to me—something that you have done to me,' he said. 'Something I cannot reverse, although in truth I have tried—*mais oui*, I have tried! I thought the confusion in my head was because I'd discovered my father—but soon I saw that this was not so.'

'You're not making any sense.'

'You think I don't know this?' He shook his head as if he were clearing his thoughts—or marvelling that he should have them in the first place. 'I realised that the things you said to me were true—that I cared more for *things* than I did about people. And I don't want to live that way any more. You made me look at things differently, Laura,' he continued, when still she said nothing. 'You made me want more of what I had with you—something I'd spent my whole life running away from.'

'And what was that?'

There was a pause. 'Emotion,' he said eventually. '*Oui.*' And, seeing her look of amazement, he shrugged and gave her a look which was the closest Xavier de Maistre had ever come to being helpless.

'I kept remembering your face,' he said, in a voice which was almost dreamy. 'When something happened which amused or angered me I found myself wanting to tell you. I would lie in bed at night, reliving the moments I had with you—both erotic and tender moments, and not nearly enough of them.'

His eyes were intensely black as he stared at her, the blackest she had ever seen them.

'It's driving me crazy. *You're* driving me crazy.' He swallowed. 'I've missed you, Laura.'

Her heart lurched with excitement, hope, fear. 'Missed? Past tense?'

'Always the lawyer's precison with words,' he mocked. 'Okay, I miss you. I *miss* you,' he repeated, slowly and deliberately. 'How's that?'

Laura could feel the swirl of uncertainty, and she was afraid that he would see her terrible need, her desire—all the things which made her feel vulnerable around him—and be turned off by them. Was she grown-up enough to handle an affair, which was presumably what he was offering?

'I want to be with you,' he continued, and then his face became dark with passion, intent with something else. *'Je t'aime,'* he said softly, and then added, 'I love you.'

Laura knew what it meant—everyone who had ever learnt French at school knew what it meant. And if someone had asked her what she wanted most in the world, then Xavier had just given it to her in those three words. But she was frightened. Terrified, in fact. She was like a unsure skater who had been told it was safe to go on the ice—yet some instinct of self-preservation made her want to test how solid it was.

'How many other women have you said that to?'

'None. Only you.'

'We haven't known each other for very long.'

'I know that.'

'And we've never been together in normal circumstances.'

'I know that, too.'

'Well, what if it won't work?' she said desperately.

For the first time he touched her—reaching out to brush away a stray lock of hair which had fallen onto her pale cheek. 'What if? What if?' he murmured softly. 'Why don't you come to Paris and we'll make sure it works? Together.'

The Laura of a few months ago would have baulked at the suggestion of throwing caution to the wind and taking a step into the unknown. But that had been before Kharastan—an experience which had affected her profoundly and for which, ultimately, she had the cheating Josh to thank. And Xavier too, of course. In Kharastan he had wanted her on his terms, but she had resisted going for the easy fix. She had grown a new self-respect—and was no longer victim or coward.

She stared at him and then pointed to her old clothes, her gesture taking in the sweet little cottage room, which was a million light years away from his sophisticated urban style.

'But this is the real me,' she said. 'That expensively clad woman you met doesn't exist.'

He laughed softly as he shook his dark head, and his fingertips traced her eyelids, her nose, her lips, and then came to rest at last over her pounding heart.

'No,' he demurred. '*This* is the real you. The woman who has touched my heart and body and soul. The woman who made me look at myself, who made me think things I sometimes cared not to think. The woman who haunts my waking and sleeping hours and the woman I long to kiss once more.'

'Then kiss me,' she breathed.

He took her into his arms and groaned as he brushed his mouth over hers.

'Where's the bedroom?' he growled, after a few frantic moments.

'You won't need a route map,' she gasped. 'There's only two, and it's upstairs. Come with me.'

He had to dip his head again to enter the miniature bedroom with a bed which was a little small for his taste, but he laid her down on it, pulling off her underwear, throwing it aside with the rest of his own clothes with none of his usual teasing restraint, uncaring. In fact, uncaring of anything other than the urgent need to join with her completely.

It was only a brief interlude of sanity which reminded him to protect himself—and *that* near-slip dazed him, too, for it was always at the very top of his agenda.

Laura sobbed as he entered her, and he licked her tears away with his tongue as he slicked in and out of her. She whimpered with pleasure, wanting to hold onto it—to cherish the feeling and the movement and the moment—but she was fighting a losing battle.

'Oh, Xavier!' she cried, and tightened her arms around him as if she would never let him go.

He had known it was about to happen—had observed

it from the rosy flowering at her breasts—and he knew he wanted to be with her, the same journey at the same time, leading to the same place. He had never had simultaneous orgasm before—the icy control at the very core of his being had never wanted to make himself quite that powerless—but this time he craved it with a hunger which overwhelmed him.

Xavier let go, letting his orgasm take him up, and he followed it—swooping upwards just like the falcon who chased the lure. For a moment he felt at one with her— just as the sound of the wind seemed part of the desert itself—which was part of him.

Never had his peak lasted for so long, and never had the sweet spasms taken so long to subside—so that for a moment he felt as though he had wandered into some unknown place of such enchanting beauty that it could not possibly exist. A place a little like Kharastan? Yes!

When he looked into her eyes he could see the glimmer of another tear on her cheek, and he wiped it away with the tip of a gentle fingertip.

Laura bit her lip. 'Oh, Xavier,' she gulped. 'I love you so much.'

He looked down into her emerald eyes, so clear and bright, shining with an emotion she no longer had to hide, and his heart turned over with love. 'I know that, too,' he said softly.

EPILOGUE

DESERT WEDDING FOR *SHEIKH'S ILLEGITIMATE SON!*

THE press had gone wild—it was the biggest international story in years. Xavier's Parisian apartment was staked out by representatives from the media, so that in the end he and Laura had to employ a firm of heavies to keep them away.

They had tried to keep the wedding and its location a secret, but inevitably—with an event of this magnitude—it was bound to leak out. Kharastan was set to have its first big royal wedding in decades. Its people had taken the Sheikh's son to their hearts, and they adored his beautiful bride-to-be, with her sunset-coloured hair and eyes the colour of the forests.

'Did that surprise you?' Laura asked Xavier curiously one morning. 'That they should so quickly accept you, in view of the strange circumstances of your birth?

Xavier shook his head. 'During the month I spent

there after you had gone they got to know me a little, and as time goes by they shall know me better still.' He smiled. 'But their approval has been my father's reward for his loyalty to his late wife, and for the just and fair way he has ruled the land.'

They were lying in bed, in the huge apartment whose windows reflected the shimmering light of the Seine, and every so often Laura would hold up her hand to admire the whacking great square-cut emerald engagement ring which glittered on her finger—and which Xavier said mirrored perfectly the colour of her eyes.

In a month's time—when the plans were ready to be finalised—the two of them would fly out to Kharastan for their wedding, and a honeymoon in the countryside afterwards.

She turned to him and stroked the bare flesh of his shoulder thoughtfully. 'Is this all happening too quickly, do you think?'

'No. Do you?'

She shook her head and smiled. 'I want to be your wife, Xavier. More than anything else in the world.'

He smiled, touched his fingertips to her lips. 'Well, then—I want that, too. I want to make you legally mine—to bind you to me for the rest of our days.'

Laura shivered as she heard his masterful intent and snuggled up to him, thinking that life couldn't get much more perfect than this.

She had gone to Paris with the intention of finding

her own apartment and her own job—but work had quickly come her way, courtesy of Xavier, and surely only a stubborn fool would have turned it away?

She had tried looking for an apartment on her own, too—and, interestingly, the area she'd liked best was the Marais, where Xavier had grown up which was now one of the smartest areas in the city! But then she'd realised that she didn't want to spend nights apart, and neither did he. She wanted to be there in the mornings, and there in the evenings, and at all the other times in between. The two of them together seemed almost pre-ordained—as if anything else but Xavier and Laura as a couple was unimaginable. And when Xavier had asked her to marry him one sunlit morning as they walked out to buy baguettes for breakfast, she had burst into tears of joy.

It *was* soon—she knew that and he knew that—but there was a reason for that, unspoken but understood. His father was still alive, and Xavier wanted to show the Sheikh that there was going to be continuity in his illegitimate son's life. That he was marrying someone the Sheikh had met, and of whom he approved.

At least the question of inheriting the kingdom was not an issue—Giovanni was older than Xavier.

'Thank heavens for that,' Laura had murmured with genuine gratitude when she'd found out. 'I wonder if he's going to reply to the invitation to our wedding? I really hope he does come—I'd like to meet him.'

At the mention of Giovanni, his half-brother, Xavier

felt his heart leap with a joy tempered by trepidation. But Laura had taught him not to fear his feelings any more—to let them in and just go with the flow.

She had taught him that, and so much else. But the most important thing she had taught him was how to love.

The Sheikh's Unwilling Wife

SHARON KENDRICK

To Andy Thompson, dear friend –
who reminds me of cool cathedral squares
and almond croissants!

CHAPTER ONE

You didn't have to be drowning for your life to flash before you. Nor to be sleeping to feel you had stumbled into a nightmare.

And this was her worst.

Alexa blinked her eyes rapidly, like someone emerging from the water—their vision blurred so that they couldn't see clearly—and found herself thinking that maybe it wasn't him. For a split second a fragment of optimism floated before her as she narrowed her eyes to watch the man who sauntered with such careless grace down the cobblestoned street. But hope died as he grew closer and she saw a group of women stop talking mid-sentence and turn their heads to follow his path.

He walked like the leader he undoubtedly was—a man born to money, as well as having made more than enough of his own. Tall and striking, he had crisp dark curls, hard black eyes and a proud and haughty look on a face which in repose looked faintly cruel.

His olive skin was dark—even for a Southern Italian—and a shamelessly exotic air had only added to his mystique in his native city of Naples. Glamorous mother; father unknown.

He was wearing a perfectly cut pale grey suit over a lean, hard body, and as he walked the women watching him almost melted on the spot. It would almost have been comic if it hadn't made Alexa's heart ache with a pain which should have disappeared a long time ago and yet deep, deep down was a feeling far more acute than pain.

Fear.

She licked her lips. Giovanni.

Giovanni—her husband.

Jealous, possessive, unrealistic, idealistic. Giovanni…

Silently she said the name she had tried to forget but never would—for how could she, when she was still tied to him by law, unresolved feelings and by something deeper still? Something so precious that if…if…

Alexa swallowed. Had he seen her? Her heart skipped a beat as that stupid hope flared into life once more. Did he know she was here?

But even before she met the ebony glitter of his eyes, training themselves on the shop window like a hunter's gun, or watched him beginning to cross the road towards the building, she knew that it was a dumb question to ask.

Of *course* he knew she was here. Why else would the black-hearted millionaire be wandering down a quiet English road instead of swanning around his hot and noisy Naples in that sleek little sports car he used to drive, with all the men shouting Gio! and the girls smiling and swaying their hips as he passed?

What else did he know? Had he…*found out*?

Oh, please. The world began to blur again, and she clutched the flimsy piece of silk she was holding. Please don't let him know.

Skin icing and heart beginning to pound, Alexa could feel the palms of her hands growing damp, and she put down the silk T-shirt she had been folding with shaking fingers. No wealthy customer would part with cash for an over-priced item if it was covered in splodges of her sweat. She licked her dry lips, telling herself it was insanity to try to second-guess the situation. Just see what he has to say and play it cool—surely you can do that, considering what's at stake?

The shop door pinged, and she looked straight at him as he walked in, fixing a smile to her lips which she hoped was just the right mixture of formal politeness and mild curiosity. The kind of smile that any estranged wife would give to a husband who had given the dictionary a new definition for 'unreasonable behaviour'.

'H-hello, Giovanni,' she said, but she heard her voice tremble, and he heard it too, for she saw the black eyes briefly narrow as he tried to interpret its origin. 'This is a—'

'What?' he questioned, deadly as a snake.

'Surprise.' She swallowed, feeling her throat constrict on the word.

'Ah! Such understatement, *cara mia*!' he murmured 'Did you really expect to go through the rest of your life without ever seeing me again?'

'I hadn't really given it much thought.'

'I don't believe you,' he said softly, and his eyes

flicked her a mocking look. Not think about him? The moon would fail to rise in the heavens before that should happen! 'All women who have known me are obsessed with me—and in many ways you have known me better than most, for you are the only woman I ever married.'

But Giovanni knew that it had been more than just the legal tie of their marriage which made her knowledge of so unique—a marriage which had been far stronger and less easy to shrug off than he had anticipated. It was because Alexa had seen him with his guard down—she had witnessed Giovanni veering towards the vulnerable—and she had taught him a lesson that he should have known all along: women were never to be trusted.

Alexa's fixed smile became a grotesque kind of grimace. 'Did you…did you want to speak to me?'

Jet-black brows were raised in arrogant query. 'The alternative being that I want you to sell me some women's clothes—perhaps shopping here for one of my mistresses? What do you think?'

If only he knew! If only he had an inkling about the crazed thoughts which were swirling around in her mind like an out-of-control whirlwind. *Because you know that what you have done to this man is wrong?*

She willed the voice of her conscience to cease—dampening down its clamour with a reminder of the harsh and bitter words he had spoken to her. *Everything she had done, she had done for a reason.* 'I can't talk now. I'm working.'

'So I see.' He glanced around the shop's interior, affecting interest—but in reality it was to allow the beating of his heart to steady. He was taken aback by its thunderous pounding—for he had underestimated her impact on his senses. Or maybe he had simply forgotten.

Hungrily, he let his eyes feast on her. Her bright hair was caught back in one of those severe French plaits you rarely saw these days, and she was wearing a black pencil skirt and white blouse—presumably some kind of uniform for working. Yet it didn't look anything like a uniform when she was wearing it. With the slim skirt skimming the gentle curve of her hips and the silky shirt caressing the swell of her breasts, she looked like a favourite male fantasy—buttoned-up, yet red-hot and hungry underneath. Giovanni swallowed. Later.

'Still a shop assistant?' he questioned sardonically. 'Isn't this where you came in—unless you own the place, of course?'

'No, I don't own it.'

So there had been no sudden change in her fortunes. No lover to lavish his wealth on her, having been reeled in with that unique blend of supposedly innocent sensuality. Those pale green eyes which could range from serene to feisty and a hundred expressions in between. She had the kind of body you wanted to cover in diamonds—and then slowly remove them, one by one.

Had it surprised him that she had not approached him for a hefty divorce settlement? He supposed it had—but maybe her lawyers had advised her that a mere three-month marriage would not yield much in the way of alimony.

'Hardly what you'd call rapid promotion, is it?' he

mused. 'Shop assistant in some small backwater of a place you grew up in.'

How effortlessly fluent was his English—and how brutally accurate was his contempt for her situation! Alexa gave him a non-committal smile. 'Well, we can't all be captains of industry,' she said quietly. 'Listen, Giovanni—no one was ever going to be in any doubt that you were the achiever in our relationship, but I really *don't* have time to stand around and chat.' Especially about something as painful and as potentially explosive as their past.

He glanced around the empty shop. 'But you don't have any customers!' he observed caustically. 'If this were my place then I'd give it a dramatic overhaul.'

'Well, fortunately for me, it isn't. So what is it that you want, Giovanni?' She blinked up at him, wondering if he could hear the slight crack of pain in her voice—because sometimes emotions just crept up on you, whether you liked it or not.

What if he had come to tell her that he wanted his freedom? That he had met someone new and fallen in love—only this time it was the real thing, not some youthful cocktail of lust and unrealistic expectations. 'You can tell me quickly.'

Giovanni heard the note of hope in her voice and gave a slow smile. 'You think I've travelled from Italy to *tell you quickly*?' he echoed silkily.

He had her senses spinning and she wanted it to stop. She wanted the rapid hammering of her heart and the feeling of faintness to pass, along with the regret and all the other things he had stirred up inside her within the space of a few minutes.

Alexa drew a deep breath. 'You should have warned me you were coming,' she said, in a low voice. And how would she have reacted if he had? Run away until she was certain the coast was clear, taking Paolo with her? But you couldn't keep running away all your life. Suddenly, an intimation of terror began to whisper its way over her skin. 'You should have warned me,' she repeated, more urgently now.

Giovanni looked at her trembling lips. Not for a moment had he thought she might have grown immune to him—but Alexa's reaction was *very* interesting.

She was edgier than he might have expected in the circumstances. And why was that? he wondered. Because she'd realised what she had thrown away? Or because she wanted him to take her into his arms and kiss her—to press his hard heat against the pliant softness of her body and drive his throbbing hardness deep inside her until she begged for release?

Giovanni's sensual lips curved into a cruel smile as he felt the rush of heat to his groin and the powerful beat of anticipation—yet he experienced slight dismay, too and the faint prickle of anger, because the feelings she provoked in him defied all logic.

Memories of betrayal and deceit washed over him when he looked at the pale oval of her face, and yet there was lust, too—a fierce sexual hunger which he had never completely satisfied. Surely that must account for the sudden strange lurching of his heart?

The agenda which had brought him here today was simple: the invitation burning a hole in his pocket and a desire that his wife accede to his wishes. And yet there had been curiosity, too. A sense of something never quite completed, nor put to rest—a question that everyone whose marriage had failed must ask: *what if?*

Giovanni's mouth hardened. But that was pure unnecessary sentiment—and he was not a man given to sentiment. Putting that aside, he knew what he really wanted, and it was more than her agreement to accompany him on such an important occasion. Ah, *si*. He intended to have her one last time. He would feast on her body and take his fill from it—and then… He swallowed. Then that last lingering legacy from their ill-fated marriage would be satisfied and he could move on.

Inside the luxurious interior of the store, the lights shone down and transformed her hair into pure spun gold. Yet the light played tricks just as the heart did, for her hair was not really gold, but a strange colour somewhere between red and gold—the colour they called strawberry-blonde. Such a rare shade to adorn a head, and especially so in his native Southern Italy.

Her eyes were the fresh colour of pistachio and her skin looked like creamy vanilla. The first time he'd met her he had told her she looked like an ice cream sundae, and only just stopped himself from adding that he wanted to lick her all over. Much later he had teased her that he wanted to dip his spoon in her—and her corresponding blush had sealed her fate. His face darkened.

She was his.

Alexa.

Alexa O'Sullivan. A name as unusual as her hair, as her soft curving body, pale with silken skin. She looked as innocent now as she had done on the day they had met. But innocents did not lie, nor did they cheat.

He was prepared for the anger, but unprepared for the regret. That he had ever married her in the first place? Or that he had let her pale green eyes and berry-coloured lips lull him into believing a fantasy?

'What time do you finish?' he said softly.

For a moment Alexa hesitated, recognising that he wasn't going to go away until he'd got what he came for, no matter how much she wanted him to. The most sensible thing would be to arrange to meet him for lunch the next day—which would give her time to compose herself, prepare herself for any verbal battle. But that would mean him hanging around—maybe even staying in one of the local hotels—and then what? Giovanni asking questions—smarming his way into the confidence of adoring women staff, or—worse—local people beginning to look closely at his stunningly dark Mediterranean looks and putting two and two together.

'I finish at six,' she said quickly.

'Good. Good.' Giovanni's black eyes glittered with satisfaction. The first part of his mission was accomplished—the second would be to decide where to take her. A hotel? With the convenience of a bedroom within walking distance? Why not start as he meant to go on? Hunger curved the edges of his mouth into a hard smile. 'I'll pick you up here.'

'No!' The word flew out before she could stop it, but Alexa wanted neutral territory—a bland, safe environment. Though was anywhere really safe with Giovanni? Didn't the power of his presence subtly dominate his surroundings, so that no matter where you were all you were aware of was him? She met his questioning stare. 'My boss doesn't like anyone else in the shop while I'm emptying the till,' she babbled. 'I have to look after the takings.'

'I shouldn't think there'll be much in the way of *takings*, judging by the lack of customers,' he observed sardonically, raising his eyebrows. 'You will have to do better than that for an excuse, *cara*.'

It was arrogant of him to suppose that she *needed* an excuse not to talk to him—but then, his arrogance had never been in question. 'I won't be able to concentrate if you're breathing down my neck.'

He smiled. Better. Much better. 'No, I can see that might be a problem,' he agreed evenly. 'So, where shall I see you?'

Alexa's mind was racing. She would have to phone the childminder, of course, and arrange a later pick-up, but that should be okay.

She ran through all the possible venues to come up with the one where she was least likely to know anyone—but as a woman who rarely went out in the evenings she had a pretty big field to choose from. 'Meet me in the Billowing Sail,' she said. 'Just after six. It's a little pub, tucked away in the corner of the harbour.'

'A pub?' he echoed.

'That's right.'

'But I don't like pubs, Alexa,' he said softly. 'You know that.'

And *she* didn't like being forced into a meeting with a man who could still turn her emotions upside down. He—like she—would just have to put up with it. 'I'm afraid that pubs are part of English life—and none of the coffee shops will be open at six.'

'Then let's have dinner instead.'

'D-dinner?'

'The meal that people eat in the evenings,' he enlightened her sarcastically. 'You know.'

Alexa felt her heart slam nervously against her ribcage. One thing she knew for sure—no way could she endure the forced intimacy of a restaurant, with its subdued lighting and leisurely service.

She shook her head. 'No—not dinner.'

His black eyes narrowed. 'You mean you don't want dinner, you don't eat dinner—or you're having it with somebody else?'

For a second she was tempted to say yes—that the man of her dreams would be waiting at home for her, with a warm smile and an even warmer bed. Because most men would give up and go away if they thought she'd moved on and found herself another man. But Giovanni wasn't most men, and his jealousy was legendary. It had helped destroy their relationship with its warped, dark poison—and Alexa didn't think she could face seeing it activated now.

She shook her head. 'No, I'm not having dinner with someone else. But I'm tired,' she said truthfully. 'It's

been a long week, and I don't imagine we're going to
have a lot to say to each other—certainly not enough to
fill a whole meal-time. A quick drink should do it.'

For a minute their eyes met in a silent battle of wills,
and he thought about trying to impose his on her—but
wouldn't that put her defences up? Alexa had something
he wanted, and so for now he would play this her way.
And besides, he would soon talk her out of her dismissive suggestion—or maybe kiss her out of it. His heart
began to race in anticipation. *A quick drink*, indeed!

'Very well,' he agreed. 'I will see you in there, soon
after six. *Ciao, bella.*' And he turned his back on her and
walked towards the door, seeming to take all the light
and the colour with him as it shut behind him with a
little pinging of the bell.

In a daze, Alexa watched him go, her knees feeling
as if they were about to give way, scarcely able to believe
that what she had most dreaded had just taken place.

Only it isn't over yet. Not by a long way.

She turned round and reached for the box of tissues
she kept beneath the counter, for customers to wipe off
their lipstick before they slithered into costly items of
clothing, and dabbed furiously at the tears which couldn't
seem to stop welling at the corners of her eyes. She didn't
even register that the shop door had opened again, and it
wasn't until she heard a voice behind her that she whirled
round and saw her boss standing there—an elegant
blonde in her fifties, a concerned look on her face.

'Teri!' she gasped. 'I was miles away. I didn't—'

'I know you didn't. That was your husband, wasn't

it?' guessed Teri perceptively. 'The Italian Stallion currently wowing the female population of Lymingham?'

Alexa nodded, trying to compose herself. 'Ex-husband,' she corrected, swallowing back the tears.

'I didn't think you were divorced?'

'We're not—officially—but divorce is just a piece of paper,' said Alexa fiercely. 'Just like marriage.'

'You think so?' questioned Teri wryly, and then a note of curiosity crept into her voice. 'How come we've never seen him before?'

Alexa tensed. 'Because he lives in Naples and I live here, and we don't have a shared life together.'

'That's not what I mean, Lex,' said Teri gently. 'He's Paolo's father, isn't he?'

There was a pause. It was just as Alexa had thought—the resemblance was as unmissable as a dark cloud suddenly obscuring the sun. The boy was a carbon copy of the man. 'Yes,' she whispered.

Teri's eyes narrowed in a slowly dawning comprehension, and she raised the tips of her fingers to her mouth. 'And he doesn't know, does he?'

There was a terrible silence.

'No.'

'Oh, Alexa.'

But Alexa shook her head, remembering Giovanni's bitter words. The torture of living with him once he'd decided she didn't measure up to his exacting standards of what a woman should be. The accusation he had flung at her as she had left his house and his city and his life. And she remembered his immense wealth and determination. Oh, no. She would be a fool to start having some kind of euphoric recall about the man she had married—and an even bigger one to underestimate his power.

'He would take him away from me if he knew,' she said flatly. 'And that's the truth.'

'But how...*why?*' asked Teri in confusion. 'I mean, how on earth has all this happened?'

How, indeed? Why did some people's dreams get smashed to pieces while others merely faded away like the end of a film?

She could tell Teri that she had travelled to Naples and fallen in love with that vibrant, chaotic city which was flanked by Mount Vesuvius, the island of Capri and the crystal-blue waters of the Tyrrhenian Sea. Just as she had fallen in love with Giovanni—or *thought* she had. With his dark good looks and dangerous charm and his determination to possess her—yes, *possess* her— who could have resisted him?

Fresh out of university, and undecided about a future which had seemed to have a gaping hole in it since her mother had remarried and emigrated, Alexa had gone to Italy to brush up on a language at which she was already passably fluent.

It hadn't taken her long to decide that Italian men were after one thing—easy, uncomplicated sex with women who were prepared to offer it to them on a plate. And Alexa hadn't been. Her one foray into matters sensual had been enough to make her cautious— because the man to whom she had lost her virginity had

had all the sensitivity of bull. But then she'd met Giovanni, and all her best intentions had flown out of the window.

Working in the air-conditioned splendour of the city's biggest and plushest department store, Alexa had become a bit of a novelty. A foreigner who spoke cool and fluent Italian—and there certainly weren't many English shop assistants in Naples! Customers had been charmed by her accent, and men in particular had come to purchase soft leather gloves from the pale-skinned creature with the green eyes and red-blonde hair and the pale, poised air. Sales had increased. She'd been given a raise and moved onto handbags.

And then one morning Giovanni had walked in, and everything had changed. In an instant she had become the victim of the feeling which had swamped over her— a feeling she'd never really believed in until it happened to her. But then no one ever did.

The world had stopped spinning, became suspended and frozen—and everything in it had blurred into insignificance except for the man who had sauntered in, seemingly oblivious of all the eyes upon him as he homed in on her like a moth to the flame. And Alexa had fallen in love.

She had not known that he owned the store, and several like it throughout Italy, or that he featured on all the Best-Dressed and Most Eligible lists—usually somewhere near the top. All she'd known was that he had eyes like ebony and skin which seemed especially dark—like sleek, polished wood—and that the suit he wore did little to conceal the hard, honed perfection of his body. Her mouth had dried, but she'd hidden it behind her polite shop assistant's smile.

'So, you are the woman who is causing all the excitement,' he murmured.

Alexa glanced around the shop, taking deliberate note of all the women who were watching him, and she smiled as she answered him in Italian. 'And you are the man who seems to be doing just the same!'

He was slightly taken back—as much by her retort as by her fluency. Giovanni had been told that she spoke his language, but he had not expected it to be so…so… perfect. 'I have been told that you are very beautiful,' he said huskily. 'But words do not do you justice. I have never seen a mouth so begging to be kissed.'

Alexa's eyes became shuttered. Because these were the kind of glib phrases she knew were meaningless. In the past weeks she had become a dab hand at spurning the advances of amorous men—though it had never seemed remotely difficult before. 'Are you interested in buying a handbag, sir?'

Giovanni thought of a hundred ways he could react to her question. He could say yes, go through a flirtatious little pantomime of asking her advice and then buying the one she liked best—probably the most expensive one— and presenting it to her with a theatrical flourish before asking her out for dinner. But some cool reserve in the pale green eyes told him that this strategy would not get him the result he wanted. She was not flirting with him, he realised with a certain astonishment. *Not flirting with him*!

'No, I am not interested in handbags. I am interested in showing you Naples.'

'I have a map.'

'And I have a car.'

Alexa glimmered him a smile. 'I like to walk. But thank you all the same.'

'I am used to getting my own way,' he purred.

'Then I have a feeling that this time you're going to be disappointed.'

'I am never disappointed when I set my heart on something.'

Alexa discovered that he was rich, and that he changed his women more often than his cars. She told herself that the best thing would be to avoid him—but Giovanni da Verrazzano laid siege to her, and the more she refused his invitations, the more ardent became his pursuit.

If she'd had been older and more experienced she would have realised that her unwillingness to go out with him was only increasing his determination, and his admiration. But she wasn't doing it to play games. She was doing it because she was frightened of being hurt.

So that by the time she could refuse him no longer, and agreed to have a chaste lunch in a tiny restaurant scented with jasmine and overlooking the city, Giovanni had placed her on a pedestal as high as Vesuvius itself.

He swept her off her feet with a masterful arrogance which left her reeling—and yet it was his surprisingly tender restraint which ensnared her and fuelled the fires of a passion she hadn't known she possessed. The almost reverential respect he showed for her determination not to fall into his bed meant that Alexa could relax.

For the first time in his life Giovanni listened to a woman, and talked with her—and it was a novel experience. She made him laugh—while he showed her that a sexy and virile man could have the soul of a poet.

He fell in love—was blown away by it—as innocent as a child beneath the onslaught of this powerful feeling. The cynical man of the world who had seen and done everything was as susceptible as the next when it came to the age-old vulnerability of the heart.

But nobody told them about brevity of the *colpo di fulmine*—the thunderbolt of love—which crashed into lives for such a brief moment before crashing out again. If anyone had tried, they'd have never believed them.

'Marry me,' he said one day.

Alexa's heart lurched, and threatened to deafen her with its sudden wild pounding.

'But—'

'Marry me, Lex,' he said again—softly, sweetly—his lips brushing over hers in way which made her want to faint with pleasure.

Maybe it was madness, but in Giovanni Alexa saw her glorious future. He wanted to take care of her. Her beautiful, strong, old-fashioned Italian seemed to be the answer to something she hadn't even been aware she was looking for.

So they married, in a ceremony which was intended to be simple—until Giovanni's mother arrived back from a spending spree in Monte Carlo to turn it into

something of a spectacle. But nothing could destroy
Alexa's slightly disbelieving pleasure in the unexpected
twist her life had taken. It felt like a dream—it *was* a
dream, she thought happily, forgetting that dreams
didn't stand up to the cold light of day.

And hers crumbled on their wedding night itself,
when Giovanni made the discovery that his bright-
haired and perfect bride was no virgin. He stilled,
staring down at her in disbelief, words torn from his lips
moments after he entered her.

'There has been another?'

It was a question designed to break the bubble of her
passion—though for a moment Alexa wasn't quite sure
she had heard properly. But then he repeated it—or rather,
he shouted it—and the lovemaking which up until the
moment of penetration had been like her wildest expectations come true—suddenly mushroomed into something else entirely. Something ugly. Something shameful.
Giovanni's face closed up—closing her out—but he didn't
stop what he was doing. He carried on moving inside her,
and the only chink in his armour came in that brief
moment when he lost control and cried out her name.

Afterwards, she lay back against the pillows, feeling
as if he had ripped something from her heart and her
soul, staring up in the moon-washed silence as his terse
and furious interrogation began.

And the first night of their honeymoon was only the
start of it—for his discovery had awakened the dark
green serpent of a jealousy which up until that moment
had lain dormant. Every move she made was watched;

every statement she uttered was analysed. She had slept with five men, no—ten. Or was it more than that? And how many was she sleeping with now, other than him? She must tell him, for he needed to know!

Yet he seemed determined to give her satisfaction—almost as if he was demonstrating a master-class in sex. As if he wanted to show her how good it could be. And in some ways it was. In his arms, Alexa gasped out her pleasure time and time again, but the lack of emotion and the simmering anger on Giovanni's face made her feel empty afterwards. Like a beach, when the tide had turned and flowed away.

It was a slow kind of torture, and Alexa lasted only three months of her doomed marriage. Then she had fled vowing never to revisit that black landscape of despair ever again—but she would never forget Giovanni's snarled and angry words ringing in her ears.

At least we must give thanks that you aren't pregnant—for how would we ever know the identity of the father?

Yes, the facts were simple—it was what lay behind them which was complex. She had been too young to know the difference between love and lust, or between protection and possession. She should have known something about Italian men—and Southern Italian men in particular—before she committed herself to marriage.

'Are you going to tell him?' asked Teri now, her concerned voice bringing Alexa back to the present. 'That he has a son?'

Alexa wiped away the last tear and shook her head. 'I can't,' she said, swallowing defiantly. 'I can't afford to.'

CHAPTER TWO

AFTER Teri had left the shop, Alexa forced herself to deal with practicalities. She phoned the childminder, who said that, yes, of course Paolo could have his tea there.

'I'll pick him up at about seven-thirty,' said Alexa, in a voice which suddenly sounded shaky. 'Will you...will you send him my love?' She heard the emotion trembling in her voice as the childminder said she would, and that they would see her later.

Alexa put the phone down. Her proud and beautiful little son would not be happy to have his normal routine changed, but he would soon have the childminder acceding to his every wish just by looking at her from beneath the thick curtain of his dark lashes and twisting her with that heartbreaking smile.

What would Paolo say if he knew that his daddy was in town? She bit her lip with pain and guilt—but it was pointless allowing her mind to go there. Hadn't she gone over this, over and over again, and decided this was the only way that her son could be guaranteed a life that wasn't filled with acrimony and trauma?

But by the time Alexa finally locked the shop door at the end of the day she was a bag of nerves, and knew she had to pull herself together. It was pointless trying to predict what she would say or how she would behave until she knew the reason why Giovanni had suddenly turned up here today. And if she walked into the pub looking like a shivering wreck, then his suspicions would only be alerted.

Changing out of her working clothes, she pulled on jeans, sweater and jacket, and stared back at her image, knowing that she was dressed in a way which was practical and smart rather than feminine. But appearances mattered—particularly to a man like her husband. He would judge her by what she was wearing and she would not, *not* be found wanting. So she brushed her hair and added a touch of lipstick, and rubbed her finger against her cheeks in an attempt to put some colour there.

At least the crisp breeze which blew in from the sea took her breath away and made her feel properly alive— even if her heart felt dead. She walked along to the harbour, where little boats bobbed in the water with their masts chattering and where seagulls cawed in their relentless search for food.

On such a cold evening there were few people hanging around, and it seemed so desolated and so very English that for a moment Alexa could scarcely believe that her estranged husband was sitting waiting for her—here, in this little town. Her territory, she thought. Not his.

The pub sign creaked, and Alexa hugged her coat

tightly to her as she dipped her head to walk into the warm, beamed interior and look around for Giovanni.

He wasn't hard to find. The pub was fairly quiet, with just a few office workers having a quiet pint before setting off home for the familiar evening routine, and Giovanni looked overwhelmingly exotic in comparison.

On a table in front of him stood two glasses of red wine, and his long, muscular legs were stretched out in front of him—pulling the material tight over his groin and unashamedly accentuating his masculinity.

Alexa thought how deeply olive his skin looked beneath the soft lighting—yet it gave off a soft golden radiance which contrasted with his thick hair, as black as the coal which lay waiting to be thrown onto the roaring fire.

And suddenly she felt a terrible yearning—like someone standing in an icy waste who had just sighted a thick cashmere blanket. For how long was it since she had looked on a man and felt anything approaching desire?

Not since Italy.

And she had never desired anyone the way she had Giovanni—how could she? Who could possibly follow a role model like him?

Well, she wasn't going to think of that now. Keep focussed. Find out why he's here and keep it simple. Pinning a smile to her lips, she began to walk towards him.

Giovanni's eyes narrowed as he saw her, and again that alien and unexpected feeling wrenched at him. How pale her face looked, he thought with a frown. And how did she always manage to project that image of being all alone in the world—so that a man wanted to reach out and safeguard her? His frown deepened. Because that was the game she played—one that all clever and beautiful women engaged in. His own mother had excelled at it. Alexa was simply capitalising on her assets—emphasising her strange fragility and her pale, doe-like beauty.

Forcing himself to concentrate instead on the darkened bow of her mouth, the sway of her hips, and the thought of her breasts hidden beneath the bulky jacket, he was rewarded with a familiar leap in his groin. He rose to his feet as she approached, because his manners were always impeccable, even if the dark light flashing from his eyes was anything but conventionally polite.

'Here I am,' she said flatly.

'So I see.'

They stared at one another like two new boxers in the ring, who were trying to psych the other one out.

He would never have allowed her to go out wearing such a bulky, waterproof jacket as the one which now sparkled beneath fine droplets of seawater, he thought. Yet the dilemma with someone who looked like Alexa was that on the one hand you wanted her to display that magnificent body of hers—while on the other you did not want other men seeing it. But they were separated now, and none of the normal rules counted. How she dressed was nothing to do with him, for he was interested only in seeing her without any clothes on at all.

His eyes flickered over her, to where her glorious

hair tumbled down in windswept strands over her breasts. 'At least you've let your hair down,' he observed softly.

'Giovanni, we aren't here to…'

'To what, *cara*?' he questioned innocently.

'To—to make personal remarks like that.' To make her feel like a real woman for the first time in years and remind her of his consummate skill as a lover. And wasn't she in danger of regarding even *that* through rose-tinted spectacles? She must force herself to remember the reality of their wedding night and its bitter conclusion. 'It isn't appropriate,' she finished.

Giovanni heard the slightly despairing note of appeal in her voice and bit back his smile. This was good. What was it that the English said? He was *getting under her skin*. Just as she had once got under his, playing disingenuous games in order to hook him, as women had been attempting to do since he'd first started shaving.

'Sit down,' he said, his eyes narrowing at her look of genuine hesitation.

'I don't know if I should.'

His mouth curved into a mocking line. Did she really imagine that he would let her walk away from him a second time?

'I said, sit down,' he repeated silkily.

Come to think of it, she wasn't sure she could walk straight out again—even if he'd told her she could. The feelings which had surged over her since he'd entered the shop suddenly took their toll, and with legs which were suddenly weak Alexa sank down onto one of the overstuffed leather sofas, glancing around her as nervously as if she was a woman on a blind date.

Sometimes when she was out she felt self-conscious, or paranoid as if people were staring at her. But today they really were. And it was nothing to do with a windswept woman on her way home from work—but everything to do with the exotic man who had just sat down opposite her. He was lounging back in his chair like a dangerous, undiscovered species who needed a warning notice attached to him.

He pushed a glass of wine towards her. 'You look as if you could use it.'

Alexa took the drink but didn't touch it. Just looked straight into his eyes and willed herself not to respond to all those potent signals he was sending out. But most potent of all was the heartbreaking similarity between him and Paolo. The same thick forest of black lashes, and the slash of high, slanting cheekbones. The same dark curls—though Paolo's were more of an ebony tumble and Giovanni's had been expertly clipped to lovingly define the proud shape of his head. She shook the thoughts away.

'How did you find me?' she questioned, curling her fingers around the glass, as if doing that would warm their frozen stiffness.

'Oh, finding you was simple, *cara*—far easier than I expected.' He shrugged. He had been surprised she was still here—but then, didn't women always go back to somewhere they'd known? She had lived here before she had come out to Italy. Before her mother had moved off to live in the wilds of Canada, and before he had foolishly decided that Alexa needed looking after and had married her.

His mouth hardened. 'I tried your old phone number and got your voice on the answer-machine.'

'And if you hadn't?'

He shrugged, but his eyes glittered. 'Then I should have had to employ someone to find you. Anything is possible.'

'A…detective?'

'Something like that.'

'But you didn't? Get a detective, I mean?' she questioned, until she saw his face and realised that she'd said too much. Underestimated his razor-sharp intelligence. He must surely have noticed her wide-eyed fear and be questioning its source. So better start back-tracking before it was too late.

'Whatever is the matter, Alexa? Anyone would think you had something to *hide* from me.'

'Oh, don't be so melodramatic!' she said brightly, though inside she hated herself for the unspoken lie which fell from her lips. 'I'm just fascinated to find out what has brought you here.'

'Are you?' He traced his forefinger along his bottom lip thoughtfully. Of course she was going to be jumpy— what woman wouldn't be, in her situation? Was she looking at him now and realising what a stupid mistake she had made? But *she* was the one who had to live with the consequences of her own stupidity—and that was not the reason he was here.

'Yes, in truth it is a fascinating story,' he agreed, but for once in his life the words did not come easily—there was no template for this kind of situation. He ran his finger around the rim of his wine glass and realised that although they were separated he was still treating her like a wife. For simply by marrying they had forged a deep bond he had experienced with no other woman— no matter what had happened between them subsequently. Why else would he be about to confide in her an incredible story he had told no other? 'You remember my mother?' he asked suddenly.

It was not the opening Alexa had been expecting, and it took her off guard. 'Yes, of course I remember her,' she answered slowly. 'She's a pretty unforgettable character.' Natala—his glamorous, gorgeous mother, with her penchant for diamonds and those slinky black satin dresses which were as tight as a second skin. Until Alexa had met Natala she hadn't realised that mothers could look like film stars.

'How is she?' she questioned, not quite sure of the etiquette in asking after a woman who had once been overheard pronouncing her as—'*ordinary*. And she has no *money*, Gio!'

His lashes came down, concealing all but a dark gleam of light in his eyes. 'She died last year,' he said bluntly.

Alexa gasped, everything else forgotten—because his mother had been relatively young. 'Oh, Giovanni— I'm so sorry,' she said instinctively, and only just stopped herself from leaning forward to touch him.

Giovanni's eyes narrowed and she saw in them the

brief chink of pain. But then it was gone—clicked out—
like the shutter of a camera.

'Did you come here just to tell me that?' she questioned uncertainly.

His black eyes hardened. 'No. Of course not.'

There was a pause as he seemed to search for the right
words. It was so uncharacteristic of Giovanni to hesitate
that Alexa felt herself stiffening with apprehension.

'What, then?' she said nervously, because precious
minutes were ticking away—and it wasn't just that she
wanted to be back on time for Paolo and not to alienate
the childminder by taking advantage. She also wanted
to be away from the still-powerful sexual pull her
husband exerted—away from the foolishness in her
heart which made her want to put her arms around him
and draw him close in a gesture of comfort.

He tapped his long olive fingers against the polished
surface of the table. 'After she died I was going through
her papers and I made a discovery.'

'What...kind of discovery?'

Sifting and sorting through the files of information
in his mind, Giovanni began for the first time to place
them in some kind of coherent order. 'The unwelcome
kind—that informs you that you have been labouring
under an illusion for most of your life,' he said, and his
voice sounded suddenly harsh.

'What *illusion*?'

His voice hardened. 'As you are aware, I grew up believing that my father was a Spanish aristocrat—one
who refused to publicly acknowledge me, even though

he was prepared to pay generously for my upkeep and
my mother's jewels. My mother told me that her silence
about his identity to the rest of the world would guarantee her a lifetime's riches. And it did.' The stony expression in his eyes matched the sentiment at the heart
of his words. 'She also led me to believe that he had
died—and I had no reason to distrust her.'

'You mean she was lying?'

Giovanni threw her a look of mockery. 'Why? Would
you feel an affinity with her if you knew that to be the
case?' he questioned acidly.

'I'm not interested in raking up old scores, Giovanni,'
she answered quietly. 'What are you trying to say?'

'That my father is not Spanish at all—and he is not
dead. Though he is very old, nearing the end of his
life, and—'

'And?' she prompted, on a whisper.

'I am the son of a sheikh,' he said at last, aware even
to his own ears—how bizarre his words must sound. He
could see his own reaction mirrored in her widened eyes.

'What?'

'My father is a sheikh.' But through the haze of un-
reality bubbled a feeling of intense...*satisfaction*. It was
as if he had found the missing bit of himself—which,
in a way, was exactly what had happened. 'More specifically, he is Sheikh Zahir of Kharastan,' he added.
And then, as if to lessen the emotional impact of his
words, he raised his jet brows in question, as if he were
a university professor quizzing a student. 'You have
heard of it, perhaps?'

For a moment Alexa forgot their history, forgot her own dark secret and her fear of the man she had married—because his startling piece of information wiped all other thoughts completely from her mind. She didn't even stop to question it—Giovanni wouldn't lie about something like that. Why on earth would he? He had the riches and the power that most men hungered for—he wouldn't invent royal blood unless it were true. And wouldn't that just make him a million times more attractive to the opposite sex? she thought, with a sudden pang of wistfulness.

'Of course I've heard of it,' she breathed. 'The papers have been talking of nothing else for weeks. There's a big royal wedding taking place there soon, isn't there?'

She tried to remember a bit more, but she had mainly looked at photos of the handsome groom and his beautiful fiancée while she'd been sitting in the hairdressers. What with working full-time, looking after her son and running a home some things had to give—and reading the foreign news section of the papers was unfortunately one of them. Alexa frowned. 'But I thought it was the Sheikh's *son* who is getting married. And isn't he half-*French*?'

Giovanni gave a grim smile, for in a way she had made this easier for him. 'Yes. He is. The Frenchman's name is Xavier,' he said. 'And he is—as you say—the Sheikh's son. He is also my half-brother.'

'You mean there's more than one son? I...don't understand, Giovanni.'

Hadn't he thought exactly the same thing himself,

when the incredible facts had first been presented to him by the Sheikh's aide—the man they called Malik? For in one swoop Giovanni had gone from being a man with no family to finding himself a father and a half-brother.

'Although he had a long marriage, it seems that the Sheikh had two illegitimate offspring who were born in Europe during that time. Xavier was one and I am the other,' he explained slowly. 'Neither of us was acknowledged publicly, for fear of offending the Sheikh's wife, but after her death it was his dearest wish to be reconciled with both sons, and for them to meet each other.' Giovanni's face was implacable. 'And that is what has happened.'

'You mean—you've met them?'

Giovanni nodded, his black eyes brilliant -seeking, restless, almost yearning. As if starting out on this bizarre quest had wakened some kind of dormant wanderlust in his blood. As a man who—apart from his one ill-fated experience with Alexa—was used to encasing his feelings in ice, it was strangely unsettling to feel this way.

'*Si*,' he said, his voice now rough with a passion he had not expected to feel for any country other than his Italian homeland. 'I have met them. I flew to Kharastan. To a palace which is bluer than the brightest sky of high summer. To a land where falcons dominate the stark desert and hunger waits around every corner for the unwary. And there I was introduced to my…' He toyed with the word *family* as a cat might play with a mouse before striking. But Giovanni did not strike. His lips curved, for the intimate title seemed inappropriate for a couple of men he barely knew—no matter what their blood-tie was. 'I met the Sheikh and Xavier,' he said carefully. 'And the woman Xavier is to marry. They want me to go to their wedding.'

There was a pause while Alexa tried to digest the incredible facts he had told her. In any other circumstances she might have flung her arms around his neck and told him she was happy for him. Or she might have delved deep into his mind and asked him how he felt about suddenly discovering that he had a ready-made family?

But Alexa could not afford to do any of those things—even if their relationship had been the kind which would allow it. They had parted bitterly—with too much said which could never be unsaid. And there was too much at stake for her to risk asking him anything other than the time of his flight back to Italy.

'It's a very interesting story,' she said carefully, and put her glass down on the table. 'But I don't understand why you've come all the way from Italy to tell me about it when we're…'

'When we're what, Lex?' he prompted softly. 'Neither married, nor divorced? What is it that you say in England—neither fish nor fowl?'

'We're separated. Estranged.'

'But still legally bound—so in theory we are still family. Why is that, I wonder? Why did you not file for divorce, *cara*?' he questioned softly. 'Did some clever lawyer advise you to bide your time—telling you that *il tempo viene per chi sa aspettare*?'

'All things come to those who wait?' Alexa translated slowly, for her command of the language had grown rusty. She hadn't used it for years. Hadn't wanted to—just the sound of it took her back to a place too hurtful to reside in.

'*Bravo, bella*,' he applauded softly. 'Yet—while you may go to the top of the class—you have avoided answering my question. *Have* you been advised by a divorce lawyer? Closely watching my business dealings and then slowly closing in to make the maximum financial kill?'

Alexa felt the rapid skitter of her pulse, sensed a sudden and unknown danger. 'You're a cynic, Giovanni.'

'Maybe life made me that way—and still you avoid my question.'

Because if she answered him then the whole story of Paolo would come tumbling out. Yet she could not avoid divorce for ever, could she? She'd somehow imagined that Giovanni would file for divorce early on after their split, and that whole subject would come up within the sanctity of a legal framework. Protected by lawyers, she would have been safe. But now too much time had elapsed—and that created its own problems. She honestly couldn't see a way out of the maze she had helped create.

How could she tell him the truth when it was so blurred in her mind and in her heart that she wasn't really sure any more about what was real and what was not?

And if you show him any weakness he will pounce on it.

'I saw no reason in filing for divorce.'

'Not even for the settlement?'

Alexa hesitated. She could have done with a settlement. But pride had stopped her. She had chosen independence and freedom from his obsessive jealousy over all else—so in the circumstances could hardly ask him for any money. If she did that then the truth would come out, and the chance of a generous settlement was too high a price to pay if it meant that Giovanni could wrench Paolo away from her.

'Perhaps you wish to remain married to me?' His black eyes were gleaming as he continued with his relentless line of enquiry. 'Maybe you regret that the division of our relationship ever occurred? Did you walk out thinking that there might be a million other men like me out there, only to discover just how wrong you could be?'

Alexa opened her mouth to question his arrogance—to remind him of his unrealistic expectations of her which could never be fulfilled. But not only were accusations and recriminations futile, they also had the potential to be dangerous. Because was there the tiniest intimation of truth behind them? Just go. Get up and go.

'There's no point in making inflammatory remarks, Giovanni.' She bent down to retrieve her handbag, repressing a sigh of relief that her ordeal was almost over. Yet there was some part of the feminine psyche—and hers in particular—that made her experience a terrible, tearing pang at the thought that this really might be the last time she saw him. And part of her was longing to ask him a stream of questions about his discovery. But it's none of your business, she reminded herself. He's not part of your life.

Isn't he?

The goading question inside her head disturbed her more than it should have done, and Alexa gripped the strap of her handbag as if her life depended on it. 'If that's everything you wanted to say, then I really must be on my way. It really was...' She shrugged a little helplessly. 'Fascinating.'

'Do not be absurd, Alexa,' he warned silkily. 'You can't just get up and leave.'

'I can do anything I please,' she returned. Because now the hammer of fear was beginning to strike at her heart—until she reminded herself that not even Giovanni would dare to keep her there by force. 'That's the joy of being single!'

Stung to anger, she had given away the fact that there was no man on the scene—but Giovanni did not feel it necessary to allow himself a quiet smile of satisfaction. Even if she's had a lover he would soon have been dispatched—for who on earth would ever win a woman over Giovanni da Verrazzano?

'You still haven't heard the reason why I have come here today, Alexa—surely you are a little bit curious?'

She feigned uninterest but suddenly her senses prickled. There was an air of thinly veiled excitement about him. And something else too—something she couldn't put her finger on.

Was *he* going to ask for a divorce? she wondered, and to her astonishment felt her heart plummet like a coin dropped from the top of a tall building. Wasn't it strange how something as sensible and as irrevocable as the legal termination of a long-dead marriage should have the power to hurt, even after all this time? 'Okay, I'm curious. Tell me.'

He smiled. 'I want you to accompany me to Kharastan. I want you at my side for the wedding of my half-brother.'

CHAPTER THREE

ALEXA stared at Giovanni, her heart now beating very fast.

'You want *what*?' she echoed incredulously, as if somehow she might have misheard him—though in reality every silk-dipped word had been as clear as the look of enjoyment on his dark, rugged face. He was getting a kick out of this, she thought.

'Stop playing for time, Alexa—it really is very simple. Come with me to Kharastan,' he murmured, and his eyes narrowed in sardonic query. 'You can afford to be so blasé about it?' he mused. 'I confess myself surprised—after all, it isn't every day that a woman gets an invitation to a royal wedding. Doesn't the prospect of that tempt you?'

She guessed that there were women who would have been thrilled to bits by the prospect of such a high-status event—no matter what the price they had to pay to get there. But Alexa wasn't the kind of woman who could be swayed or seduced by money or trappings. Hadn't she left every item of clothing and jewellery behind in Naples when she had fled the marriage?

'You have to be out of your mind!' she choked. 'Give me one good reason why I should accompany you *anywhere*?'

'Because you are my wife.'

'In name only.'

'In name is enough.'

'Not for me, it isn't.'

'But I am talking about *my* needs, *cara*—not yours.'

Alexa picked up her wine glass and managed to successfully negotiate a mouthful of wine before putting it tremblingly back down on the table. She felt it burning its way down to her stomach, but at least it gave her a little bit of courage.

'You're not making sense, Giovanni—and even if you were the answer would be the same. It's no. How could it possibly be anything else, in the circumstances?' She could see that stony, obdurate look she knew so well on his face. 'There must be women who would queue up around the block to accompany you!'

He stilled, and when he spoke his voice was as cold as ice. 'You would not care? It does not bother you to think of me taking another woman?'

She injected bravado into her voice. 'Why should it?'

So she *did* have the calculating heart of a woman who could just walk away from a marriage without a backward glance or single regret. Hadn't there been some small and crazy part of him which thought she might *react*—that she might have *cared*?

Giovanni's face darkened with a rage which made him want to hurt her. 'It does not concern you to think of me kissing her? Nor to imagine me deep inside her body, with her legs wrapped tight around my back, until she cries out her pleasure?'

Unprepared for his sexual taunt, Alexa was not expecting the hot swell of nausea which rose up within her. She flinched. 'Giovanni—'

His mouth curved and he made no attempt to hide the triumph which washed over him in a heady wave. 'Of course it does!' he gloated. 'You would have to be made out of stone for it not to affect you.'

And nobody could accuse her of that. Her body had been soft and warm. It had trembled violently beneath his touch as if he'd been a virtuoso playing a brand-new instrument. Where he had led, she had been content to follow—he had drawn up the boundaries of their sexual relationship and she had seemed happy to comply with them. When she had nodded in flushed agreement to his stern suggestion that they wait until after the wedding before they consummated their relationship, he had known a thrill of expectant pride like no other.

He had been searching for innocence, and Alexa had led him to believe that he had found it. Not until their wedding night had Giovanni discovered what a sham it all was, and by then it had been too late to do anything about her deceit. Other than to despise her for making a fool out of him. And Giovanni had never been made to feel a fool before.

Something in his heart had died on their wedding night. Yet through his hurt and his anger Giovanni had been determined to take the pleasure he deemed rightfully his—and he had taken delight in coaxing from Alexa her own reluctant response. She had known that he despised her for what she had done and yet she had been unable to resist him. For her, every time she'd sobbed out her orgasm it had been a kind of defeat; for him, a kind of victory.

'Admit it,' he urged softly. 'You do not like the thought of me lying with another woman!'

Of course she didn't like it—it made her feel violently sick. She swallowed down the bitter taste in her throat and hoped her face didn't reflect her inner turmoil.

'Just as *I* do not like the thought of you lying with another man,' he breathed.

So nothing has changed there, thought Alexa. 'This is ridiculous,' she said, clasping her hands together and resting them on the table in front of him as if in silent appeal—like a handcuffed prisoner in the dock. 'We're separated. We haven't seen each other for almost five years—one of us ought to get around to filing for divorce. It's not exactly a textbook description of an easy relationship—yet you turn up out of nowhere and ask me to go with you to this wedding? You can't honestly want that on such an important occasion.'

'Ah, but that is where you are wrong,' he contradicted. 'I want this very much. In fact, it is you I want and only you.'

For a moment Alexa wondered if her ears were playing tricks on her—for weren't those the very words she had once dreamed of Giovanni saying? Coming to her with a contrite and heartfelt declaration that he had been wrong to treat her like a *thing*. A possession. Someone he had seen as perfect, but not quite real. A woman who could only be judged by his own archaic standards. And what woman in the world could have lived up to them?

But of course he would not have changed. Men like Giovanni considered themselves always to be in the right—to admit otherwise would go against every arrogant atom of his alpha-male make-up.

'Well, you can't have me.'

Carefully he placed his palm over her clasped hands, covering them entirely with his warm skin, and he felt her start, saw the pistachio-green eyes darken and her lips part in unconscious invitation.

'Can't I?' he said softly.

For a moment Alexa let herself go there—to the place where sensation dominated everything else. The touch of his hand made her tightly locked fingers relax—unfurling as if they were sticks of ice thawing under the unexpected heat of a winter sun. Such a seemingly innocent contact, and yet it brought all those long-suppressed and forbidden feelings flooding back. Skin against skin. The sensation of being touched, stroked, cajoled. Entered. Pleasured.

'Why would you want to take me to the wedding with you?' she whispered.

Deliberately, he lifted up her hand, to let his thumb begin a slow, sensual circle around her palm. 'Because I want a lover while I am there—a sexual partner for the duration,' he murmured. 'And it will be less offensive to Kharastani sensibilities if that woman is my wife.'

There was a short, disbelieving pause.

'A sexual partner *for the duration*?' she bit out, as if he might suddenly turn round and say that he was sorry—he hadn't been thinking straight and hadn't meant to say it. But of course he didn't. His black eyes just glimmered with amusement, and Alexa realised that he was actually *enjoying* himself. 'Are you out of your mind?'

She hadn't even noticed he was still holding her hand, he realised, and leaned a little closer. 'Let me be honest with you, Alexa, in a way you were never honest with me. We should never have married—I accept that. But there's still a lot of sex which didn't happen between us—I feel it and you feel it too. I can tell just by looking at you, by the way you tremble beneath my touch. So why fight it?' He gave a short laugh as he looked down at the fingers which were lying so compliantly cupped in his. 'I don't imagine you're ever going to get an invitation like this again.'

Snatching her hand away, Alexa shuddered and scrambled to her feet. There was, she realized, no diplomatic way to do this—there never had been, not with Giovanni. He would forge ahead until he got what he wanted. Only in this case he wasn't going to get it—and the sooner he realised that, the better.

'The answer is no,' she said in a low voice, fighting her instinct to shout it out—but she didn't want to draw any more attention to them. 'It's over, Giovanni. It should never have begun. Please—let's just leave it. We've said all there is to say. Except maybe goodbye.'

She walked out of the pub, her head held high and her cheeks burning—glad that her lifestyle meant she rarely ever went to places like this, and neither did her customers. At least it wasn't likely that she was going to run into anyone asking *Who was that gorgeous man we saw you with last night*?

But once outside she started running as if her life depended on it. She risked a quick glance over her shoulder, but thank God—oh, thank *God*—Giovanni hadn't followed her.

She was out of breath by the time she had reached the quiet cul-de-sac where Paolo's childminder lived, but at least she had begun to relax. Of course he wasn't going to follow her. He might want a 'sexual partner for the duration'—to use his own sickeningly cold-blooded choice of words—but he wasn't so desperate that he was going to start haranguing her to get her to agree to accompany him.

'Mamma!'

Paolo hurled himself straight into her arms the moment the neat little front door was opened, and Alexa's heart turned over the way it always did when she saw her handsome and clever little son.

But for once her joy was measured by other, uncomfortable emotions as she helped him into his duffel-coat.

Fear, yes—but guilt, too.

Because the huge brown eyes which gazed up at her so trustingly were so like Giovanni's? Was it seeing him for the first time in nearly five years which had made the similarities so apparent? Or was it the vague stir of her conscience which troubled her—a conscience she could usually manage to push away to the corners of her mind during the busy blur of everyday living?

'Where have you been, Mamma?' Paolo asked, his little hand firmly clasping hers as they walked up the narrow track leading to her tiny cottage.

'I went for a drink after work, darling.'

'Who with?'

'With…' What did she say? What could she possibly say? Oh, just with someone I knew a long time ago. Your father, actually. She felt her cheeks burning hot and red, but whether it was with guilt or shame at the heavy secret she carried, she couldn't be sure. *There was nothing else you could do—no alternative open to you— you would have lost your only child if you had tried!*

'Look, we're almost home, darling—shall I make us cocoa when we get in?'

'Oh, yes, *please*, Mamma!'

Alexa was so preoccupied with her swirling thoughts, and with opening the front door and switching on the light, that she didn't see the figure emerging from out of the shadows behind them, before it was too late.

Instinctively, she pushed Paolo inside—but that was probably a mistake, for the child stood in the full, illuminating glare of the light, staring up with fearless interest at the man whose powerful body almost filled the doorframe.

'Who are you?' her son asked innocently.

But Giovanni was staring at the child with a look of incredulity—frozen into astonishment by the sight of himself as boy—but the shock slowly left him, and he looked up and met Alexa's eyes.

A silent question was asked, and she nodded her head. For how could she do otherwise?

Yes, her eyes told him. *He is yours.*

'How old is your little boy?' he questioned, in a voice which somehow stayed steady. Because even though he knew the answer somewhere deep inside him, Giovanni was too much of an operator not to want to assemble all the facts before him. And it gave him time to think…

There was a pause. 'Paolo's four—and a quarter,' she said

Maybe he wouldn't believe her—why should he, when he had thrown all those accusations at her, his fevered and jealous mind imagining a whole catalogue of men she was supposed to have been intimate with? But five years on and he had changed, Alexa realised. Maybe it now suited him to see beyond the distortion of his own prejudices, or maybe he just could not deny the evidence of his own eyes—for she knew at the precise second when he accepted Paolo was his.

A brief shining moment of exultancy which was quickly replaced by a much darker emotion as he looked at her.

If she thought that she had seen bitterness there before then Alexa hadn't even come close to it—and now she almost recoiled from the vitriolic light which flooded over her in a dark blaze.

'Are you going to tell him?' he questioned softly. 'Or am I?'

CHAPTER FOUR

'TELL me what?' demanded Paolo.

Alexa bit her lip as she looked down at her son—at his beautiful, dark, oh-so-innocent face—recognising that once he was told his world would never be the same again. And shouldn't that be done with a little forethought?

She glanced up at Giovanni and his icy black gaze lanced through her like a sabre—but the recriminations which were bound to come her way were not important. Nothing was—except for Paolo. Deliberately she projected appeal from her eyes.

Please don't hurt him, went her silent message. *Hurt me, but please not him—for none of this mess is his fault.*

There was an almost imperceptible narrowing of Giovanni's eyes in response, a slight nodding of his dark head—or had Alexa imagined that?

'I am a friend of your mother's,' he said softly.

'I don't know you,' said Paolo stubbornly, and Alexa recognised that this strange man was stepping on the young boy's territory—or at least that was how Paolo was interpreting it. Would Giovanni be sensitive enough to do the same? she wondered. 'I've never seen you before. Are you Mamma's boyfriend?' he demanded, with a suspicious scowl.

'Why, does *Mamma* have a lot of boyfriends?' questioned Giovanni, and sent Alexa a look of pure, shivering malice.

How could she stop this? He would never believe her if she tried explaining that she'd never actually *had* a boyfriend, because Giovanni took real delight in imagining the very worst about her.

'I knew Giovanni a long time ago,' said Alexa, in a bright voice which sounded as if it was cracking open, like a smashed nut.

The black eyes glittered with another *just-you-wait* message.

Paolo nodded his dark curls energetically, the dark eyes huge in his face as he stared up at the tall Italian. 'Are you staying?'

There was a tense silence, until Giovanni gave a soft laugh which might have convinced Paolo that he had found something amusing, but which failed to do the same for Alexa.

'You'll have to ask your mother that,' he said, in a soft voice which sounded like a threat.

'Look, we ought to shut the door—we're letting all the warmth out,' said Alexa desperately, telling herself that she must not go to pieces. She couldn't just *couldn't*—not in front of her son. 'Giovanni—' This time there was a new appeal in her face, a subtle but dignified pleading in her voice. 'Why don't you come back tomorrow? You could come for tea—you'd like that, wouldn't you, Pao—'

'I'm not going anywhere,' said Giovanni smoothly. 'As long as Paolo doesn't mind?'

Openly fascinated by such an exciting-looking man, and enchanted to be included in an adult decision, Paolo shook his head. 'Can you play games?' he questioned, tugging at Giovanni's dark cashmere overcoat.

'Just try me,' Giovanni murmured.

Alexa watched him follow Paolo into the sitting room with an expression which bordered on disbelief, wanting to pinch herself, to tell herself this wasn't happening, none of it—from the moment he'd strolled into the shop this afternoon, leaving a trial of emotional havoc in his wake to now. Hadn't she imagined there could be nothing as bad as his reappearance? How naïve could you possibly get? Because this was far worse— Giovanni discovering the truth in this way.

But there's a reason you didn't tell him!

It was imperative that she didn't forget that and stayed strong—because her strength was her only defence, and she needed every bit of it to protect Paolo.

Ignoring the hostility in his eyes, which bored into her whenever there was an opportunity during Paolo's sweet but unfair domination of the dice game they were playing, Alexa lit a couple of lamps and set about making up the fire. Only when there was a cheerful blaze crackling in the hearth did she venture into the cubby-sized kitchen to make the promised cocoa.

She couldn't imagine the sophisticated and urbane Giovanni sipping the milky, chocolatey drink—but she included a third mug, and some of the gingerbread men she'd made with her son, which were nearing the end of their life but were still just about edible. And Paolo would be so proud of them, she thought, as she slid them onto a plate—before pulling herself up short and slumping against the kitchen wall in horror.

What was she *thinking* about?

She wasn't thinking—that was the trouble. For a moment back then she had slipped into some kind of normal programmed response of a mother serving drinks to a guest. But she wasn't. This wasn't an exercise in Happy Families—not by any stretch of the imagination. Showing off Paolo's creative attempts at cookery was one thing—but that was as far as it went.

Except that she didn't have a clue what was going to happen next. Alexa wasn't stupid, and she had a measure of the man she was dealing with. The very last thing Giovanni da Verrazzano was going to do was jump back on a plane and disappear out of their lives again.

So what, then?

So she needed to have all her wits about her, that was what.

By the time she brought the tray into the sitting room the fire had really taken hold, and the whole room was lit with a crackling warmth. Firelight was not just forgiving—it was as flattering as candlelight. It flickered and danced and created all kinds of illusions, and it hid

the shabby and rather ugly reality of the room—
cloaking it instead with the golden-orange glimmer of
flames. The cheap rented furniture glowed as deeply as
any antique, and you didn't notice the rug was thread-
bare beneath the glimmering light.

'Here we are!' said Alexa, her smile stretching so that
she felt it might split her face, feeling as if she was performing in some horrible, cruel farce.

Two faces were raised to hers, so heartbreakingly
similar—but while Giovanni's eyes glittered with unashamed enmity Paolo's were filled with love and trust.

Trust.

Would he still trust her after he had found out what
was now screamingly inevitable? That he had a father.
Why had she never stopped to think about that before?

Handing out drinks which nobody really wanted, she
could see Paolo trying desperately not to yawn. And,
although she was dreading the moment when she would
be alone with Giovanni, Alexa knew that she couldn't
put off her son's bedtime any longer. Scrambling to her
feet, she held her arms out.

'Come on, sunshine—time for bed!'

But Paolo didn't leap up for a monkey cuddle, the
way he usually did—instead he slid his hand into hers
in a newly grown-up way which tore at her heartstrings
and turned to look at Giovanni.

'Will you be coming back?' he questioned.

Giovanni nodded his dark head. 'Oh, yes,' he said.
'I'll be coming back.' And then, lightening his voice and
his mood by a conscious effort of will, he dazzled the

child with the full-wattage smile he rarely turned on. 'Shall I teach you an Italian game next time?'

Paolo nodded. 'Are you…Italian?'

There was a frozen, split-second pause, and Alexa had to turn her gaze away from the bitterness in Giovanni's face.

'*Si*,' he said. For now was neither the time nor the place to explain that he also had Kharastani blood running through his veins and so, by implication, did Paolo. Because that was a very big subject for a little boy to take on board. 'I am Italian—and it is the most beautiful language in the world. Did your mother never teach you any?'

'Mamma doesn't speak Italian!'

'Oh, I think you will find that she does—don't you, Lex?'

Alexa's eyes were drawn back to his face—like iron filings drawn irresistibly towards a magnet. She swallowed.

'Not any more—I've grown rusty.'

'What a pity,' he murmured, but the platitude was laced with steel. 'Every child should speak more than one language.'

Alexa ignored the silken threat underpinning his words. All she had to do was get her son safely to bed without some kind of terrible scene erupting. 'C-come on, darling,' she murmured unsteadily.

She went through Paolo's bedtime routine on autopilot. No time for a bath tonight, but tooth-brushing, hair-untangling, face-washing and story-telling took on their uniquely calming rhythm. It isn't *his* fault that stupid grown-ups had made a mess of their lives, she thought to herself fiercely as she pulled the duvet back.

But as she covered up his wiry little body—clad in soft blue pyjamas with little trains on them—she was struck by the guileless innocence in his face. Had Giovanni once looked at his mother in such a way—as if she could answer any question he put to her, solve any problem which came his way?

'I *like* that man,' confided Paolo sleepily, as he snuggled down beneath the covers and gave in to a yawn.

'Night-night, darling,' prevaricated Alexa, and wondered why her guilt should feel so intensely strong—as if someone had just flung a dank bucketload of it at her and left her dripping in it.

I did it for you, Paolo, she thought, as she gazed at where his lashes had fluttered down to form two dark arcs on his smooth, pale olive skin. *Only for you.*

Had she somehow hoped that by spinning out her goodnights Giovanni might have gone? Slipping away into the night like a bad dream?

But he had not gone anywhere. He had risen to his feet and was standing in front of the fire, with the flames behind him transforming him into a towering and threatening silhouette. She could not see the expression on his face and she didn't need to—because pure anger was radiating from him in waves almost as heated as the fire itself.

'Shut the door,' he said softly.

'Paolo—'

'I said, shut the door,' he repeated, his mouth hardening. 'Just do it.'

Alexa's hand was shaking as she complied, and she needed every bit of courage she had ever possessed as she turned round to face him.

Giovanni stared at her, observing the dark-fringed eyes and the berry-coloured mouth which trembled in dismay.

Had Alexa been hoping that by the time she came downstairs he would have gone?

His eyes bored ebony holes into her.

'So, were you ever going to tell me?' he questioned in a voice of dangerous silk.

'Giovanni—'

'Were you?' he continued. 'And—if so—when would it have been, I wonder? When he was eighteen? Maybe when he graduated? Or would it have been when he got married? Would I have been the spectre at the feast, Alexa—the unknown father turning up to curse the woman who had denied him his flesh and blood for all these years?' He lowered his voice and began to walk towards her. 'And if he had died—'

'Stop it!' she choked, clamping her hands over her ears.

'If he had died,' he continued brutally, enjoying her distress and her discomfort because, damn her—*maladizione!*—she had not cared about *his*, had she? If he could wound her with his words then he would aim for the jugular! 'What then? I would never have known, would I, Alexa? That my son had been born and had lived and died without me ever setting eyes on him?'

'No!' she moaned, because no matter how much she

tried to block the sound out his words came filtering through, hitting her like a persistent, heavy hammer.

Brutally, he wrenched her hands away from the side of her head.

'How can you live with yourself?' he continued remorselessly.

'I did it for *him*!'

'No, you lying little bitch—you did it for *you*! You did it because you wanted to keep him all to yourself!' He caught hold of her elbows, imprisoning her, and Alexa wriggled like a snake caught in a corner—wanting desperately to escape. But Giovanni was quicker than her—his reactions more alert. Without warning he levered her powerfully close up against his body, and as Alexa's eyes widened with fear and with a terrible yearning sense of recognition, he nodded his dark head.

'*Si*,' he agreed grimly. 'You feel the hardness of me? You feel how much my body wants you, even while my soul despises you for what you have done to me and to my son?' And, in a gesture born more out of anger than frustration, he drove his mouth down on hers.

For a second she struggled, but the grappling brought her even closer—so that she could feel the hard, seeking heat of his body, imprinting itself on the softness of hers. With expert pressure he prised her lips open and drove his tongue inside her mouth with a violent, stabbing movement which surely should have had her gagging, not responding—wanting greedily to kiss him back.

'Oh!' Astonished, dismayed, and so hot that she squirmed, she felt the way he arrogantly pushed up her jumper—his fingers homing in on a nipple which was almost indecently erect through the fine lace of her bra—while his other hand cupped itself over her buttock. She heard herself moan against him, felt her knees give way as a wild thought flew unbidden into her head.

Might this not absolve her from what she had done? If she gave him this, might he not find a tiny piece of his heart to forgive her? To see it her way—to try to understand the terror of losing her child to a man infinitely more powerful than a young girl on her own?

Giovanni felt his hard heat threatening to explode, and the temptation to tear down her jeans and impale her right there and then, against the wall, was overpowering. He could kiss her fraught cries quiet—feel his own power and domination as he brought her to orgasm. And as she shuddered around him he could draw comfort from his own swift conclusion—for surely the temporary obliteration of sexual pleasure was the only thing which would banish the black thoughts threatening to drive him insane?

But something stopped him. And it was not the thought that his son might hear. His *son*. Giovanni's hands dropped from her as if they had been contaminated.

'*Donnaccia!*' he hissed. Clenching his fingernails into the ball of his clenched fist, he winced, just stopping himself from drawing blood—and only then did his dark torrent of accusation flow over her. 'Slut! How many men have you allowed to take you against the wall like this, while my son slept upstairs unaware?'

CHAPTER FIVE

IT WASN'T Giovanni's abuse which brought Alexa to her senses—after all, him calling her a slut was nothing out of the ordinary, and if she didn't want him to think of her that way then she shouldn't have gone to pieces in his arms like that, should she? No, it was those two small words of utter possession which had sent hackles of fear prickling down her spine, as if someone was jabbing her with a million tiny needles.

My son, he had said. And the powerful words had been underpinned with both threat and determination.

Alexa's world was threatening to implode, and if she didn't do something soon—if she didn't take back some kind of control— then it might very well happen, and it would be too late for her to do anything about it.

'*Get away from me,*' she choked, gasping in a shuddering breath of air.

'You have a sudden change of heart? Isn't it a little late for that?' he drawled witheringly. 'Why, I could be inside you now if I had not stopped!'

His contempt was so overwhelming that Alexa felt

faint—until she forced herself to think straight. You did nothing that he didn't do, and *you are not a victim*, she told herself fiercely. And the sooner you stop acting like one, the better for all concerned—Paolo most of all.

'Can't you see why I didn't want to tell you, Giovanni?'

'No, I cannot,' he snarled. 'Never in a million years!'

'All through our marriage you accused me of sleeping with loads of men,' she said shakily.

'On the evidence of what just nearly happened, can you blame me?' he said, his mouth curving with disdain. 'Or am I to flatter myself that you've been waiting for me to walk back into your life to turn you on again?'

She tried to imagine his disbelieving scorn if she said *yes*—but that was a pointless path she had no intention of trying to set off on. Yet she had to try to make him see it from her point of view—she *had* to. Alexa steadied her breathing. 'Do you remember the last thing you said to me as I left Naples?'

'*Ciao?*' he bit out furiously.

'You said: At least we must give thanks that you aren't pregnant—for how would we ever know the identity of the father?'

There was silence for a moment while he stared at her incredulously. 'Are you telling me that you used a statement I flung at you in anger as a reason for *not telling me* that I had a son?'

'It was one of my reasons, yes.'

'And the others?' he demanded. 'Perhaps you'd like to enlighten me about what you felt gave you the right to play God with other people's lives?'

'Like your black jealousy, you mean?' she returned. 'The ridiculous accusations you kept throwing at me?' she continued steadily. 'The fact that you had me on a par with a hooker—'

'You should have *told* me you weren't a virgin!'

'I didn't realise that an unbroken hymen was a condition of marriage—or have I just been living in a different century?'

'It was your *deceit* which initiated my reaction,' he cut in icily. 'And today you have proved beyond any reasonable doubt that I was right not to trust you.'

Shaking her head with frustration, Alexa could see the great communication chasm which lay between them. They had fallen straight back into the pattern of charge and counter-charge, and nothing was going to be resolved—not in an emotionally charged situation such as this.

'I think we'd both better calm down a bit, don't you?' she questioned shakily.

At that moment Giovanni could have taken her by the shoulders and shaken her, demanding how she dared speak to him in such a way—like a teacher in charge of a naughty pupil.

Abruptly he turned on his heel and walked over to the window, which looked out onto the star-spattered night, and tried to will away the lump which had welled up in his throat and was threatening to suffocate him.

His son.

His *son*.

He stared at the tiny garden, his slow gaze taking in

a small plastic tractor which looked unreal in the silver-soaked light of the moon—and that cheap little toy seemed to symbolise all that he had lost. Or rather, all that she had stolen from him.

How long he stood there he did not know—but only when he considered he could face her without wanting to utter a torrent of invective did Giovanni turn around.

She was watching his face carefully, the enormity of her actions slowly beginning to dawn on her. She wanted to cry—but wouldn't her tears look like a self-pitying gesture from the woman whom Giovanni had always judged detrimentally and continued to judge still?

'I'm sorry—' she began, but he stanched her flow with the flat of his hand, slicing dramatically through the air—as if he was decapitating her words as she spoke them. And suddenly the path she had chosen seemed a blurred one, and she felt a great shuddering of regret. 'Maybe I should have told you about Paolo.' Her eyes searched his face in silent appeal. 'I didn't want it to turn out this way, Giovanni—honestly I didn't.'

'Oh, spare me your lies,' he grated. 'You didn't tell me, and you probably never would have done. It was only chance which brought me here today!'

'But I wrote to you once—when I was…pregnant.' She saw him flinch at her use of the word. 'Do you remember?'

His eyes narrowed. Memories were always dis-torted—*had* she written? Or was it now convenient for her to imagine she had? But, no, he *did* recall a letter—a stilted little thing, received when he was still angry and hurting and cursing his own stupidity and lack of judgement. In it she had wondered whether they might be able to have a meeting, and he had sworn, crumpled the cheap paper into a ball and hurled it into the bin.

'That bald little *note*?' he questioned. 'There was no mention of pregnancy in that, was there?'

She had been testing the waters, wanting to see if they were grown-up enough to be civil to one another. And she had been aching, too—broken by the shattering of her dreams, her heart missing the man she loved. His silence had seemed so final—and to her mixed-up way of thinking it had seemed to be for the best. He had wanted her out of his life, so why complicate matters further?

'No,' she admitted quietly. 'But you didn't reply.'

'And so for that one omission I was to be punished by being kept in ignorance of my son?'

'Giovanni—'

'No! You have no defence against my accusation because there is no defence,' he said viciously. He could see the shimmer of tears in her pale green eyes, but he hardened his heart against them. 'Why did you do it, Alexa? Do you really hate me so much?'

Hate him? She could have wept at how wrong he was. She had loved him with a passion she had never felt before, nor since.

'Not as much as you seem to hate me.'

But he seemed distracted, his eyes narrowed, as if he

were trying to keep up with his racing thoughts. 'The past is past and we can't bring it back,' he clipped out. 'The question is—what are we going to do about it?'

She could see the calculating look in his eyes as he though went a list of options, and Alexa felt her blood grow cold in her veins. '*Do* about it?'

He heard her fear, and suddenly Giovanni was filled with a sense of his own power. Did she think that she was in complete control—the one who could make the big decisions and have everything her own way? Up until now, maybe—but she was about to wake up to a lesson in reality.

'Do you really image that I am about to just walk away?' he demanded softly.

She tried to stay calm, even though the tone of his voice and the implacable look of determination on his face were making her begin to panic. 'No, of course not. But…but…'

'But what?' he queried.

'Well, it isn't going to be easy, is it? If you want to see Paolo.'

'*If* I want to see Paolo?' he echoed dangerously.

'Well, yes—I mean, you live in Italy and I live in England. We're going to have to consult lawyers about access, aren't we? Draw up some kind of agreement.'

A nerve flickered in Giovanni's cheek. Did she realise that with her dust-dry statement about lawyers she had concentrated his mind perfectly? he wondered. That her tentative but lukewarm attempt at appeasement had helped seal her fate?

His black eyes glittered. 'You have had things your way for far too long, *cara*, and that is all about to change.'

'What do you mean?' She could hear the fear in her voice, and she saw from the glint of triumph in his eyes that he heard it too.

'I want to take my son to Kharastan to meet his grandfather,' he stated flatly.

Alexa stared at him. Her first thought was that she had played this all wrong—and please couldn't she have the time-tape back to rewind it? But how far back would she go? To before this afternoon? Or before she had her baby? Maybe she would take it back even further than that—so that she would never have gone to Italy and never met him in the first place.

She could hear the pounding of her heart, and feel the corresponding dryness of her mouth. 'Giovanni, please let's not be hasty.'

'Hasty? You have some kind of nerve! You've had nearly five years, and now you're trying to waste yet more time?' He took a deep breath, enjoying the sudden panic which had clouded her eyes. 'Well, I'm sorry— that isn't an option. I've missed enough, and I don't intend to miss a second more. I'm taking Paolo with me.'

Giovanni realised that the subject which had dominated his thoughts until a couple of hours ago had now begun to develop different repercussions.

He was son and heir to a sheikh. But this was no longer just an isolated piece of information, to do with as he wished. The momentous discovery of his own birthright would impact on his son, he realised.

His *son*!

'You can't just pluck a child from the English countryside and transplant him to some exotic place he's never even heard of!' she protested.

'I want to take him to Kharastan,' he repeated stubbornly. 'And I'm going to.'

Alexa could see from the obdurate look on his face that he meant it, and she realised that she was going to have to be very careful. 'He won't come without me,' she pointed out softly.

His answering look could have withered at ten paces, but she forced herself not to recoil beneath its onslaught.

'Then you shall come too,' he said silkily. As he had originally intended—and, sweet heaven, she would pay for what she had done.

'And if I refuse?'

'You can't refuse.' His mouth curved. 'You have no choice, Alexa. Unless you want an all-out war, with our son as the spoils, then I advise you to co-operate with me.'

'With our son as the *spoils*?' she echoed. 'Like some kind of *trophy*? If that's how you see him—'

'That is enough!' His voice cut through her protest like a guillotine. 'You have been playing God all his life— you can hardly blame me if I've now decided to do the same.' He raked his fingers through his thick dark hair, his hard-edged smile laced with triumph. 'The wedding is early next week. We shall fly out there together.'

She felt dizzy and frightened at his use of the word *we*—because it almost made them sound as if they were a real family, and nothing could be further from the truth. How words could paint such false and haunting images inside your head, she thought, as a great wave of sadness overwhelmed her. 'What about my job? And what am I going to tell Paolo?'

With uncharacteristic hesitation Giovanni mulled over the possibilities—but he had not added to his monumental success without knowing that sometimes you had to step back. At the moment he was nothing other than a curiosity to the boy, and he had no influence on him. At least, not yet—though all that would soon change. Again he felt the clench of something like pain around his heart, and his eyes gleamed dark accusation at her.

'That is your problem, *cara*, not mine.'

CHAPTER SIX

'WAKE up, darling. Wake up.'

Jet-black curls moved beneath Alexa's stroking hand, and Paolo stirred as the sound of the jet's engines changed, indicating that they were beginning their descent into Kharastan.

'He'll come to in a minute,' she said, aware that Giovanni was watching her every movement, those keen black eyes weighing up everything she did, as they had done for the whole seven-hour flight, and before that as well. She felt as if she was undergoing some silent and tough assessment—as if he was examining her behaviour as a mother to see if she came up to his exacting standards. No, Giovanni hasn't changed, Alexa thought despairingly—but you aren't going to let him get to you.

He had picked them up first thing that morning, in a shiny black chauffeur-driven car which had had all the neighbours gawping before it whisked them off to a nearby airstrip, where one of Sheikh Zahir's private jets had been waiting for them.

It was the first time Paolo had ever been on an aeroplane—and Alexa sincerely hoped that he wasn't going to measure every future flight against this one. She was no experienced traveller herself, but this aircraft of the Sheikh's fleet was something outside the experience of most people—herself included. The exterior of the plane was dazzling white and sleek as a bird, while its interior was all restrained luxury, with gleaming woods and pure gold fittings.

There were low divans on which you could sleep, a dining area complete with table and overhead chandelier, a seating section where pure silk embroidered cushions were heaped upon squishy sofas, and a bathroom which wouldn't have looked out of place in a luxury hotel.

It seemed that everything they desired could be catered for—from soft-boiled eggs to lamb chops—but Alexa had asked if they could try some typical Kharastani cuisine, thinking that it might be a good idea to get Paolo used to the local food, while he was slightly over-awed with the lavishness of the plane.

She had seen Giovanni's eyes narrow as they'd met hers, and he had given a reluctant nod of his dark head in response. Alexa hadn't been looking for his approval, but she wouldn't have been human if she hadn't enjoyed it when it came.

Yes, Paolo had loved every second of the flight—which was more than could be said for her. Because for her the most part had been like tiptoeing through a minefield of unasked questions and forbidden subjects—made worse when their son had decided to nestle in his seat and sleep.

At least while he was awake there was some degree of civility between her and Giovanni—rather than the thinly disguised friction which was bubbling away beneath the surface like a cauldron of unwanted and unexpressed emotions. It was almost as if neither of them dared approach the more difficult topics—as if to do so might start some mid-air row which would embarrass them and frighten Paolo, or give the discreet crew something to frown upon.

The sudden drone of the engines told Giovanni that soon they would be stepping into a strange and beautiful land—peopled by an exotic nation of strong, black-eyed men he might have ruled had Fate not decreed it differently.

'What have you told him, Lex?' asked Giovanni softly, as he watched the boy begin to stir from sleep and he felt the increasingly familiar pang of disbelief and delight that this long-limbed child should have sprung from his loins.

She heard the urgency and the faintly proprietorial note in his voice, and once more it gave Alexa cause for concern. How far would he go to get what he wanted? she wondered. And how much of Paolo *did* he want? What if he decided that a four-year-old boy was a pain, and he most definitely *didn't* want to be a hands-on parent?

Yet deep in her heart Alexa knew this was a no-hoper—she had only to see the rapt look on her estranged husband's face to understand that. It was as if he couldn't get enough of staring at his son—displaying that sense of a newly formed love-affair which almost every parent had for their child.

'So, what have you told Paolo about me?' he repeated.

'I haven't mentioned you specifically.' She saw the look of simmering fury which hardened his dark face. 'He knows we're going to Kharastan—I told him we're going to a very special wedding in a royal palace. With you.'

'And what did he say?'

'He asked when we were going.'

'He didn't ask *why*?' he questioned incredulously.

Alexa shook her head. 'Children think differently to adults.'

It was the wrong thing to say.

'I wouldn't know, would I?' he declared hotly. He saw the colour flare in her cheeks and he knew that his barb had thrust home. 'So, how exactly are you *going* to explain to him? He needs to know who I am, Alexa—and we need to agree some kind of strategy for telling him.'

She felt her blood run cold. How quickly things could change. Twenty-four hours and he considered it his right to be included in decision-making. *We*, he had said— and just the sound of it had sent shivers running down her spine. But how could she prevent it?

'Not yet,' she said.

'You're hedging.'

'I'm thinking about Paolo.'

'No,' he contradicted forcefully. 'You are not. If you were thinking of Paolo then you might have stopped to consider his needs—and all children need a father!'

'Even if that father has judged a woman and found her wanting in a way that they used to do in Medieval times?' she declared. 'Who puts a woman on a pedestal so high that there is no way for her to go other than crashing down?'

'But you played the innocent to ensnare me, didn't you?' he accused softly. 'And I was fool enough to fall for it—mesmerised by the bewitching fall of red-gold hair and those green eyes which sparkled so innocently.'

'I did not *lure* you,' she said proudly. 'I never *said* I was a virgin.'

'Yet you knew how important it was to me.' Was it the fact he had grown up to the sound of men creeping in late at night as his mother brought her latest young lover home which made him place a higher price than most Italian men on the question of purity? 'You tricked me!'

'No.' Alexa bit her lip. 'I was too young and inexperienced to ever *dream* of concocting such a fabrication.' Too much in love and in awe of this masterly man.

'So why didn't you tell me, Lex?'

'Because our relationship was about *romance*—or at least I thought it was. Not a clinical breakdown of past partners—and don't forget I'd had only one!'

A nerve flickered in his cheek. His time with Alexa had been the only time in his life he had allowed himself to believe in the supposed fairytale of love. 'Not romance,' he snapped. 'I'd call it fantasy. You *pretended*, Lex—you know you did!'

'You never asked! It seemed somehow...*tacky* to discuss something so clinical. You made me feel like the only woman who mattered. I thought you wanted to prolong the anticipation—the glorious agony of making us wait,' she whispered. 'I didn't realise that you would have such double standards—that it was okay for you to have had loads of lovers, but my one solitary sexual encounter would be the launching pad for a whole heap of unreasonable accusations. I was either virgin or whore in your eyes, Giovanni—a stereotype, not a real woman.'

'A *real* woman would not have kept my son hidden away from me,' he said stonily.

Alexa drew a deep breath. 'I did what seemed best at the time. I was wrong. I'm sorry.'

He flashed her a cold black look. 'You've decided that now is a good time to apologise?' he mocked. 'Buying yourself brownie points while you can, are you, Lex?'

Oh, what was the use? Alexa sat back in her seat, closing her eyes tiredly as she thought of the sleepless nights she'd spent since he had walked back into her life.

For nights now she had lain awake and seriously pondered the possibility of just gathering up a few vital belongings and fleeing from Lymingham with Paolo—away from Giovanni and all the complications his return had thrown up. It hadn't been a lack of adventure which had stopped her, but the certain knowledge that she could have run to the ends of the earth and he would find her, now that he had discovered his son. And something else had stopped her, too—something that she had not expected to strike her so forcefully.

The fact that she could no longer deny Paolo what was rightfully his—a father.

But how did you *tell* a child something like that? How did you explain in words a four-year-old could understand just why she had never mentioned him before—and in such a way that she would not paint a black picture of Giovanni? Because that wouldn't be fair to either of them. And wasn't another reason behind her reluctance to tell Paolo the slight fear that her son would lash out and be angry with her? Was Giovanni right, after all—was she letting her own self-interest govern her behaviour to the detriment of her son?

'You're going to have to say something to him soon!' Giovanni's voice broke into her troubled thoughts. 'Because other people already know.'

Alexa opened her eyes. 'What do you mean? Which people?'

'I have told Malik—the Sheikh's aide. Some explanation was necessary,' he said grimly. 'How else could I explain why I suddenly wanted to bring a child with me? And Sheikh Zahir will also have been told by now. And word will get out, particularly when we arrive.' His black eyes sparkled with a hurt he hid behind the patina of a readily accessible anger. 'Even if I had said nothing onlookers would have to be pretty unobservant not to make the connection—given the likeness between us.'

'No, I guess not,' she said slowly, her mind full of conflicting thoughts. Because—if she was truthful— wasn't that another thing which freaked her out? Similarity was perhaps the wrong description—mirror-image might be more accurate, because Paolo was a lminiature version of his father.

Alexa glanced down at the dozing child. True, Paolo's skin had not quite the same dark lustre of his father's—but the jet hair with the hint of a curl to it, and the elegant and patrician features were the same. And the eyes... It was the deep dark eyes which matched most precisely—slanting and intelligent and framed with a thick sweep of black lashes which most women would have paid a fortune to possess.

With her contrasting pale and golden looks Alexa could not detect a single physical characteristic that she shared with her son, and it left her feeling something of an outsider. Like the unsuspecting bird who had nurtured a cuckoo's chick in her nest. *And now she was afraid that Paolo was going to fly away—to a glamorous new life of palaces and sheikhs—while his shop assistant mother faded ever more distantly into the background.*

'So, what are you going to say to him?' he demanded.

Alexa cast a fleeting look at Paolo, who had fallen back into a deep sleep in the way children seemed able to do in the blink of an eye. She was sure he couldn't hear—but didn't they say that hearing was the most acute of all the senses?

She placed her finger over her lips, but Giovanni shook his head.

Did she think she could shush him because of the child's proximity, and thus avoid discussing topics which needed addressing? Nice try. His mouth curved into a hard smile.

'If you don't want to be overheard, then come and speak to me in private.' He rose to his feet and walked over to the far end of the luxury cabin, well out of earshot of his son—and arrogantly beckoned to her.

For a moment she thought of defying him. But almost in the same moment realised that it would be a complete waste of time. Because Giovanni held all the cards, she realised. They were on one of the Sheikh's flight and he was the son of the Sheikh: the honoured guest. Whereas she was merely a means to an end.

She had something he wanted—his initial desire for a sexual partner had been superseded by something far more important. Now he wanted their little boy. With a sinking heart, Alexa realised she was effectively trapped—and it had nothing to do with being in the enclosed space of an aircraft. She was going to be as trapped when they landed in Kharastan as she had felt during her short, ill-fated marriage.

But in the meantime she had her son's feelings and welfare to consider, and the question Giovanni had asked was important. How *was* she going to tell him? If Alexa could have buried her head in the sand and prayed for the whole issue to just disappear, then she would have done. But it wasn't going to, because Giovanni wouldn't let it—and even Alexa recognised that it would be wrong to do so.

She recognised too that the most damaging way it could emerge would be if it was blurted out during a row just before they landed. So there was little choice other than to unclip her seat-belt and walk reluctantly over to join the man she had married, trying without success to ignore the fact that her heart still clenched with longing whenever she looked at him.

Today he was dressed entirely in black, in an exquisitely cut suit which hugged his lean body and emphasised the long, muscular shaft of his legs. His shirt was dark too, and he wore no tie. He looked expensive and dangerous, with the faintest suggestion of shadow at his jaw—a potent symbol of his virility.

As she grew closer to him she could smell the faint yet distinctive tang of the aftershave he had always used, and even as it prompted some terrible yearning deep inside her Alexa despaired that she could even be thinking of something like that at such an emotionally fraught time.

'So, what are you going to say and when are you going to say it?' he demanded softly. 'I suggest soon—the sooner the better.'

'With…' Alexa swallowed. 'With you present, you mean?'

He stared at her from narrowed eyes, and at that moment Giovanni's anger became a rage which threatened to explode like champagne from a bottle which had been shaken furiously.

'What did you imagine?' he breathed. 'That I would conveniently allow you to give him your version of 'the truth' in secret? To paint me as some dark monster from your past?'

'I wouldn't dream of doing something like that!' she defended on a whisper.

'No? Just what *have* you told him about the fact that he doesn't have a father?'

In a way she had been expecting this question, in all its painful complexity. 'I just told him the truth. That his

Mummy got married, but sadly the marriage didn't work out.' Alexa shrugged her shoulders in a brittle movement, because the matter-of-fact statement did nothing to convey her deep sadness and the sense of failure she felt that their marriage had disintegrated.

'What a perfect explanation,' he put in sarcastically. 'Did he never ask questions?'

Alexa shook her head. 'He seemed to accept that. Lots of his friends have parents who are divorced—'

'Ah, yes, of course! What a conveniently disposable world we live in,' he interrupted, in a low, savage voice. 'Maybe the reason he didn't ask any more was because he could see you didn't want to talk about it. Children are very good at picking up on the mood of adults and acting accordingly.'

Alexa opened her mouth to stand up for what she had done but thought better of it—and it had nothing to do with fearing Giovanni's wrath, but a with sudden insight as to where some of his anger might be coming from. Because for the first time she realised that she had denied Paolo a father in the same way that Giovanni's own father had been denied him, and the enormity of that now hit her.

She whispered her words. 'I acted the only way I could at the time—'

'And I've told you before,' he cut in viciously, 'that I neither want nor need your expedient explanations. Don't start coming over all penitent now, Alexa—just to make life easier for yourself!'

'What would *you* have said?' she questioned painfully.

Verbally, he wanted to rail and lash out at her with the might of his tongue. But the sleeping child on the other side of the luxurious cabin inhibited him.

'Alas, men are rarely in the privileged position that women occupy in a child's life. They cannot spirit their offspring away and airbrush the other parent from history!'

She wanted to explain. To tell him that she had been frightened—genuinely frightened—of his rages and his power and possessiveness. But if she admitted that fear now then wouldn't it acknowledge a weakness which still existed today? And surely Giovanni would simply capitalise on that weakness, using it as a springboard to exact some kind of revenge for what she had done?

'I'll tell him when the moment is right,' she promised.

'You will tell him when he wakes up.'

'Is that an order?'

'What do you think, *cara mia*? That I would beg and plead or wait at *your* convenience?'

Their gazes locked. Ebony fire sizzled from his and seemed to burn into her soul itself. But Alexa knew that she had to be strong or Giovanni would try to take everything. A long time ago he had already stolen her heart—but she would not let him have her son, or her sanity.

'Mamma!'

Alexa smiled. 'What is it, darling? Did you sleep well?'

'Are we nearly there yet?' asked Paolo, blinking his eyes open and looking around him.

'Nearly,' said Alexa. 'Why don't you come over here and have a look out of the window?'

Paolo jumped up and came to stand next to her. 'Look, Mamma!' He pointed his finger excitedly. '*Look*!'

'They're mountains,' said Alexa, looking down and realising they were flying over the a place she had thought existed only within the prohibitively expensive sections of travel magazines. 'Huge, snow-capped mountains.'

'And, look—there is the desert,' said a soft, deep voice.

Alexa swallowed, for Giovanni had come to stand behind them, and she could feel his presence—could almost touch it and taste it. The scent of him—his own unique, musky scent—pervaded her nostrils and replaced the air with the essence of *him*.

Didn't they say that women were attracted to alpha-men by some subtle processing mechanism which happened on a subliminal level? Was that what had happened—her body had taken into account all the factors which would ensure that she picked the strongest, most virile of the bunch? She wanted to shout at him—*please stay away from me!* Yet she wanted him to gather her in his arms too. To pull her close to his hard, seeking heat and cover her mouth with his kisses. Rough kisses that would not give her clamouring conscience time to resist.

'Can you see it, Paolo?' he murmured, leaning closer in, for he could tell from her posture that she was acutely aware of him. Was she uncomfortable with him standing so close to her? Did she want him? Good!

Their son's attention was completely taken up with the flash of silver and white buildings, and deliberately

Giovanni pushed his body into hers. Could she feel the hard ridge of his erection pushing against her bottom? He heard her barely perceptible intake of breath, felt the briefest shudder of her slim body, and knew an answering moment of heady triumph which more than made up for the ache of frustration. Yes, she wanted him!

Moving away from her, he heard the faint hiss as she expelled the breath she had been holding, and he bent his head close to his son's. 'Do you know why we're going to Kharastan, Paolo?' he asked gently.

''Cos there's a wedding!'

'Do you know whose wedding it is?'

Paolo shook his dark curls, and more of them fell around his head in disarray. 'No.'

'It is Xavier's wedding.'

'Who is Xa-Xa-Xavier?' stumbled Paolo.

'He is my brother.' Giovanni reached down and tangled his fingers in the silken mop of curls, and to Alexa's astonishment Paolo let him. 'Well, he is my half-brother—we have the same father, but different mothers.'

'Two girls in my class have that!'

Giovanni nodded. 'Lots of people have that these days—but I only found out that I had a brother very, very recently.'

Paolo's eyes widened as he stared up at Giovanni. '*Did* you?'

'*Si*,' said Giovanni softly, and then crouched down so that his eyes were on a level with the boy's. He felt his heart lurch. 'Sometimes families get all complicated for all kinds of reasons.'

He smiled at the little boy then, and Alexa was taken aback by the affectionate brilliance of that smile. It hurt when she compared it to the way he looked at her. But this isn't about me, she reminded herself. This is about Paolo, and the best way to tell him, and if you don't act now then Giovanni is just going to go right ahead and tell him.

'Paolo, what Giovanni is trying to tell you is that—'

'I am your father.'

The words rang out, and seeming to echo around the enclosed space, and Alexa bit her lip so hard that she felt the salt taste of blood. So he had done it anyway.

There was silence, and Giovanni was appalled that he should feel suffused with such *triumph* when he saw the hurt and the pain which clouded her green eyes. But she hurt me too, he thought viciously. She has hurt me more than I ever thought possible. She doesn't have the monopoly on inflicting pain.

Swiftly, he cast these reflections aside and stared into Paolo's little face, hoping—no, actually *praying*— that coming straight out with the truth had been the best way to handle it.

Alexa stood waiting too, feeling like an outsider—a shadowy interloper who was intruding on a very private conversation.

'Paolo?' she questioned tentatively.

Her son looked up at her then, and on his face was an expression she had never seen before. It was a mixture of emotions—of curiosity and relief and very definitely *delight*—but it was a troubled and faintly reproachful face, too.

'But Mamma doesn't have a husband,' he protested.

'Yes, I do,' she said, in a low voice she prayed would not tremble and crack. 'Giovanni is my husband. We got married—'

'In a fever?' Giovanni cut in cruelly.

'A long time ago,' Alexa followed on evenly. 'And we kind of…well, we lost touch.' She waited for Giovanni to contradict her, but to her surprise he did no such thing. The glint in his black eyes told her he had not forgiven her—but he had no intention of letting their son suffer because *their* relationship was in a mess.

Paolo seemed blissfully unaware of the undercurrents of tension sizzling in the air all around them, and the huge implications behind why she had *not* told him. His eyes were the size of chocolate saucers as he stared up in wonder at the tall, elegant man with the dark, rugged face. 'You're my *daddy*?'

There was a lump, and it was a pretty big one, which had just lodged itself right in the middle of his throat, so all Giovanni could do was nod, his lips pressing hard against one another as he attempted to keep his feelings in check.

'Yes, I am,' he said eventually. 'I'm your Papà.'

Alexa stood frozen, looking at the unfamiliar sight of his arrogant and beautiful face struggling beneath the weight of unfamiliar emotions. Like a spectator at some shamelessly weepy movie, she watched as he held his arms open and Paolo went straight into them—like someone coming home after a long absence—and she wondered just where they went from here.

From the things he'd said—and the contempt which had snapped from his voice—she guessed that Giovanni would never find it in his heart to forgive her.

The question was, would Paolo?

CHAPTER SEVEN

THE hot Kharastani sun beat down on Alexa's head, and she blinked as the young woman wearing a filmy veil over her moon-pale hair joined the tips of her fingers together as if in prayer and bowed deeply from the waist

'May I have the honour of welcoming you to the Blue Palace, Alexa?' she said, in a soft, low voice. 'My name is Sorrel, and I shall be looking after you while you are here.'

Just when Alexa had reassured herself that there couldn't possibly be any *more* surprises lying in wait, she had been proved wrong yet again—because here was another. And maybe it was good to have something to focus on other than all the possible repercussions of Paolo finding out that Giovanni was his father. 'But you're English!' she exclaimed, looking at the blonde in surprise.

Sorrel—who looked about the same age as Alexa—gave a wide smile. 'You can tell? I don't have any trace of a Kharastani accent?'

Alexa shook her head. 'Not to my ears,' she said, and

then looked around her with a slightly uncertain air, as if she expected to wake up from this crazy dream at any minute and find herself back in her little rented cottage in Lymingham. But, no, she was here—with an imposingly domed and turreted building behind her, the largest of all the royal residences in Kharastan.

On arrival at the palace Paolo had immediately wanted the bathroom. He had insisted that Giovanni take him—not her—and Alexa had fought an inner battle before giving in gracefully.

'It is easier that way,' said Sorrel softly, as they watched a silken-robe-clad servant lead Giovanni and his son through some carved doors. 'For there are areas of the palace which are still off-limits to women.'

Alexa nodded, telling herself that her son's behaviour was understandable in the circumstances—even if it was with a conviction she didn't really feel.

Paolo had just discovered a father figure and he wanted to make the most of it. Like a child who had been given a wonderful new toy—he simply wanted to play with it non-stop. And, if you considered that they had just arrived in an exotic, very different country from the one he was used to—a country which seemed to be dominated by the male of the species—then surely she could understand why her son wanted to look and act like one of the men?

So why did she feel so alone and so excluded? As if she was standing on the very edge of a cliff which was slowly crumbling beneath her feet? Because the balance of power had changed, she recognised painfully. It was all now heavily weighted in Giovanni's favour—and, oh, hadn't he just taken to his new royal status as to the manner born?

A fleet of cars had met them at the airport when they had touched down in the capital—long, low cars, with tinted windows and bullet-proofed bodywork—and from these had emerged men with bulky jackets and dark, impenetrable eyes whose gaze never quite met hers.

They had been welcomed by an official who wore flowing ivory robes. His name was Fariq and he was secretary to Malik—the Sheikh's most senior and trusted aide. He had bowed to Giovanni.

'The Akil Malik bids me tell you that he is currently in discussion with Sheikh Khalim of Maraban, prior to the royal wedding. He sends his most abject apologies and will see you later, at dinner.'

As they climbed into one of the luxury cars, Alexa turned to Giovanni with a frown.

'Everyone's treating you as a member of the royal family,' she said in confusion.

Giovanni shrugged, determined to remain friendly towards her—at least outwardly, and especially when they were with Paolo. The boy would not know a moment of disharmony if Giovanni could prevent it—and neither would he be told how close he had come to never knowing the identity of his father. It had been Alexa's doing, but no blame would be apportioned there. What was the point, when the child adored his mother? To demonise her would only make Giovanni the monster in Paolo's young eyes.

No, he would make Alexa pay for her deception in

his own particular way—and he knew exactly how he was going to do it. Anticipation heated his blood. He could feel it flaring warm over his cheekbones. But the glance he threw her was nothing but mocking as he enjoyed her obvious discomfiture, the fact that she could not seem to relax beside him.

'That is because they have *accepted* me as a member of the royal family,' he said coolly.

'So soon?' she asked.

'It was decided that waiting would serve no good purpose,' he drawled, as Paolo climbed on to his knee and snuggled into him like an eager puppy. 'Thus my identity as the second son of the Sheikh has been revealed in the last few days.'

But Giovanni's cool air disguised his own utter astonishment at the news which had reached him via reports sent directly by Malik. The Kharastani people—who adored their ruling family and anyone connected to it—had taken to Giovanni immediately.

No matter that the circumstances of his birth had been unusual, to say the least—it made no difference to the enthusiasm of the country's reaction.

The *Kharastan Observer* had produced a thoughtful editorial, celebrating the new blood being brought to the line by Xavier and now Giovanni.

Any son of Zahir with Kharastani blood running through his veins is sheikh enough for the people of this land. And if two heirs have been produced, then our people will know the meaning of a true bargain!

It had been planned that Giovanni should make his first official appearance on the balcony, following the royal wedding. His mouth hardened into a determined line. And he fully intended to hold Paolo aloft in his arms!

Alexa grew silent during the car journey to the palace—feeling as if she was at the beginning of a process intended to edge her towards obscurity. Paolo was wriggling on Giovanni's knee, chattering excitedly as they passed strange flowering trees through which they could see skies much bigger than the skies back home.

'Look at the soldiers!' cried Paolo. 'They've got *guns*!'

Alexa shot Giovanni a beseeching look.

His eyes narrowed, but he touched Paolo's arm lightly. 'See over here instead,' he murmured. 'There is a little monkey—playing on an accordion.'

'Oooh!'

'And do you know that there are snake-charmers in the main square of the city?'

'*Real* snakes?'

Giovanni nodded. 'Black cobras—and pythons.'

'Can I see them?'

'I'm sure you can, and, look—here we are. Just coming up to the palace.'

'A palace?' questioned Paolo, who had only ever seen them pictured in his story books.

'A palace,' agreed Giovanni solemnly. 'It is where the Sheikh lives, and soon you shall meet him for yourself.' Across the top of Paolo's head, his eyes once more met Alexa's. The child wouldn't have made the association, but had she? Sheikh Zahir was his grandfather. Paolo too had royal blood running in his veins. And to the people of Kharastan this connection would be valued more highly than the purest gold.

'Is *that* it?' Paolo piped up excitedly.

'It certainly is.' He smiled.

Giovanni had stayed at the Blue Palace during his last visit, but this time he was stunned into a kind of dazed silence—as if the true magnificence of the building was only evident on a second careful viewing, and by imagining it through a child's eyes. He realised with something of a start that he was not used to looking at something from another person's perspective.

'Oh, it's beautiful,' breathed Alexa as she looked out of the limousine window, all her troubles momentarily dissolved by the impact the building made on her senses. 'Utterly beautiful.'

Every shade of blue she had ever seen—and a few more besides—was there, culminating in a soaring dome which tantalised the eyes. The combination of blues made a colour so intense that it rivalled anything produced by nature. But, in contrast, the flowers which grew everywhere were many-hued—pinks and reds and purples and creams, and the deep saffron shade of egg yolk. The powerful scent from the massed blooms pervaded her senses as they climbed out of the car, and made her feel weak.

And that was when the blonde woman called Sorrel had appeared from within the shadowed sanctuary of the palace to welcome them—looking so cool and ethereal in her gossamer-fine veil that Alexa had half wondered if she might have dreamt her up.

Alexa found herself wishing that she had worn a hat, or something a little cooler than the linen trousers and jacket she had worn—but she had been too self-conscious to wear anything more ethnic to Heathrow Airport.

'Come inside, into the cool and the shade,' Sorrel urged. 'You look hot.'

'I *am* hot,' Alexa confessed. And tired and disenchanted—and terrified that I'm going to lose my son to a man who once said he loved me but now looks at me with nothing but hatred in his black eyes. Licking her dry lips, and feeling ever more disorientated, Alexa looked at the blonde woman. 'H-how come you speak English so perfectly?' she enquired, in a voice which sounded wobbly.

A faint crease appeared between Sorrel's brows. 'I shall tell you everything you wish to know—but you are in no fit state to ask or answer questions at the moment. Come with me and I shall direct you to your suite. There you can bathe and change into something more suitable for our climate.'

'But I'm waiting for my son,' protested Alexa.

'Your son will be fine,' soothed Sorrel. 'I promise you. One of the servants will bring him to you—the best thing that you could do for him would be to have yourself some rest. You look dead on your feet.'

Could Alexa trust Sorrel? More importantly—could she trust Giovanni to look after Paolo? Alexa was feeling light-headed now, and yet she knew with a bone-deep certainty that Paolo would be safe.

'Maybe you're right,' she said shakily.

Sorrel led her along a series of seemingly endless and interlinking marble corridors. Alexa felt as if she was in a honeycomb. At the very heart of the palace was a central courtyard, which contained the most exquisite garden Alexa had ever seen.

Yellow flowers tumbled down through the branches of tall trees which provided welcome shade, and there were waxy white flowers which filled the air with their heady scent. The paths which divided the garden into a series of rooms were of blue and white mosaic tiles, and the sweet, swishing sound of a fountain playing made Alexa long to jump into the refreshing water.

'These are your rooms,' said Sorrel, throwing open a set of double doors.

Inside was a huge salon, with faded silk rugs and exquisite inlaid furniture, and chandeliers which glittered like a million diamond icicles suspended from the ceiling.

'There are two bedrooms and three bathrooms,' said Sorrel softly. 'Perhaps,' she added gently, 'you might wish to freshen up?'

There was a part of Alexa which was past protesting at the way her life seemed to have been taken over. She was so weary—emotionally *and* physically, that even putting one foot in front of the other seemed to take the most monumental effort.

'But Paolo—'

'I suspect that Xavier is on his way to meet him and Giovanni to give the child a quick tour of the palace— it will help him get orientated—so you certainly have time to change.' Her face softened. 'Better Paolo sees his mother refreshed and with a smile on her face.'

A smile? Was it possible to smile whole-heartedly when inside you felt as if your heart was breaking?

'Look,' said Sorrel softly, and guided her towards a lovely oval mirror which hung on one of the walls. 'See for yourself.'

Alexa stared back at herself, and if she hadn't already been as white as a wedding veil she might have blanched from the shock. She looked *frightful*. Apart from the dispirited set of her shoulders, her eyes were tired, and there was a dark streak of something across her cheek, where she must have run the back of her hand—now, why hadn't Giovanni told her about *that*? Because he wanted her to look a fool? The shop girl she really was—out of place in such lavish surroundings?

Was he hoping she would make such a bad impression that the Sheikh and other members of his new-found family would consider her unfit to be the mother of a child with royal blood?

If Alexa had thought Giovanni powerful enough to snatch her son away from her—she hadn't even considered what it would be like to have the full might of the Kharastani royal family banked against her.

But along with her fear came a renewed wave of determination. Was she just going to play into his hands? To sit back and let it happen?

Like hell she was!

'Why is an Englishwoman such as yourself living in this strange and exotic place, Sorrel?' she questioned quietly, because the other woman's kindness was making her warm to her.

'My father was the British ambassador here in Kharastan for many years,' said Sorrel. 'I spent all my vacations out here, and I quickly learned the language and a love for its people.' A cloud passed over her beautiful face. 'My parents were killed in an aircraft over the mountains of Maraban when I was sixteen, and I was made the ward of Malik, the Sheikh's aide—a very important man, whom you will meet later.'

'You didn't want to go back to live in England?' questioned Alexa, fascinated by a story which momentarily made her own troubles fade into the background.

Sorrel shook her head. 'Not a bit. I felt an indescribable *affinity* with Kharastan,' she said earnestly. 'Maybe I learned that from my parents, who taught me much about its culture and its turbulent history, and I was lucky enough to be fluent in the language, which is rare for a Western woman. Whenever I was in England I seemed to live for my time here—so I decided to complete my schooling and university here.' She shrugged her narrow shoulders and gave a shy smile. 'And here I am.'

'So what is your role here now?' asked Alexa tentatively.

'Ah, my role.' Sorrel gave a dry laugh. 'I work at the British Embassy and live within the palace walls. I do not think a definition exists for my role here!'

Alexa wondered about the slightly acid tone which had coloured Sorrel's voice, but told herself it was none of her business. She certainly had enough on her own plate to worry about. Yet the other woman's words had been kind and encouraging—she had not appeared to mind Alexa's interest. Was it too much to hope for a tentative sisterhood between herself and her fellow countrywoman? An alliance, perhaps?

'Are Giovanni, Paolo and I all staying in this suite together?' she asked Sorrel softly.

'Yes.' There was a barely perceptible pause. 'That was what Giovanni requested.' Sorrel's face was impassive and she gave a helpless shrug. *Don't blame me*, it seemed to say. *Don't ask me questions I cannot in conscience answer.*

And Alexa understood perfectly. Sorrel's silent gesture was telling her something she had already guessed—that Giovanni had all the power here, and his wishes would be paramount. There was little choice for Alexa other than to go along with it.

But that didn't mean that he could actually take her child from her by force.

If she was about to have a custody fight on her hands, then Giovanni had better realise that a mother's love could move mountains. Yet, just as a general going into battle would not do so if he was weary and unkempt, so neither could Alexa meet anyone while she was looking like this.

'Can I have a quick bath?' she asked Sorrel.

'A quick bath!' Sorrel laughed. 'I haven't heard someone say that since I was at boarding school in England, many years ago! Yes, of course you can—I took the liberty of having one drawn for you in preparation.'

And, despite her distracted state, Alexa couldn't help but exclaim out loud when Sorrel opened the door to one of the bathrooms and she saw the vast circular bathtub, lined with inlaid mosaic. The water within it was sweetly scented, and there were rose petals floating on the steaming surface.

'Like something out of the *Arabian Nights*?' guessed Sorrel, with a smile. 'It's not exactly asses' milk, but I think you'll enjoy it.'

Enjoy it?

After Sorrel had left, Alexia pulled off her crumpled clothes and slipped into the perfumed waters, letting out a long, instinctive sigh of pleasure. The bath was almost deep enough to float in, and never had the sensation of warm water embracing her wearing limbs seemed so utterly pleasurable. She could have stayed there all day. But she didn't have all day—so she washed her hair and then pulled on a fluffy towelling robe and tried not to compare this to her small bathroom at home, where she had to contort yourself like an ostrich to dry herself off, and where Paolo's socks and pants hung on a drying stand during the winter months.

Her case had been produced and unpacked in the dressing room, and hanging in the wardrobe were Alexa's brand-new clothes. Before the trip she had gone online and discovered what was acceptable garb in Kharastan—and then she'd left Paolo with the child-minder and hit the fabulous Asian bazaar which visited her corner of southern England once a month.

For a song, Alexa been able to purchase swatches of

silks in different colours, which she had made up into close approximations of the long, floaty tunics Kharastani women wore. Now she picked out one of them and ran her fingertips over a light material, the most delicate and gossamer-fine silk, and couldn't wait to slip it on.

Pulling on the delicate fabric, she heard it whisper in a silken kiss over her warm skin, and just at that moment she felt almost decadent—not like the responsible and nun-like single mother she had become out of necessity. *This isn't real*, she told herself in slight desperation. *None of this is real.*

With one final glance in the mirror, she walked back through into the dim light of the suite and went to find her son.

Narrowing her eyes against the bright light which blazed outside, she looked around to see Paolo sitting at a table on the wide terrace, drinking through a straw from a glass of juice the colour of a sunset, watched by a young Kharastani woman who was clearly some kind of nanny figure.

At the sound of Alexa's footsteps he turned his dark head, his eyes lighting up as he scrambled down from the chair, running full-pelt into her arms and squealing with excitement.

'Mamma, Mamma! The garden is much bigger than the park at home!'

'Is it? Oh, Paolo.' She tightened her arms around him and closed her eyes. 'How are you, my darling?'

He wriggled free from the constriction of her

motherly embrace. 'I saw the palace an' it's *huge*, and I met Uncle X-Xavier, an' there's a toy box in my bedroom, an' we can have sore-bet for dinner!'

'What's sore-bet?'

'He means sorbet,' came a low, silky voice from behind them, and Alexa whirled round to see Giovanni emerging from the shadows of the room. 'I told him it was a dessert which tastes like an ice lolly.'

Her heart skipped, a beat and then began pounding as if it had only just learned how to. He looked like some dark, sensual predator, and Alexa hated the instinctive prickle of her skin and the tingling of her nerve-endings as her body instinctively acknowledged his. Because he was the father of her child—was *that* why she felt this bond which was almost tangible?

'Papà!' squealed Paolo in delight, as he extricated himself from her arms and jumped down, rushing over to Giovanni to attach himself with all the easy confidence of young puppy.

Papà? thought Alexa weakly. Already? When the hell had *that* happened?

Giovanni reached down to rumple the dark curls, and smiled. 'Did you drink lots of water? Because it's hot, and because—'

'*Water makes lions strong!*' put in Paolo enthusiastically, and went running back out onto the terrace as if he had lived in a palace all his life.

The unfamiliar expression threw her, and Alexa wondered what else Giovanni had managed to teach him in such a short space of time. That Italy was a much

warmer and more hospitable climate than England? Or
had Giovanni dangled the carrot of his wealth—telling
Paolo that he owned a turquoise rectangle of a
swimming pool which was as big as their local lido. And
more. Much, much more.

'How quickly you have influenced him,' she said softly.

'Can you blame me?' Giovanni's mouth curved into
a cruel line. 'I have four years' catching up to do.'

Face your fears, she told herself. Face them head-on.
'Are you working towards getting full custody of him,
Giovanni? Is that what I'm fighting against?'

'Whoever said anything about fighting?' The sight of
her—all bathed and fresh and sweetly scented—had
just begun to register on his senses. 'That's the very last
thing on my mind at the moment,' he murmured huskily,
his black eyes sliding over her in a look of pure sexual
scrutiny. 'How perfect you look, *cara*.'

Alexa sucked in a breath, trying to claw in enough
oxygen so that she wouldn't do something unforgivable—like crumpling to the ground in front of him.
Because that look was sheer, sizzling temptation. And
because beneath the delicate silk of her new and unfamiliar robes she felt curiously naked. She felt the sudden
melt of longing—was terrified that he might be able to
detect from the subtle perfume of heightened sexual
desire how much she wanted him. Through dry lips, she
swallowed. 'Giovanni…'

He raised arrogant black brows. 'What?'

'Your son is out on the terrace,' she whispered, alarmed.

'So?'

'So stop trying to be provocative. He might see us.'

'What do you think most married couples do?' he demanded softly. 'They send silent messages with their eyes, and they whisper just what they plan to do when their child is safely tucked up in bed.'

It was both a warning and an invitation.

'But we're not married. Not properly.'

'Improperly, then. And maybe that's better. Marriage complicates things with emotions—this way we are free from such constraints. We can just enjoy the sex for what it is.' *Just as I originally intended*, he thought. Deliberately, he ran his tongue over his lips, and watched her eyes following the movement with a greed she could not hide, no matter how much she wanted to. 'Want me to do that to you, *cara mia*?'

'No.'

'Liar.'

He was right, damn him—but that didn't mean she was going to give in to what she really wanted. 'Please don't do this, Gio.'

He smiled. But it was a cruel, hard smile. Let her squirm. Let her plead. And then later let her gasp his name out loud in a different kind of plea altogether. 'I am not doing anything other than looking at you.'

How could she tell him that his looking at her was enough to set off a whole series of complex reactions to him—both physical and psychological? That the blaze of his ebony stare was making her turn to mush, drying her mouth to dust and making her knees shake? And her heart was hurting, as if he had taken a long sabre and stabbed it right through, because she could see the naked hostility which shone through his heavy-lidded desire.

Alexa opened her mouth to protest, but no words came. She felt as helpless as a newborn. He took advantage of her momentary weakness, snaking his hand out to capture her waist and pull her into his body.

It was an arrogant gesture of ownership which he had demonstrated many times with many women over the years. But this was different. Against her hair, Giovanni briefly closed his eyes, uncharacteristically weakened, just for a moment. It felt different. Because it *was* ownership? Because she was his wife, who had borne him a son? Yet she had cleverly run away and built herself a life without him—she who should have been closest to him was in fact a million miles away. But not for very much longer.

With the fingers of his free hand Giovanni jerked her chin up, so that her face was staring directly at him—the pale green eyes wary, the full lips trembling under his burning scrutiny.

'But you are right,' he conceded huskily. 'This is neither the time nor the place for love. Our son, as you reminded me, is out there on the terrace, and I must go to meet with Xavier, my half-brother.'

His mouth hardened. From being a man who had considered himself all alone in the world—it now seemed that he had relatives. He had already decided to make his claim on Alexa for Paolo—but how would having a half-brother impact on him? Would his sudden new royal status bring any influence to bear on his life? He forced himself to concentrate on that which he could control, and as he felt the distracting soft silk of her skin beneath his fingers he felt the sudden urgent leap of hunger. 'Have you seen the sleeping arrangements yet?'

'I'm afraid I have.' Turning her head, she wrenched her face away from his touch, from all the dangerous messages it was sending skittering along her skin.

'It will be quite like old times to share a bed, will it not, Alexa *mia*?' His smile was one of mocking triumph as he sensed her obvious discomfiture—enjoying the fact that she was fighting her feelings and trying to suppress her own desire. 'I, for one, cannot wait.'

'Well, I can—and I will. 'She drew a deep breath, knowing that this needed to be said. 'It doesn't matter how you've plotted or planned or connived to put us in the same bed—proximity means nothing in the face of my own determination. You won't have me, Giovanni— it would only complicate things,' she vowed softly, and she turned to walk outside.

Giovanni began to laugh softly as he watched her moving towards the terrace, seeing the pert thrust of her buttocks pushing against the fine, filmy fabric of her robe. How pointless her protest! How wasted her words!

Soon he would possess her in the most fundamental way possible. But this time he would use his prowess as a lover to tie her irrevocably to him.

When they had been married the stakes had been much lower. His pride had been badly hurt when she had left him—but in the end all he had lost had been a lying bride.

But with the discovery of Paolo everything had changed.

Alexa would never be allowed to run away from him again—because what she possessed was too valuable. She had something he wanted.

Their son.

And Giovanni was never going to lose him again.

CHAPTER EIGHT

ALEXA dressed for dinner with a cold feeling of dread at the pit of her stomach. How ironic that she found herself in a state which many women would find enviable—dining in a royal palace—and yet inside she was a bag of nerves.

But it wasn't etiquette which was bothering her—the fear that she might not curtsey to the right person, or might inadvertently use the wrong knife at dinner, or eat something she wasn't supposed to, or not want to eat something she *was* supposed to. No, she was worried about Giovanni—about what schemes were simmering away behind that implacable dark mask of a face.

And she was worried about her own unpredictable and volatile emotions. It was one thing to keep telling herself that he was the wrong man, but that didn't stop her heart racing when he was near. Or the stupid, senseless longing to have him hold her, and look at her—with that melting look softening his hard black eyes—the way he'd once done such a long time ago. But—let's face it—he wasn't about to do that again, was he?

She felt as if she was in one of those subtle psychological thrillers, knowing that he was playing on her weakness and his strength. On the fact that a fiercely strong sexual attraction still burned between them. Even when they had been living together, and he had taunted her and despised her supposedly louche morals, he had still known exactly how to please her—even though his own particular brand of sexuality had been like making love to a man with no heart.

'Are you ready, *cara mia*?'

Just the sound of that soft Italian accent was enough to send whispers of awareness shivering all the way up her spine. Alexa looked up to see Giovanni standing at the door of Paolo's bedroom. She had been doing up the last button of Paolo's long silk tunic, worn with matching trousers, which their son had been given to wear by Sorrel. It had been a bit of a battle to persuade him to put them on, until Giovanni had reassured him that he, too, would be wearing traditional Kharastani dress for the evening meal.

'Why?' Paolo had wanted to know.

'Because it is courteous,' Giovanni had replied solemnly. 'And because surely you would like to look like a little prince for the night?'

That had swung it as far as Paolo was concerned, and Alexa's worries about how looking like a little prince might turn the child's head were instantly forgotten now, at the sight of Giovanni himself in the promised Kharastani costume.

He wore a robe of the finest silk she had ever seen,

coloured a deep sunset-red which made him look like a moving flame. A headdress in pure gold, held in place with a knotted scarlet circlet, completed the outfit. Alexa guessed that some men—if they carried a little extra weight, perhaps—might be in danger of looking ridiculous. But the way that the fabric flowed over Giovanni's hard and muscular body—he looked like a shimmering study in masculinity.

'Papà!' squealed Paolo. 'Do I look like a prince?'

'You look like a bold warrior,' Giovanni replied gravely.

'*Do* I?'

'Indeed you do. Now, come along—for we must not be late for dinner.'

Paolo rushed past him, and Alexa had no choice but to follow. But Giovanni did not move, just continued to stand in the doorway, as if he'd been fashioned from some hard, pure steel. She could feel the shivering of her skin beneath her gown.

'Let's go,' he said huskily, tearing his eyes away from the sudden thrusting points of her nipples against the fine silk of her gown. If only he were not constrained by palace rules and their child—he would be pinioning her up against the wall and thrusting into her.

The formal banquet for heads of state and visiting dignitaries had been held the night before—but this, the pre-wedding dinner, was a 'family' affair. It was held in a dining room which Malik had described as 'intimate'—but which was the size of a small ballroom, lined with gold and mirrors and priceless paintings.

The table was round, and set lavishly with crystal and

silver, and bowls full of richly scented roses. Tall white candles guttered and cast intriguing shadows, while robed figures slipped silently in and out of the room, carrying dishes which catered to the diners' every whim. In one corner was a small group of musicians who plucked on strangely shaped instruments to produce a sweet keening sound which was oddly haunting.

There were seven of them in total. As well as Alexa, Giovanni and Paolo sat Malik, with Sorrel close by. Next to her was Xavier, with Laura—his English fiancée.

'We don't usually eat this early,' said Malik, his hard black eyes momentarily crinkling in a smile down at Paolo. 'But then we are not usually honoured with such important guests as young Paolo.'

'But I can stay up late!' boasted Paolo, and followed this with an enormous yawn, which made everyone laugh.

Putting his heavy silver goblet down, Giovanni looked around the table, thinking what a disparate group they made. And that Malik seemed to be acting as host tonight, despite the presence of the royal groom.

Giovanni's eyes narrowed with curiosity. Perhaps Malik had taken over because Xavier and his fiancée were at that stage of being so much in love that they could barely tear their eyes away from each other.

Even today, when he and his half-brother had met in an attempt to piece together their patchy pasts, to see if they had anything in common, Xavier had been keen to get back to the woman who tomorrow he would make his wife.

Giovanni watched while the Frenchman poured water for her, touched his hand to her hair almost in wonder, and mirrored her body language in a way which would have pleased the most critical of behavioural psychologists.

His mouth twisted into a cynical smile. Had he ever felt like that about Alexa? He tried to think back, but his memories were tainted with bitterness and a sudden sobering dose of insight—that all of them were subject to the capricious whims of their hormones.

Love was just a word used by society to regularise a much more basic instinct—nature's imperative to continue the human race. What Xavier and Laura were experiencing right now was just a heightened state of sexual awareness—coupled with a compatibility which might or might not last. It probably wouldn't—if you took the time to study all the statistics. And marriages of mixed race fared even less well. His mouth hardened into an implacable line as he stared across the table at his deceitful wife. Just look what had happened to him and Alexa.

Did she feel his eyes on her? Was why she looked up and their gazes locked? Yet for a moment he felt a victim of the tricks that time sometimes played, losing himself in the softness of her green gaze, seeing a fleeting sadness there which briefly weighed heavy on his heart.

He saw her bite her lip as she turned her face away, the movement making her lush breasts move beneath the fine fabric of her tunic, and he had to swallow down his frustration as he felt the springing of his erection. How dared she affect that sad, almost mistreated air? She who had taken it upon herself to deny him his son!

Dampening down his anger, he turned instead to

speak to Malik—who seemed to be having some kind of uncomfortable exchange with the sassy blonde they called Sorrel. She was Malik's ward, and acted as if she was part of the family.

'The Sheikh will not be joining us for dinner?' Giovanni asked softly.

Malik shook his head. 'Unfortunately, no. These days, His Imperial Highness retires early—but he wishes to meet with you and Paolo tomorrow, before the wedding takes place.' Malik paused. 'And your wife, of course.'

Giovanni pondered this for a moment, hearing the unspoken question in the other man's words. He had not actually confirmed to Malik or anybody else that he and Alexa had long been estranged, though he suspected that it was common knowledge. He wasn't naïve enough to think that they would have admitted him to the close confines of the royal circle without having him thoroughly investigated—indeed, they probably knew everything about him, right down to his shoe-size. 'I see.'

'You are a man of few words,' Malik noted, raising his dark brows in query.

Giovanni smiled. He approved of a world where protocol forbade the asking of direct questions; a world where feelings could be acceptably buried and forgotten. 'I believe in keeping my own counsel,' he said softly.

Malik nodded. 'A wise strategy, for that is the Kharastani way—particularly for its royal men,' he observed sagely. 'I trust that you find your rooms adequate?' he added.

Giovanni smiled as their eyes met. How perfect! A

polite question about accommodation which disguised the real question underneath. 'More than adequate,' he murmured, and the eyes of the two men met in a moment of unspoken understanding.

Alexa heard the exchange between the two men, and her head jerked up in indignation as Giovanni spoke.

More than adequate? What would the select assembled group say if she suddenly blurted out that, no, they were *not* adequate—that in fact they were quite the opposite? That she had been put in a room and was expected to share it and a bed with her estranged husband, and she wasn't sure how she would be able to resist him?

But she knew how to behave at a royal banquet—or rather, how *not* to behave—and her generous hosts would learn nothing of her inner disquiet. Instead, she smiled at Laura. 'Are you nervous about the wedding?'

Laura shot a look at Xavier—but he was busy recounting a story to Giovanni about one of the Sheikh's famous racehorses, and not paying the two of them any attention. She bit her lip with an excitement which was almost palpable.

'I *should* be nervous,' she confided to Alexa. 'What with just about every royal family in the world being represented—not to mention all the politicians and filmstars, and the fact that I'm going to be photographed from just about every angle, and I'm terrified I've got a spot brewing—but the thing is…' Her voice tailed off and her eyes grew misty and dreamy. 'I love Xavier so much that none of it seems to matter—we could be standing barefoot on a deserted beach, for all I care!'

'*Fantastique!*' interjected Xavier silkily, who had clearly heard the last part of the sentence. He shot Alexa a mischievous look. 'They are calling it the wedding of the decade, and yet now I realise that we could have eloped to the Maldives for all Laura cares!'

'Because it's *you* I'm marrying!' pouted Laura. 'And you're the only important person.'

'Am I, now, *cherie*?' he questioned softly.

Their love was incandescent, and Alexa was glad of their glowing happiness, but it was hard not to feel a twinge of envy. She remembered her own engagement. That had been equally ecstatic. But she could see now that all their idealistic expectations had made it seem unreal—as different from Xavier and Laura's easy familiarity as chalk was to cheese.

Giovanni had behaved with almost exaggerated regard for her, and Alexa had let him, not having the self-confidence to do anything other than accede to his wishes. She had been so in love—and so disbelieving of the fact that he seemed to feel the same way—that she honestly thought she would have dyed her hair green and walked on burning coals if he'd asked her to. *Or let him believe you were a virgin by implication?* an inner voice questioned painfully. Alexa winced. How could anything so unequal ever have lasted the course?

But she did her best to put such futile introspection out of her mind, and to concentrate on an experience she was unlikely to repeat once the wedding celebrations were over. Dinner in a palace!

Course after course was placed before them. Meats and fruits and figs and pastries—and a huge fish which had been cooked with raisins, carried in by two people on an enormous golden platter.

Alexa thought that Paolo had behaved extremely well during the protracted feast—every adult around the table had been paying him lots of attention and he had revelled in it—but when he demanded a grape and added, somewhat imperiously, "And you must peel it for me, Mamma!" she knew it was time for a reality check.

'I think you've had enough to eat, darling,' she said gently. 'And I think it's time I took you to bed—it's been a long day.'

'I don't wanna go to bed!'

Alexa winced, guessing that this rare tantrum had been long overdue in light of the dizzying array of events which had taken place—but that didn't stop her cheeks from burning with embarrassment as she scrambled to her feet, wondering if Giovanni would try to cite this untoward scene as an example of her poor mothering skills.

Yet when Giovanni looked up there was no expression of recrimination on his face, though his black eyes remained enigmatic. 'You want me to come and help?'

Such a simple question—yet it had the power to tug unbearably at her heartstrings. Because it was just the kind of thing a normal husband might have asked his wife and Alexa could have wept for what might have been. Theirs wasn't a *normal* relationship, she reminded herself fiercely—it never had been and it never could be. And Giovanni wasn't stupid—on the contrary, he was an operator *par excellence*. His remark had probably only come out as being caring and solicitous because they were in company, and he was aware that the others were watching, listening.

How much *did* the others know about their situation—how much had he told them? Had he painted her as the hard-hearted bitch of some of his more heated accusations? But, if so, then Xavier and the others were showing no sign of disapproval. On the contrary, she had been shown nothing but consideration and courtesy by everyone here this evening, and it made her feel pensive. How she would have loved to be a proper part of a group like this—feeling she belonged somewhere.

Giovanni's black eyes were still trained on her in glittering question, but Alexa shook her head.

'No, honestly—I'm fine on my own, thanks. Goodnight, everyone.'

'You look tired,' said Laura, frowning.

'I am. Completely bushed,' admitted Alexa.

Maybe Giovanni would take the hint, she thought—more with hope than conviction. Maybe he would sit up late, talking and drinking with Xavier and Malik—and by the time he came to bed he would find her sound asleep and leave her alone.

Maybe.

A servant was there to guide her through the cool marbled corridors back to their suite, and in an effort to quell the relentless chatter in her head Alexa forced herself to concentrate on the small things while she got Paolo ready for bed. The wash of moonlight on the floor. The heavy scent of roses in a gleaming vase. The trace of jasmine as it floated in through the open shutters on a gentle breeze. What a beautiful place this was, she thought wistfully as she squeezed a blob of toothpaste onto Paolo's brush.

She lit a couple of low lamps, and Paolo was so exhausted that he was almost asleep by the time she pulled the cotton sheet over him. None of her fears about him being freaked out by such strange, new surroundings were fulfilled.

Hadn't there been a part of her which had hoped he might be a little fractious and unsettled, causing her to have to stay with him in a kind of motherly vigil?

Lovingly, she stared down at the dark lashes which formed two soft arcs, brushing against his olive skin. Oh, Paolo, she thought.

'Night, Mamma,' he murmured sleepily.

'Night-night, darling—sleep tight.' But his breathing had already settled into a soft, deep rhythm.

So now what did she do?

There really wasn't a lot of choice open to her. She did not want to sleep with her husband, that was for sure. Far too dangerous—on so many different levels. But she was equally certain that Giovanni wouldn't dream of camping out on one of those low divans in the sitting room—which meant that she would have to. He could have the huge bed to himself and get on with it!

Quickly she undressed, and took out a long night-gown which Teri had insisted on giving her for the trip, along with two matching bra and knickers sets.

'Nightwear and lingerie can *never* be done on the cheap,' her boss had said, and when Alexa had shaken her head in protest, she had added firmly. 'Take them, Lex—and look on it as a bonus for being such a good worker.'

Wasn't there a part of every woman which adored luxury? Alexa hadn't needed asking twice. With its soft layers of oyster silk-satin and lace, the gown felt like heaven—but at least it swept the ground in a relatively demure way. So if she needed to get up in the middle of the night, then at least Giovanni wouldn't be able to accuse her of provocation.

Brushing her long hair so that it spilled in a golden waterfall all the way down her back, she took a pillow and a heavy satin coverlet from the four-poster bed and made herself a makeshift bed on a divan, then climbed into it and prayed for the solace of sleep.

Outside, she could hear the sound of some unknown bird calling in the palace gardens—was that the Kharastani equivalent of an owl? she wondered sleepily. Moonlight crept in through the slatted shutters, reliev-ing the darkness with muted silver stripes of light. The divan wasn't soft, and the one pillow was woefully in-adequate—but maybe the emotional maelstrom of the last few days had been enough to completely exhaust her because, almost with a sense of disbelief, Alexa quickly felt herself sinking into the dark embrace of slumber.

But if she slept then she had no recollection of it—

because it seemed almost as soon as her eyelids had drifted wearily down she was startled by a soft sound in the room, and her eyes fluttered drowsily open.

Which of her senses was engaged first?

Was it his presence she felt, or did she hear the sound of his breathing?

Or was it the gradual readjustment of her eyes to the flickering light which began to register on her consciousness? Giovanni was standing by the divan, a beautifully intricate silver lamp in his hand.

For a moment she thought she must be dreaming as her eyes made the visual connection before her brain had time to decipher all the implications of his presence. His torso was bare, and around his waist was knotted a long piece of material which gleamed golden and scarlet in the lamplight. He had told his son that he looked like a warrior king, but in that moment he looked like a king himself.

Almost in slow motion, she watched him put the lamp down and then unknot the heavy gold brocade at his hip, so that it fell to his feet with a heavy sigh.

And suddenly he was naked.

He stood there, dark and haughty, comfortable and unashamed by his nakedness—and who could blame him? The glimmering light emphasised the long, tawny limbs, the broad, hard chest and flat belly. He really was the most perfect example of the male of the species, she thought, with an aching sense of longing.

Unwillingly, but irresistibly, her eyes travelled slowly down his body- to the very fork of his masculinity. Amid the coiled dark forest of hair was the paler hint of his manhood, and Alexa found her lips drying, knowing that she should feel appalled at the sudden longing which caught her by the throat and by the heart. *Was* she dreaming?

'Giovanni.' She swallowed.

Carefully, he sat on the edge of the divan—close enough for the animal warmth of his body to radiate its heat, but not close enough to threaten her. In the soft lamplight, she lay back, her eyes wide and dark and her face a pale blur. But it was her hair which captivated him—all red-gold satin which spilled out over the pillows around her. That and the dark petals of her lips which had parted in unconscious invitation.

'You were sleeping,' he said, but there was a sudden and unexpected lump in his throat.

What was it? The softness of his voice which lulled her, or the building ache of hunger which threatened to silence her every objection?

'I feel like I still am,' she said, and part of her wanted him to destroy this spell that the darkness had woven around them. To make her safe to reject him. To *want* to reject him.

'Why are you in here, Lex?' he murmured. 'All alone on this hard and unforgiving divan?'

'You know…you know why,' she said, hating her hesitancy—the stammering uncertainty of her response—and the hunger to have him touch her even though every fibre of her being told her unequivocally that it would be wrong.

'No, I don't.'

'Giovanni…'

'What is it?'

'I—'

'*Bella*,' he murmured. '*Bella mia.*'

His words were cajoling, coaxing—seeming to beg all kinds of confidences. But she dared not begin to speak, for fear that she would blurt out just how beautiful he was. And how much she had missed seeing his hard dark and golden body naked like this. How the absence of the intimacy of marriage could leave you bereft—even if that marriage had not been one which was made in heaven.

He wondered if she was aware that her nipples had begun to peak through the fine material of her nightgown. That the soft silk clung to her thighs, skated over the flat plane of her belly and skimmed over the narrow curve of her hips. Had ever a woman both tantalised and disappointed him as much as Alexa?

Dio, but he wanted her!

Reaching out, he placed the tip of his thumb beneath her chin, rubbing it in a slow, enticing movement, tempering his hunger with careful, unthreatening seduction. 'You're tense,' he murmured, as the thumb slid along the curve of her jaw. 'Relax.'

Relax? When just the touch of him was beginning to scramble her senses? How long had it been since a naked man had stroked her skin in the middle of the night like this? All her reasons for being kept awake in recent years had been of a far more practical nature.

She remembered the sleepless nights of Paolo's

childhood fevers. The mopping of his hot brow and the sharp tear of panic and fright—until the crisis had passed and the pale light of morning had crept in.

She remembered too the time when there had been no permanent job—before Teri had opened the shop in the village—and the worry about how she was going to support the two of them without the indignity of having to ask the State for support.

Her mother was living so far away that she might as well be residing on a distant planet—and she had made it very clear that she thought Alexa was a fool to have ended up as a single mother with no alimony. There had been no one to ask and no one to share her growing dread, and during that time Alexa had learnt the harsh definition of how it felt to be completely on her own.

Did the barren quality of her life since Giovanni explain why she was lying there now, as compliant as a cat being stroked by its master?

Alexa tipped her head back, and her protest seemed to be torn reluctantly from between dry lips. 'Leave it, Gio. Please.'

But she might as well not have spoken, for he did not heed her words, nor loosen his hold on her, just continued to stroke reflectively at her flesh as if he had all the time in the world.

And how was it that even a touch as innocuous as that could weave such a powerfully sensual spell, sending whispering little messages of need and desire skittering over her skin? Alexa could feel the sudden acceleration of her heart, the heated flush to her face as he arrogantly moved his hand down to cup her engorged breast, and she looked at him, startled, even while the nipple sprang harder still into pert life beneath his questing fingers.

'You want me,' he whispered. 'You want me, *cara mia*. You always did and you always will.'

It was an outrageous sexual boast, and Alexa wanted to deny him—to deny to herself the fundamental truth contained within it—but the expert caress of his fingers was making her melt beneath him.

'Gio…'

Her eyelids fluttered to a close, and Giovanni allowed himself a small smile of triumph as he bent his dark head and began to kiss her, his mouth grazing hers, feeling her lips part and the warmth of her breath as it mingled with his.

'Don't you?' he persisted, his voice muffled against the sweet taste of her skin.

The pressure of his lips stopped her from replying—or was she simply fooling herself? Because from where could she summon up the strength to tell him to stop what he was doing when it felt as if she had been fast-tracked into paradise? And now he was moving his hand down, so that it lay on the flat of her belly, circling there reflectively. For a moment Alexa froze, waiting for some kind of recrimination—as if he would suddenly start berating her for what that belly had carried within it without his knowledge.

But he made no such accusation. Instead, he drifted his fingers downwards, over the slippery silk, and then further still—heading inexorably but with agonising slowness towards the centre of longing at the fork of her thighs.

'Don't you?' he said again, drawing his mouth away from her by a fraction as he felt her body stiffen in anticipation.

Alexa swallowed. In the dim half-light she could see the feverish glitter of his eyes, and she lifted her hand to touch the hard contours of his face with its fierce look of intent. She could say no, that she didn't want him—but wouldn't that be one more lie to add to the pile? And in a way wasn't this inevitable? Hadn't it been inevitable since he'd walked into the shop and back into her life last week? 'Yes,' she admitted brokenly. 'Yes, I want you.'

Giovanni knew then that he had her—and that he could make her beg for him if he so desired. Yet if this was victory, it seemed a hollow one—and for once in his life he wasn't sure why.

His mouth hardened, for confusion was an emotion he could do without. 'Come. We must not wake our son,' he said, and he bent to lift her into his arms, holding her up against his bare chest.

Was Alexa imagining the sudden disapproval colouring his voice? She must have been—because why else would he be stroking his fingers teasingly over the silk-covered globe of her bottom as he carried her through to the master bedroom? Yet, although his hands were gentle, his face was implacable as he carried her into the bedroom and laid her down on the bed.

For a moment he just stood, towering over her, staring at her with an expression she had never seen on his face before. Then with a cruel smile he reached down, catching hold of the delicate fabric with both hands and tearing it apart with a single wrench to lay bare her pale and beautiful body.

Alexa gasped as she heard it rip, and felt warm, scented air rushing onto her bare skin.

'What did you do that for?'

He did not know. To destroy something which was hers? Or to remind himself that ultimately everything was disposable? Silk-satin was no different from the vows made during a marriage ceremony—they could both be torn to shreds. 'Let's just say I couldn't wait,' he said, in a dangerous voice.

Alexa knew she should have protested—told him that he had just destroyed an expensive gift which might not mean much to him, but sure as hell meant a lot to her. But it was too late for that. Too late to do anything other than gasp again—only this time with pleasure. For he had begun to kiss her again, and his warm naked form was lowering itself on top of her—it seemed that he had spoken the truth and that he couldn't wait. Or didn't want to. Because he was big, and hard, and—oh, heavens—now he was stroking on a condom.

'Gio!' she gasped.

Hard, honed flesh was melding with the soft, giving nature of hers. His hand was between her legs—fingers luxuriating in her honeyed wetness—and she could feel the tip of him nudging against her as he said something in Italian that in her befuddled state she could not understand.

What was it that made her wrap her legs around his

back and push her hips up invitingly towards him—as if all the harsh words and bitterness between them had not happened? Was it simply a sexual hunger which had gone too long unfed? Or was it because deep down, in spite of everything, it was Giovanni who had dominated her waking thoughts and night-time dreams for so long, even though she had done everything in her power to try to forget him?

The man she had loved.

And loved still?

'No!' she whimpered in denial.

He stilled. 'No?' he drawled, in disbelief.

'Yes,' she whispered, and brushed her lips to his shoulder, her fingers tangling in the dark silky waves of his hair. 'I meant…yes.'

Perversely, her slurred words of incitement made him hold back. To show that *he* held all the power, and not her. To prove to himself that he could make her beg and make her wait while *he* had the self-will to resist the wanton thrust of her hips

But then she touched her lips to his throat, licking at the hollow there, the way she'd used to, and that one small gesture took him right back to a time when he had seen in her all his hopes and dreams of a glorious and golden future. For a split-second Giovanni felt as if she had ripped his chest open and was watching his raw heart pumping there.

Furiously he thrust into her, harder and deeper than he had ever thrust into a woman before, as he forced himself to forget that he had married her, that she had ever been more to him than she was at this moment. Just a perfect and willing body sharing his bed. She is *nothing* to you, he told himself fiercely, and shut his eyes to blot her out.

'Giovanni—'

'What?' he growled.

Alexa's fingers bit into his broad shoulders as he moved inside her, seeming to stab at her heart itself as he took her further and further towards the peak of glorious fulfilment. Yet somehow it seemed like an *empty* pleasure. Even as she felt the encroaching rush of desire lapping at the edges of consciousness she realised that he was no longer kissing her.

Above her, his face was a mask—his closed eyes were not seeing *her*—and even though his body moved with such sweet and piercing accuracy inside hers the whole act somehow felt *mechanical*.

He wasn't making love to her—he was having sex with her. Physically satisfying, but cold and functional sex.

She felt a silent anguished protest scream from deep within her, yet it was too late to back out now. Too late to halt the great building whoosh of pleasure. Her own body seemed like a traitor as it came to shivering completion in his arms.

Yet try as he might—in the dark, flowering moment of his own release -Giovanni could not shake off the thought that this *did* feel different. That he had once desired her in a way which had taken his breath away—and, even if you discounted that, his child had been nurtured within her womb in the interim. A part of *him* had grown inside *her*.

Unexpectedly, emotion ripped through him as a ragged cry was torn from his lips. He felt as if the universe was imploding behind his eyes. As if he might die at the very height of it—and that such a death would be matchless and perfect.

He had planned to distance himself afterwards, to roll away from her and to sleep on the other side of the vast bed until his desire returned once more and he could reach for her with nothing other than passion on his mind. But somehow it didn't happen. He couldn't move from where he lay, still locked inside her, with his dark head cradled on her breast as he felt the last of the blissful spasms dying away.

'Gio?' questioned Alexa, wondering just where the hell they were going after this. But her one-word question fell on ears that did not hear, and she blinked her eyes with something like surprise.

For Giovanni was already asleep.

CHAPTER NINE

ALEXA spent a fitful and apprehensive night while Giovanni slept beside her—the sheets rumpled beneath one hard, dark thigh while his hand rested carelessly at the dip in her waist.

She lay still as their naked bodies brushed together and her ripped nightgown lay in tatters on the floor, and wondered how she could have behaved in a way which was so horribly *predictable*.

It wasn't even as if she had been coerced into it. He hadn't brutally crushed her into his arms the way he'd done that time at her little house, when he'd gone all out to demonstrate his whole repertoire of sensual skills, had he? In fact, he had simply appeared by her bed and let his wrap flutter to the ground—like some cheesy stripper. And she had let him stroke her face and touch her breasts and then practically gone down on her hands and knees and begged him to make love to her.

Make love?

If it wouldn't have risked waking him then she would have let out an ironic laugh. She had placed herself in enough emotional danger without adding to it—and if she started imagining that what had happened between them last night had been *making love* then she would be in real jeopardy.

Resisting the urge to wriggle her body restlessly, for fear that it would disturb the virile form of the sleeping man beside her, Alexa stared at the patterns on the ceiling—at the shimmering movement of moonlight reflected through the crystal drops of the chandelier—as night-time drifted slowly into day.

What had she done?

She had compromised herself utterly and completely, that was what she had done. Had had loveless sex with a man who had made no secret of despising her—or of his macho view of the world and a woman's place in it. Wouldn't he despise her even more now? The easy virtue he had always accused her of—and which she had always hotly denied—would now seem to have been explicitly confirmed by her actions.

She wasn't stupid. She knew what he wanted—something which all his wealth and power could not buy him. His son. And if he went ahead with a legal battle to gain custody then what chance would she have? What kind of picture would he have his clever over-paid lawyers paint of her? A wanton? A slut? A *puttana*, as they said in Italy.

In the end, she went to sleep at the worst possible time—dozing off just before daybreak and thus having to abandon her plan to slip quietly from the bed and get showered and dressed in time to wake Paolo, and not risk him having to see…

'*Papà*! What are you doing here, Papà?'

Paolo's delighted little voice broke into the cloud of her disturbed dreams and Alexa opened her eyes in time to see her son's pyjama-clad figure hurtling towards the bed—where an indolently Giovanni lay like a watchful black panther against the bank of pillows.

'What does it look like?' Giovanni questioned indulgently as the child hurled himself at him, like a tiny steam train. He smiled as he held his arms out and cuddled the child to him, then yawned. 'Waking up.'

Paolo stared at him. 'Will you always sleep with Mamma now?'

Black eyes glittered from over the top of Paolo's head in Alexa's direction, but they were watchful, wary. Last night had shaken him. Had left him feeling a way he had not expected to feel. Light-headed, and not quite real. His voice hardened as he closed his mind to it. 'You will have to ask her that yourself.'

The look she returned to him simmered with an unspoken fury. She was hating her son having to witness her looking like this—with her bedhead hair. Paolo was used to seeing her in an oversized T-shirt, and her nakedness beneath the bedclothes made her feel vulnerable and defenceless—as well as diminishing her opportunities for flouncing out with her dignity intact.

She clutched the sheet to her chin with one hand and ruffled Paolo's dark curls with the other. 'Um, darling, would you mind passing Mamma the dressing gown I left lying over there on the chair?'

'Allow me,' interposed a silken voice.

And, to Alexa's horror, she saw Giovanni gracefully uncurl the child from his arms and get out of bed—completely naked himself—and saunter over to the satin kimono as if it was perfectly acceptable for him to pad around the place with nothing on.

Her eyes flashed a message at him. *Put some damned clothes on.*

He met the look and smiled, his eyes dilating by a fraction as he picked up the green gown and carried it over to her, subtly kicking her ripped nightgown out of sight, which made Alexa's cheeks flare with mortification. He had torn that expensive nightie from her body—and she had just *let* him!

'Paolo, why don't you go and brush your teeth and Mamma will come and find you in a minute?' Alexa suggested furiously, though she was trembling so much she was amazed that the sentence sounded coherent.

'Okay!'

She waited until he had run out of the room before she rounded on Giovanni. It was as much as she could do not to beat her fists on his chest—but she wasn't naïve enough to risk something as provocative as *that*. 'How dare you?' she breathed. 'How dare you?'

'What, in particular, are you objecting to?' he drawled.

'Parading around with *no clothes on*!' she choked.

'What's the matter—has he never seen a naked man before?'

'Of course he hasn't!'

'Ah!' He bit back a smile of unmistakable satisfaction. 'He hasn't?'

She had walked straight into a trick question, and Alexa glared at him. She knew it was perverse—but some misunderstood demon inside her wanted to tell him that, yes, Paolo had seen a thousand naked men pass through her bedroom. That she entertained lovers with all the unembarrassed ease of an ancient courtesan!

'Of course he hasn't!' she said again crossly. 'Not that you're likely to believe that, of course—you just believe what happens to suit you at the time, don't you, Giovanni? So therefore a woman who's not a virgin *must* be a slut—because there's never any room for grey in your world, is there? Only black and white! Always bending reality to suit your vision of it!'

He thought how magnificent she looked. How, if it weren't for a list of royal engagements and their young son waiting for them nearby, she would be writhing beneath him by now. Cursing the fact that he had slept right through the night without taking advantage of the opportunity for more sex with her, he spread the palms of his hands out in a gesture of admission. 'You may have a point,' he said softly.

Alexa stilled, not sure if she'd heard him properly. 'Let me get this straight. I no longer top your list of sexual predators? You're *agreeing* with me?' she questioned suspiciously.

Giovanni was astute enough to recognise that more accusation would work against him. Last night had been a one-off—an undeniably powerful coupling, driven by hurt and anger and bitter memories of the past as well as by sexual hunger. But in a way the act had been ca-

thartic—washing everything away—and if he wanted a
repeat performance, then he was going to have to
employ a completely different strategy towards her.

'I am saying that you have a point,' he conceded, as
careful with his words as any lawyer.

Once, the acknowledgement might have filled her with
a sense of victory—but it was far too late for that. It didn't
matter that he might have misjudged her and been harsh
on her—all that was irrelevant now, and only their son
counted. 'But all of that is completely beside the point.
What about Paolo walking in like that, to see—?'

'Two grown adults doing what comes completely
naturally?'

'Don't wilfully misunderstand me, Giovanni!' Alexa
clenched her fists. 'I can understand that you weren't
going to be satisfied until you got what you wanted—'

'Whereas you didn't want it at all, I suppose?' he
enquired sardonically. 'I really had to fight to get you
to submit to my wicked way, didn't I?'

She ignored the interruption and its wounding
accuracy. 'But you could have had the decency to creep
away before it got light and sleep on one of the divans. At
least that way Paolo wouldn't have had to witness—'

'To witness what? A husband and wife waking up in
bed together?' he queried silkily. 'You think that is such
a terrible crime, *cara*?'

'Yes, I do—in our case!' She darted a look towards
the bathroom door, but thankfully there was still no sign
of Paolo. Alexa pulled on the dark silk kimono and
knotted it tightly at her waist, raking her hand through

her tumble of hair and thinking what a sight she must look. 'We aren't even supposed to be married any more—just in case you'd forgotten!'

'I am having trouble remembering anything right now—especially with the golden silk of your hair tumbling down over your breasts like that,' he said huskily.

She would have had to be made of ice not to respond to the sensual compliment, and she had already proved beyond reasonable doubt that being glacial was not in her nature—not around Giovanni. Alexa drew in a deep breath. 'Can you *please* put some clothes on?'

He shot her a mocking look. 'That's the first time I've ever been asked *that* particular question.'

He walked into the bathroom and returned wearing a white towel knotted around his narrow hips, but even that could not disguise the unmistakable outline of his rapidly growing desire. He saw her eyes drawn to it convulsively, and then dart away again before they fixed themselves on his face. 'Frustrating, isn't it, *bella*?' he murmured.

'What the hell are we going to do?'

'About the frustration, or about the day's plans?'

'Gio!'

He touched his fingers to the rough rasp of new growth at his jaw, thinking that he needed a shave and feeling—uncharacteristically—that he was out of his depth. He was a man who considered that he knew all the rules of sexual behaviour—yet this was entirely new territory for him.

For a start, he didn't usually bed women who had children—not unless they were older and safely out of the way. In fact, he didn't involve himself with anything which threatened to cramp his style—and that included jealous husbands or mothers-on-the-make who wanted an assurance that he would marry their daughters if he happened to conduct an affair with them.

In all these matters he was obdurate and determined—never allowing himself to be swayed, no matter what the provocation. And if that was considered selfish, then so be it—at least Giovanni was honest; he never promised something he couldn't deliver. Pleasure without strings. If the woman didn't like it, then *duro*—tough—there was always another, just as beautiful, waiting to be given whatever Giovanni da Verrazzano was prepared to offer.

But with Alexa...the child in question was *their* child—and that put an entirely different perspective on the situation. He found he didn't *want* to demand coldly that she hire in a babysitter. He *wanted* to share breakfast with their son. Yet wouldn't admitting that show him as vulnerable—expose a side of himself which she might use against him in any future battle for their son?

His hard, dark face gave away nothing of his conflicting thoughts. 'We are presenting our son to the Sheikh, and then going to the wedding of Xavier and Laura, as planned.' He gave her an icy smile. 'Nothing has changed, *cara*—did you really expect it to?'

Alexa stared at him. 'Nothing?' She had asked him to stop making allusions to sex, but she had not expected all the vigour to suddenly drain from his face, leaving the eyes cold and the mouth cruel. 'Are you saying that last night isn't going to impact on us one way or another?' she questioned slowly.

He raised his dark brows. 'That is up to you,' he said. 'It can impact on us any time you like—you have only to say the word and we'll enjoy an action replay.' Black eyes danced a sensual message. 'Satisfaction guaranteed.'

'You arrogant—'

'But it's the truth,' he murmured sardonically. 'You know it and I know it.'

'*Bastard!*' she hissed.

'Keep your voice down, Lex—I don't want Paolo growing up around bad language.'

Rarely had Alexa felt so frustrated or so angry, but presumably that was his intention. Not trusting herself to reply and give him the satisfaction of knowing that, she turned on her heel and went to persuade Paolo to wear the outfit she'd brought for him.

He submitted fairly peacefully to her ministrations, and afterwards, while he was being served with fresh fruit and pastries on a terrace already warm from the sun—though it was not yet high in the sky—Alexa pulled out her own wedding outfit. She tried to be enthusiastic about the accessories which Teri had recommended to match the full-length sheath dress coloured an unusual shade of cobalt green.

Large dangly green earrings and a clutch of bangles clattering at her wrist brought the whole outfit together, and when she looked in the mirror it was with the satisfaction of knowing she looked her best. That the reflection which stared back at her was of a young and

attractive woman in her prime—not a hard-up shop girl
for whom every penny counted.

But above the unusual garb Alexa's face was drained,
and she sighed. What on earth was she going to say to
Giovanni's father, the Sheikh?

'Lex?' came a voice from behind her.

She turned round to see Giovanni, looking as if he
was born to live in a palace—his dark skin and black
eyes standing out in stark relief against the pale, fluid
robes he wore.

'What's up?' he asked.

Like he *cared*! 'Oh, you know.' Affecting nonchalance,
she shrugged. 'Someone should write an etiquette book
along the lines of: *How To Cope When the Father of Your
Child Announces He's Royal*!' And, of course, the follow-
up volume: *Meeting His Father For the First Time*!

The merest glimmer of a smile curved the corners of
a mouth more habitually seen set in a forbidding line.
'You're nervous?'

'What do you think? That I meet sheikhs every day
of the week?'

'I think you look beautiful and that you are a good
mother. That's what I think,' he said unexpectedly.

The compliment took her by surprise, and warmed
her far more than it should have done. Was that because
he hadn't paid her one for such a long time? She blushed,
and then hated herself for blushing. *Just because he's
stopped being nasty to you for a split second, it doesn't
mean you should read anything into it.*

She stared instead at his white robes and headdress,

the purity of the garments broken only by the splash of
colour on his headdress and sash. 'I thought only the
bride was supposed to wear white.'

'Not in Kharastan. Apparently she's in red and
gold—lavish embroidery and lots of jewels. Are you and
Paolo ready to see Zahir now?'

Alexa knew she couldn't put it off for ever.

'Yes,' she answered quietly.

'And have you told Paolo?'

Again, she nodded. 'I have.' Her expression was wry.
'If there's one thing I've learnt from all this, it's that total
honesty is best where children are concerned.'

'Only children?' he mocked softly. 'You mean that
lies are acceptable when you're dealing with adults?'

She looked at him, wondering how the face she had
touched with such rapture under the concealing darkness
of the night should now seem so distant and remote. 'I'll
never lie to you again, Giovanni,' she vowed.

He turned away. Words were so easy. They could be
plucked from out of nowhere at will. And he had no
need of her reassurances. 'Let us go and find our son,'
he said harshly, hardening his heart against the faint look
of disappointment on her face.

The three of them went off to the Sheikh's private
quarters. The rooms were large and cool, and there were
treasures here more stunning than anything else she'd
seen in the palace, but in a way Alexa was oblivious to
everything other than the significance of the occasion.

The Sheikh was very old, and was seated on a beautiful cushion-scattered seat by a window overlooking a

rose garden. He beckoned to them to approach. Paolo's hand slipped quietly into hers, and when they grew closer Alexa surprised herself by dropping a deep curtsey she hadn't been aware she knew how to do.

'Please.' The Sheikh smiled and patted the space on the divan beside him as he looked at the boy. 'Do you want to sit down beside me?' he asked Paolo.

To Alexa's astonishment, Paolo went immediately, hopping up easily and swinging his little legs as if he was sitting on the wall outside school! Was that because he had been starved of extended family from the word go? Only a grandmother in Canada whom he saw maybe once every couple of years, if he was lucky?

For a moment she felt stricken with a heavy kind of guilt and turned her head to see Giovanni's gaze, expecting to find accusation firing from his black eyes. But, no. Instead, she was startled by a brief glimmer of admiration in their ebony depths—or was she imagining it? But no, he had told her that he thought her a good mother, and there was no reason for him to tell lies about that—especially not when he had been so brutally honest about everything else.

The Sheikh began to talk softly to Paolo, telling him about what it had been like growing up in Kharastan, and Alexa thought that the tale was as much for his son as his grandson. He talked about the desert, where flowers bloomed only once in a century and where camels walked for unimaginable amounts of time, and he described the ancient art of keeping falcons—the wild, savage beauty of these birds of prey. With an expression of unmistakable pride, he described the fine racehorses he kept in his stables. 'Do you ride, Paolo?'

'No, sir.'

'Would you like to?'

'Oh, yes, please, sir!'

Afterwards, they all took sweet mint tea and the ordeal was nothing remotely as terrifying as Alexa had feared. But when they were about to leave, the Sheikh summoned for her to remain behind.

She looked beseechingly at Giovanni, but his black eyes glittered unperturbed as he placed his hand on Paolo's shoulder.

'Want to go and see all the acrobats practising?'

'*Acrobats?*' squeaked Paolo.

The Sheikh gave a smile. 'Indeed, there are acrobats,' he said gravely. 'And magicians, musicians and dancers—for in Kharastan a royal wedding is rare, and something to be truly celebrated!'

After they'd gone, there was silence for a moment. Alexa wasn't experienced in handling royals, but she knew that you were never supposed to initiate conversation—especially so in a country where it seemed that women were submissive. Remembering something else she had read, she dropped her gaze so that her eyes were downcast.

'You have a fine boy,' said the Sheikh at last.

His words made her look up and, inspired by surprise as much as relief, Alexa's face broke into a wreath of a smile. 'Why, thank you.'

The Sheikh nodded, and there was a pause. 'But he has had a hard life, I understand?'

Alexa stilled. 'Hard? I'm not sure that I understand, your Imperial Highness.'

'Giovanni tells me that you live in a small cottage and that you work in a shop.'

Oh, did he? Never considered particularly tall, Alexa now instinctively drew herself up to her full height, and sucked in a breath of angry air through her nostrils. 'We may not have much in the material sense,' she said, with quiet dignity, 'but Paolo has never gone short on the things that matter. He's always had sustenance, play and comfort—but more importantly than anything he's always had love. An abundance of love. So I don't think his life has been at all hard, Your Highness—I must disagree with your son.'

The Sheikh's eyes narrowed with a glint of humour. 'From what I understand, there are many disagree-ments between the two of you—but your relationship with Giovanni is not my concern. My grandson, however, is. The sentiment that money cannot not buy love has always been true—but money *can* buy you comfort,' he said.

'It can buy *material* comfort,' Alexa emphasised. 'Emotional comfort is far more elusive.'

'Only women place importance on such things,' he said dismissively.

But Alexa was not one of his servants—there to be banished because her views didn't happen to coincide with his. Yes, he was all-powerful within his kingdom—but surely it was morally wrong to agree with him just because of that?

'Women are usually the ones left caring for the family,' she argued. 'And we recognise the importance of emotion.'

He stared at her. 'You are stubborn,' he said suddenly.

'No. I'm passionate about the things I believe in, Your Majesty.'

'We sometimes have to live without the things we believe in,' he said softly, and then shut his eyes and leaned back, suddenly weary. 'Thank you for talking to me. Now, go and enjoy the wedding.'

Was he sending her a silent message? Telling her that she was *wasting her time* if she was hoping for a show of emotion from Giovanni? Well, you needn't worry, Your Imperial Highness, she thought—I'm under no illusions where Giovanni is concerned.

A servant took her to where Paolo was standing, down in the courtyard, being given a private performance by a set of jugglers. Giovanni was standing a short distance away, beside an orange tree which bore both fruit and flower.

He looked up with a questioning stare as she approached. 'Your meeting with the Sheikh went well?'

'Surprisingly well, considering.'

'Considering what?' His voice was cool.

Alexa narrowed her eyes. 'Did you describe Paolo's life as hard?'

There was a pause. 'Of course.'

Count to ten. Keep calm. Don't lose it. But it wasn't easy when she wanted to scream her outrage to the rooftops. 'How could you say that? It's not *hard*,' she defended breathlessly. 'Your son is loved and wanted. Even the Sheikh acknowledged that much.'

'My son does not have a father,' he said coldly. 'Nor all the advantages that my wealth could bring him—'

'But—'

'Hear me out, Alexa!' His words cut through her objections like a knife through a ripe peach. 'I had not intended to bring this up until after the wedding, but since you seem determined to have the discussion I have no choice.'

'Choice? What are you talking about?'

'Considering all the odds which have been stacked against Paolo—'

'What *odds*?' she questioned, in a dangerous voice.

'The fact that you are a single working mother and that you cannot afford to buy your own home.' He saw her look of objection and shook his dark head. 'These are not things that I am simply *making up*, *cara*,' he intoned fiercely. 'They are known obstacles to a child's proper development. You know that. I know that.'

She jerked her head in the direction of their son, who seemed to be giggling and having a whale of a time, despite the fact that he didn't speak more than a word or two of Kharastani. 'You think he looks deprived?'

'Not at the moment, no—but he will, Lex.'

'Oh, really?'

'Yes, really! He will become one of those fatherless boys who hang around on street corners and smoke cigarettes,' he said witheringly.

'Oh, ye of little faith! Where did you get your knowledge of the world from, Gio? The international book of stereotypes? And anyway—' She fixed him with a triumphant look '–You grew up without a father yourself!'

His smile told her that she had walked straight into the trap he had carefully set up for her. 'Exactly!' he breathed. 'And I have seen what it's like!'

Alexa frowned, confused now. 'You're saying that you don't like the way *you've* turned out?'

'I am saying that I have turned out the man I am *in spite of* my upbringing—but Paolo may not be so fortunate. I have seen what it is to have a mother who hungers for the company of men.'

'I've had *two* lovers in my life!' she returned furiously. 'And I've told you that until I'm blue in the face—when are you going to get it through your head, and believe that I'm not about to start entertaining the troops in my bedroom?'

'But you are still very young,' he parried. 'Your life is taken up with the mechanics of everyday life with Paolo. Yet there will come a time when he does not need you quite so much—and you will think about fulfilling your own sexual needs. That is when he is likely to go off the rails.'

'You didn't,' she pointed out. 'And you were the child of a single mother!'

'Because I was lucky!' he stormed, feeling a knife twist deep in his heart as he remembered all those nights waiting for his mother to come home. Not being able to settle until he heard the sound of her high heels as they clattered their way across the hall floor. Sometimes he would fall asleep, only waking with a start as he heard the front door being pulled to a close and realised that it was past dawn... 'But it's a lottery we're talking about,' he added. 'And Paolo might not be as lucky as I was.'

'*All* life is a lottery,' she said dryly, wondering if she had imagined that sudden bleakness which had clouded his eyes. She must have done—for now his face had resumed that flinty and obdurate expression. 'Having two parents isn't a surefire recipe for happiness, Gio.'

'No, but I want to maximise his chances,' he said stubbornly.

She shook her head in frustration, the bright sunlight making her squint. She wished that she could just grab her son and run. 'Were you always such a pessimist?'

'Pretty much,' he said softly. 'You base your behaviour on personal experience.'

She looked at him, trying to be objective—but it wasn't easy. His attitude riled her, and his words infuriated her, but that didn't stop her wanting to tangle her fingers in his thick black hair and pull his head down to kiss her. She swallowed. 'Look, you've given me plenty to think about, and I will,' she conceded. 'When I get back to England.'

Giovanni gave a grim kind of smile. She still hadn't realised, had she? That when he wanted something he went all out until he had got it.

'I don't think you understand,' he said silkily. 'The decision has already been taken.'

Alexa blinked, scarcely aware that in the distance could be heard the sound of pipes and drums, and that haunting, reedy instrument again. 'What decision?' she breathed, as the musicians began warming up.

'Things have moved on. I now accept that you are not a woman of loose morals, but you are still a woman, with all a woman's needs—and I am not prepared to tolerate my son being brought up by another man,' he said flatly.

'But this is all hypothetical, Giovanni,' she objected. 'There *isn't* another man.'

'Not at the moment, there isn't.'

Being told you couldn't have something often had the effect of making you want it more, and it provoked in Alexa a sudden defiance. 'You can't make me do anything I don't want to,' she said.

'Oh, but I can, *cara*,' he demurred softly. 'And I want Paolo with me.'

'Paolo lives with *me*,' she pointed out, aware that they were discussing their son as if he was a piece of furniture. Her cheeks began to burn with shame and terror.

'Then it is obvious that you must come and live with me as well,' he said silkily. 'You are a good mother, and I want the chance to be a good father. We proved last night that we've never stopped desiring one another— so where's the stumbling block?'

She wanted to blurt out and ask him what about *love*? Or even—if that was aiming too high—what about the emotional security she had discussed with his father? But his father had been as dismissive about it as Giovanni inevitably would. It would be as useless as chasing after rainbows—their colours always appeared so bright and solid from a distance—but when you got up close they were nothing but air.

Maybe what she and Giovanni had briefly shared all those years ago *had* been love—or the tentative beginnings of love—but it had been smashed by circumstance. Yet her heart still burned for him as much as her body did, and he was the father of her child. They were tied together through both their lifetimes by shared flesh and blood.

What he was offering was a compromise—but how would she have the strength to live a lifetime of compromise with the only man she had ever loved?

Alexa shook her head. 'I'm sorry, Giovanni, but I can't do it.'

There was silence for a moment, and when he spoke his words had all the deadly cutting power of a razor's edge.

'It isn't a proposal I'm making,' he said. 'It's a statement of fact.'

Alexa blinked. 'I don't understand.'

'Then you are being remarkably slow, if I might say so. I am not *asking* you to come and live with me, Lex— I am telling you that you have no alternative if you wish to remain with your son.'

Did he imagine that by coming to a country like Kharastan—where men dominated and women obeyed—he could simply dictate his terms and she would meekly accept them?

'There is *always* an alternative, Giovanni,' she said proudly.

His smile was one of cold, pure power.

'Yes, you are right,' he agreed softly, and for a moment saw her relax. 'You can hire yourself a lawyer to fight me—if you can afford to. But no matter how much money you were to pour into it, it would be to no avail, Lex. You see, if you do not accept my terms then there will be a custody battle—that I do not want but which will go ahead if it comes to it.'

His black eyes glittered with a determination which made her skin turn to ice. 'And I will win.'

CHAPTER TEN

GIOVANNI'S silken threat rather spoiled the rest of the day for Alexa. It wouldn't have mattered what had happened during the marriage celebrations—a rocket could have flown down from the moon in the middle of the ceremony itself, for all the notice Alexa would have taken. She guessed that there were worse places to worry that you were going to lose custody of your only child, but right then she couldn't think of one.

She forced herself to try and concentrate, so that the memory of such a magnificent day wouldn't be just a blur—and so that the royal family wouldn't consider her a churlish and ungrateful guest, or Paolo be ashamed of his Mamma for looking glum. And concentrating on the occasion worked well as a distraction technique.

The service took place in a circular courtyard in one of the most innermost sanctums of the palace, with tiered seating all around—especially constructed, according to Sorrel to accommodate all the visiting dignitaries. Alexa recognised two members of the British royal family, as well as three ex-presidents, and it was the strangest sensation to be sitting close enough to touch people she had previously only seen within the pages of a newspaper or on television.

Because, of course, given the Giovanni connection, they were sitting in the very best seats, listening to vows made in Kharastani, French and English, repeated in all three languages. She sat there with a fixed smile as thousands of fresh rose petals fluttered down from the balcony and there was a burst of applause and triumphant music.

Somehow she managed not to flinch at the blinding wall of flash from the cameras which exploded into life as Laura was officially made a princess. Afterwards, the wedding party walked on brilliant blue carpets, beneath garlands of jasmine and deep-scented lilies, to the feast itself—where every conceivable Kharastani delicacy was being served on priceless gold dishes inlaid with real jewels.

Alexa found herself wondering if any of the guests would be tempted to pocket one of the teaspoons, which looked as if they'd each be worth a small fortune—and the inappropriate thought made her smile properly for almost the first time.

'You're very quiet, *cara*,' observed Giovanni, as they walked towards the table.

'What did you expect?' she demanded in a low voice. 'That I'd be dancing with joy after the threats you made earlier?'

'I believe there *is* dancing later,' he observed evenly. 'So why not?'

'Oh, very clever. Well, count me out!'

Of course heartfelt declarations made to your estranged husband when you were having a row didn't always stand up to gentle pressure from well-meaning members of your brand-new 'family'. Thus, when the Sheikh made it known after the meal that he would like to have a photograph of himself with his two sons, their wives and Paolo, how could Alexa have possibly objected?

Then he called 'my most loyal and trusted aide' Malik' into the shot—though the reason for *that* was a little confusing. And when the entire wedding party had adjourned into the grand ballroom—which was bedecked with flowers—the Sheikh raised his hand to order the dancing to begin.

It was started by the bride and groom, and soon Zahir waved Alexa and Giovanni onto the dance floor—though she held herself as stiffly as a frozen piece of wood in his arms.

'It won't work, you know,' Giovanni said softly.

'What won't? I don't know what you're talking about.'

'Yes, you do. I'm talking about sulking, my *bella* Lex. It won't change my mind, and it will only make things unpleasant for Paolo—and ultimately for you.'

Alexa raised her eyebrows. 'So not only am I being blackmailed into remaining as your wife—I'm also being instructed on how to behave?'

'That all depends.'

'On?'

'How good you're going to be.'

'I don't *feel* like being good!'

'Ah!' He started laughing. 'That's better,' he murmured approvingly. Giovanni's hand moved down to the small of her back and began to massage its knotted tension with expert caress. 'Don't fight it, *cara*.'

He meant *Don't fight me*. And, oh, it was so tempting to obey him. To sink into his embrace and let the hard heat of his body send little sizzles all the way down her nerve endings. Especially when the rhythmic movement of his fingers was easing all the rigidity out of her body, making it feel as squishy as marshmallow.

Alexa closed her eyes and ran her tongue over dry lips with something approaching despair. What was it about Giovanni, and only Giovanni, that he could make her feel this way? She hadn't lived *completely* as a hermit during her time as a single mother. There had been the occasional social function—some of them with dancing, and some of them even with eligible men had who seemed keen to dance with her. But it had never felt like this.

'How long is it since we've danced?' he questioned unsteadily.

'I...don't remember.'

'Don't you? It was the night of our own wedding.'

Of course she remembered—she had just been trying not to. Though she was surprised that *he* did. Her head seemed to want to fall into the hollow of his shoulder, just as it had done back then. She could feel the slow build-up of sexual hunger. Much more of this and she would be incapacitated by it. Alexa wriggled, but the movement brought her body into frighteningly erotic proximity to the ridge of hardness she could feel quite clearly through the fine silk of his robes. Her eyes widened into saucers. 'Giovanni!'

'Can you feel what you do to me?' he questioned idly.

'Stop it!'

'How? There's only one way to get rid of it, and I don't think it's going to happen right now—in the circumstances.'

'You're disgusting!'

'You didn't seem to think so last night!'

'That was different.'

'*How* was it different, Lex?'

'Well, for a start I didn't realise then that you were planning to fight me for custody of Paolo!'

'You thought that after the wedding we'd all go back to our separate lives—as if nothing had happened?'

'No, of course not.'

'What, then?'

The music changed tempo and mercifully picked up speed, so that Alexa could move her body marginally away from the aroused distraction of his. 'I thought we'd do what other couples in similar circumstances do. We'd make access arrangements.'

'*Access* arrangements? You want to fly a young child out to Italy on alternate weekends.'

'Or…well, there's always holidays.' As soon as she saw the darkening fury on his face she knew that she had said the wrong thing.

'A part-time father, you mean?' he snapped. 'Still, I suppose that's an improvement on an absentee father.'

'That's not what I'm suggesting. I'm just not sure how Paolo would feel about being uprooted to Italy.'

As usual, she was tagging her own misgivings onto Paolo, he thought. 'Why don't you ask him? Or don't you dare to hear the answer he may give you?'

'Oh, Gio.' She looked up at him with wide eyes. 'It's not like that at all.'

'Isn't it?' He pulled her back into his arms—only this time she was aware of his strength, rather than his sexuality as he bent his head to look directly into her beautiful face. Did she think for a second that all she had to do was to bat those amazing pale green eyes at him and he would accede to whatever she wanted? 'I don't think you appreciate how *lenient* I'm being with you—considering that I have been kept on the sidelines for all these years,' he hissed. 'Maybe it's about time I laid down a few ground rules.' His black eyes glittered with pure rage. 'You will co-operate with me, and you will do so at once.'

'At *once*?'

'On your return to England, you will make the necessary arrangements.'

'*Arrangements*?' she echoed again, sounding like one of those language tapes where you repeated the words so that you would never forget them.

'For your move to Naples,' he finished, with a gritty kind of smile

Her knees felt suddenly weak as she recognised that he meant every word. He wasn't going to back off now, or have some miraculous change of heart—and even if he did would access ever really work? What if Paolo became enraptured of his macho daddy, seduced by his power and his money? Wouldn't a tiny rented cottage with underwear drying in the bathroom begin to pale as he became old enough to make comparisons—as label-conscious teenagers inevitably did?

Afraid that she might do something unforgivable—like cry at a wedding when the slushy part was over—Alexa pulled away from him. 'I think I've had enough dancing for now. It's late. I'm…I'm going to find Paolo and put him to bed.'

He traced a thoughtful finger around the outline of her lips. 'You can run from me all you like, but it will be to no avail,' he said softly. 'Because soon you will be with me in Naples—exactly where I want you to be, Lex. Just as later you will be in my arms and in my bed.'

Alexa felt her mouth tremble beneath his touch, even though her heart rebelled. Did he think that because he was the son of the Sheikh that he could imperiously impose his desire upon her?

'No, I won't,' she vowed, and went to move away. But he stayed her with a hand to her arm, his hard fingers biting into the soft silk of her skin.

'And while we're at it let's get something else straight—which is that I'm not prepared to play cat-and-mouse with you over sex,' he hissed. 'Especially when we've established just how much you want it. Last night was an exception—but I have neither the time nor the inclination to go through that kind of pantomime night after night.'

'You ripping off my nightie, you mean?' she accused.

Giovanni froze. 'It pleases you to make it sound like an aggressive act, doesn't it, Lex—even when such things are done within the bedroom and only serve to heighten sexual pleasure?' Like it did yours, he thought bitterly—and then wondered if she would be too much of a hypocrite to admit it.

'Well, I don't want you near me tonight,' she said, terrified that her voice would crack, and that tears would start spilling out of the corners of her eyes to show him that beneath it all she was just a vulnerable and pathetic walkover. 'So stay away.'

Giovanni's face hardened in a proud and arrogant look. Did she really believe that he would beg her? Or weaken when she called his bluff? He bent his head close to her face, so that all she could see was the ebony blaze of his eyes. 'If I don't find you in our bed tonight, I shall not come to you. You can attempt to withhold sex as a bargaining tool, but it won't work—for believe me when I tell you that I shall not change my mind about Paolo.'

He walked off the dance floor, with every female eye following him, and Alexa was shaking as she went over to lead the over-excited and exhausted Paolo to bed. After she had tucked him up, she ran herself a bath and lay there in the cooling water, telling herself over and over again that she would *not* be intimidated and that there was no way she was going to be an easy conquest. Not any more.

How much loveless sex could she endure before she blurted out something unforgivable? Like telling him that she wanted the kind of intimacy she had once thought was hers for the taking because he had loved her enough to marry her? Would Giovanni meet her halfway if she dared try? Or was he too hard and unforgiving to ever be able to let go of the past?

Her skin was pink and her fingertips as wrinkled as starfish by the time she emerged from the bathroom in her nightgown.

The salon was empty, and in the bedroom the vast bed lay uninhabited—mocking her with its bareness. Alexa knew that she just *couldn't* go in there and wait for him like a sacrificial lamb. Instead, she crept silently towards the divan, where last night he had begun his seduction, and there she lay, waiting for what seemed like hours as her heart skittered with apprehension. When he came should she suggest that they talk—properly—and try to do so without blame or recrimination?

As the minutes ticked by, her nervousness began to seep away slowly replaced by the drugging onslaught of sleep. And Alexa welcomed it—embraced it, almost—for at least sleep would rob her of these tortured thoughts and the aching sense of realisation that the control over her own life seemed to be slipping away from her. Could Gio *really* force her and Paolo to stay with him in Naples? was her last conscious memory.

Giovanni walked towards the silent suite, rubbing his fingers against tired temples. After meeting with various Italian dignitaries, his father had summoned him to his private quarters and offered him land on the eastern reaches of the country—and a permanent home if he so desired. But inheritance had been the last thing on Giovanni's mind. He had been more stirred by the impact of sharing time with this man who did not have time on his side.

They had talked long into the night, until the Sheikh had grown tired and there had been only one thought dominating all others in Giovanni's mind.

That Paolo should never experience the absence of a father figure as he had done.

'Do you blame me for not having acknowledged you sooner?' the Sheikh had asked him quietly.

Giovanni had given his father a rueful smile. 'It is not my duty to apportion blame—only to learn from the experience.' He had agreed that he would return soon to Kharastan and to discuss the future then. He yawned. A wedding, a true reconciliation and the proud presentation of his only son to his brand-new family. Yes, it had been one hell of a day—and it was not over yet. Symbolically, Giovanni knew that one final test lay ahead, and he felt the sudden anticipatory hammer of his heart.

Did Alexa wish to be his wife in the fullest sense of the word?

The corridors to their suite were almost deserted, and when he walked through the dimly lit rooms he found her lying curled up on the divan, swathed in bedlinen. He felt the knife-twist of anger and frustration deep in his gut, and a sudden weariness, too. Oh, foolish woman! Did she not realise that he had made a vow, and

that his arrogant Neapolitan pride would never allow
him to go back on it?

Did she not realise that up until now he had been
handling her with kidgloves?

And that now she stood to lose everything?

CHAPTER ELEVEN

THOSE last few days in Kharastan taught Alexa the true meaning of isolation—and she was quickly made aware that her refusal to share Giovanni's bed had effected a kind of stand-off between them. Something was different, and it was her husband's attitude towards her. Gone was the gleam of desire, and the teasingly provocative remarks, and Alexa realised the truth in the saying that indifference was death.

His demeanour was haughty and icy towards her. If he was sexually frustrated then he was too proud to show it—and much too proud to ask her to change her mind, or to try and change it for her. She was left in no doubt of how it felt to be an outsider.

In a world full of privilege—to be royal was always to be top of the heap, no matter which society you were in, and in that Kharastan was no different from any other.

Giovanni was the favoured son. The Sheikh's son. Yes, she was afforded courtesy and respect because she was his wife, but more importantly because she was Paolo's mother. Yet deep down she knew that if

Giovanni chose to withdraw his support then she would be cast aside. Cut socially adrift and left to flounder.

No one was actually *rude* to her, but she sensed a certain coolness and a sense of detachment—almost as if they considered it a waste of time to include her in any important discussions about the future, because she would not be part of that future.

Alexa began to question whether she had been too hasty. Whether she *was* using sex as some kind of weapon. And so much of sex was in the head, wasn't it? At least that was what they said, especially about women. By deliberately sleeping on the divan on the night of the wedding itself, she seemed to have wounded Giovanni's macho male pride in a way she hadn't really appreciated. His eyes had glimmered at her coldly the following morning, and Alexa had been left feeling strangely empty and confused—questioning whether she'd done the right thing.

After that, he remained exaggeratedly cool towards her as they made all the preparations for her trip to Naples, and she supposed that his demeanour was perfectly understandable in the circumstances. So why did it niggle away at her? Wasn't this what she'd wanted? To show him that she would not be bought, like some kind of modern-day concubine?

But it went much deeper than just the act of sex itself. Of course the sex worked—it always had done—and she suspected there wasn't a woman on the planet who wouldn't be turned on and satisfied by Giovanni. It was what the sex *stood* for that scared her. Functional, emotionless sex was scary—it felt insubstantial. After it was over it left her feeling *less than*—as if she would disappear if she wasn't careful—and maybe that was what he really wanted.

But, nonetheless, she caved in to his wishes to go to Italy—because she didn't have the strength or the resources to do otherwise. Arrangements had already been made for Paolo to transfer to a small bi-lingual school in Naples, which had lemon trees growing all around it and a white rabbit called Blanco, which the children took in turns to pet and which her son had fallen in love during their visit. And *that* was the main reason she intended to give Naples a chance. She tried to put it into words to Teri, during their brief return to England to tie up all the loose ends.

'My happiness is all linked with Paolo's,' she admitted tentatively. 'It's not something separate from him. And he *wants* the change, Teri—he wants it badly. He loves his…Papà…which is exactly as it should be.' She said the words with determination, as she knew they should be said—though wasn't there a tiny, horrible part of her which wanted Paolo to declare that he never wished to see Giovanni again? It would certainly make life easier.

'And he loves Italy, too,' she continued. 'Who wouldn't—especially when you're his age? Everyone makes a fuss of him out there, and not just because he's Giovanni's son—they genuinely seem to love children. They pinch his cheeks and try to give him sweets. Then there's the weather, of course—and the swimming pool. It's going to be like a permanent holiday for him.'

No, the decision had been made. They were going to Naples—and no amount of avoiding sex with Giovanni in Kharastan was going to change his mind. He had made that quite clear. Thus the court case and custody battle would now be avoided.

Paolo was excited—desperately—and Alexa knew she should not minimise the impact of such a gigantic lifestyle-change on her son. At the moment he saw only the rich and exciting aspects of the move, but doubtless he would miss his homeland, and all his little friends. She had to make the transition easy for him, and bury whatever *she* was feeling deep inside her.

But when they arrived in Naples and Giovanni drove them through the winding streets—past cafés, cathedrals and archaeological excavations—Alexa began to relax a little, remembering the bustling and colourful impression that the city had made on her when she'd arrived as an impressionable twenty-something.

Paolo was gazing wide-eyed out of the car window, but Alexa found that she kept wanting to snatch a look at the hard, chiselled lines of Giovanni's dark profile.

'It doesn't look as if it's changed much,' she observed, trying to concentrate on the lively chaos outside and not his cool manner towards her.

Giovanni shot her a glance as he hit the flat of his hand on the horn, in typically Neapolitan fashion. 'Look beneath the surface and you'll find that everything changes,' he said obliquely, as the car began to climb the hill which led out of the crowded city centre towards Vomero, and the family home. 'A lot of money has been poured into the city. The poorer areas are being regenerated—a huge clean-up campaign has been instigated. Napoli has had a face-lift—and she wants the world to see it.'

'Are we nearly there, Papà?' piped up Paolo.

Giovanni smiled. '*Si, mio bello*. Nearly here,' he said, glancing down at his son, his heart turning over with love—and then he caught sight of Alexa's pale face in the driving mirror, and his hands tensed on the wheel. 'Remember this?' he questioned harshly, as a tall pair of electronic gates opened to reveal the elegant façade of the *palazzo* beyond.

Alexa had only visited the place once, years ago—the cool, dark villa where he'd grown up, which nestled in the hill as if it had always been there. 'Yes,' she answered uncertainly.

Giovanni felt a shiver momentarily chilling his skin. The house had been empty since his mother's death, and just the smell and feel of it now made him apprehensive as the ghosts of his past floated before him.

But his waterside apartment was not suitable for the three of them, and this was one of the best locations in which to bring up a family. So he had hired a cook, and a housekeeper who had a son, Fabrizio, who was just a year older than Paolo. At least there would be plenty to keep his son amused, he thought. He could learn football, and Italian, and some warm southern sun would bring the colour to his pale English cheeks.

'He can start school as soon as he likes,' Giovanni said, during dinner that first evening.

And what about me? her eyes asked him silently, her fingers crumbling an unwanted piece of bread.

'You can decorate the house and improve your Italian,' Giovanni said carelessly. 'Or shop.'

He made her sound as dispensable as yesterday's newspaper—which presumably had been his intention.

The meal was being served outside on the terrace, which looked down the hillside. Stars like bright lamps hung suspended from the night sky, and Naples glittered like a jewelled brooch in the distance.

Alexa kept looking down to the city, thinking, *This is my home now*. She wondered if it would ever feel that way—but the thought of the future scared her. What if it stayed like this—with her and Giovanni skirting round each other like strangers who had just met at a cocktail party?

But that was precisely the pattern of the days to come— with Alexa feeling like the water which had been pushed out to the edge of a whirlpool, while Paolo was sucked further and further into the centre of his father's life.

To see her son blossom beneath the sun and the approving eye of his father was both sweet and poignant, and Alexa began to understand that a moral obligation could be far stronger than a legal threat. Because she wasn't stupid.

Now that she had stepped back from their heated exchanges she realised that there was no way Giovanni could *force* them to stay—and that no court would wrench her son away from her simply because his father was rich and powerful.

But how could she wrench Paolo away—when he was clearly so happy here—take him back to a life which would always seem like a half-life in comparison?

At night she lay in the cool, scented room she had been given, listening to the massed sound of the cicadas whirring outside her window—but really listening out for Giovanni. Wondering if she would ever hear the creak of his footstep outside, or the sound of her door slowly opening—and then cursing herself for her own foolishness.

Did she really picture him walking into her room and climbing silently into bed beside her? When he'd already warned her that if she rejected him a second time he would withdraw from her? When he was a combination of two proud and stubborn races—probably the least likely candidate in the world to backtrack?

Or had she somehow thought that his was an idle threat, and that he'd change his mind and stroke her hair and tell her it was all going to be okay? Hadn't she realised that the ice she had been skating on was so thin that it was almost transparent?

Night after night she would turn over, pulling the fine sweet-scented Egyptian cotton sheet over her narrow shoulders and asking herself, couldn't *she* go to *him*?

But the longer Alexa gave the matter consideration, the more daunting a prospect it seemed. To have to creep into the bed of a man who had only offered you sex as part of an irresistible package to gain his son wouldn't fill even the most confident woman with much in the way of self-esteem. Wasn't that settling for crumbs when she wanted the meat of a real relationship, with love and closeness and all the other stuff which went with it?

But Giovanni didn't *do* love. He did jealousy, suspicion and distance. When he was having sex he held something back—hell, he *always* held something back, whatever he did. Would some women be content with that? Would *she*?

She stared up at the ceiling. It was funny how you could tell yourself you wanted x, y and z out of a relationship—but in the end you were defeated by the ache in your body and the emptiness in your heart.

CHAPTER TWELVE

'MAMMA, did you *know* that Naples football pitch is called Stadio San *Paolo*?'

Alexa smiled. 'No, darling, I didn't.'

'Is that why you called me Paolo?' her son demanded.

Alexa's fingers trembled slightly as she put her coffee cup down in the saucer and met Giovanni's enigmatic black eyes. 'N-no. I called you Paolo because it's a lovely name.'

Giovanni heaped some *marmellata di albicocche* onto his bread . 'I thought I'd take Paolo down to the stadium this morning—Fabrizio, too. Then maybe have some pizza down by the waterside.' He paused. 'You want to come?'

She could see the effort it took for him to ask her, and knew the effort it would take her to maintain a façade of contentment for a whole day down in the city. Sometimes she could carry it off almost without thinking, but others— like today—it felt like a weighty burden which was chained her shoulders with no chance of shaking it off.

Alexa shook her head. 'No, thanks. I thought I'd

carry on going through the swatches of fabric for the library curtains—and I've found a book on fifteenth Century wall colours.'

Giovanni shrugged as he finished his breakfast and put his napkin on the table. Naturally she would prefer to sit alone in a dusty library than to spend any time with *him*. 'As you wish,' he said coolly, and stood up. 'We'll be back around five.'

'In time for a swim, Papà?'

'*Si, bambino*.' Giovanni's eyes crinkled automatically. 'In time for a swim.'

But Giovanni's heart was heavy as the two of them went off to find Fabrizio—the golden promise of the day ahead tainted with the certain knowledge that he could not go on like this. He stared up at the cloudless blue sky. None of them could. It was not fair—but especially to Alexa. He had seen the sadness behind her smile—a sadness she did her best to conceal, but in a way that only made it glaringly more apparent. Unexpectedly, her silent suffering hurt. Made him feel a tyrant—like some throwback to another time, when powerful men could get their own way by sheer force of will and power.

Had he really imagined that they could carry on like this—into an unknown future—with Alexa here only on sufferance?

Yes, he wanted his son full-time—but that was never going to be the case. Not when he had blackmailed his mother and coerced her into staying. No wonder she recoiled from him whenever he walked into the room.

If it had been any other woman than Alexa he might

have tried to seduce her into staying—but that was not an option. And not simply because as a measure to keep her here it would be only temporary. No, it was because he had grown to respect her—to admire her quiet dignity and the way she conducted herself around him and around their son.

She deserved that respect, but she deserved something else too—and that was her freedom.

Giovanni's eyes narrowed against the sun as a cloud passed over his heart.

After they'd gone, Alexa set to work. She suspected that Giovanni had been being flippant when he'd first suggested she decorate the villa, but she had seized the task with vigour—partly as a kind of displacement activity, but also knowing she would never get an opportunity like this again.

The *palazzo* was old, with dim, muted rooms abounding with superb eighteenth-century art, multi-coloured marble and Majolica tiles which were worth a small fortune. There was a formal *salone*, the dining room, and a more informal room which overlooked the garden, where tall cypress trees rose like stately dark green flames. But it was the library which had captivated her, with its row upon row of leather-bound books—all with their own delicious scent and texture. It was the kind of place she could get lost in—allowing her imagination to run riot among the well-loved novels in different languages and the reference books—some with rich and wonderful illustrations.

The decor had been badly neglected, and was crying out for some tender loving care. Alexa had managed to find an oil-based paint which exactly matched the original tempera which had adorned the walls. Later, she would show it to Giovanni, to see if it met with his approval.

And will you be around to see it painted? mocked a small voice in her head. But she shushed it quiet and sat back on her heels to drink in the room's beauty, and at that moment a shelf which was almost hidden by the fireplace caught her attention.

She could see the corner of a book sticking out, and closer investigation revealed it to be a photo album. As she pulled it out Alexa stilled, with shock because... Well, because it was a pictorial record of Giovanni's childhood.

And it was like staring down at her own son.

Wasn't it funny how she could know something on one level—that Paolo's resemblance to his father was uncanny—but seeing it captured on the page for the first time took her breath away?

There was Giovanni at a circus, standing in a sweet little coat next to an elephant. Were elephants safe? Alexa wondered inconsequentially, as she turned the page.

There was Giovanni smiling next to his mother, by the seaside down in Chiaia, and there they were in Paris, walking among the flowers in the Tuilleries. There was a record of Gio in just about every country in Europe, and every photo was distinguished by his mother gazing into the eyes of a tall and handsome man.

And it was a different man in every photo.

She looked closely at the image of the child who so

resembled Paolo and saw the confusion and vulnerability in his young face. This wasn't a boy enjoying a rip-roaring series of holidays—this was a boy who was an appendage, an extra. A boy who funded a rich and expensive lifestyle. A little boy lost.

Oh, Gio, she thought.

'What the hell do you think you're doing?'

The words broke into her thoughts, and with a start Alexa looked up to see Giovanni framed in the doorway of the library, an implacable look darkening his face, the whole stance of his body tense and watchful as his black gaze swept over her.

She sat back on her heels again, her heart beating very fast. 'Looking around.'

'*Impicciona!*' he accused.

The word shot out like a bullet—an obscure word, but wasn't the human memory a strange and selective thing? For its meaning came back to her as if she used it every day of the week. Alexa shook her head. 'No, I'm not snooping.'

His glance swept over to the window—to the panorama of the verdant countryside, culminating in that heart-stopping aspect of Naples which was so beautiful that you could understand where the expression *See Naples and die* came from. Some views were almost priceless, such was their beauty—and this was one of them. A stunning vista bought by a sheikh in order to guarantee his mother's silence. Buying a woman's compliance was not a trait he admired in his father—and yet wasn't he guilty of attempting to do the same with Alexa?

This morning, when he had gone with his son down to the city and felt the grip of the child's trusting hand in his, he had felt his heart breaking open with happiness. Only to be left with a sickly scar of realisation in its wake.

It had hit him like another thunderbolt—that what he desired above all else was love. And love could not be bought, nor forced, nor demanded. Love was like a plant—it needed nurturing and light and space in order to thrive. All the things he had denied Alexa when they'd first been married, because of his stupid, arrogant pride.

He wanted the kind of authentic, warm family life that he had never had for himself—but he couldn't have that without the mother of his only child there. And Alexa didn't want to be there. Being there, with him, in Naples, was the *last* thing she wanted—she had told him that herself—and could he blame her? For he had tried to keep her there as an emotional prisoner—tied to him by false threats of how he would ruin her if she failed to comply with his unreasonable demands.

He had been angered by her failure to tell him about his son—but in view of his behaviour both before and since the discovery could he really blame her? How could he possibly berate her for her deception when she must have known that once he found out he would move heaven and earth in an attempt to possess Paolo in the way he had once tried to possess her?

For all the mess they had made of their own relationship, no one—least of all him—was denying that she was a good mother. So was *this* how he was attempting to reward her for her exemplary care of his son? By intimidating her?

He would tell her now that he would be generous with her. 'You can have the alimony you deserve. Enough to guarantee you a life of comfort in England. I won't try to keep you here against your will any longer, Lex.' He shrugged. 'You can go.'

Alexa blinked, taken aback. '*Go?*'

Did she wish to twist the knife? To make him beg for her forgiveness? 'Yes—go!' he said angrily. 'For that is what you wish!'

The freedom and the financial security he was offering her beckoned, and Alexa suddenly realised that these things meant nothing. But then she was beginning to understand what motivated this powerful but ultimately lonely man.

Alexa stared into his face for a long moment. His jealousy had started the chain of events which had led to her keeping their child a secret—but she had never stopped to question *why* it was etched so sharply on his character. It was almost as if she had imagined he'd been born with it—in the same way that he'd been born with black eyes and olive skin.

But people didn't just inherit jealousy—it wasn't up there with eye colour and long, lean legs. It developed for a reason—and the reason was there in black and white, and in colour, too—locked within the pages of his childhood photograph album.

A different man on every page—with Giovanni's discomfiture plain to see. Alexa knew that little boys were notoriously protective of their mothers, and that children often over-simplified life, based on their own experience of it. Paolo had taken to Gio perhaps because he'd felt some primitive bond straight away, but his acceptance had almost certainly been helped by the fact that he was the first man—the only man—she'd been intimate with since his conception.

She tried to imagine Paolo's confusion and rage if she had brought in a succession of 'uncles' to part-share his life. Was it any wonder that Giovanni had grown up thinking that women liked variety rather than constancy?

That was why he had overreacted on their wedding night she realised. Not because she wasn't innocent—but because of what her lack of virginity stood for. Virginity implied inexperience. Virginity was *safe*—from it he would know as much of her back-story as he needed to. He had thought her a goddess and discovered that she was just a woman. And the role-model he'd been exposed to as a child had made him uneasy.

Emotionally, he had flailed out at her like a little boy, and her *perceived* deception about her virginity had then been compounded by her *real* deception over their child. Both of them had acted rashly and selfishly—but as she stared into his eyes Alexa realised that she couldn't keep hiding behind her fear and the mistakes of the past for ever. Someone had to cross this ever-widening chasm, and if she had to embrace humility to do so—well, there were a lot worse things than that.

'I'm sorry, Giovanni,' she whispered. 'So...very sorry.'

He had been mentally assessing how best to work at

formalising their separation, and her words came as a shock. He froze, his black eyes narrowing into ebony shards. 'Is there something you've done that I should know about?'

'No. It's nothing like that.' She hesitated. 'I meant for the pain I've caused you. For the years of Paolo's life I've denied you.'

He shook his head, angry now. He wanted her to leave well alone—to leave him to come to terms with his decision. 'You don't have to say these things, Alexa. You can have your freedom. You can go home to England as soon as you wish.'

Was he sending her away in any case? Alexa stared at him aghast. 'And what if...?' Flicking the tip of her tongue around her lips, she swallowed. 'What if I don't *want* to go home to England?'

'Don't,' he said flatly. For the steel barriers around his heart had been in place for too long to be vanquished by a stumbled denial, however prettily she made it. 'Don't say things you don't mean.'

'But I *do* mean it! I...' She hesitated, knowing that she had to put her feelings on the line, and knowing also that there was no guarantee he would treat them with anything other than mistrust or contempt. This was the hardest thing to say when the face you were saying them to looked like a stony mask. 'I love you, Giovanni,' she whispered. 'Deep down I've never stopped loving you, and I never will.'

The words shot through him like little darts. Deliberately, he turned his back on her, blocking out the look of naked appeal in her eyes and concealing the hunger in his own eyes, too—such a raw and savage hunger. Not for her body, nor even for their son—but for the dream which had eluded him all his life.

He wanted to turn back to her, to tell her that *he* was sorry too, for the twists and turns their lives had taken, but he was scared—strong, powerful and autocratic Giovanni da Verrazzano was actually *scared*. What if these things were simply being said carelessly—here today and forgotten tomorrow?

Yet as he turned and looked into her face he found himself believing her. The truth blazed out like a beacon from those shining green eyes. Maybe it had been there all along—he just hadn't known how to look for it. He had something wonderful within his grasp, but everything to lose—and he didn't think he could bear to lose it. Not for a second time.

'I don't want your words,' he said harshly. For how could words undo all the bitterness of the past, all the wounds they had knowingly and unknowingly inflicted on each other?

'Then take my heart,' she said softly, walking up to him, touching her fingertips to his tense face. 'Take everything I have. But please, Giovanni—take me with you on your journey through life. I don't care if you don't love me back—just so long as you stay a good father to our son. And I will stay faithful to you, my one true love— as I have done since the first time you took me into your arms. And, besides, I have enough love to go round.'

There was a pause. He felt the slam of his heart and

the kick of some powerful emotion deep inside him—
as if some great block of ice had suddenly been melted
by the furnace within. For a moment he didn't move,
and then, when he did, so did she—and they clung to
each other like two survivors from a shipwreck.

A sigh shuddered from his lips and washed over her
mouth as they began to kiss, and it was a kiss like no
other they had shared. For it was not one of lust or anger
or frustration, it was a symbol of their love—real, adult
love—and it was their commitment to their future.
Because through the tears and the joy Alexa sensed that
they would never again be parted.

At first neither of them noticed that a small boy had
crept into the library, and when they did they saw the look
of tentative hope on his little face. Together, they opened
their arms to their son—and he went right into them.

EPILOGUE

SHEIKH ZAHIR was delighted but apparently not surprised that Alexa and Giovanni had quietly renewed their wedding vows in Naples—and he insisted on throwing an enormous party for them in Kharastan. Teri was invited, and naturally Alexa's mother—*'Darling! You've done better than I could ever have dreamed!'*— as well as some of Paolo's little school friends and his old childminder.

But during the six months since they had last seen him, the Sheikh had grown more frail. Alexa remarked on it to Giovanni when they were lying in their huge palace bedroom, with the faint smell of jasmine-scented breeze wafting over their naked bodies.

Giovanni stared at the ceiling. 'I know,' he said, in a sombre voice. 'I do not think that he has long left.'

Alexa was aware of the bond which had been forged between father and son, two proud men who had difficulty expressing emotions—one because the starchy formality of duty forbade it, and the other because he had never been shown how. But Giovanni was getting better at it every day. Oh, yes. She turned to him and stroked her finger softly over the hard contours of his lean face.

'Do you want to come and live out here, *caro*?' She asked Giovanni softly. 'You're older than Xavier. Do you think Zahir wants to pass the kingdom on to you? Has he said anything about it?'

He turned and smiled and kissed the tip of her nose, marvelling in this woman who was his wife in every sense of the word. This woman who cared not for the trappings of wealth, nor for status, nor trinkets—her heart's desire lay in those closest to her, and mirrored his. Her family. He shook his dark head. 'Don't worry about it,' he murmured.

'You can't just pass it off like that, Gio!' she protested. 'And I'm not worried about *it*—I'm worried about *you*! What if—'

'Shh,' he whispered, and silenced her with a kiss. 'Just wait.'

The following day a formal announcement was made—that the last of the Sheikh's three sons was to be identified.

'*Another* son?' demanded Alexa, as the excited buzz of chatter grew around the capital. 'You mean the Sheikh's got a *third* son?'

Giovanni nodded. 'The third and *final* son, I am assured,' he said dryly.

Alexa stared at Giovanni with wide eyes. 'You aren't surprised?'

Giovanni laughed. 'No, I'm not—for the hell of me I can't work out why, but I was kind of expecting it.

Xavier and I were informed just before the announcement was made.'

'And do you know who it is?'

'No—although I was given the opportunity to do so. But Xavier and I said we would prefer to find out at the same time as our wives.'

'Oh, *Gio*!' she gurgled delightedly.

'Anyway, I've guessed. It's Malik.'

'*Malik?*'

'I'd stake my fortune on it.'

But he didn't have to. Because he was right. The Sheikh's loyal and trusted aide—the only one with pure Kharastani blood running through his veins was—in fact, the oldest son and Zahir's true heir.

Alexa had grown fond of Malik, but her first and most fervent loyalty was to her beloved husband.

'Did you imagine that you might have ruled Kharastan before you found out about Malik? And would you have done it?'

'I would have had no choice,' Giovanni said simply. 'Destiny is not something which can be chosen at will— like goods in a supermarket—and if my destiny had been to take over the mantle from my father, then I would have embraced it wholeheartedly.'

She would have been a sheikha, thought Alexa fleetingly—and their son would, have one day worn the crown. Suddenly she was glad for Paolo—rejoicing that such a great burden would not be placed upon shoulders which had already carried much in their young life. 'You don't mind?' she asked her husband anxiously. 'That you won't be Sheikh and rule this beautiful land?'

Giovanni smiled as he lifted his hand to her face with an air of wonder of his own—but then, he still hadn't lost that *Am I going to wake up in a minute feeling?* she always induced in him. How had she so transformed his life? he wondered. But he knew the answer—love had a transformative power like no other. For both of them. He had seen Alexa blossom and bloom like a flower as she basked in the warmth of his love.

'No, *amata mia*, I do not mind—for I have riches far greater than those contained in any kingdom.' His black eyes crinkled with their now-familiar smile as he raised her fingertips to his lips in the regal gesture which came so naturally to him. 'I have you, and I have Paolo—what more could any man ask from his life than that?'

The Desert
King's Virgin
Bride

SHARON KENDRICK

To Chris and Cerys – may there be many,
many sunny days to follow.
With love from your favourite cousin. xxx

CHAPTER ONE

'MALIK, I'm...' There was a slight pause as Sorrel struggled to push the words out. She cleared her throat and tried again—forcing a smile which felt as if it was slicing her face in two. 'I'm leaving you,' she said, and then wished she could have bitten the words right back, wondering why the *hell* it had come out like that.

Malik looked up from the document he had been reading and a spark of undisguised irritation flashed from his black eyes. Eyes which had been described by the press as cold, or intimidating, or even—in the more colourful publications—as being like those of a lithe predator, about to strike its helpless victim. 'What?' he questioned impatiently.

'I mean...' Sorrel stared at the dark-skinned Sheikh, sitting in his shimmering silken robes at his desk. He had barely noticed her entering the room and he was barely looking at her now—and worrying about how her words had been interpreted was obviously a complete waste of time, since he obviously hadn't been listening either! 'That I'm leaving Kharastan,' she finished huskily.

A frown creased Malik's olive brow—for he was too preoccupied with affairs of state to have heard her. More importantly, he had no desire to bother himself with the internal domestic squabbling of the palace. Surely she knew that? 'Not now, Sorrel,' he growled.

Not *now*? If ever Sorrel had needed confirmation that she was doing the right thing, then it came in the Sheikh's moody and offhand response to her. He spoke as if she was a troublesome fly who had buzzed into his large office suite and he was just about to carelessly swat it.

Amber sunlight slanted in through the window, turning the sumptuous apartment into a tableau of pure gold and illuminating the man who sat at the desk like some glorious living statue. As always, just the sight of him made Sorrel's heart yearn—but the sooner she got out of the habit of doing *that* then the sooner she would recover from the impact of his potent charm. Instead, Sorrel tried very hard to ignore his physical attributes, and fixed him with a questioning look instead. 'When, then? When *can* we discuss it, Malik?'

'Look!' Impatiently, he waved his hand at the large pile of paperwork awaiting the royal stamp and the royal signature. Beside them lay his open diary, crammed with engagement after engagement. 'You know that there is an important border issue with Maraban which needs to be resolved quickly—and I have a new ambassador to welcome later this morning. Can't you see how busy I am?'

'Yes, Malik,' she said, with a sigh. 'Of course I can

see.' It hurt that he should even ask—for surely he must know that she always had his interests at heart? Once, she had been alone in looking out for Malik—in the days when he had been nothing more than the Sheikh's most valued and trusted aide—but now all eyes were fixed on him.

In the royal palace—and in the desert lands beyond—he was the centre of the universe. To be a desert king was considered irresistible in the eyes of the world. When Malik said 'jump', people leapt—usually with a smarmy and obsequious smile pinned to their faces.

It hadn't always been that way, of course. Malik was a late starter in the royal game—he hadn't even realised that he was the illegitimate son of the Sheikh until two years ago, when the bombshell announcement had been made. The old ruler had died, and Malik had been crowned—from aide to king in a simple ceremony—from commoner to royal in an instant. And yet Malik seemed to have adapted to his new status like a falcon which took its first solo flight in the desert sky.

His always haughty air had become fine tuned—but now he had developed a cool dismissiveness towards others. The practical side of Sorrel's character acknowledged that he needed distance—literally, to stop anyone from getting too close to him and to attempt to claw back some of his most precious commodity: time.

Yet, deep down, hadn't Sorrel been hoping that in her case he might make an exception? Didn't it occur to him that she was itching to tell him of her decision and to get on with it—to start making something of her own life, instead of just existing as some invisible satellite of his? No, of course it didn't!

Ever since Sorrel had known him Malik had been an autocratic and supremely dominant man—but since he had inherited the Kingdom of Kharastan his pride and his arrogance had known no bounds. His wishes were always paramount—nothing else mattered except what the Sheikh wanted—and Sorrel had come to the heartbreaking conclusion that there was simply no place for her in his life any more.

Everything had changed—he had, and she had. Suddenly she no longer felt she belonged—certainly not in the land where she had lived most of her life.

Then just where do you belong? The question which had haunted her for so long popped into her head, even though she had been trying to ignore it—because every time she let herself think about it she was frightened by the vision of a great gaping hole in her future.

Malik's black eyes were now scanning the cream parchment pages of his diary and, knowing that he could be seen by none of his servants, he scowled. It was unlike Sorrel to add to the burden of his work.

'There is no appointment for me to see you marked out in my diary.' He frowned, and then he looked up again. 'Did you make one?'

Once, Sorrel might have wanted to weep at such a matter-of-fact statement coming from the man she had idolised ever since she could remember. The man who had in effect 'rescued' her, who had become her legal guardian after the sudden and tragic death of her parents and allowed her to remain in Kharastan instead of being carted off back to England. But this harsh new attitude towards her hurt more than she could have thought possible, and even though she tried very hard to tell herself he wasn't being unreasonable—it wasn't easy.

'No, I didn't make an appointment,' she said flatly.

Malik's eyes narrowed. What was the *matter* with her lately? From being someone he could talk to and relax with, she had become…*edgy*. 'Well, be quick,' he said impatiently, flicking a glance at the modern watch which looked so at odds when contrasted against the fine silk of the flowing robes he wore. 'What is it?'

Sorrel wondered what he would say if she blurted out *I think you've become an arrogant and insufferable pig.* Would he have her taken away for treason?

She flicked her tongue out over lips which had grown suddenly dry. 'I want to go to England,' she said.

'England?' Malik frowned. 'Why?'

'Because…' Where did she begin? Not with the truth, that was for sure.

Because I'm in love with you. I've been in love with you for years, Malik, and you've never even deigned to notice me as a woman.

No, the truth would horrify him. Sorrel had no real experience of men—but the palace library was stocked with the world's greatest literature, and she had read enough classic love stories to realise that she was wasting her time with the black-eyed Sheikh of Kharastan, who had steel for a heart.

'Because I am now twenty-five.'

'No, Sorrel,' he negated. 'You cannot be.'

This was the kind of remark which once she would have found sweet, and amusing—but which now rankled as if he had just insulted her. And in a way he had—for his failure to know her real age went some way towards explaining why he treated her as if she was about six years old.

'I really think that if anyone happens to know how old I am, it's me,' she said, as near as she came to sarcasm with His Mightiness these days.

'Yes. Of course. Twenty-five,' he repeated wonderingly, and for a second he met her gaze full-on. 'How can this be?'

Sorrel steeled her heart against the sudden faraway look in his ebony eyes. A sad, wistful, almost dreamy look—as if he had lost himself in the past.

Which just proved how unrealistically sentimental she had become—*as if* Malik would be longing for the days when he had been just the aide to the Sheikh, instead of the Sheikh himself!

'The years go by more quickly than any of us realise,' Sorrel said briskly, realising how *prim* she sounded—but that was the trouble: she *was* prim. Basically, the years were zooming by, and with them her youth, and she was wasting it pining for a man who never noticed her. Well, not as a woman.

One day—probably in the not-too-distant-future—Malik would start casting his eyes around for a suitable bride. A woman of Kharastani stock who could provide him with pure-bred Kharastani babies. 'And I can't stay here for ever,' she finished.

'But you don't know England,' objected Malik. 'You haven't lived there for years.'

'Not since I was at boarding school,' Sorrel agreed. 'And even then I didn't what you might call *live* there. Being allowed out to the sweet shop in the village every Saturday morning to spend my pocket money hardly counts as interacting with the country of my birth!'

Malik's hard mouth momentarily softened. He had known her since she was a child—a blonde-haired poppet, as her father had used to call her. And he had been right. Sunny little Sorrel had charmed everyone.

Her parents had been diplomats—clever academics with a hunger for facts and experience which had ended over the treacherous peaks of the Maraban mountain range which bordered the Western side of the country. There, one hot and stormy evening, their plane and their dreams had crashed and lain in pieces on the ground, and the sixteen-year-old Sorrel had been left an orphan.

Perhaps if she had been younger then she would have been unable to refuse to return to her homeland, to be cared for by a distant relative. And if she had been older then there would have been no need for a protector. But she had needed someone, and Malik—a great friend and confidant of her ambassador father—had been named as guardian in their will.

He had been more than a decade older, and in a more liberal country than Kharastan questions might have been asked about whether such an arrangement was appropriate between a teenage girl and a red-blooded single man. But no questions had been asked. Malik's reputation where honour and duty were concerned was unimpeachable. He had overseen her education and her upbringing with a stern eye, far stricter than that of any father—though Sorrel had never given him cause for concern, not even a hint of rebellion.

Until now.

He stared at her. She was almost completely covered in pale silk, as Kharastani custom dictated, so it was almost impossible to known what her figure was really like, though from the drape and fall of the cloth, and the perfect oval of her face, it was easy to recognise that beneath it she was a slim and healthy young woman.

Only a strand of moon-pale hair peeped out from beneath the soft silver lace which covered it, and the only colour which was apparent was the bright blue of her eyes and the natural rose gleam of her lips. For the first time Malik began to realise that somewhere along the way she had become a woman—and he hadn't even noticed.

Should he let her go? 'Can't you just have a holiday in England?' he enquired moodily. 'And then come back again?'

Sorrel sighed. He was missing the point—only she couldn't really tell him what the point was, could she?

'No, Malik,' she said patiently, aware from the sudden narrowing of his eyes that few people said 'no' to him since his sudden elevation in status. 'I've spent my whole life having *holidays* in England—I haven't lived there properly for years. Why, I even went to university here, in Kumush Ay—'

'Which has a fine reputation the world over!' he interrupted, with fierce pride. 'And which enabled you to become possibly the only Western woman to speak fluent Kharastani. Why, you speak it almost as fluently as I do!'

'Thank you.' Briefly, Sorrel bowed her head—aware that the Sheikh had just paid her a compliment and that to fail to acknowledge it would be seen as discourteous. But it was yet another example of how much had changed since his elevation into the royal ranks.

There was a time when she would have playfully teased him—or perhaps challenged him about who was right and who was wrong—but not any more. And the longer you stay, the worse it's going to get, she told herself.

'I don't want to become a stranger to the land of my birth, Malik,' she said fervently. 'And if I leave it much longer then I will be. I'll become one of those people whose only knowledge of their country is through the rose-tinted glasses of memory.'

His eyes glinted as he nodded his black head with slow consideration. 'Yes,' he conceded. 'The ties to our homeland are one of the strongest of all instincts known to man—for they link us to our forebears and make up our very history.'

Sorrel could have kicked the leg of his ornate writing desk in rage, wanting to tell him not to be so damned *pompous*, but she couldn't do that either. He might be speaking to her as if he was aged about a hundred and three, but what he said made sense—and in this instance at least he spoke from the heart. *His* heritage was of huge importance to him, and so he would naturally understand her need to go and investigate *her* roots.

After all, it wasn't his fault that she had stupidly nurtured a rather different fantasy about their shared future over the years...

'Sorrel?'

His voice butted into her thoughts and Sorrel blinked, her heart leaping in spite of everything, the way it always did when he said her name in that uniquely honeyed way of his.

'Yes, Malik?'

'Just what are you proposing to do? In England?'

Try to start a new life. Do the normal stuff that a twenty-five-year-old woman would have done by now if she hadn't been all caught up with trying to fit in somewhere where she didn't belong. Maybe even find herself a boyfriend along the way.

'I'll look for a job.'

There was a pause. 'A job? What kind of *job*?' he demanded, as incredulously as if she had just started doing cartwheels around the state apartments.

'I can do plenty of things.'

'Oh, really?' He sat back in his chair and, interlacing his long dark fingers in front of the silken shimmer of his robes, fixed her with a piercing black look. 'Such as?'

'I'm a good organiser.'

'That much is true,' he admitted, for she had been co-ordinating palace functions ever since she had graduated. No royal banquet was ever complete without Sorrel quietly manoeuvring behind the scenes to prevent delicate egos from clashing.

'And I am also versed in the art of diplomacy.'

He could see exactly where this was leading, and as he was reminded of just how protected and innocent she really was Malik shook his head. 'If you think you'll just be able to walk straight into a job without any formal training, then you are wrong, Sorrel.' Thoughtfully, he drummed one long finger on the polished surface of the exquisite inlaid desk. 'However, I may be able to speak to a few people on your behalf. Perhaps,' he mused, 'I could arrange for you to stay with a family. Yes, that might be the best solution all round.'

'A *family*?'

'Why not? Girls do it all the time.'

Girls, he had said. Not women, but *girls*—and enough really was enough! For the first time in her adult life Sorrel looked around the high-ceilinged palace room and saw it not as a place furnished with priceless antiques and glittering chandeliers and wonderful artifacts but as a kind of elaborate cage. Except that even a bird trapped in a cage could be seen, while she was hidden away like a guilty kind of secret. Prevented from freely mixing with men, covered from head to toe in robes designed to conceal the female

form from all eyes. Never before had she minded about
the camouflage of the national dress—but lately she had
been looking at fashion sites on the internet with a
yearning which surprised her.

'I am not a g-girl,' she said, her voice shaking with
an emotion she wasn't sure she could identify—even if
she had been in the mood for analysis. 'I am a *woman*—
not some teenage *au pair* who needs looking after.'

Malik's eyes were caught by the sudden trembling
of her lips and his pupils dilated—for it was as if he had
never seen them before. Like petals. Provocative and
rosy. Did she have any idea what Western men might
do when confronted with a pair of lips like that? He
glared at her.

'I would feel happier if I knew that you were in
capable hands,' he said stubbornly.

It wasn't easy, but Sorrel knew that she had to start
standing up for herself if she wanted any kind of independent life. 'Strangely enough, this isn't about *you*,
Malik—this is about *me*, and my life. We've been
dealing with yours non-stop ever since you became
Sheikh, haven't we?'

For a moment he stilled, every instinct alerted to the
presence of something he wasn't used to—at least,
never with Sorrel—and that something was discord.
Black eyes gleamed. Was she daring to *criticise* him?
Or to imply that she was not happy with her lot?

His hard mouth flattened into an implacable line of
anger which Sorrel had seen before—many times—
but never directed towards her.

'Well, do forgive me if you've been *bored*,' he said, in an arrogant drawl which disguised the outrage he felt. Ungrateful little Westerner! He had willingly taken her under his wing, had ensured that she had a stable education and a secure home-life, and she was now throwing back his protection in his face—like some spoilt little child.

How he would like to teach her a lesson!

But as he felt the blood fizzing heatedly through his veins, Malik rose quickly from his desk, momentarily confused by his reaction—if such a state could ever have been said to exist in a man who was a stranger to the very concept of self-doubt. Why, for a moment back then…

Aware that her eyes followed him, he walked over to the window—his back ramrod-straight as he stared out into the manicured grandeur of the palace gardens—and stifled a sigh. When had he last had the freedom to just wander around its scented splendour—without a care in the world?

Not since his last few innocent days as a free man—before the announcement that he was the eldest of the late Sheikh's three illegitimate sons and that the crown of Kharastan was to be placed on *his* head.

In many ways Malik had been well-prepared for the very specific burdens of kingship, for he had been the trusted aide to Sheikh Zahir for many years, and was well-versed with the intricate customs of the Kharastan court.

But knowing something as an advisor—no matter how highly favoured—was completely different from *becoming* the ruler, especially with very little prior warning. Malik had known that the changes would be much more subtle and far-reaching than the mere swapping of roles.

Gone was the relaxed status he had simply taken for granted. Suddenly he had been hurled into a world where he was no longer able to express an opinion without first carefully thinking it through. For his words would be seized on—twisted around, or analysed for a meaning he had not intended. Yes, he had been able to turn to Fariq—his own assistant—and elevate him to the position of Sheikh's aide, but Malik still felt as if he was on trial. As if he had to prove to everyone—to his people and the world and to *himself*—that he was capable of shouldering this mighty responsibility of power.

Only with Sorrel had he not had to bother—and yet now there was to be another change, and Sorrel wished to leave.

He turned round again to find her eyes wary. And something in that fearful look shook him—seeming to click reality into sudden focus. As though the trepidation in her big blue eyes emphasised more than anything else had done to date just how different his life had become.

She who had never looked on him with anything other than serene and smiling acceptance was now surveying him as if he were some cruel sultan who had stepped out of the pages of the *Arabian Nights*—he, Malik, who had shown her nothing other than kindness!

Well, let her go! Let her see how she enjoyed an anonymous existence in England!

But he saw the faint clouding of her eyes and he relented, giving her one last opportunity to see sense. 'A role could be found for you at the Kharastani Embassy,' he mused.

'I...realise that.'

He heard the unspoken reluctance in her voice, and with anyone else he would have quashed any further enquiry—but this was *Sorrel*, for mercy's sake, who as a child had brought him back a little box covered in seashells from a place called Brighton. 'You do not wish for any assistance?' he questioned proudly.

Sorrel hesitated—for the very last thing she wished was to insult his honour. Kharastani customs were incredibly complex, and it had taken her a long time to understand that the possibility of an offer was always suggested before an offer was made. Thus, the possibility could be rejected and not the offer itself, ensuring that nobody's pride would be hurt.

'I just think it's better if I do it myself. Stand on my own two feet, for the first time in my life.' She turned her face up to his beseechingly, but his eyes were as cold as stones. 'Surely you can understand that, Malik?'

'I think you forget yourself,' he remonstrated cruelly. 'It is not my place to understand one of my subjects— nor theirs to suggest that I should!'

He drew his shoulders back and iced her a look, and Sorrel could have wept—for never in a million years could she ever have imagined Malik pulling rank on her. And *was* she one of his subjects? Perhaps she was— technically, at least.

Once again, the sensation of being enclosed and trapped enveloped her like a velvet throw.

'No, of course it isn't,' she responded stiffly, momentarily lowering her eyes—not so much in a mockery of submission but more so that he would not see the fury reflected in her eyes. When she looked up again, she had composed herself—enough to even curve her lips in a polite little smile. 'Then I shall make the necessary arrangements.'

'Indeed,' he said, deliberately cold and unhelpful, picking up his golden pen in a gesture which was obviously intended to dismiss her.

But Sorrel was not prepared to be so pushed aside—not any more. For Malik himself had just demonstrated how he rewarded loyalty and unswerving affection—with disdain and contempt.

'I believe that there was a little money set aside in a trust for me by my father?'

He stared at her, tempted to use his power as trustee of her late father's estate. Let her see how long she would last in the world if she had to go out and earn her living like other mortals—*then* she might appreciate her cosseted life within the walls of the palace!

But Malik was not foolish, and he would no more seek to deny Sorrel what was rightfully hers than he would contain her in a place of which she had clearly grown tired. Just a few minutes ago he himself had shuddered at the sensation of being trapped—so why would he inflict it on someone else?

Because he would miss her?

His mouth hardened. Perhaps for an instant, but no more than that—in the way that you might miss your favourite horse if you went to live in the city and found you could no longer ride. But doubtless Sorrel would visit Kharastan from time to time. He would watch her blossom as she embraced her new life—and that was exactly as it should be.

'Yes, Sorrel,' he said, surprised by the sudden heaviness in his voice. 'The money your father left in trust for you was invested by the financial advisors of the late Sheikh.' He paused for emphasis, to let the words sink in, but also to gauge her reaction. 'Thus the amount he left has grown considerably.' He saw her eyes widen, and he knew that he must move quickly to quash any ill-founded dreams that she might have. 'That does not mean that you are now a wealthy woman—but that there is adequate provision for you. I advise you to spend it wisely—cautiously, even—until you are used to dealing with money.'

Sorrel stared at him. What did he think she was going to do? Blow it on hundreds of pairs of shoes or start buying diamonds? 'Thank you for your advice,' she said stiffly.

Malik relaxed slightly. So she was prepared to listen to him! 'Shall I have one of my people talk to you— guide you through all the possibilities of budgeting?'

For a moment Sorrel was tempted—and then some dormant streak of rebellion sprang out of nowhere. All her life, people had 'guided' her and helped make her decisions—and that didn't happen to other people of her age. Why, how many other young women had never paid any rent, nor shopped for groceries—or had to cook their own supper? And were *they* given the benefit of the palace's financial advisors?

Besides, what advice could they possibly give that was going to be relevant to her new life in England? They could hardly tell her how to make savings on the central heating bill!

'Thank you, Malik—but no. I would prefer to stand on my own two feet.'

His eyes narrowed. 'How stubborn you can be sometimes, Sorrel,' he said softly.

'It isn't stubbornness, Malik—it's called independence.'

He hesitated, and then asked the question, knowing that by doing so he was breaking protocol. 'You don't want my help?'

Sorrel shook her head, and as she did so she felt her veil shimmer around her shoulders. She had worn it for as long as she could remember, and yet soon the veil would be lifted and removed—her head bare in a way which was considered unseemly here. It would be freedom in more ways than one—and most important of all she wanted to be free of this one-sided adoration she felt for the Sheikh.

'I want to do it my way.' She should have felt excitement, but at that moment she felt the clammy clamping of fear around her heart as she looked up into Malik's hard black eyes, realising that despite everything she wanted his blessing—his assurance that her actions would not damage their friendship. That once she had got him thoroughly out of her system a residual affection would remain. 'If that's okay?'

He shrugged, deliberately disdainful. 'Do as you please, Sorrel,' he said coldly, and picked up one of the documents he had been working on in a gesture which said quite clearly *I wash my hands of you.* 'But if you don't mind—I think we have exhausted the subject, don't you? And I happen to be rather busy.'

Sorrel stared at him. She had been dismissed as he would a servant, and she had to bite back her rage and her pain as he deliberately bent over his work. Yet somehow she kept silent, her head held high as she walked towards her apartment, telling herself that his reaction to her news after a lifetime of friendship was nothing less than *shameful.*

Well, she would show Sheikh High-and-Mighty Malik! She was going to get right out there in the world and start living her life as it *should* be lived!

So why did her heart feel so heavy as she walked into her sumptuous apartment and looked around? At the delicate inlaid furniture and the paintings whose frames gleamed softly with gold. At the row upon row of beautifully bound and rare books she had inherited from her diplomat father. And at the view over the palace gardens—the emerald lawns leading down to a long rectangle of water, with a fountain pluming in feathery display in the distance.

Against the glittering silver surface she could see the flash of the orange-pink feathers of flamingos—birds

so fantastic that they looked almost unreal. Wild ducks
and geese landed here sometimes, *en route* to the wide
Balsora Sea, and many times Sorrel had seen astonishment on the faces of Western visitors—as if they simply
couldn't imagine that such a variety of wildlife existed
in a land which was dominated by desert. But
Kharastan was a land of constant surprises—its beauty
and richness and complexity seeped into your bones
almost without you realising it, and she was going to
miss it.

Sorrel turned away from the window and stared
down at the group of photos which sat atop the baby
grand piano. Among the old black and white collection
of distant relatives there was a wedding-day photo of
her parents, and a later shot of the three of them,
laughing on a visit to the Balsora Sea—shortly before
their death.

Yet one portrait alone dominated her vision, and she
picked it up and drank it in, her heart beating fast as she
looked at the formal coronation day study of Malik—
his beloved face so stern and so determined beneath the
heavy weight of his crown and his destiny.

Rogue tears pricked at her eyes, and a feeling of
strange apprehension threatened to overwhelm her as
Sorrel quickly put the photo down on the piano and
turned away.

CHAPTER TWO

'It will not be as you imagine it to be. And people will treat you differently there. Come back to me if ever you are in trouble, Sorrel.'

Those remembered words echoed in Sorrel's ears— the very last words that Malik had spoken to her just before the door of the dark limousine had closed and shut her off from him.

For ever?

Now she was just being ridiculous! Of course she was going to see him again—and she hadn't come all the way to England and fundamentally changed her life around simply to spend her time thinking about Malik, had she?

The problem was that it was difficult *not* to think about him, not to keep comparing her new life in England, which was so different from the way she'd lived in Kharastan. After the enclosed world of an English boarding school and her cloistered life at court, for the first time in her life she was tasting freedom.

It was just that freedom seemed to come with a price…

Recognising that she was lucky to have the funds to do so—she'd begun looking around for somewhere to rent. She had rejected London—on the grounds that it was too big and too busy, and it would probably swallow her up and spit her out again—but she didn't want to sink into obscurity in some tiny little English village.

In the end she'd chosen Brighton, because it was a bustling and beautiful seaside town, and she recalled spending a wonderful holiday there when she'd been a little girl.

She had found an apartment on the seafront—with huge floor-to-ceiling windows which let the most amazing light flood in. It was one of several owned by Julian de Havilland, a very successful local artist, who only let the rooms out to people who had 'good vibes'. Sorrel suspected that the stark and bare layout of the apartment, with only the barest minimum of furniture, would not be everyone's cup of tea—but it was by far and away the nicest one she had looked at.

'I'll take it!' she said, her attention caught by the sunlight dancing on the sea outside the vast windows.

'There's no curtains, I'm afraid,' he said, raking hands which were stained with Indian ink through an already tousled mane of hair.

'Who needs curtains?' said Sorrel lightly, thinking that she would undress in the bathroom, which featured an enormous great boat of a bath and a noisy cistern.

'Are you working in Brighton?' he asked curiously,

watching as she ran her fingertips along the edge of the
marble fireplace.

'No, I haven't got a job,' she said, and then, seeing
the heightened curiosity on his face and not wanting to
come over as some little rich-girl—which she wasn't—
and realising that only by working was she going to get
to know people, she gave him a bright smile. 'Not yet,
anyway. I'm going to have to start looking.'

'What do you do?'

Ah. That was the question. What *did* she do? Sorrel
screwed her face up and came up with her one most
marketable asset. 'I can speak French. And German.'

'Fluently?'

'Oh, yes.' She was determined to play down her
knowledge of Kharastani. Sorrel had already decided
that she wasn't going to publicise her background—
mainly because it wasn't fair to Malik. He was
powerful, and he was a king, and while some people
might actually think she was fantasising about even
knowing him she must never forget that others might
wish to make his acquaintance for all kinds of reasons.
And she could never presume on their friendship by
daring to make introductions to him.

Friendship?

Some friendship!

He hadn't bothered replying to her e-mails and
neither had he once picked up the telephone, or in any
way acknowledge the couple of jaunty postcards she
had sent, with a deliberately cheerful tone—as if she
was having the most wonderful time in the world with

her newly acquired freedom. As if she wasn't missing him and her life in the exotic and complex country which was Kharastan. But she did.

She missed it all like mad—the apricot-soft dawns and the fiery sunsets, the stark beauty of the desert and the warm, scented air of the palace gardens. And didn't she miss her exceptionally privileged lifestyle there, if she was being completely honest? Hadn't she become rather too accustomed to servants who acceded to her every whim? To having her clothes laundered and her meals cooked and served to her? Why, by the time she had left Kharastan she had actually had her *own* aide!

Most of all she missed Malik. The sight of his beautiful mocking face at state banquets—the sound of his rich, resonant voice as he made a speech to welcome visiting dignitaries. She missed the expectation of bumping into him. The thought that at any moment he might suddenly appear—sweeping through the wide, marbled palace corridors with his silken robes swishing and a cluster of aides scurrying in his wake, because his long stride seemed to cover so much more distance than anyone else she knew.

But didn't that speak volumes about how hopeless her longing for him was? If she analysed the actual *substance* of her relationship with him, it was nothing. A few daily snatched glimpses of him and being a member of an adoring audience as he delivered a speech was not a *real* relationship—hardly even a friendship. She sounded more like a starstruck fan than an equal. For she would never be his equal. Not now.

In the years before the bombshell had dropped that he was the true and rightful heir to the Sheikh there had been hope that he might love her back. But he never had and now he never would. Perhaps deep down Malik had always sensed the true magnitude of his destiny, and she had to accept hers. And hers was here. Now. And she must learn to adapt to this completely different way of living.

It was a shock to the system—but one that she needed if she was to achieve any degree of contentment, she decided, as she signed a cheque and handed it over to Julian.

He took it, folded it, and slid it in the back pocket of his jeans. 'Well, if you need a job and you're a linguist, then why don't you try the Alternative Tourist Office?' he questioned, and saw her puzzled look. 'It specialises in places of interest which are off the beaten track—as well as the usual attractions—but they get loads of foreign tourists who don't speak much English. They've got a crazy little office down the road on the seafront.'

'And they're looking for someone?'

Julian grinned. 'They're always looking for someone! They don't pay great money—but the atmosphere's pretty relaxed.'

It certainly seemed that way. The office was situated a mere shell's throw from her apartment, sandwiched between a clothes shop and a wine bar. A few wilting plants sat on the windowsill, and there was free coffee and a pile of magazines with most of the advertisements cut out—plus music playing from a deck in one corner.

Sorrel was asked a fairly basic question in French and given the job on the spot—mornings only and every other Saturday. She would be working with Jane, who had just left university and couldn't decide what to do, and a very good-looking male model called Charlie, who told her he was currently 'resting'.

'Oh, you're always "resting"!' accused Jane, with a giggle.

It was such a relief to be in a friendly atmosphere with people her own age that Sorrel found herself relaxing for the first time since her plane had taken off from Kumush Ay airport.

The job was also so easy that she felt she could have done it with her eyes shut, and when she wasn't working she kept the plants watered and read everything there was to know about Brighton, because she was determined to do well.

And when Jane and Charlie asked she told them simply that she'd been working in the Middle East but had wanted a change—and that was the truth. It was a gentle shoe-in to the working world, yet Sorrel felt incredibly nervous—given that just a few months ago she had been rubbing shoulders with political leaders and queens. Where had that serene and unflappable Sorrel gone? She seemed to have left her behind.

She guessed that her anxiety stemmed from more than just setting out on her own in a land which was like a foreign country to her—it was as if she had to acquire a whole new identity to cope with her new life.

For a start, she had to go out and buy clothes which

were suitable for her new appointment, and how strange that felt—not having to follow the strict dress-code of her adopted country which had become second nature to her.

Without her neck-to-ankle silk gowns she felt almost…exposed—even though she wasn't, not really, and certainly not compared to everyone else. She bought a couple of floaty long skirts and a pair of jeans—but the jeans hung disturbingly low on her hips and the T-shirts she wore with both clung to her breasts in a way she was not used to.

But this is England, she reminded herself—not Kharastan.

In fact, the clothes she wore were very modest— especially considering that the weather was blisteringly hot, since England was having the kind of freak summer heat-wave which Sorrel would never have anticipated. Even though they left the front door wide open, the office was like an oven—and during the still nights when she lay in bed Sorrel found herself longing for the air-conditioned coolness of the palace at Kumush Ay.

'Aren't you baking, dressed like that?' asked Jane one morning, as flung her handbag down onto one of the desks. 'You're not in the Middle East now, you know—and these little sundresses are much cooler!'

'Yes, they look cooler,' agreed Sorrel, with a slight longing in her voice as she glanced at Jane's bare thighs. 'But my legs are so pale. Not like yours.'

'Didn't you sunbathe in…Kharastan?' asked Jane.

'It wasn't really encouraged,' said Sorrel, with wry understatement.

'Well, my tan isn't real,' confided Jane—and when she saw Sorrel's blank look she burst out laughing and began rubbing her hands together. 'Oh, *yes!*' she breathed, with gleeful enthusiasm. 'I've always wanted to do a real-live makeover on someone!'

It was an experience that Sorrel would never forget. First came the beauty salon—where fake tan was sprayed all over her. When she emerged, she shrieked with horror at the blotchy, muddy mess her skin presented—until she was assured that the colour would flatten out. Next she had her toenails and fingernails painted in an iridescent shade of rose-pink.

'You've *never* had a pedicure before?' shrieked Jane in amazement.

'Never,' agreed Sorrel, pushing away her nagging feeling of doubt as she tried to imagine what Malik would say if he could see her now, lying back on a leather couch as if she was awaiting a medical examination, while the nail polish dried. He probably wouldn't even deign to comment. She had taken her chosen path and was now a Western woman who could do exactly as she pleased—no longer under his protection or control. And he had moved on, too, eradicating her from his life completely—which presumably was why he hadn't even had the courtesy to reply to her.

Hot tears stung at her eyes and she blinked them away, willing it not to hurt—not *wanting* it to hurt.

But it did hurt—and Sorrel despised herself for

feeling a pain that had no justification in reality. Because nothing had gone on between her and Malik—absolutely nothing—except within the fertile planes of her imagination. Not a nod or a glance, nor a snatched look—and certainly never a kiss or even a touch. Sorrel swallowed. That was true. Unless you counted the times when as a child she had been learning to ride and he had first lifted her onto a horse and gently put her feet into the stirrups, Malik had *never even touched her!*

Even at the weddings of his two half-brothers—when the opportunity had been there—he had not danced with her. Much of the time he had been busy—like her—with the sheer mechanics of organising two such fancy functions, but when there had been a lull... No. She frowned in recall.

He had not actually danced with anyone—even though some of the more blatant female guests had been circling him as she had sometimes seen vultures circle a fallen leopard amid the blazing waste of desert sands.

So why was she allowing him to clog up her thoughts? And why was she continuing to dream this dream, which should have been growing more distant by the day—not featuring in glorious Technicolor in her mind.

It was time to move on, and there were practical ways she could do that. She'd found the apartment and the job—maybe it was time to stop standing on the side-lines of life in her homeland and to embrace the culture as would any other single young woman of twenty-five.

She glanced up at Jane, who was working her way through sample bottles of moisturiser. 'Could we go shopping after work?'

'*Can* we?' Jane giggled. 'I thought you'd never ask!'

Sorrel had never really hit the shops with a credit card before—her parents had not been big spenders, and had actively discouraged what they'd called *the feeding frenzy of consumer spending*. After their death it had simply not occurred to her to shop. While she'd been at the palace all her clothes had been paid for by the Sheikh—and she had discovered that a very generous salary had been paid into her bank account during those years.

So why shouldn't she splurge a bit? Chainstore dresses weren't exactly going to break the bank, were they?

And Jane was like a child who had been let loose in a dressing-up box.

'Try this!'

'No! I can't—scarlet is not my colour,' protested Sorrel.

'How do you know until you've tried it?'

How indeed? To Sorrel's surprise, Jane was right— not only did scarlet suit her, but the little cotton sundress looked rather good when teamed with some clashing orange beads. It was the last thing she would have worn in Kharastan—but surely that was a good thing? New life, she reminded herself. New woman.

In the end she bought four dresses, a denim mini-skirt, and some cool tops—some with teeny spaghetti

straps and others with no straps at all—and a pair of ver-
tiginous wedge sandals which made her legs look
almost indecently long.

'You'll get a chance to show them off tonight,' said
Jane.

Sorrel blinked. Had she missed something? 'What's
happening tonight?' she asked.

'You are,' said Jane firmly. 'I'm not asking any questions, since you obviously don't want to talk about it,
but I can tell just by looking at you that you're trying
to get over *some bloke*—the only way to do that is to
find another one, and that's exactly what we're going
to do!'

Sorrel's first impulse was to recoil in horror at the
very suggestion. To protest that finding a man was the
last thing on her mind—until she began to worry that
maybe there was something *wrong* with her. There must
be—if she was objecting so strongly. In twenty-five
years she had *never* had a boyfriend—never even kissed
a man—and how sad was that? But there were some
things you didn't confide—and, much as she liked Jane,
that was one of them.

She needed to break the cycle of emotional depen-
dence on the man whose affection for her was based on
his obligation as her guardian.

Swallowing down her panic, she nodded. 'Where
will we go?'

'The wine bar. Tonight—at seven.'

Sorrel got ready, feeling mixed up and a fraud—but
knowing that she should be experiencing the sense of

excitement she suspected most other women her own
age would be feeling if they were wearing brand-new
clothes to go for a carefree night out on a hot summer
evening. But she felt as if she was outside her own
body, looking at herself with the detached eye of an
interested observer instead of being the participant.

Part of her was aware that the itsy-bitsy floaty blue
dress looked good, and that her blonde hair had never
looked so pale or so shiny as it cascaded down her back
to her waist. And that her tanned brown legs did look
so flattering—especially when she wore them with
open-toe sandals which showed off her dazzling
pedicure.

There was an extraordinary moment when she
walked into the crowded wine bar and every head
turned in her direction. She looked behind her—
thinking that someone famous must have followed her
in. But, no, they were looking at *her*.

'Why is everyone staring?' she hissed at Jane,
rubbing her finger underneath first one eye and then the
other—in case her supposedly smudge-proof mascara
hadn't lived up to the extravagant claims made on the
packet.

'Oh, come *on*!' reprimanded her friend acidly. 'You
look a knockout—that's why. Charlie—get Sorrel a
drink, will you?'

Sorrel accepted the glass of white wine Charlie
pushed into her hand and took a sip. And here was
another problem. Alcohol was not taken freely in
Kharastan—although it was always provided in the

palace for foreign dignitaries. But Sorrel had only ever tasted champagne at the royal weddings of Xavier and Giovanni—Malik's two half-brothers—and she hadn't been mad about it. It had made her feel a bit too dreamy on two dangerously romantic occasions, and she had looked up and found Malik glaring at her and had hastily put the glass down.

Well, not any more! Why shouldn't she have a drink like any other person in the civilised world? It wasn't as if she was knocking it back—not like some of Jane's friends.

But a couple of large glasses of rough wine bar plonk was having a profound effect on a someone who wasn't used to drinking and who hadn't eaten anything since lunchtime. The wine bar had started to get hot and stuffy, with smoke drifting in from outside, where all the smokers were gathered, and Sorrel felt herself swaying slightly.

'You okay?' questioned Jane.

'I need to eat something,' said Sorrel woozily.

'Yeah. Me, too. Tell you what—let's get a curry and take it back to your place.'

It seemed churlish to object—especially when Jane had gone out of her way to help her buy clothes—and Sorrel didn't even protest when several of the others they'd been talking to decided to tag along. They seemed a nice, if slightly noisy bunch, and she was going to have to learn about entertaining sooner or later, wasn't she?

In the end, twelve people stumbled into her beautiful flat and took silver cartons of curry into the kitchen—ladling out heaps of yellow rice and chicken in shiny sauces and great wodges of bread. There weren't enough plates to go round, so some people were eating out of cereal dishes and pouring wine into mugs. After they'd eaten someone found a non-stop music station on the radio—and what Sorrel would have loosely described as dancing began.

Jane was swaying with her arms locked around someone whose name Sorrel thought was Scott, though she couldn't be sure, and then another couple flopped down onto one of the sofas and began kissing quite openly. Sorrel started wishing that everyone would leave so that she could go to bed. And what was that sickly sweet smell of the smoke drifting in from the balcony when she had most definitely said that there was to be no smoking?

It should have been wonderful—especially as outside the uncurtained windows the moon was beginning to illuminate the sky with a pale terracotta sheen. But it was the opposite of wonderful—particularly when Scott stumbled up to Sorrel and tried to pull her into his arms.

'Come and dance with me,' he mumbled.

'I can't... Scott, will you please let go? I happen to be holding a plate of curry—' And then the doorbell rang, and Sorrel felt a mixture of relief and alarm at its piercing shrill—relief because it meant that she could extricate herself from Scott's arms, and alarm because she wasn't expecting anyone. She didn't *know* anyone.

Apart from the landlord!

Heart pounding, and a chilly, clammy feeling in her hands, Sorrel put the plate down and made her way out into the hall. When she pulled the door open her knees threatened to give way.

Because there—with a small phalanx of bodyguards standing clustered around him—stood the formidable and disapproving figure of Malik.

CHAPTER THREE

FOR a moment Malik and Sorrel just stood staring at one another, and for a couple of moments longer she almost didn't recognise the Sheikh, yet wasn't sure why. But there was no time to deal with that—not when she was having to confront the burning look of rage which sizzled black fire from his angry eyes. His narrowed gaze was sweeping over her dishevelled appearance, and she realised what a sight she must make.

'What is *this*?' he choked, in a disbelieving voice she had never heard him use before.

'Malik—'

But he silenced her with an imperious wave of his hand and a terse command made in Kharastani as he glanced over her shoulder to the scene behind and flinched as if someone had punched him.

'What is this scene of utter *debauchery*?' he iced, in disgust.

He didn't seem to want a reply to his question, because he uttered a few more terse commands in his native tongue and the burly-looking men who were with him moved quickly into the apartment and took control.

It was like watching a team of soldiers going into enemy territory, Sorrel thought weakly, as she watched one of the guards march over to the radio and silence it. With the cessation of music everyone in the room froze, and then stared in disbelief at the group of dark-skinned men with black eyes and a shimmer of strength about them which seemed so at odds with the men who were partying.

'What the hell?' Scott lurched over towards Sorrel, and she wanted to yell at him to stop, to go away—to not let himself be annihilated by Malik's strength and power.

'Want a hand, baby?' he slurred.

Sorrel could feel the disgust emanating from every pore of Malik's impressive frame as he stepped into the hallway.

'Get rid of him,' he bit out.

She knew that there was no point in arguing with him, and she hoped that Scott and company would have the sense to realise the same.

'*Now!*' Malik roared.

Scott scuttled away like an insect who had just been revealed beneath a stone.

'Can you all go, please?' urged Sorrel quickly, and she could see that they needed no second bidding as they scurried round to find handbags and shawls which had been deposited around the flat, and then started trooping out.

Only the couple standing smoking the sickly sweet substance on the balcony seemed oblivious to the uproar in the apartment, and Malik's eyes narrowed in their direction before he nodded briefly to one of his guards.

If she hadn't already been panicking about just what Malik would do when the flat was emptied, it would have been almost comic, thought Sorrel, as she watched the guard striding towards them, whereupon he plucked the joint from the woman's fingers and crushed it between his own.

'Call the police!' ordered Malik imperiously.

'Malik, no, please—'

'You have been *taking drugs*?' he hissed.

'No!'

'Drinking, then?'

'Two or three glasses, that is all.'

'All?' With an effort Malik steadied himself, sucking in a deep draught of air and only just preventing himself from hauling her into his arms and…and… He watched as the last of the pathetic-looking men shuffled sheepishly from the flat, and then he barked out an order to his guards. In a daze, Sorrel watched as they too disappeared—until it was just her and Malik alone in the flat.

'Shut the door,' he said softly.

'Malik—'

'I said, shut the door.'

There was something in his tone which was making her feel quite peculiar but it was also a tone which broached no argument—and at that precise moment Sorrel felt about sixteen again.

Until she looked into the dark mastery of his eyes and realised that he had never looked at her like *that* when she was sixteen—with a combination of simmering fury and something else which she didn't dare start to analyse, because it was only threatening to make her light-headedness worse.

So she closed the door and then stood looking up at him, a hopeful expression on her face. Maybe he had finished venting his wrath, and now that he had would quietly forgive her.

But there was no forgiveness on the dark, rugged face with its alluring shadows cast by his amazing bone structure—nor in the almost fevered glitter of his ebony eyes. His features were set in a stony mask, and then Sorrel realised what it was about him which had made him look so different when she'd first opened the door.

He was wearing a suit!

Sorrel swallowed. She had never seen him wearing anything other than his traditional robes—which seemed less like clothes and more like an extension of him—and this new and different Malik took a little getting used to. Somehow it made her feel uncomfortable to look at him in such traditionally Western clothing, and at first she couldn't quite work out why.

The pale grey trousers did not exactly cling to the hard sinew of his legs, but they certainly emphasised the muscular length of his thighs—just as the jacket highlighted the broad shoulders and torso, tapering to a narrow waist and hips.

An open-necked shirt gave her the faintest glimpse

of a whorl of crisp black hair at his chest, and Sorrel felt faint as she realised just what it was that was making her feel so uncomfortable—the Western clothes accentuated his masculinity in a way which his Kharastani robes never had. Those merely *hinted* at the body which lay beneath—but now, for the first time ever, she could actually *see* it.

'Look at you,' he said softly, and Sorrel's eyes widened—for it seemed that he was as taken aback by *her* appearance as she was by his. Was he actually going to compliment her? she wondered, as she heard that husky note in his voice. But from the oblique look in his black eyes it was impossible to tell.

He let his gaze rake over her—slowly—in a way he had never done before. But then she had never provided him with the inclination to. Yet the outfit she wore tonight virtually screamed *Look at me*!—so who could blame him if he did?

It was not a Sorrel he recognised—in a dress that skimmed her tanned thighs, which gleamed faintly like oiled silk, and beneath the filmy fabric he could see the lush movement of her breasts. The shimmer of her hair—like pale, spun gold—cascaded in a gleaming waterfall down her back. But it was not simply the blatant display of her body which had made him stare at her in disbelief—but the make-up which so marred her beauty.

Yes, the sweep of black mascara curving her long lashes made her blue eyes look enormous in her heart-shaped face, and the gleam of lipstick made the petal-softness of her lips even more provocative. But where was her innocent beauty gone?

Had it gone?

Malik felt his heart slam against his ribcage, and a feeling halfway between rage and despair as he moved his face closer to hers.

'So, did you achieve your aim, Sorrel?' he questioned unsteadily.

What riddle was this he was testing her with? Sorrel wondered. But she wanted to do something—any-thing—to remove that obdurate look of anger from his face, and so she played along.

'What aim?' she questioned back.

The slam of his heart increased. 'Did you dress like a...*tramp* in order to lose your virginity to the first man who would take you?'

Lose her *virginity*? Sorrel swayed. Only this time it had nothing to do with the wine but with sheer, disbeliev-ing anguish that Malik could utter such damning words of criticism against her and look at her with such contempt.

Fiercely, she bit her lip, and the self-inflicted pain brought her up sharply—what *right* did he have to chastise her in such a way? He had been her guardian, yes, and a remarkably good one for many years. But the years had now passed and his little bird had flown the nest—and she would not be insulted like that for behaving just as any other young woman of the same age would do.

'I am *not* dressed like a tramp!' she defended.

'Really? That is a matter of opinion.' He saw the way
her breasts jiggled when she moved—like some
damned belly dancer! Controlling his angry breathing
only with a monumental effort, he flicked her a disdainful look. 'And you haven't answered my question!'

She stared at him and he stared back, a silent
exchange going on between their clashing gazes—his
black and accusing and hers indignantly blue. But she
was damned if he thought he could quiz her about her
innocence. 'And neither do I intend to!'

He sucked in an outraged breath. Did her refusal
mean an admission of guilt? But he could not force her
to answer—and certainly not when she was standing
there wearing…'Just go and change your clothes,
Sorrel.'

For a moment she really thought she had misheard
him.

'I'm sorry?'

'No, Sorrel—it is too late for apologies,' he ground
out.

This was even worse! 'I wasn't *apologising*!' she
spluttered. 'I just can't believe this is happening. You
storm in here, asking me personal questions, and then
you order me to get changed—as if I'm a five-year-old
who has spilt paint on her overalls!'

Oh, that she *was* five years old again—she would not
be in a position to defy him! What a stupid little fool she
was being, he thought furiously. Did she not realise her
bare legs and tiny skirt were making him want to…to…?
Appalled at the progress of his thoughts, he swallowed.

'Do not play games with me, Sorrel,' he said unevenly. 'Don't you realise the power a woman has over a man when she puts her body on display? Is that what you want? For me to have difficulty concentrating on what I have come to say to you since you are dressed—or rather *un*dressed...' deliberately, he tempered his words '...in such a provocative manner.'

Sorrel blinked. Was Malik actually admitting that he had *noticed* her? Yet could she blame him for his censure? He was judging her by Kharastani standards, which were far stricter than any she had found here, and to be honest the dress was a little short—she had thought so earlier, only Jane had persuaded her otherwise and Sorrel had let her.

For the first time since he had walked in she bowed her head very slightly, in respect of his title and his status. 'Very well,' she said quietly. 'I will go and put on something more...*suitable*—if you would like to make yourself at home, Malik?' It was only as she left the room that she realised what a ridiculous thing it had been to say. As if this was anything *like* his home—the palace.

Once she had gone Malik relaxed—freed from the unexpected physical temptation which the sight of her had dramatically provoked. He shook his dark head, briefly perplexed—a state that did not sit readily or easily with him—but just as quickly the sensation vanished. It must have been caused by tiredness—by the unremitting weight of duties which had fallen upon him. And yet...

Unseen by the eyes which usually followed him, Malik allowed his tongue to flick over his lips, moistening their dryness, and then wished he had not—for the action made his body ache. Fiercely he tried to wipe out the image of Sorrel standing there in front of him, all legs and breasts and flowing silken hair—but it wasn't easy.

In his mind she had always been a child, and then a vivacious teenager. She had somehow made a seamless and unseen transition into womanhood, almost without his noticing. The robes she usually wore had helped disguise her very attributes, of course—and wasn't that one of their functions? Not to put unnecessary temptation in the way of men?

He could not be seen with a woman who looked that way, he realised, and for a moment he questioned the advisability of the proposal he was about to make to her. Yes, she had acceded to his request that she put on something more suitable—but what if that was a one-off? What if Sorrel had already embraced her new freedoms with a passion—what if she had changed and moved beyond the behaviour expected of those who associated with the Sheikh of Kharastan?

Malik sighed. It was yet another example of how much was different since he had found out about the accident of birth which had suddenly transformed him from high-ranking royal aide to ruler of a vast and affluent desert nation—with all the joys and burdens which went hand-in-hand with such a responsibility.

His late father, Zahir, had enjoyed a long, dynastic

marriage, but his wife had been unable to bear him
children. Many in Zahir's position would have taken
another wife—instead he had taken lovers, each of
whom had borne him a child. His youngest son, Xavier,
was half-French. Giovanni was half-Italian. Only
Malik, the oldest, was of pure and true Kharastani
blood—his mother a noblewoman who had died in
childbirth.

Malik had been a lonely, motherless child who had
become the Sheikh's right-hand aide. Yet he had been
denied a father—for the momentous discovery of his
lineage had come too late for him to enjoy a relationship with the man who had sired him.

Yet as he glanced around the apartment he acknowledged that his solitude had helped to forge his character—to make him the man he was today. In reality,
there could have been no better training for the role of
king—for to rule was to exist in isolation from other
men.

And women.

He walked through into the kitchen, and for a
moment he studied the debris there as an archaeologist
might study the ruins of some unknown civilisation he
had stumbled upon. What lay before Malik now was a
scene completely outside his experience.

Food lay congealed in silver containers—some of it
spattered on the surfaces—and half-empty bottles stood
in warm puddles of beer. In his country food—even
when it was simple—was always served with a certain
amount of ceremony and respect. Fine wines would ac-

company meals, if requested, but Kharastani subjects tended to prefer the juice of a pomegranate mixed with crushed limes and mulberries and a spoonful of honey—the beloved concoction which was known as *labbas*.

His eyes flicked to where a spoonful of rice lay co-agulating on the side. And now Malik's lips curved with distaste—never in Kharastan would there be such an undignified mess daring to masquerade as entertainment.

Was this what Sorrel had wished for when she'd demanded to leave Kharastan? This the destiny she followed—the dream she chased? This casual and rather depressing sight of excess combined with little elegance or formality?

Abruptly he turned away and walked back into the large sitting room—though he did not put any of the lamps on. The windows were open to the world, and his bodyguards would have a fit if he did—and besides, it was strangely soothing to look at the room in the moon-light. At least here he could see a certain amount of beauty—mainly provided by the living backdrop of the sea directly opposite. Moonlight danced on the little waves, making them silver and slick. And the sea was the sea….as fundamentally beautiful here in Brighton as it was by the shores of his beloved Balsora where as a child he had learnt to swim—as slippery and as agile as an eel.

He sighed, lost in the non-threatening landscape of the past—where all the rough corners of authenticity could be rubbed away with a little help from the imagination—until a soft and familiar voice broke into his thoughts.

'Malik?'

He turned then, and the breath caught in his throat—like dust.

For Sorrel was standing before him—looking at once like Sorrel, and yet not like her at all. Gone were the over-short dress and the high-heeled shoes which had made her look so outrageously available. Now her shapely body was covered—not with the familiar robes of Kharastan, but with Western clothes which served the purpose almost as well.

A ruffled skirt fell to the ground, worn with some kind of T-shirt—but unlike her traditional garb this top hugged her lush young breasts, emphasising their thrusting curve in a way which was making him hard.

He bit back his despair at the effect her appearance was having on him—aware that this was *his* problem, not Sorrel's, and accepting that perhaps it was time he turned his mind to the delights of the flesh. Not with *her*, naturally, but with someone beautiful and willing and eager to be his lover—someone who would make no demands on him in any way. Because he had allowed pleasure to become a distant memory. He had done nothing but work, he recognised now, ever since the solemn glory of his coronation day. No wonder there had been a chink in his armour—allowing inappropriate thoughts of Sorrel to surface.

Since his accession he had not dared to relax—not

for a single moment—afraid that he would be found
wanting by a people still reeling from their beloved
Sheikh's death and the colourful reality of his private
life! And neither had he wanted to fail—to let his people
down in any way—so he had put everything into taking
over the formidable reins of his kingship.

It was not the kind of role you could ever really be
prepared for—no matter how well you knew how the
'job' functioned. Because it was far more than just a
job—it was a complete and all-consuming way of life,
and it was one which required the very definite stamp
of his personality to make it uniquely his. No wonder
there had been no time to think of women....

'Is this better?' asked Sorrel softly.

Much better, he wanted to purr, and then, with the
iron-hard resolve which had made his enemies and
admirers alike dub him Malik the Steely, he let his dark
lashes flutter down to partially conceal the hectic glitter
in his eyes.

'Is there a room which isn't overlooked?' he
demanded. 'Somewhere more private?'

Sorrel's heart began to race—because wasn't this a
desire she had nurtured since as long as she could
remember? Of the forgiving shadows of the night, with
only the romantic glowing disc of a huge moon outside,
and Malik there, with her. Only him, and only her...

Yet she was scared. Terrified, even—and her
stomach was contracting with the aching conviction
that this was what she wanted.

'Malik?' she breathed uncertainly. 'Are you sure?'

'Of course I am sure!' Malik frowned. 'You suggest that we conduct this talk in a room which brazenly omits to have drapes at its vast windows? Allowing time for some sniper to take a pot-shot at me?'

Thank heavens for the dim light which hid her blush of shame from him. How could she have got it so very wrong?

'Oh, Malik,' she whispered, and her heart turned over as she thought of the selfish nature of her thoughts when compared to the mortal danger at which he hinted. Was that how shallow and selfish she had become? 'Is that...*likely*, then?'

He gave an impatient shake of his dark head. 'It is not a *probability*,' he said shortly. 'But it is always a *possibility*.' And besides, a slightly scaremongering tactic might help click her onto another kind of wavelength—one which could entertain all kinds of scenarios which simply would not have happened if they had been on home territory, back in Kharastan. Because she needed to think differently if she was to be part of his plan.

A plan about which he had still mentioned nothing!

'Please,' she said quickly. 'I know where we can go.'

Having demanded somewhere more private, he could now hardly back out of it—but he prayed that it was not a bedroom. To his relief and perplexity, it was not.

'The bathroom?' he questioned in disbelief, as she snapped on a switch which illuminated a circle of lightbulbs set in theatrical style around a mirror.

'I know it isn't....conventional.'

'You can say that again,' said Malik faintly, but for
the first time in weeks a brief smile curved his lips.

'But look—it's windowless. Unobserved.' And she
needed to repair the damage of earlier, to put their relationship back in its proper box. To try to convince
herself that it felt as easy and as relaxed with him as it
used to.

'Yes. So it is.' Malik looked around, taking in the
clutter of the room, aware with a sudden poignant pang
that this feminine intimacy—which would be the habitat
of most men, once they married—would never be his.
He let his keen gaze commit the whole scene to
memory—all the bottles lining the windowsill, along
with candles and a curved glass jar of something
coloured green which he assumed was destined for her
bath.

Her bath.

Malik swallowed as once again he was haunted by
that insistent pulse—beating relentlessly at his temple
and now throbbing deep within his groin, too. Why the
hell had she brought him in *here*?

Because she was following his orders!

And it was time he assumed the upper hand.

'I cannot talk in here,' he snapped—his sweeping
hand movement managing to convey his disdain and incredulity that he had ever allowed himself to be lured
into such an unsuitable setting in the first place. 'Have
you eaten?'

Food had been the very last thing on her mind, and

in truth she hadn't had a thing—mainly because he had burst in with all his guards before she'd managed to get a forkful of curry into her mouth. Sorrel shook her head, and Malik slid a phone from his pocket, punched out a number and issued a curt directive to the person who answered immediately.

'Bring the car round, would you?' he said, his black eyes fixed to her face. 'And reserve a table for two for dinner.'

CHAPTER FOUR

SORREL had forgotten what it was like to be a part of royal life—to be whisked along by its smooth and efficient machinery. There were never any blips when you were with a king—or if there were, then you were shielded and protected from them.

Cars turned up when they were supposed to, and no traffic jams ever impeded progress—since roads were cleared just to make the journey trouble-free. Planes took off on time, trains ran to within seconds of their predicted timetables, and tables in restaurants magically became available at a moment's notice—no matter how exclusive the eatery, nor how crowded.

At the exact moment that Sorrel and Malik stepped out of her apartment block, a limousine with tinted windows slid to a halt. It moved with all the importance and weight of a heavily bullet-proofed vehicle, and of course it demonstrated to Sorrel the downside of a privileged and royal life.

Sorrel hadn't put up any objections when Malik had 'suggested' they eat out—not just because her stomach was empty, but because she knew it would be pointless to argue with him when he was in this kind of mood. And perhaps because she could see his point, that the ruler of Kharastan could not be expected to have an un-chaperoned conversation in a single woman's bath-room!

He still hadn't given her any clues about what it was he wished to say to her.

'So what's this talk you want to have with me?' she asked, forcing a casual note into her voice that she was far from feeling as she slid onto the car seat next to him.

Malik's black eyes glittered her a warning. Had she always spoken to him so freely, he wondered, or had he simply forgotten? Certainly there was no other person than Sorrel in his court who would have dared address him in such a blasé manner. And since she had left Kharastan he seemed to have become aware of the starchy formality of his life as never before.

Yet he was momentarily distracted by the faint outline of her leg through the filmy material of her skirt, and the subtle fragrance of the perfume she wore, and he leant back against the soft leather of the seat so that he could avert his gaze without appearing to do so. 'I do not intend to discuss it here and now,' he cautioned coolly. 'You must wait until we get to the restaurant.'

Oh, *must* she? Once she might have bristled at the rather *pompous* way he was speaking to her, but Sorrel was still feeling unsettled—as much by the way he had been looking at her back there as by the unexpectedness of his appearance. And now they

were closeted together in the back of a limousine and
suddenly it felt *different*. Awkward. As if the old ease
which had always existed between them had somehow been obliterated and replaced with something
darker—something she didn't recognise and wasn't
sure she wanted to.

Swallowing down her nerves, she started to make
conversation, as she had done innumerable times with
visiting diplomats to the palace, but never with Malik.
'So where are we going?' she asked, because talking
distracted her from the awareness of his male heat and
his hair, which gleamed like the wing of the Black Kite
which flew so powerfully over the desert sands.

'Does it matter?' he queried carelessly.

'Bet it's the Etoile de la Mer,' she hazarded, and
then, in answer to his questioning look. 'It's the best
hotel in Brighton.'

'You have visited it before, perhaps?'

She hesitated, wondering if she could possibly
convey how different her life here was from the privileged existence she'd enjoyed in Kharastan. 'Hardly. It
isn't really in my price league.'

'No? I'm sure that there must be a queue of men
eager to take you out for an expensive supper, Sorrel,'
he murmured silkily.

His soft words made it abundantly clear what he
thought those men might be granted as a reward for
such an expensive supper, and Sorrel was conscious of
his insulting implication. Yet she was also aware that it
would be an unforgivable breach of protocol to risk the

driver hearing her snap back a comment at the Sheikh, and so she merely allowed her mouth to curve into an enigmatic smile.

'Yes,' she agreed dreamily. 'A queue that stretches right round the block and back again.'

'This is true?' he hissed.

The look she sent him was one of pure challenge, sparking blue from her eyes. 'Wait until we get to the restaurant,' she retorted softly, replicating his own words. 'I do not intend to discuss it here and now.'

There was a short and disbelieving pause as he registered her insolence, and Malik felt his blood on fire with an unfamiliar heat. He felt himself hardening beneath his robes, cursing the sweet-painful throb of desire, and silently cursed that it had been Sorrel who had brought him to such a point and at such an inconvenient time.

If it had been any other woman he would have slipped his hand beneath her skirt. Would have tapped sharply on the driver's window and alerted him to the fact that he had changed his mind. That he was no longer hungry. Well, not for food. But it was not any other woman. It was...

'Malik!'

Her soft voice broke into his erotic thoughts and he knew that he must take control before he did something unforgivable—like kiss her.

'Yes?' he snapped.

How moody he could be, Sorrel thought. And what a timely reminder that it might hurt a bit—sometimes more than others—but ultimately it was better to be out of his life and living her own on the other side of the world from him.

'We're here.'

The limo had drawn up outside a hotel and it was as Sorrel had predicted—for the sign outside read Etoile de la Mer.

'Bravo, Sorrel!' he applauded softly.

As the name suggested, the Etoile de la Mer was situated overlooking the sea—the kind of venue which played host to visiting politicians and stars who performed at the local theatres. A minor member of the British royal family had been conducting an extramarital affair for many years within its luxurious walls. It was discreet, luxurious, and very expensive.

Outside, it was unremarkable only in its quiet restraint. Two perfectly clipped bay trees stood sentry, and several burly-looking doorman with calculating eyes stood beside the revolving door, ready to keep the unwanted away.

Inside, however, it was apparent why the Etoile de la Mer had achieved a small fame of its own. The view from the restaurant itself was simply breathtaking—a stunning sweep of the English Channel, whose watery-smooth surface reflected the moonlight.

Malik's people had obviously been hard at work before their arrival, and Sorrel knew that the intention would have been to ensure the maximum security with the least fuss. Few inside the restaurant would realise who had just walked in—until after the Sheikh had been ushered to the best, most carefully shielded table in the room.

Even if they *were* noticed it was doubtful whether they would be disturbed. Restaurants like this counted on their clientele being well-connected and famous enough to be diplomatic about their fellow-guests—certainly not crass enough to slip out to the restroom to telephone the gossip column of one of the national newspapers and announce that Sheikh Malik of Kharastan was dining alone with a blonde!

Waiting to greet them was Rafiq—one of Malik's closest aides and a man known to Sorrel since childhood, for he had often advised her father on Kharastani policy. He must now be in his late forties, she decided—but her instinctively friendly smile of greeting froze in her face when it was met with a perfunctory cool nod from the learned Kharastani advisor.

'How are you, Sorrel?' he enquired with heavy formality, as if he had met her only minutes before.

'I am well, thank you,' she returned faintly.

'If you will allow me to show you to your table, Highness?' said Rafiq in soft, rapid Kharastani—presumably so that he would not be understood by the Maître d', who had just materialised by his side with a look of barely restrained excitement. 'I have organised everything to your pleasure.'

They moved towards their table, and unexpectedly Sorrel blinked in surprise as she caught sight of herself in one of the mirrors which reflected the sea back into the room. Her rose-pink T-shirt and flouncy gipsy skirt were just about presentable enough for a place like this—though they certainly did not carry the expected price-tag for a royal dining companion—but it was her expression which momentarily startled her. The way her eyes looked like giant blue saucers in the pale-gold of her face and her lips formed a rather anxious-looking 'O' shape.

Was that because she was nervous of Malik and what he was about to say to her—or because she had never been more glaringly aware of how tall and dynamic he looked? How the fluid cut of his very Western suit seemed to emphasise his dark beauty, the dark olive of his skin and the sensual promise of his hard, muscular body.

Two waiters appeared as if by clockwork to pull their chairs back, and menus were brought, dealt with and dispatched again—the wine list imperiously waved away and the waiter hurriedly sent to bring back a selection of soft drinks for the Sheikh to choose from.

Fariq, too, had melted away, and Sorrel folded her hands in her lap, like an obedient child—though in her case it was to prevent Malik from seeing how much they were trembling. And no wonder. It wasn't easy, sitting opposite him like this and trying not to drink in the pleasure of looking at the high, angled slant of his cheekbones and the lush black lashes which shielded the glitter of his eyes. Her heart was pounding as if she had been running in a race, and she knew that she had to pull herself together.

'So, Malik?' she said slowly.

For a moment he said nothing. He had learned to bide his time. To wait for the precise moment to strike. Just as the falcon did when it floated seamlessly on a warm current of desert air...circling, circling...until its prey was foolishly lulled into believing that it was safe.

And then it pounced.

He studied her face dispassionately. Her lips were parted, so that he could just make out the moist gleam of her tongue through tiny white teeth, and he found himself having to swallow down a sudden thickness which was threatening to constrict his throat.

And suddenly it was not so easy to think strategy. To think like the falcon. He was thinking like a man, and it was not appropriate—not with Sorrel. For the first time since he had conceived the idea he began to question it. And yet what was he, if not a man of strength and resolve? If he was sexually frustrated then he would take a temporary lover—and it would not be the flaxen-haired innocent who sat before him so expectantly.

'Do you ever miss Kharastan?' he asked.

Sorrel hesitated, but she knew that she had to answer this one truthfully—because anything else would be a betrayal of all the love and affection she had for his home. 'Yes, I miss it,' she said quietly. 'I feel like there is an empty space in my heart sometimes.'

He suppressed his sigh of triumph. 'And you enjoy your job here in Brighton?' he queried with a careless air, as if it didn't matter, but Sorrel knew that Malik never wasted words.

'It's okay,' she said truthfully. 'Very different to what I was doing at the palace, of course!'

'So I understand,' he said coldly. 'It seems that you

cater for the needs of backpackers.' He bit the last word
out as if it were poison.

Sorrel felt that she ought to stand up for the great
majority who didn't live in palaces. 'We have a varied
clientele,' she said primly, 'who just want to see a different side of things.'

'It is not the kind of job which has any future,' he
accused.

She considered this—knowing that it was pointless
saying something she didn't mean, because the razor-
tongued Malik would slice through her argument like
a knife through a ripe melon. 'Not long-term, no,' she
admitted.

He lifted his glass to his lips and sipped some soda,
and then put it back down again, his eyes never leaving
her face. 'I don't want you working there any more,' he
stated flatly. 'I want you to accompany me on my
European tour instead.'

Her heart was pounding beneath her breast, but bizarrely Sorrel's initial reaction to Malik's suggestion
was indignation that he had said it in the tone of
someone who was marshalling his troops. I *want*, he
had said. An order, not a request. She guessed there was
a difference between *want* and *like*, but Malik had never
had to worry about the most diplomatic way of asking
for something. What Malik wanted, Malik got.

Playing for time, she stared at him. 'And why on
earth should you want me to do that?'

He thought he must have misheard her. 'Why?' he
echoed. 'You dare to ask me *why*?'

'That's right.'

Malik frowned. He was used to acquiescence. Subservience. She had already got her way over this ridiculous request to find independence in England—and even though he had been forced to rescue her from that disreputable crowd it seemed that she had still not learnt her lesson. While sometimes he might think to himself that it was tedious never to be challenged—he now realised that he might have been mistaken. When would she learn that he was *always* right?

'Is it not enough that your Sheikh commands it?' he queried softly.

For a moment she didn't respond—because, despite his unashamedly autocratic tone, Sorrel was woman enough to thrill to that masterful entreaty. Yet it's *wrong* to react like that to his arrogance, she reminded herself. You know it is.

'Not really, Malik. No.'

For a moment he thought that she was joking—why else would she even hesitate over the opportunity he was offering her?

'You mean you are turning down my offer?' he demanded, outraged that she should even try.

For the first time since they'd walked in Sorrel smiled—for this was Malik at his predictable best. How black and white he always made everything seem! But wasn't that always the way of Kharastani men, and of the ruling class in particular? This went some way towards explaining why Fariq had behaved so frostily towards her—she doubted that he approved of Malik's wish to have her by his side.

'Do you consider me an intelligent woman?' she mused.

'Intelligent?' His eyes glittered as they surveyed her. 'You were not showing much evidence of it in your apartment earlier, with that bunch of—' His lips curled in derision. '*Drunks.*'

'Is that a yes or a no, Malik?'

Malik stared at her cool blue eyes. She had taken a First in Middle-Eastern studies at Kumush Ay University, and had been offered a research post there—nobody could deny that she had a brain and that she could use it. But having a brain was different from having common sense. 'Yes,' he admitted grudgingly—although he could not see what bearing this had on his original request.

'*Thank* you,' she said sarcastically. 'Just as I think of you as an intelligent man.'

'Why, thank *you*!' he returned, and for the first time in a long time Malik realised that he was enjoying himself—he was impatient for the waiter to deposit the plates of fine seafood and the raspberry cocktails on the table, so that he could continue with this verbal sparring which was so rare for a man in his position.

'So if I were ever to offer you some kind of position in *my* life, as an intelligent man I would expect you to ask me all kinds of questions about it before you agreed to take it.'

Malik stared at her in amazement. 'All that to make a point, Sorrel?' he queried faintly.

Sorrel shook her head. 'All that to try and make you see *my* point of view,' she corrected. 'So, will you please tell me what it is you want of me?'

For one moment he very nearly told her—until he pulled himself together, reminding himself that it was the frisson of their disagreement which had renewed this terrible sexual aching. Malik found himself glaring at her, as if she had aroused him deliberately. Did he still want her help? he wondered. Was it worth risking?

But then his mind leapt ahead as he envisaged the whistlestop tour his advisors had worked out for him, and he knew that, yes, it was.

He inclined his dark head slightly. 'I want you behind the scenes, helping me—just as you used to help my father, the Sheikh.'

'But you have proper advisors to do that,' objected Sorrel.

How could he begin to explain that the formal and older Fariq and his younger but equally formal assistants were like robots? That the thought of major cities—even Paris, which he had once visited as an impressionable boy on the cusp of manhood—no longer held any allure for him. Not now. It would be all signing papers and starchy meetings. Although surrounded by hordes of people eager to accede to his every whim, he would be alone in the truest sense of the word.

'Yes,' he said, more heavily than he had intended to—and then his black eyes narrowed slightly, as if he had shown her an unexpected chink in his defences that she might store up to use against him. But Sorrel was not a manipulator—she did not have enough experience of the world to have learnt *how* to manipulate—and wasn't that one of the reasons he wanted her with him? 'I am not expecting you to suddenly take on the role of political advisor,' he said testily.

'Well, what *would* my role be?'

Malik thought about it. 'As a kind of social companion,' he said carefully.

'Which sounds like the kind of post you might offer to a woman over fifty!' Sorrel stared at him. 'Would you mind elaborating, please?'

He tried and failed to think of another woman—or man, even—he would allow to get away with speaking to him in such a manner. 'I will have functions to attend. Long dinners. Cocktails. Afternoons at the races. Visits to museums. War memorials. It would lessen the burden considerably if I had someone I knew well to accompany me. Someone with whom I can discuss and assess afterwards.' He opened his eyes a fraction wider, like a cat which had just been awoken from a long sleep. 'Someone who can stop people from getting too close to me. Especially women.'

Sorrel ignored the implied boast, even though she felt a sudden stab of jealousy. 'A kind of gatekeeper, you mean?' she questioned coolly.

'Precisely.'

'Fariq could do that just as well.'

'Fariq isn't quite so easy on the eye.'

For a moment Sorrel didn't quite believe that she'd heard him properly. Malik, saying that she was *attrac-*

tive? She stared at him suspiciously. 'And what's that supposed to mean?'

Malik lowered his voice, even though they had both been speaking in Kharastani. 'Oh, come, come, Sorrel,' he murmured, mock-reprovingly. 'Don't be disingenuous—for it scorns the intelligence you hold so dear! Flaxen hair and blue eyes on a pretty and shapely young woman are the hallmarks of beauty, as well you know.'

Defiantly, she speared a seared scallop and ate it— partly to defuse her annoyance at his remarks and partly to give her time to answer a compliment which he had managed to make sound like an insult! Disingenuous, indeed! What did Malik know?

She might tick all the right boxes in attributes that men seemed to want—but the outside stuff had nothing to do with what was going on *inside*. And inside she was as mixed-up and as wobbly on self-esteem as the next woman. She'd had no real boyfriend. No lover to reassure her that she was gorgeous—though maybe she shouldn't be relying on a *man* to booster her feelings of self-worth. Maybe she should dig deep and find them within herself.

'So you want some arm-candy?' she questioned flippantly.

Malik scowled. 'Such a short time in England and already you are conversant with slang!' he accused.

'It's all part of my education to enter the modern world, Malik. I can't go on living in an ivory tower for ever.'

'And just how *comprehensive* an education are you seeking?' he enquired dangerously.

'Who knows?' She saw his eyes darken with rage, and with something else she didn't recognise—and suddenly Sorrel felt empowered by her own sense of freedom. 'That's my business,' she answered softly, and the words hung and shimmered on the air like morning dewdrops on the web of a spider.

'Mine also,' he said, and his words were equally soft.

Their eyes met—hers questioning the grim certainty in his.

'You think so?' she questioned.

'I know so! I cannot abandon a lifetime's habit and wash my hands of you as if you no longer exist,' he grated.

'Is that why you're offering me the post?' she demanded. 'So that you can keep your eye on me.'

'I can assure you that my motives are far more selfish than that, Sorrel.' He leaned forward just a little—so that she could see the black glitter of his eyes, as dark and as hard as jet itself. 'You could prove very useful to me on this trip—for you *know me* better than anyone.'

Once she would have agreed with him. He had not known the identity of his father until just before he died, and his mother had slipped away in childbirth—so, yes, during her growing up Sorrel had been close to him. But that had been before he had inherited the Kharastani crown—an event which now seemed so long ago that it was like a lifetime.

Yet it was only two years, she realised with a start.

Sorrel bit her lip as an immense wave of sadness washed over her—hating the inevitable changes which time had wrought.

What had he just said—that she could prove very *useful* to him? What a damning testimony *that* was. A bullet-proof car was *useful*, and so was soft pillow on which to place your weary head at night—but Sorrel would have hoped to have had a more flattering word than that applied to her. And that was where the trouble lay—she was a fool where Malik was concerned. Deep down she hankered after much more than he would ever be prepared to give her.

If took him up on his request—went with him to all his glamorous destinations—then wouldn't she just get sucked into his life once more? Only next time find it even harder to grab the courage to say goodbye?

'I notice that still you make me wait for your answer,' Malik observed slowly, but his eyes gleamed with the anticipation of a certain victory.

Grabbing all the pluck she possessed, Sorrel met the soft dark blaze of his eyes and steeled herself against its hypnotic beauty. 'I can't do it, Malik,' she whispered.

'Can't? Or won't?'

'Doesn't it amount to the same thing?'

A muscle began to work in his cheek. 'Would you mind telling me why?'

And Sorrel suddenly realised that she was going to have to come up with something about which there could be no argument—something he couldn't try to talk her out of. Something *true*—but something shocking. So that the Sheikh would regret ever having asked her. But she recognised as she opened her mouth to say the words that they would change his opinion of her—and damn her for ever in his fierce and puritanical eyes.

'Because I need a lover, Malik,' she said huskily. 'That's why.'

CHAPTER FIVE

FOR A MOMENT, Malik could not quite believe what he had heard—and he stared at her for a long and disbelieving moment. Sorrel—his sometimes feisty but always innocent ward—had just announced that she wanted a lover! Which was as inconceivable as the morning sun rising a sickly shade of green instead of its habitual gold.

'*What* did you say?' he questioned unevenly.

Never had Sorrel heard the Sheikh's voice sound so dangerous, so forbidding, so...*scary*. But she told herself that she was an adult—free to do as she wished—and she did not have to answer to *him*! Nevertheless, she backed away from actually repeating the words to the formidable presence who was seated opposite her, simmering with a quiet dark rage.

'You know what I said.'

'That you want a *lover*!' he sneered. 'How can this be?'

They were speaking in Kharastani, and their voices were so low that even the bodyguards seated a discreet distance away would not have heard what they were saying—but the venom in Malik's accusation must have carried across the room, because several of the well-heeled diners jerked their heads up and frowned, before tactfully returning their attention to their meals.

The accusation which burned angrily from his ebony eyes washed over her in a black fire, but Sorrel knew that she could not allow him to psychologically defeat her. She was a woman, for heaven's sake—not some little doll which was dressed up and brought out on state occasions. 'What's wrong with that?' she said, more airily than she felt inside.

'Wrong? *Wrong*?' Rarely had Malik remembered feeling such a raw and blinding rage. He wanted to lash out. He wanted…

His long olive fingers briefly flexed, made an even briefer claw-like shape, before clenching into tight and angry fists on the starched white linen tablecloth. Could it really be *Sorrel* who was saying this? Sorrel—his ward—the young ward he had watched over like a hawk. Sweet, flaxen-haired Sorrel, who'd used to run around the palace gardens—indulged by all who came across her sunny smile. Sorrel the innocent…the…

Or was that an assumption too far? Like the ones he had stupidly made about her unquestioning obedience and her loyalty to him as her Sheikh? Did her desire for a man to know her in such a way mean that she had already tasted the fruits of intimacy? Enjoyed the pleasures of the flesh in a way which had made her hungry for more? A shaft of something which felt like pain but which he put down to outrage caught him by the throat. She had denied it once, but that did not mean she had spoken the truth!

'You are no longer a virgin?' he demanded hoarsely.

Sorrel felt the stain of a blush flare up from the base of her throat to burn in tell-tale spots upon her cheeks. How bizarre that he felt he had the right to ask her something as intimately personal as this *in a restaurant*!

But didn't you ask for it? mocked a small voice in her head. *By stating your crass desire to find yourself a lover?*

Reminding herself that she *did* want to live like any other young woman, she stared at him.

'You've already asked me that, Malik.'

'And I am giving you the opportunity to retract your statement.'

'We are *not* in a court of law!' she stormed.

He ignored that, leaning across the table towards her. 'Do you speak the truth, Sorrel?' His black eyes bored into her. 'Are you still a virgin?'

Their eyes did furious battle—until Sorrel realised that it was a pointless one. What was the point of pretending an experience that was sadly lacking if it would damn her even further in his opinion?

'Yes,' she admitted. 'I am. And the one thing I am *not* is a liar, Malik!'

He was unprepared for the flame of triumph which blazed through him, surging in a heated stream through his veins, but he did not show it, merely sucked a still-angry breath in through his nostrils—like his most tem-

peramental stallion when he was thwarted. He must, he
realised, play this very carefully—for Sorrel was *not*
being obedient. Far from it. But she would be made to
bend to his will, without even comprehending that she
was doing so! He uttered a silent prayer of thanks,
without understanding why it should be so important
to him. Because it meant he would have failed in his
role as her guardian?

'So why the urge to change that state?' he questioned, in a cool voice which was a million miles away
from the inner turmoil of his feelings. But he was good
at disguising his feelings—as a child it had been a necessity, and as aide to the Sheikh he had quickly learned
that it was inappropriate to *have* feelings. And hadn't
that been the most invaluable training for his new
position? 'It sounds rather an *impetuous* decision,' he
drawled.

How cold his eyes. And how disapproving his demeanour, which had the power to make her feel like a
gauche young girl—or maybe that was his intention?
Suddenly Sorrel wanted him to hear the truth, not a
sanitised version of it told to protect the precious royal
ears.

'Because….because I'm twenty-five years old and
I feel like I've spent the whole of my live in a convent!'

'You mean you have been protected from the carnal
desires of men?' he elaborated savagely.

Sorrel licked her lips nervously. Had she been expecting such an angry response? The answer was that
she hadn't really thought it through properly.

'I mean that I want to live like other women of my age!' she declared. 'Or rather I want to *live*! I'm fed-up with conforming to other people's standards. I want to be able to show my legs without feeling that I'm breaking some kind of moral code, to dance late at night and drink alcohol, and...and...'

'And have sex?'

Why the hell was he making something which was perfectly healthy and normal sound so fundamentally wrong?

'What's wrong with that?' She sighed. 'Other women my age do.'

'Other women your age are not *you*.'

Sorrel shook her head in frustration. 'And just what is that, Malik—huh? Who *am* I? Someone who is like a stranger in her own country and yet can never fit into her adopted country.'

'Why not?' he questioned coolly.

'Because...because....' *Because I adore you and there can never be any future with you—and that's even if you had ever bothered to look at me as a woman rather than as someone who just fits in with your un-realistic wishes.* 'Because I can never have true independence in Kharastan.'

'And that is what you want? That is what matters to you? To wear the revealing clothes and have the sex?'

She had never heard him sound so...*foreign*... But then she had never seen him so het up before. And the truth was that these things were not really what she wanted—but what they represented. If she had carried on living in Kharastan then she would have spent all her youth and her life living in the shadow of a man who would one day marry another. And Sorrel knew that she couldn't have stood there and watched it happen.

Malik was so egotistical that it wouldn't even occur to him that it might hurt. Why, she could even imagine him thoughtlessly requesting that she help his new wife settle in—maybe even help with any progeny they might produce. And she couldn't do that—she really couldn't. It would rip her heart in two if she ever had to deal with Malik's beautiful black-eyed children by another woman.

'Maybe these things *do* matter,' Sorrel said, expecting another furious tirade—but to her surprise there was none. Just that narrow-eyed and considering look from those glitteringly intelligent eyes which those who knew Malik had learned to be wary of.

'And you think that if you accompanied me on my tour I would prevent you from doing these things?' he questioned.

Was he *kidding*? Or was it just one of Malik's devilishly clever plans which had made him one of his region's most feared and respected rulers in just two short years? Sorrel decided to call his bluff. 'Are you really implying that you'd give me your blessing to start living a liberal life if I decided to join you?'

For the first time he partook of a little food—crumbling a bread roll between his fingers and eating a piece of it thoughtfully rather than eagerly. He ate little, Sorrel realised—he always had—and she guessed that explained why his body was harder and leaner than those of other men. It was like the difference between a pampered domestic cat and a predator that existed on its wits in the forest. He picked up his water glass and drank from it, so that when he put the glass down and lifted his gaze to hers his lips gleamed, as did his black eyes.

'That depends.'

Sorrel blinked, putting down her fork, which still speared a half-gnawed piece of fish—because this whole situation was so bizarre that she had completely lost what little appetite she'd had.

'Depends?' Her voice trembled as she looked at him, and so did her body. 'Depends on what?'

'On just who you elect to be the lucky recipient of your sexual favours.'

'Malik, you make it sound so…'

'Vulgar?'

'Well, yes.'

He shrugged. 'I agree entirely. But surely you have only yourself to blame? You did not express a wish for the hearts and the flowers that I assumed all young women yearned for when they lost their maidenhood—you simply made it sound like a mechanical act.'

Now he was humiliating her. 'I don't want to talk about it any more!' she vowed fiercely. 'Let's just forget it.'

Malik shook his dark head in a resolute and decisive movement that Sorrel had seen many times before.

'I cannot forget it,' he said simply. No indeed—for

now he was haunted by vivid and graphic and infinitely disturbing images of her pale, bare body tangled with that of a man. Being penetrated by another...her beautiful, sunny and innocent face crying out first her pain and then her pleasure. Her long, shapely legs—which he had only seen for the first time himself tonight—wrapped around the back of an interloper. Someone else who would fill her with his seed... He winced, halfway himself between pain and pleasure, and having to suppress a small sound of protest. 'But I have a solution which I think might suit us both.'

Sorrel's senses prickled with alarm, and with something else, too—something she wasn't really sure she recognised. 'I'm not with you.'

He smiled, but it was a calculating, almost cruel smile. 'You want a lover?' he said softly. 'Well, so do I. You want to learn the delights of lovemaking? Then let me be your tutor—for you will find none better.'

Her heart was pounding fit to deafen her—but a thousand nebulous dreams exploded into a shivering feeling of fear as they became a possible reality. 'You mean...you...*you*...would...?'

With a grim kind of satisfaction he noted the rosy colour which had bloomed in her cheeks as he listened to her stumbled words. How naïve she was! How the hell was she expecting to cope in a world of sexual predators? he thought soberly. With her flaxen hair and her delicate blush she looked heart-stoppingly innocent. Why, he should throw her to the lions and let her discover for herself just how foolhardy she was being.

But then he felt the hard weight of his erection pressing against his leg and knew that he could not bear for another man to touch her. Not before he did…

'Yes, I would be your tutor,' he agreed softly, drinking in the blue confusion of her widened eyes. 'Would that be so reprehensible a gesture?'

She was about to say yes, when he spoke about it like that—with all the lack of emotion he might employ if he were reading out a shopping list. Except that Malik would never have to even *look* at a shopping list, she reminded herself. 'I just hadn't…' But her words tailed off. She knew that he might detect the lie in them if she said she hadn't ever thought of him in terms of lover when she'd spent years fantasising about just that.

'Hadn't what, Sorrel?' he prompted throatily. 'Hadn't got around to picking a candidate? Well, then, you have the very best available.' His black eyes glittered with anticipation of pleasures to come. 'For every woman I have bedded has told me that I am the greatest lover of all,' he murmured, totally without shame.

It was stupid and illogical, but this *hurt. Really* hurt. Of course somewhere in the back of her mind Sorrel knew that he'd had lovers—and that there had probably been lots of them. Malik was certainly no innocent— he exuded an air of sexuality which was as natural to him as breathing. He was bred to be sensual in the same way that the falcon was bred to move in for the kill— but she had never heard it voiced before, and his boast made her picture him with other women. How many? she wondered jealously. How *many*?

He noted her hesitation and, oddly enough, it pleased him—for a man would take little joy in a prize easily won. 'What I am offering you is a scenario that most women would yearn for,' he mused, and traced the tip of his finger along the lush pad of his bottom lip, knowing that her eyes followed the movement and knowing perfectly well what effect it would have on her. 'You will be taken to the most glamorous places in the world and you will stay in the lap of luxury—and there you will be given the most comprehensive education possible in the art of seduction.'

It was a cold-blooded itinerary for something so significant, and Sorrel knew that she ought to say that it was a preposterous idea—but she was distracted by the erotic gesture of Malik stroking his mouth like that. Was he doing it deliberately? she wondered. Aware that her eyes would be mesmerised by the slow and tantalising gesture—that she would be imagining him stroking *her* lips like that…

But could she bear to have him as her lover? To give him her body when he had already captured her heart? Wouldn't that be a risk too far? Say no, urged the calm, inner voice of reason—but reason was vanquished by a sudden and unexpected source.

A svelte redhead was sitting on the other side of the restaurant, at a table which afforded a perfect view of Malik's hard and autocratic face.

Sorrel had noticed the woman staring over—but that was nothing new and she had paid her little attention.

With his dark, slightly dangerous good-looks people were always staring at Malik.

But some transformation had occurred at his suggestion that he could fulfil the role of Sorrel's sensual tutor—and it felt awfully like *possession*. That he was *hers*—or rather he *could* be hers—and wasn't that almost as dangerous as the unrequited love she had felt for him for years? Because Malik could never be hers—not in any real sense. He was too proud and too cold to give himself to her emotionally, even if strict Kharastani custom meant that he could never marry a woman not of his own blood.

Marry him! Now, where the hell had *that* come from? Age seemed to have taught her nothing if she was having the kind of bizarre fantasy that she wouldn't even have been foolish enough to entertain at the age of sixteen!

Malik had been studying her with the kind of detached interest with which a scientist might peer into a test tube as he waited for her answer—but the new focus of her gaze in the direction of the redhead made him frown, and his eyes narrowed as he glanced over at the Titian-haired beauty.

The woman had clearly been to a colour expert who must have advised her that green was the way to go—her very womanly curves were squeezed into a luscious mint-green cocktail dress which provided a wonderful backdrop for the rich lustre of her hair. Her scarlet lips were pouting, and she didn't seem to be listening to a word that her dining partner was saying to her.

For one second—like an invisible observer—Sorrel watched the interplay between the stranger and the Sheikh. *I want you,* the woman's eyes said—as clearly as if she had shouted the words out at the top of her voice.

Sorrel sneaked a glance at Malik, who had allowed a small and rueful smile to play around the curved perfection of his mouth. Was she imagining it, or was his glittered look a silent acknowledgement, *I want you, too,* or was she just going crazy? Crazy or not, Sorrel felt a tug of an emotion so primitive and powerful that for a moment she couldn't breathe. She looked at the naked hunger on the beauty's face, and knew with certainty that *she* would have taken up Malik's offer without a moment's thought.

Malik had no need to pick up strange women in restaurants—no matter how stunning they were—but he had already said that he wanted a lover.

Sorrel bit her lip perplexedly. So, did she turn down his offer—make the wise decision and just walk away?

Or did she give in to her heart and body's desire and take what was so beautifully on offer—even if it risked the complete wreckage of all her dreams?

But maybe dreams had to be smashed to allow you to carry on living with some degree of contentment in the real world?

'Okay,' she said, shrugging her shoulders like an awkward schoolgirl and wishing that they were alone somewhere, so that the arrangement could have been sealed in the traditional way.

'*Okay?*' Malik frowned. It was not the jubilant acceptance which was his due, and clearly she had no idea of the great honour he was affording her. But she would soon learn, he thought grimly.

Sorrel shifted in her chair as practical considerations began to rear their heads. 'What will…? Well, what on earth is Fariq going to think about the arrangement?'

Malik gave a short laugh. 'I'm not exactly planning to go on national television to announce it.'

His sarcasm should maybe have warned her that she was playing with fire—and everyone knew what happened to people who did that—but it was too late to back out now, even if she'd wanted to. But if their sexual arrangement was to resemble some sort of business arrangement, then they really ought to establish ground-rules right at the beginning.

'You mean it's going to have to be a secret? Fariq won't know?'

'Of course he will *know*,' he said softly. 'But, as usual, he will turn a blind eye, and we will be discreet.'

His words made it perfectly clear that this was how these things worked. Smoke and mirrors and discretion. 'Of course.'

Her lips were trembling, and he found himself swamped with an overpowering desire to kiss them. He turned towards the aide seated unobtrusively at another table and glimmered him a look—and the whole machinery for the Sheikh leaving a restaurant was set into motion.

He signalled for her to follow him out, but her hands were clammy with nerves as the small cluster of hotel management who were mingling with his staff moved forward to accompany them to the executive lift.

'Leave us now,' Malik ordered his bodyguards, once the door of the penthouse apartment had been opened, and Faliq, who had silently appeared from within, gave a short bow and followed them—though Sorrel knew she hadn't mistaken the faint look of shock and disapproval on his face.

Malik closed the door behind them, and put his hands on her shoulders.

'So, we are alone at last,' he murmured, and his voice was thick with desire. 'Your lesson must begin.'

She could feel his hands burning into her flesh through the T-shirt she wore, and suddenly Sorrel felt unprepared—unworthy of her sheikh lover.

'You mean...*now*?'

Her face was a mere hand's width away, and never before had he been so aware of the sapphire blueness of her eyes—as gleaming and as bright as the colour of his beloved Balsora sea on a hot summer day.

'Now?' he echoed huskily, not quite understanding.

'You want us to go to bed now?'

Malik's mouth hardened, first with anger and then with a grim determination. She was wise to have adopted him as her tutor—but would he soon be regretting his swift folly in having offered himself?

'This, of course, is the trouble with modern women,' he said witheringly. 'They wish to devour the feast without tasting the food—like snacking straight from the fridge—and, pray tell me, where is the pleasure or the enjoyment in that?'

It sounded like a reprimand—indeed, it *was* a reprimand. Sorrel stared at him, hoping that she was hiding her hurt feelings, but she found herself blurting out words of reproach. 'You can't expect me to be an expert on these matters, Malik.'

'No.' Bizarrely, he found himself wanting to kiss her—even though she had not prepared herself for him. And despite his reservations, and his certainty that he should send her away to bathe, Malik gave in to his desire. 'Come,' he commanded, and pulled her into the warm circle of his arms, her handbag falling to the floor as her face turned automatically up to his, like a flower to the sun. 'Come let me kiss you,' he murmured, his lips driving down on hers with a raw hunger which was outside his experience.

She tasted of elderflowers and she smelled of lilacs and her trembling body sang of her purity—and Malik found himself trembling too, as her mouth opened beneath the seeking insistence of his.

'Oh, Malik!' she breathed, her arms flying up uninhibitedly to his neck, coiling around him as you sometimes saw a sleeping snake coiled around the charmers in the heat-dazed market square of Kumush Ay.

She pressed her body eagerly against his, so that her soft pliancy was moulded against the hard contours of his, and Malik could scarcely breathe—for he was taken aback by the openness with which she offered herself. For one split second he imagined her honeyed warmth and tightness, and the hardness of his body felt too close to torture to be bearable.

He could take her here and now. Kiss her into an easy submission and lay her down on the carpet. Why, he would not even need to undress her—because none of his aides would dare enter until he gave them permission. He could push up that filmy gipsy skirt and rip off her panties and…and…

'Malik!' she breathed once more.

He gave a little moan and pushed her away from him, glaring as he released her. 'What did I just tell you?' he demanded.

Dazedly, Sorrel stared at him. Now what? She'd thought he'd been enjoying the kiss as much as she was. 'Did I…did I do something wrong?'

'Yes! No!' He shook his head in frustration. 'These are supposed to be exercises in sensual restraint—a slow build-up to eventual delights—not that…that *frenzied* demonstration.' A demonstration which made his own lovemaking boasts sound distinctly hollow. The best lover of all? Why, he had responded like an eager schoolboy!

Abruptly, Malik turned away and stalked down the corridor towards the vast salon. Sorrel stared after his angry back for a moment, before deciding that there wasn't a lot of choice other than to follow him.

Lost in thought, he stood staring out of the window, at the dancing sea which was coloured inky and indigo by the night, except where moonlight topped the waves with little slicks of silver. He heard the sound of her footsteps, and he steeled himself to demonstrate the fine balance between control and need which would be necessary for him to conduct this somewhat unconventional liaison.

Arrangements must be put into place—and quickly—because they would be leaving for Madrid almost immediately.

'There are many preparations which need to be made,' he said softly. 'But not tonight. Tonight you need to go to bed.' Reaching out, he traced the pad of his thumb over the shadows beneath her eyes, meeting the startled look which darkened her blue eyes and shaking his head in answer to her unspoken question. 'Alone.'

A hurt look which she managed to twist into a wry smile curved Sorrel's lips as she left to retrieve her handbag. She very nearly said *So what else is new?* For hadn't she spent the whole of her life alone?

CHAPTER SIX

THE NEXT morning, Sorrel wondered if she had dreamt
it all. Malik gate-crashing her party and then whisking
her away from it and telling her that he would teach her
everything she needed to know about love. But then she
touched a finger to her kiss-bruised lips and knew it had
all been real.

She'd woken with the scent of the Sheikh on her
skin—tasting him on her lips—and she shivered as she
showered herself with a brand-new self-awareness. As
she pulled on her underwear and fished out the one
long silk Kharastani tunic she'd brought to England
with her she wondered if she was doing the right thing.

But who could she possibly ask?

There was no one. She was—and always had been—
a lone agent. Even when her parents had been alive she
had felt very much in the background. They had loved
her as best they could—but had been consumed by
their passion for foreign culture and the adventure of
exploring inaccessible terrain.

She looked around the rented flat. In a neat pile on

the desk was her passport and a few papers. Her clothes filled two suitcases, and a bag of rubbish containing a few yoghurts and some mouldy fruit was waiting to be dumped in the bin outside. Not much to show for her new-found and independent life, was it? And any minute now...

The doorbell trilled and Sorrel went to open it. Another aide, most probably.

But it was not an aide. It was Malik himself. And it was Malik looking like the man she knew—dark, elemental man of the desert, more at home on horseback or holding out one iron-hard arm to greet the returning falcon.

Gone was the immaculate Western suit he had been wearing yesterday—today he was in traditional Kharastani attire. A flowing tunic, made from the very finest silk, which shimmered as he moved and hinted at the hard body beneath. He looked as out of place on the doorstep of this very English building as a bird of paradise would appear if it landed in the centre of a city square.

'Malik,' she breathed.

'I see that you are dressed more appropriately today,' he murmured—and yet wasn't it typical of human nature that you always wanted what you hadn't got? Yesterday, he had been outraged to see those long, slender thighs on display, and yet today, when they were demurely covered, he found himself missing them.

Sorrel smoothed a rueful hand down over the flat of her hip. 'It's the only one I've brought with me. It's very old.'

'Yes. I can see that.' He frowned. 'But you had the services of the palace dressmaker—why did you not use her more?'

Sorrel met the narrowed black eyes. 'I did not feel it was appropriate.'

'Why not?'

Would it sound pathetic if she told him that she hadn't felt comfortable about dressing up for palace events? 'I was there as a functionary, Malik. To blend into the background, rather than stand out from it.'

Such an unassuming point of view had simply never occurred to him—even before he had acceded to the throne. Other than his lovers—all of whom would have had the dressmaker working for them non-stop—Malik had known few women. His mother had died in childbirth and he had been fussed over by the palace servants, but there had not been any one continuous role-model figure. If he had been asked to select the woman he had been closest to he would have plumped for Sorrel—but now it seemed that he did not know her at all. Did that go some way towards explaining her sudden transformation in England? A woman who had paid very little attention to fashion suddenly being thrown in at the deep end of modern culture?

Malik scowled. Why was he wasting his time worrying about it?

'Whilst your modesty is admirable, you will need a new wardrobe for the trip. You will be in effect, a kind of female ambassador for Kharastan.'

'I *will*?'

He nodded. 'For too long our international standing has been open to criticism. The view has been that our women are oppressed—and one of your tasks will be to demonstrate otherwise.'

'You're rather supposing that I don't go along with that view myself?'

Black eyes bored into her. 'And do you?'

Sorrel shook her head and sighed. How much easier it would be if she did. But, in a way, she could see that women had room to flourish in a culture such as Kharastan. It was true that you couldn't go around wearing a mini-skirt—but Sorrel had witnessed for herself just how much trouble that could get you into. It didn't matter if you went around declaring that women had the right to show their legs—men were programmed to react in a certain way if you did!

'No, I don't,' she said. 'Although I'm not saying that Kharastani society is perfect—'

'No society is,' he put in, a small smile curving the corners of his mouth—until he remembered that there were three cars sitting outside waiting and that Fariq would be glowering in the way he'd been doing ever since Malik had expressed the desire to have Sorrel on the trip. 'But we are wasting time.'

He had taken a step towards her, and in the cold, bright light of the morning Sorrel was suddenly fearful of his dark look of sexual stealth. She took a step back. What the hell had she allowed herself to be talked into?

'You…you mean…I've got to go shopping?'

His hand reached out to capture her tiny waist and

he snaked her towards him. 'Shopping?' he laughed softly. 'I think not—or do you imagine that the streets of Brighton could supply the best that Kharastan has to offer? No, Sorrel—you must not worry about clothes.'

Rubbing his finger reflectively at her waist, he thought that a body like hers worked best with no clothes at all. But would that not be part of the thrill for him— to have a woman he was forced to *wait* for? To anticipate, rather than have something offered to him as easily as breathing. He felt her shiver beneath his touch, and he smiled. 'I have already ordered what I want you to wear.'

Pleased to have something to distract herself from the tantalising promise of his touch, Sorrel stared up at him. 'How can you have?'

'The royal dressmaker has drawn you up a traditional wardrobe, but with a modern twist.'

'I still don't understand, Malik.'

'Well, the dressmaker knows your size—she has your measurements on file.' Black eyes roved with slow and almost insolent approval over her slender body. 'And you do not look to me as if you have gained any weight.' He frowned. 'Maybe lost just a little. I can see that I shall have to feed you, Sorrel—for we Kharastani men like our women to have some shape to them.'

Sorrel shook her head impatiently. He was being *deliberately* obtuse. 'The clothes are ready now?' And, when he nodded his affirmation, 'How *can* they be ready, when I only agreed to accompany you late last evening?'

'Because I made up my mind that I wanted you several weeks ago.'

Her heart flared with a hope which rapidly became pain as she reminded herself that he was talking practically, not sentimentally. 'But what if I hadn't...agreed?' she said slowly.

He shrugged his broad shoulders and didn't attempt to hide the arrogant complacency of his smile. 'I knew you would agree,' he said. 'You see, I always get what I want.'

Sorrel felt the alarming missed beat of her heart—anger that he had so cleverly manipulated her, but also that he appeared to show no regret for having done so.

'And what would you do if I told you that I have a will of my own?' she demanded heatedly. 'That despite the agreement made last night I have changed my mind? What if I told you that I intend to walk out right now? What would you do then?'

'Why, this,' he murmured hungrily. 'I would do this.' And he lowered his mouth to hers.

She wanted to fight it—she tried to fight it—her fists hammering redundantly at the muscular wall of his chest as she turned her head away from the hot and tempting brush of his mouth. Spurred on by his teasing little laugh, she tried to wriggle away. But the movement became something else entirely—bringing her into contact with the unmistakable hardness in the very cradle of his groin.

Her eyes widened into saucers, like an old-fashioned doll her mother had given her as a child, and she turned once more and met the mockery in his.

'Yes, Sorrel,' he said softly, watching the slow realisation dawning on her face. 'You can feel me. Feel how hard I am for you. How I could now—were I to wish it—take you in the most fundamental way possible.' He saw the flare of colour which darkened her cheekbones. 'But that is not my intention. This will be a slow and wonderful awakening—and while we may have disagreements along the way none of those will impact on your sensual education. Come, kiss me.'

Their lips were now so close that she could feel the warmth of his breath. Such a short distance—but psychologically it was a huge leap into the unknown. Sorrel knew that he spoke the truth—that he always got what he wanted. Yet she also knew that Malik might be an autocratic ruler, who governed a distinctly male-dominated society, but even he would not have dragged her back and kept her prisoner if she really *had* wanted to walk out.

If she'd wanted to walk out…

How could she possibly do that? She had crossed some invisible line and there was no going back.

'Kiss me, Sorrel,' he urged, and for the first time a note of unashamed yearning darkened his voice.

'Oh, Malik.' Instinctively she held the moment, and then gave in to it, sinking against him as if in slow motion—the soft sweet temptation of his lips contrasting with the hardness of his body and the overpowering sense of having sealed her fate.

His lips teased hers open, with the tip of his tongue lightly flicking to and fro and setting alight the flicker of desire. She could feel it building as he continued to tease her, while his hands tangled luxuriantly in her hair, using it to draw her towards him, closer into the apex of his body.

It was as if he was orchestrating her movements by using some powerful and unseen force. How else did she seem to know what was required of her? Was that stifled little cry of hunger hers? And why were her hips circling against his like that, so that he groaned in response? She wondered if he could read her mind—because how else did he pick up her silent plea of protest that he deepen the kiss? Yet she felt torn when his tongue entered her mouth—because one answered prayer quickly became another, and she wanted more. Oh, much more.

'By the desert storm!' he ground out.

He let her go. Abruptly. A fast-shuttering movement of his eyes the only outward sign that he was disturbed. For a moment he did not move nor speak; he did not dare. One word or one touch and he would forget everything he had told her about restraint and waiting and lessons and demonstrations of his finesse. He wanted her as no other!

Because she is pure, he reasoned—not the glossy breed of woman you usually gravitate towards because they always give you what you want, with no questions asked and no demands made.

Sorrel opened her eyes, aware that her breathing was laboured and so was his. His eyes glittered as if he had a fever, and his skin was flushed beneath the olive glow.

For a split-second she read the desire which fired out from beneath the heavily hooded black eyes—but in a moment it was gone, and in its place the habitual watchfulness which made people around him so wary.

'What is it?' she asked, wanting the passion back again. 'Why have you stopped?'

'You are an eager pupil,' he declared unsteadily.

For the first time she began to realise that maybe she'd made the most stupid bargain of all time. By agreeing to be tutored by Malik wasn't she in danger of consigning herself to a life where every other man would just fall into the imposing shadow of the Sheikh? For how could anyone else ever come close to making her feel the way he had just done in his arms?

'And you are an expert teacher,' she said.

He ran his eyes over her critically, knowing that the dreamy expression which still softened her flushed features was not fitting—not in these particular circumstances. She must learn that his position meant that different rules had to be in place—that she must be prepared to snap back to normality at a second's notice. To walk out to the waiting limousine as if they had been doing nothing more blameless than talking about their schedule.

'Go and wash your face and brush your hair,' he instructed, more roughly than he had intended, and to his consternation he saw her wince in response and lower her eyelashes to hide her pain. But didn't she realise that the smoky, come-hither look in her eyes was making him ache so badly that he wanted to just send the car away? To take her to bed as if they were just a normal man and woman who were allowing themselves the pleasures of the flesh?

Of course she doesn't realise, he told himself sternly. For she was innocent not only of men, but of the power of her own allure—and he must teach her how to channel it.

He touched a finger to her chin. 'Sorrel?' he said, in a voice which for him was almost gentle. 'Look at me.'

She blinked away the hint of rogue tears as she lifted her head to meet his gaze, wondering what she had done wrong—what had made him speak to her in that rough, impatient way. 'I do not please you,' she said dully.

In that one moment he wanted to forget the whole deal. He did not want to make her doubt herself. He wanted back the Sorrel that he knew—the intelligent and spirited woman he had watched grow into a beauty. But he had made the deal now, and she had bewitched him into wanting her—he would never be satisfied until he had known her intimately. Maybe making love to her would obliterate the relationship they had known—but that was a risk he had to take.

'You please me more than you could imagine,' he said softly. 'But I cannot just submit to desire when it takes me. I have a duty to fulfill and an image to maintain. And I must keep up my guard and my composure around the team who work for me. Sex weakens a man, Sorrel, and I cannot allow myself to be perceived as weak—not in any way. And that is why you must learn to switch your passion on and off.'

'As suits you?'

He shook his dark head. 'As suits us both. For—just as I need always to appear invulnerable—you too need protection. If we make it apparent that you are mistress to the Sheikh then we give my enemies ammunition with which to wound me.'

'You have enemies, Malik?' she questioned in a small voice, and the spear of pain she felt was pain for *him*.

How naïve she was! 'A ruler always has enemies.' He laughed, but it was an odd, humourless sort of laugh. 'Especially one who has had such an unusual transition into the job as I have. Now, do not look so worried, little one—or I shall not be able to concentrate on my job. Go and make yourself calm, and then we shall face Faliq. We have a plane fuelled and ready, and a deputation of dignitaries waiting in Madrid.'

She smiled at him and turned away, her heart lifting as she walked towards the bathroom. *He hasn't called me 'little one' in years.* But she banished the rogue thought, reminding herself that he had made it clear from the start that this was a practical and not an emotional relationship.

So start acting that way, she told herself, as she splashed cold water onto her heated cheeks and brushed her mussed hair.

Next stop Spain, she thought, peering one last time at her reflection in the mirror.

And then she walked out to meet the waiting Sheikh.

CHAPTER SEVEN

'WILL you be wanting me for anything else, Highness?'

In the warmth of the Spanish evening, Malik signed the last of the official papers with a flourish and then handed them to Fariq. The brooding aide had been producing document after document ever since they had returned from dinner—but even the most tedious directives could not detract from Malik's his growing sense of excitement.

'No. Thank you, Fariq—that will be all. I shall take a drink on the terrace and then I shall sleep.' He yawned rather exaggeratedly, as if to impress on his aide a tiredness he was far from feeling. Not that he would usually bother with subterfuge where a lover was concerned, but this lover was different—and propriety demanded that he be discreet about her.

'As Your Highness requires.' Fariq's face showed no reaction as he bowed deeply and left the lavish suite. 'I bid you a comfortable night, Most Serene One.'

Malik had been given the entire top floor of the luxury Madrid hotel, and his own private quarters consisted of a vast two-bedroomed suite connected by a shared drawing room. There was a separate study, from which he could work, two separate dressing rooms and two bathrooms. The place had been chosen especially to appeal to his tastes. There were Moorish-style towers on this particular building, and cool marble floors. Sandalwood hung on the air, and huge embroidered cushions lay scattered on the floor of the salon.

Silk robes shimmered as he stretched his arms above his head and walked outside onto the rooftop terrace—a fairytale haven lined with orange trees which scented the soft night air. Fat candles guttered in the faint breeze and bright stars hung in the sky like celestial lanterns, while far below came the glitter of a city still awake—but Madrid had always been a city that never slept.

Glancing at his watch, his eyes gleaming with anticipation, he walked back into the apartment just in time to hear a light tap on the door.

'Come,' he murmured, and in walked Sorrel—exactly as he had commanded that she should do when he had bent his head to speak to her at the end of dinner. In the soft light her face was a beautiful blur, but he could see its troubled expression.

A frown appeared between his black brows. 'What is it?'

She tried a smile, but it fell short of the real thing, and beneath her breast her heart was pounding. 'I feel sort of guilty, sneaking around like this—it seems so *wrong*, somehow.'

Malik's frown deepened. 'What does?'

'All the secrecy.'

'You *knew* it would have to be secret.'

His voice sounded reproving, and Sorrel swallowed down some of her reservations. 'I know. It's just… well…'

'Well, *what*, Sorrel?' he asked coldly.

Wasn't it pointless to tell him that ever since the sumptuous dinner hosted by the Kharastani Ambassador had ended she had been pacing up and down in her room in an agony of nerves—wondering how she was going to go through with it? Wondering if she had taken leave of her senses to ever agree to such a scheme.

I'm scared, she wanted to say—except that she suspected it would place too heavy a burden of responsibility on Malik's shoulders. It had been *her* decision to become Malik's lover. If she acted like a child, then he would treat her like one—and wasn't the whole point that she wanted him to treat her like a woman?

'I didn't know what to do,' she admitted huskily. 'Or what to wear.'

This was better. A few first-night nerves were permissible—as long as she had not changed her mind. Because Malik most certainly had not. His black gaze scanned over her with economic efficiency as he remembered the lavish evening they had just spent.

During dinner she had served him well—an excellent example of how perfectly a Western woman had adapted to life in such a radically different country as Kharastan.

She had looked magnificent, too—more magnificent than he could have ever dreamed, transformed into a ravishing beauty. There had been a split-second of disbelieving silence when she had walked into the crowded reception room just behind him, as part of his entourage. The Embassy had, of course, received word that Sorrel would be among his party—but he suspected that her youth and her pale blonde loveliness had taken the assembled hordes by surprise.

Her long, fitted dress, in scarlet embroidered with silver, had caused a stir, and he had seen the envious eyes of the other women calculating the cost of the exquisite emerald clips she wore in her hair and the long emerald drop earrings which glittered in green waterfalls by the side of her face. Malik had even caught a visiting British politician trying to sweet-talk her during the pre-dinner drinks.

'I did not realise that Kharastani women wore scarlet,' Malik had heard him say.

And Sorrel's cool reply. 'Perhaps you aren't aware that I'm as English as you are—and scarlet does not have the same connotations in Kharastan as it does in the West. For us, red denotes courage and fertility—not loose morals.'

Malik had watched with amusement while the man's mouth had opened and shut like a fish, and Sorrel had moved away with grace and charm to get ready to meet the Castilian Duque and his wife, who had just entered the grand reception room of the Embassy.

Yes, Sorrel had been a worthy addition to the

Sheikh's party, thought Malik with satisfaction. Even Fariq must have seen that—and, although his aide clearly disapproved of the situation—Malik knew that he would not dare to express his reservations to *him*.

'You did well this evening,' said Malik softly.

'Did I?' She had felt a bit like a performing seal—brought in to cleverly balance a ball on the tip of its nose without dropping it. Sorrel had been raised by diplomatic parents and had attended similar parties since she could remember. She wasn't worried about what to say, or drink, or even do—because it came to her as easily as breathing.

What had been different this time were the circumstances in which she'd found herself. She had been aware of the ripple of interest when she'd walked in, and of the jealous glances sent slanting over by the other women in the room. Malik was known in the Press as one of the world's most eligible bachelors—and Sorrel suspected that a lot of those women had dressed up wondering if they might be lucky enough to be able to snare the ruggedly handsome Sheikh.

'You know you did,' said Malik, but with a renewed sense of impatience. Was she going to need reassurance every step along the way—when he was busy himself with paperwork from back home which still needed the royal seal, as well as all the trade negotiations he and his team were making during this whistle-stop trip? She must learn quickly that as mistress to the Sheikh she was there to make his life easier—not to complicate it with her own issues. 'Now, stop frowning and come over here.'

Her momentary feeling of shyness was overcome by the smile on his dark face and by the thought of how long she had yearned for him. Sorrel went to him with all the greedy eagerness of someone whose aching hunger was just about to be fed. He hadn't touched her since they'd left Brighton, and she had had to endure the formality of arriving in Madrid and wondering whether she had imagined the whole bizarre pact they'd made. 'Oh, Malik,' she whispered, and flung her arms around his neck.

The breathy way she said his name set off little warning bells in the recesses of his mind, and Malik caught her by the elbows to steady her, but also to restrain her. His exuberance was sweet, but it was not appropriate. 'Take it easy,' he murmured. 'I'm not going anywhere.'

Her head jerked back at the soft reprimand, and unthinkingly she bit her lip—but that did not please him either.

'Don't,' he chided. 'Your lips should only ever be bitten by a man—when sex becomes wild and angry and exciting, as sometimes it does. But they are far too soft and sweet and inviting for that. Especially not tonight. So this is better…' And he grazed his mouth over hers, gently and caressingly—the merest brush of flesh to flesh, which made Sorrel shiver as violently as a leaf about to be torn from the tree by a storm. Malik smiled against her. 'Ah, yes—this is much better. Now, relax. Hold on to me, but gently this time.'

Slowly, she raised her hands to lie on the broad bank

of his shoulders, feeling the hard contours of muscle and bone through the silk of first his robe, and then his skin. It was a careful and considered movement—lacking all the impulsiveness of before.

Was that why he rewarded her by deepening the kiss? Making a little groan as their mouths opened together—so that the perfect synchrony of the kiss seemed to mock at her. As if he was saying, Don't show any *emotion* and I will reward you like this.

Okay, then—she thought. I won't. I will be as cool as you want me to be, Malik—I will bite back my words of adoration.

Yet although the kiss fell short of what her girlish dreams had once hoped for, on another level it exceeded every hazy wish she'd ever had. Because he *was* her every wish. Dark, powerful Malik was here—holding her and holding his hard body against her, exciting a response in her that came as easily as breathing, and she flicked her tongue inside his mouth with a luxuriant ease, as if she had been born to do that.

Her response took him by surprise—momentarily wresting the control from him so that for that one split-second he felt as if *he* was the pupil and she the teacher. 'Sorrel,' he said unevenly as he dragged his mouth away from hers, staring down at the wide-spaced beauty of her eyes and the parted dark petals of her lips.

'Do I please you, Malik?' she questioned softly.

She would please him more if she touched him where he was hard. But he knew that he could not ask her for such an intimacy—at least, not yet. Never before had such a familiarity been forbidden to him by self-restraint, and this, too, he found unbearably exciting.

'Oh, yes. Yes, you please me,' he agreed shakily. 'And you shall please me more. Come with me.'

He took her hand in his as if they were just any man and woman who could go where they pleased. But they were not. This suite—for all its opulence and luxury—was the gilded cage which confined their passions. And Malik confined them, too, Sorrel told herself as they walked in from the terrace towards his bedroom. With his rules about secrecy and appropriate behaviour.

She wanted to tell him that she was terrified—which she was—but she didn't dare, for fear that he would decide he'd taken leave of his senses and stop this madness before it went any further.

Because it *was* madness. And yet it was Malik on the only terms she could ever have him—and surely it would be madder still to turn down such a bittersweet opportunity?

'Now. Let me look at you.' He turned her to face him, his black eyes almost grave as they studied her. Unexpectedly, he pulled out the emerald clip from the pale high-piled hair and carefully put it down, then removed another, and another—and watched like a voyeur as the abundance of blonde hair spilled in satin profusion down over the embroidered scarlet gown she was wearing. 'You must always wear your hair down for me, when we are alone like this,' he said huskily. 'Will you promise me that?'

She wanted to tell him that she would walk to the

ends of the earth for him—but guessed that would be a far worse crime than hurling herself into his arms. 'I promise,' she whispered instead.

'And will you promise to tip your head to one side? Like that. There. Yes. So that I can brush my lips along your neck. Like this.' He felt the shiver of her skin, the faint tremble of her body as he did. 'Will you promise that too?'

Sorrel shut her eyes, the lids feeling heavy—as heavy as the powerful beat of her heart. 'Yes,' she whispered.

'Your neck is like a swan's, Sorrel,' he breathed. 'Long and graceful. And you bend like the wind.'

She felt like a mannequin in a shop window, standing there with her hands down by her sides, while the soft touch of his mouth against her neck was making her tremble. 'Malik,' she breathed, unable to help herself, wondering if a shuddered hint of how much she liked it was overstepping the guidelines to behaviour he seemed to have laid down.

He pulled her into his arms and began to kiss her, and it was as much as Sorrel could do not to cry out in pure delight. It's only a kiss, she told herself fiercely. But it felt like so much more. A sweet, hot leap of her heart as his mouth covered hers. One minute his kiss was urgent and seeking and then, just when she thought that she might burst into flames, he would soften it— so that it felt like an unbearably evocative exploration.

And suddenly she didn't care about what was or wasn't suitable behaviour—because the kiss had ignited a passion which she had hidden away from him for years and years. Sorrel lifted up her arms and entwined them like a vine around his neck, hearing his answering moan as she pressed her body closer to his, and seconds later he tore his mouth away from hers.

His eyes were hot and black and his breathing was ragged as he sucked in a slow, unsteady breath—telling himself that he had to take back the control. The deal was that he would teach her all about love-making, and the best lessons were all about build-up. About enjoying each new pleasure along the way, rather than dulling the appetite by saturating it. Hadn't he told *her* off for being greedy? Swallowing down his alpha instinct to take her there and then, he bent his lips to her ear now. 'I want to take your dress off,' he groaned.

'Then t-take it off,' she said shakily.

In fact, he wanted to rip the damn thing from her body—but if he didn't calm things down then he would be lost, and Malik was *never* lost. He needed to demonstrate self-control—to prove to himself as well as to her just who was in charge.

He reached round to the side of her dress, drawing the zip down slowly so that the air cooled her skin, and even though it was like every fantasy come to life to have Malik's fingers brushing against the curve of her waist she sensed that something in the mood had changed. Now it seemed so...so *matter-of-fact*—whereas the frantic kissing had felt more...

More what?

More as if it really meant something to him? Oh, Sorrel—don't talk yourself into fantasy land, she told herself silently.

'Let me see you now,' he said.

He had finished unzipping the dress and was sliding it over her head, as if he undressed women every day of the week, and then he cast it aside and took a step back to look at her—like someone in an art gallery who was studying a painting in depth.

Sorrel's instinct was to blush and to wrap protective arms around herself, but something in his black eyes stopped her.

'No. You must not be shy with your lover,' he urged. 'For coyness has no place in the bedroom. Or out of it.' His eyes glittered. 'Now, take your hands away, Sorrel, and let me see you properly.'

Lifting them away, as if she were a puppet and he were twitching at the strings, she did as he asked and stood before him—like an early painting she had seen on the palace walls in Kumush Ay, of a favoured sexual slave in homage before her beloved Sheikh. Was that what she must look like? she wondered. A slave eager to do his every wish?

Searching his face, she found his expression unreadable, but she stood there while his black eyes swept over her simple lace-trimmed cotton bra and matching pair of briefs and he gave a hard smile.

'Go and look in the dressing room,' he instructed softly.

'What am I looking for?'

'You'll see.'

Coyness has no place in the bedroom, Sorrel reminded herself of his words as she turned and walked towards the dressing room—feeling his black gaze burning into her as if he was branding her with the hot fire from his eyes.

Malik watched her go, enjoying the delicious sight of each buttock thrusting against the cotton of her panties and the sweet, slightly self-conscious way she walked— despite what he had urged her. If ever he had doubted her innocence before, her whole demeanour since they had entered the suite had been one of a woman unused to men.

She didn't return straight away—and when she did it was with an expression he had never seen on a woman's face before. Of someone who was just discovering her sexual power for the first time. A sensual awakening. She had passed the first test and done what was expected of her, he thought with satisfaction.

'I assume that you wanted me to put these on?' she questioned.

'Oh, yes,' he agreed, and swallowed. 'Yes, indeed.'

Gone were the chaste cotton garments, and in their place the frivolous French underwear he had ordered in the very colour she had defended tonight at dinner. But here the scarlet did not symbolise the courage and fertility of which she had spoken. No, indeed. Here the flimsy little bra and panties were scarlet in their other more traditional sense—a colour which was totally about sex. Her breasts spilled out over the delicate lace and the high-cut briefs made her thighs seem to go on for ever and ever. Malik felt quite dizzy with desire.

It was as though he had never seen a woman dressed—or rather, *un*dressed—in quite such a provocative way. And maybe that was true. His lovers had stripped for him many times, but there had not been this sense of the new, the uncharted.

For my own eyes only, he thought—with a fierce stab of possession.

'Walk towards me,' he said throatily.

She obeyed him, finding that it was impossible to do anything other than sway provocatively on a pair of red killer-heels so high that she felt as if she was on stilts. This is crazy, she told herself—but a wild and delicious excitement whirled her up as she saw the look of sheer admiration in his eyes. So what if it's crazy? Why don't you just do the sensible thing and enjoy it?

'Like this?' She sashayed towards him.

'Yes,' he breathed. 'Exactly like that.'

But he had seen the play of emotions which crossed her face—the uncertainty and apprehension—and Malik was suddenly assailed by a terrible sensation of doubt. Was he wrong to be doing this? Taking the sweetly innocent and unspoilt Sorrel and playing these slow, sensual games with her? Was he *corrupting* her rather than broadening her education by teaching her how to delight a man and to delight herself at the same time? Knowing all the while that it could lead nowhere?

She reached him and gave a tentative smile as she

flicked flaxen hair back over the gleaming silk of her shoulder. 'Here I am, then,' she whispered.

In that second she sounded so trusting—and so *sweet*—that the self-doubt threatened to overwhelm him. Until he reminded himself that if he were not doing this then someone else would be... The sharp spear of jealousy ruthlessly lanced the voice of his conscience.

Because if he didn't have her—then someone else would!

He picked her up into his arms in a display of strength and domination as he began to carry her towards the bed, and Sorrel closed her eyes. This bit really *was* close to fantasy—the stuff of a thousand girlish dreams—but most of the dreams had stopped at the bedroom door, and now panic had entered the equation.

She was about to lose her virginity in the most matter-of-fact way possible—to a man she had always loved, but who could never return that love.

Suddenly she felt the soft mattress beneath her back as he put her down on it, and her eyes fluttered open as she stared up at him, reaching her fingertips up before she could stop herself, touching the hard contours of his face and the grazing rasp of his jaw. Was tenderness forbidden, along with coyness? she wondered as she saw him flinch.

'Will it...hurt?' she asked tentatively.

And Malik gave a small groan—recognising the trust implicit in her question. The same trust with which she had once let him put her on the back of the palace's most feisty stallion, telling her that the only way to rid herself of fright was first to conquer it.

But this was a different Sorrel who lay on his bed—not the cute little girl who had been his ward for all those years. This was a grown-up Sorrel who was hell-bent on losing her virginity. Fiercely, he dispelled the memories of the past and concentrated on the glorious present—all soft, pale curves accentuated by sexy scarlet silk and lace—and he bent his mouth to kiss the tip of her nipple through her bra. 'No,' he said, his teeth teasing and grazing at the sensitised flesh. 'It will not hurt.'

Sorrel shivered with a wave of ecstasy so acute that it almost hurt. 'But I thought…'

He felt the rising tension in his own hard body. 'Then don't think,' he urged, his voice harsh from the recognition of just how difficult this was going to be. 'Thinking destroys pleasure, Sorrel—just feel.'

Her head fell back against the pillow as she did her best to concentrate on the waves of pleasure rather than the clear note of warning in his voice, which echoed round and round inside Sorrel's head like a tune she'd heard on the radio and found impossible to forget. Was that because thinking made you want to ask questions which would drive you mad if they were ever answered honestly?

But nothing ever turned out the way you thought it would. In her innocence, Sorrel had thought she'd lose her virginity to Malik that warm, orange-scented evening in Madrid—but the reality of the night was quite different. He didn't even undress her—well, not fully. Just reached round and unclipped the scarlet bra and then slowly removed it, flinging it carelessly to the floor as if it had been a rag.

He breathed out a long, pent-up sigh as her breasts were revealed, saying something soft in a word that Sorrel assumed was Kharastani, though she had never heard it used before.

'What does that mean?' she whispered, trying to forget that she was lying there in a nothing but a wispy little pair of scarlet panties.

But Malik shook his black head, his tongue snaking out over bone-dry lips as he drank in the creamy beauty of her skin and the rosy blush of each nipples. 'It is not a word that a woman should ever use,' he grated, and he touched one tip with his finger, circling it with a light touch and meeting the question in her eyes. 'It means that you are ready to be shown the many paths which lead to pleasure,' he relented, and his mouth softened with promise. 'Ready to be loved.'

Sorrel closed her eyes to hide the sudden fear she felt. He meant *make* love, she told herself fiercely.

'Why do you frown, Sorrel?' he questioned softly.

She let her eyelids flutter open. How much should she tell him? How much of herself was it suitable for a woman to expose? Because suddenly the idea that she might lay her raw emotions open for him to see seemed far more revealing than the fact that her breasts were bare.

'I don't know what to do,' she said truthfully.

He gave a nod of satisfaction. 'But that is exactly as it should be. I do not expect you to. It is nature's way for the man to have superior skills and to teach the woman everything he knows.' A slow smile curved his hard lips. 'And, to be honest, it is a relief to have a woman who does not start performing her entire sexual repertoire in an attempt to impress me.'

She thought that it wasn't the most diplomatic thing in the world to tell her that at that particular moment, but the woman in her was curious. 'Is that what they do, then?'

'It has happened even more since I became Sheikh,' he admitted softly. 'For they believe that men can be ensnared by sexual expertise alone.'

'And can't they?'

He stroked a wisp of hair away from the pink and white of her cheek. How innocent she was. 'Of course not. Sexual trickery is like food that has been messed around with—sometimes it ruins it—while simplicity has a charm all of its own.' Now it was his turn to frown—because what the hell was he doing, talking about such things with her? Was that not an intimacy too far—especially at a time like this? Because it was Sorrel—and she knew him better than anyone else? And did that mean she had some sort of power over him?

Never!

He renewed the stroking of her breast—only this time he ruthlessly decided to show her just what a master of expertise she was dealing with.

His fingertips teased, cajoled, excited, and his lips did the same. They traced feather-light patterns on her mouth, her eyelids, the tip of her nose and the gentle curve of her jaw, so that Sorrel relaxed into a hazy world where everything was about sensation. And through the haze she sensed that something wonderful awaited her.

Warmth began to flood through her as her heart picked up speed, and her arms reached up of their own accord to wrap themselves around his neck as Malik sweetly plundered her mouth with his.

'Malik!' she gasped.

He could feel the building of tension in her body, and he smiled as he slipped his hand between her thighs and began to stroke her through her panties, feeling her start. 'What is it?'

She wanted to ask him if it was possible to be feeling like…like… 'Something is…' Her eyes widened as the dark waves circled. 'Something is…'

He watched her as he might have watched a fledgling falcon taking its very first flight—then, as now, instinct was all. 'Don't think,' he said again, feeling the honeyed slick of her desire against his fingers. 'Just feel.'

Sorrel did as he urged, although there seemed no alternative, for by now the seemingly impossible waves of sensation dominated everything—taking her sweeping upwards towards a place of almost unimaginable pleasure.

'Oh, Malik!' she sobbed, as she reached it. 'Malik, Malik, Malik!'

'What is it?' he teased, instinctively laughing at her obvious delight.

For a moment all inhibition left her, and she stared up into the face of the man who had dominated her life since the first time she'd set eyes on him and her heart turned over. 'I love...' She saw the black eyes narrow and all the laughter leave them. Just in time she sensed his frozen withdrawal, and just in time she turned her sentence into a glowing sexual testimony. 'I *love* it,' she purred triumphantly, realising that at that moment she didn't sound like Sorrel at all.

CHAPTER EIGHT

YET just who *was* the real Sorrel?

Was she the woman who was being given a unique sensual education—who every night was brought to gasping orgasm by the silent and black-eyed Sheikh? The woman who bit back the words she knew he never wanted to hear—well, certainly not from her—and turned them into sighs of satisfaction instead?

Or was that just a temporary Sorrel, who was discovering sexual pleasure for the first time—rather as someone who had lived on another planet might greedily alight on their first taste of chocolate?

But the present didn't bother her nearly so much as what lay ahead. Because when it was over—as one day it must inevitably be—would she be able to walk away without a single pang and with a casual little wave of her fingers?

She couldn't bear to think about it.

'Sorrel!'

Just the sound of Malik's voice made her heart miss

a beat—just as it always did—but she composed her face into one of calm attentiveness.

They were now in Paris—the last stop of the tour—and she had been reading through a clutch of newspaper cuttings, some from the French dailies and some from the international press. The Sheikh had been well received, she thought approvingly, putting aside her own feelings as she heard the sound of his distinctive footsteps.

'I'm in here!'

He appeared before she had time to adjust her hair, and stood framed in the doorway of their suite with his black hair gleaming and his ebony eyes glittering in the hard, autocratic face. It was a bright Parisian day and outside the weather was just glorious—though Sorrel thought that they might as well have been anywhere for all that they saw of the cities they took in.

They had been whisked from airstrip to hotel to Embassy by air-conditioned limousines whose windows tinted out most of the natural light—so that even if, as they had yesterday, they happened to see the Champs-Elysées passing them by, it was like looking at a sepia photo of it. A postcard image.

They were cut off from the rest of the world and cut off from reality in more ways than one. Sometimes the whole experience felt as if Sorrel had wandered into a dream by mistake—and never more so than now, with the fine golden silk of his gown shimmering around the hard sinews of a body she had yet to discover.

Sorrel shivered at the expression in his dark eyes. 'Did you...did you want something?'

'I want you,' said Malik softly.

And, oh, how she wanted him, too—but no doubt he knew that. Just as he obviously expected her to drop everything and rush to him. Straight into his arms. To hold her face eagerly up to his for a kiss and to tremble with anticipation at the guaranteed pleasure. Part of her wanted to do just that, but pride made her stay her ground to confront the issue which burned at the corners of her mind whenever Malik wasn't there to obliterate everything with his kisses.

How much longer before she completely lost her identity as a person—becoming solely Malik's plaything that he could pick up and put down at will? At least when she was busying herself by helping with practical arrangements for the trip it made her feel like the *old* Sorrel. The one who had existed before she had put her life on hold and her emotions into the deep-freeze while the black-eyed Sheikh took delight in showing her just how many ways there were to pleasure a woman...

'Well, here I am,' she said briskly. Because the role of aide fitted her far more comfortably than the role of would-be lover. 'I was busy with this itinerary.' She stabbed at the papers on the writing bureau at which she sat.

'Get Fariq to deal with it,' he said carelessly.

Her voice was stubborn. 'I'd rather deal with it myself.'

He walked over to where she sat and put his hands on her shoulders, bending down to brush his lips against her bare neck. 'But I don't want you to deal with it. Your place is with me. To do as I will you. To experience pleasure in my arms. You know that, don't you, Sorrel?'

Oh, yes—she knew that. She had learnt it at his lips and in his arms. Briefly she shut her eyes, allowing the warm whisper of his lips to lull her into the heady promise of what lay ahead. What would it be today? she wondered. Which erogenous zone would he be concentrating on—demonstrating his power and his skill in bringing her silently to gasping orgasm while somehow managing to remain both physically and emotionally removed from her?

The emotional distance didn't surprise her—she would have expected nothing else of Malik and she had known him all her life. But the other distance *did*—it surprised and shocked the hell out of her, and made her wonder if there was something the matter with her. Something about her which didn't please him, since—despite her growing sensual education and his masterly tuition—Sorrel remained a virgin.

At first she had thought that he was acting out of consideration for her feelings—imagining that she'd be scared because at the age of twenty-five she was a relatively late virgin. But she wasn't scared—she was longing for Malik to make love to her in the fullest sense of all. Yet he did not.

He would give her pleasure with his hands, or his mouth, or his tongue—and afterwards he would kiss her hair and let her shuddering body still within the safe and powerful circle of his arms. And then, when she was all rosy and contented, he would glitter her a hard smile and leave the room abruptly, leaving her satisfied and yet aching. Longing for more and not knowing why he would not give her more. Or *ask* for more. Was it about control? she wondered. Just as everything else in his life was about control?

Well, she certainly wasn't going to beg him.

She opened her eyes and slowly rose from the desk to face him. 'Your brother rang,' she said.

'My brother?' There was a pause. 'You mean my half-brother,' he corrected coolly. 'Which one?'

Which one did he think? 'The one who lives in Paris, Malik,' she said sweetly. 'Xavier.'

Malik didn't react, but went over to the window to stare out at the city's rooftops, narrowing his eyes against the glare of the day and keeping his body language neutral.

He had two younger half-brothers—Xavier, who was half-French, and Giovanni who was half-Italian. One father united the three of them—but their mothers had all been different. It was a complicated history, and one which Malik sometimes wished he could forget.

Up until two years ago he had thought that he was an orphan who had been lucky enough to have been given employment and protection by the royal palace of Kharastan. But the late Sheikh had made dynamite disclosures before his death: not only was Malik his son, and thus to inherit the Kharastani throne, but he was also going to gain two half-brothers.

On balance, Malik thought that taking on a kingdom

was easier than taking on an instant family. He had been the Sheikh's right-hand man for so many years that he probably knew more about Kharastan than any other living person—and he had seen first-hand how best to rule.

The half-brother issue was different. Both Xavier and Giovanni were younger, and so there had been no question of them inheriting the Kharastan throne. Even if they had been older it was written into the constitution that only a man of pure Kharastani blood could inherit the kingdom.

The potential for discord between the three men had been there, but to his relief none had been expressed. Nonetheless, Malik had resisted the overtures of both Xavier and Giovanni for him to visit them and 'get to know them'. He did not need a family and neither did he want one.

In his unique and often lonely role at the court, Malik had seen for himself that lives only became complicated when other people were involved. It was relationships which gave rise to unrest and to dispute. Relationships made you vulnerable—and exposed you to pain.

If Malik had not been King then he might have contented himself with a solitary life—like the one he had always led, the one he knew how to deal with. But such was not his destiny. He could not take comfort in the luxury of choice. One day he must marry and produce an heir, but until that onerous burden should fall upon his shoulders he would give it no more thought.

He turned back from the window, thinking how magnificent Sorrel looked today—with her pale blonde hair tumbling down over her shoulders just the way he liked it, and in a long, white silk dress which fell in folds from the curve of her hips, so that she resembled a Grecian goddess. He felt his throat thicken with desire, but saw she was looking at him with a question in her eyes. He sighed. 'And what did Xavier want?'

Was he being deliberately imperceptive? Sorrel wondered. She put her head to one side and flicked a finger against her cheek as she pretended to consider the options. 'Let's think,' she mused. 'Xavier lives in Paris, and you happen to be visiting Paris. Any ideas what he might want—or shall we call in the palace logistician?'

His black eyes narrowed. 'Are you trying to be funny?'

'I thought you were.' She thought how forbidding his eyes looked—and how his lips were set into a hard line. But she refused to be intimidated by a man she had known all her life, no matter how much it suited him. She knew very well that he preferred to try to avoid issues such as these, and because she cared for him she wasn't going to let him. 'Malik—it's pretty obvious that Xavier and Laura want to meet up with you while you're in Paris! You haven't seen each other since Giovanni's party.'

He didn't need *her* to tell him when he'd last seen his brother! 'I don't know that there's enough time,' he growled.

'Oh, there's time,' she asserted softly, and pointed at

his itinerary. 'The drinks reception with the Foreign Minister finishes early. You could easily do dinner.' She sighed as she saw that the forbidding set of his jaw hadn't altered a bit. 'Look, Malik, we've both known what it is to lose our families—but at least you've discovered a new one! Why don't you use this opportunity to get to know Xavier a bit better?'

She stood there, looking so at ease and so *comfortable* as she gently told him what to do that Malik felt a terrible tearing pain as he caught a glimpse of another life—a life he would never lead. Where women made suggestions in order to keep the peace and worked behind the scenes to bring distant brothers together. 'Will you stop trying to fabricate a situation which happens to fit in with your idea of Happy Families?' he snapped.

'I was *not*!'

Ebony brows were elevated into disdainful curves. 'Or perhaps you are hoping to present the two of us as a couple? Get the seal of approval from my family before you try to persuade me to tell the rest of the world we're together? Is that your plan?'

It was such an outrageous accusation that for a moment Sorrel thought he was joking—but one look at the darkly thunderous expression on his face told her he wasn't. 'How dare you suggest that, Malik? When nothing could be further from my mind!'

'Because we are *not* a couple!' he clipped out. 'You know that and I know that—and what is more we never *can* be!'

'Of course I know that!' It was pretty obvious from the way he'd been hiding her away and…and… Her breath was coming in short, angry little gasps. 'You have made that abundantly clear!'

The conflict accelerated his heart and made his skin prickle, the dark flush of desire arrowing in slants down over his cheekbones. Wasn't it strange, he thought achingly, how disharmony could so accelerate desire? Anger provided an incomparable springboard for passion—which was why, he guessed, making-up sex was the very best sex of all.

The progress of his thoughts was rewarded with the hard jerk of an erection pushing against his thigh—but as always the physical evidence of his desire reminded him that this affair was different from any other. He had *made* it different—simply because it was Sorrel. He had held back and held back until he'd thought he would go insane—yet he wondered just how much more of this exquisite self-denial he could take.

'Come over here,' he instructed softly.

'No,' she said recklessly, but her heart was hammering against her ribcage. 'You think you can talk to me as if I'm an idiot, and then just snap your fingers and I'll come running?'

That was exactly what he thought. Well, not the idiot part, but certainly the rest of it. But he guessed it might not be the most diplomatic thing in the world to agree with her. 'Don't you know how much I like it when you try to oppose me?' he murmured. 'Don't you know how much it turns me on?'

Looping a strand of hair behind her ear, Sorrel stared at him. He had her tied up in so many knots that she wasn't sure about anything any more. *So ask him.* 'Malik—'

He heard the apprehensiveness in her voice—a trait that would not usually be made known to him—but then, he had never lived in such close confinement with a member of the opposite sex before. He was used to dealing with women at their glossy and most responsive best—all perfumed and ready for love. But the moment you let a woman into your life you became aware of her *moods*—and her unrealistic take on life.

'Come to me,' he ordered softly, and this time she went into his arms, her slim, soft body fitting perfectly against his. Unseen, he closed his eyes against the golden spill of her hair, breathing in its subtle fragrance before leaning back to look down at her, a stern expression on his rugged features. 'Now, tell me—what is troubling you?'

'You are.' Boldly, she lifted her hands to his face. 'You're driving me mad with questions about why...' She hesitated, and then seized the courage to say it. 'Why you don't want to make love to me.'

He traced a thoughtful finger down to the provocative swell of her breast. 'Isn't that what I've been doing to you for the past week?'

Surely it was crazy to feel embarrassed talking about sex when he had seen her writhing beneath his expert fingers and his lips in just about every major city in Europe? She hadn't felt embarrassed *then*, had she?

Yet getting carried away in the heat of the moment was a lot easier than confronting difficult issues in the cold light of day, with a man who always ran away from discussing anything resembling feelings.

'I meant...properly,' she whispered, her face beginning to burn.

'Ah!' He stroked the palm of his hand over the pale waterfall of her hair, thinking that her stumbled questions reminded him of a butterfly emerging slowly from the chrysalis before learning how to fly. He had seen her grow in confidence day by day. But that blush—redolent of a far more profound innocence—smote deep at the conscience which still troubled him.

Had he thought that one morning he was just going to wake up and find that the doubts which still assailed him over his behaviour towards her had suddenly vanished? That he would be able to take her—to pierce through to the very heart of her? And then what? To have his fill of her before casting her aside to seek a Kharastani bride?

Could he honestly, knowingly and willingly take her virginity at such a price? It was no way to treat any woman, but especially not Sorrel—not after everything they had been to each other.

And yet the alternative was to give her away to some other man!

Malik's mouth hardened. Never! His royal destiny had come to him late—but he'd now had two years of reigning over a large and influential kingdom, and some of that power had inevitably influenced him. He hungered for Sorrel with a fervour which far surpassed anything else he'd ever wanted. But he knew that he must not let sentimentality cloud his judgement.

As King he was above the rules of normal men, and this was fact, not arrogance. He could not, at present, see a way out of the dilemma which had snared him in its velvet claws, but until he did Sorrel would fit in with *his* plans and *his* desires. She would not question him, but consider herself grateful that he had taken it upon himself to educate her!

'You must not question my judgement—nor my behaviour,' he said coolly. 'Not ever. For I am the Sheikh, whose word must not be questioned!'

Maybe in matters concerning the body he was, but *she* knew a bit more about emotions and relationships than this cold-hearted King. She drew a deep breath. 'Very well, I shall not bring the subject of our sex-life up again—I will bow to your superior knowledge of the subject.' Her blue eyes sparked. 'But I would be failing in my supportive role if I allowed you to take a course of action which could be detrimental to the throne,' she said quietly.

'Meaning *what*, precisely?' he snapped.

'Just that I think it's very bad if you don't meet up with your brother while you're here. If you won't do it out of a sense of love, then at least do it out of a sense of duty. Imagine if the papers discover that you've avoided him— they'll blow it up and turn it into a feud. You know the kind of thing: *Sheikh rivalry threatens Kharastan's stability! The full story of why Malik snubbed his half-brother.*'

For a second a smile caught the edges of his mouth before he could stop it, but he wiped it away and glared at her instead.

She dared to say *this*? To *him*? 'You are nothing but a manipulative minx!' he grated.

'Or a good mediator?' she countered, feeling that, yes, she was doing the right thing—but it was more than that. For once she was wresting a little of the control away from Malik—because surely it couldn't be good for him to have everything all his own way?

Malik's eyes narrowed. Maybe she had a point. After his unexpectedly dizzy rise to power the media was still engaged in finding out all about him—and how they would love to create a scandal out of nothing.

'Very well. I will see my brother,' he conceded slowly. 'Have security check and book us a table for dinner.'

Sorrel nodded and picked up the phone, speaking into it rapidly, all the time aware that Malik had walked over to the door which connected the suite to the corridor and was ensuring that it was locked before turning back and walking slowly towards her, his black eyes glittering. 'Now kiss me,' he ordered softly.

Her lips were dry and she needed no second bidding, for she was hot and hungry for him—but her small triumph over the matter of his brother had filled her with courage. If she could assert herself over matters of state—then why the hell was she being so damned passive whenever he started making love to her?

She had been getting more and more emotionally

frustrated by the one-sidedness of these erotic encounters—when Malik seemed to know exactly which sensual buttons to press and she just responded as if she'd been programmed to do so. But all the time he was so *removed*, so *distant*.

Maybe he took some kind of perverse pleasure in just watching her climax and then afterwards coolly walking away? Almost as if he were an observer in the act instead of a participant.

And maybe it's best that way, said a warning voice in her head.

Because you love him, don't you, Sorrel?

You love him, and he doesn't feel the same way and he never will—and maybe he's doing you a favour by staying emotionally and physically cold. Because at least it isn't filling you full of false hope.

Damn you, she thought suddenly, as he snaked his hand around her and began to rub at the indentation of her waist. At this point she would normally just sigh and let him kiss her over and over, until there was no option but to surrender.

Why *did* she always let *Malik* take control? Well, there *was* an alternative! Yes, she had gone to him untutored, but surely it would only reflect badly on the teacher if sometimes his eager pupil did not show some initiative of her own?

Luxuriously, she threaded her fingers in the jet-black waves of his hair and held her face to his. Her lips were soft on his in a slow, powerful and drugging kiss when unexpectedly she thrust her hips against his—a movement she had seen some of the court dancers perform. It wasn't the most subtle movement in the book, but it worked—because as she felt the unashamed hardness at his groin and slowly circled against it Malik tensed, black eyes wary, his fingers gripping hard at her waist.

'What do you think you're doing?' he demanded.

She rubbed up against him like an alley-cat, her hands daringly reaching behind his shoulders to massage the tension-knotted muscle there—touching him as she had wanted to do for so long, only had never before dared. 'Oh, Malik,' she purred. 'I think you know the answer to that!'

'Stop it, Sorrel.' He groaned, closing his eyes as she took complete command, pushing him down onto the soft pile of floor cushions as if he was her willing captive. 'Oh, please…stop it.'

'You know you don't mean that,' she murmured, slithering her hands beneath his robes and untying the silken string woven through the loose silk trousers which all Kharastani noblemen wore. Her movements were economical, because she did not want to give him a single second of opportunity for him to stop her. But just because they were swift it did not mean that Sorrel wasn't imaginative about this unforeseen seduction— heavens, no.

Malik had taught her much—that the body was made to be pleasured and that a man and a woman could find heaven on earth together.

How easy it was to touch him and make him moan.

Not just because he had demonstrated such finesse towards *her* but because she *wanted* to please him—as he had pleased her, so many times.

She wanted to tell him how dear he was to her, how much a part of her life and her heart—but she contented herself with kisses and strokes instead, and hoped she hid her fast-mounting doubts as she slid the silk trousers off. How daunting the fully aroused sight of him, she thought! And how utterly magnificent.

'Sorrel,' he sighed, lying back almost helplessly— as weak at that moment as he had ever been. It was not the first time a woman had taken him in her mouth, nor the first time that he had been cupped with feather-light fingers at the same time—but usually he kept his eyes shut because the fantasy always superseded reality. This time he didn't.

He saw the movement of Sorrel's head, and the tresses of white-blonde hair spread out like a satin table-cloth over his thighs, and he felt himself coming. Considering that she had never done it before—he couldn't ever remember it ever feeling quite like…like…

Afterwards, she raised her head, and the sight of her sense of wonder—of delight at what she had done— nearly blew him away as much as the act itself. Her smile was almost shy—contrasting erotically with the magic she had just worked on him.

Warning bells went off in his head as she wriggled up, leaned forward and kissed him deeply on the mouth, and he moaned, because he could taste himself on her lips, and suddenly that felt like an intimacy too far.

'Sorrel,' he groaned.

Steeling her heart against her overpowering desire to sink into him, she rose gracefully to her feet, heading off towards the bathroom before he realised what was happening and could seduce her into staying.

Let him see how *he* liked it, she thought—as she ran the cold tap and thrust her wrists beneath it.

CHAPTER NINE

THE restaurant was at the top of a tall building which sat snugly on the side of the Seine and was reached through an impossibly glamorous lobby filled with flowers, its walls crammed with photographs of past politicians and film-stars who had dined there.

There were more photographs in the lift which took them up to the sixth floor. 'You're quite small fry in comparison,' said Sorrel, as she peered at a snapshot of a past president with the restaurant's owner.

There wasn't a flicker of response on Malik's face. 'Very amusing,' he said silkily, inhibited by the presence of one of his bodyguards—otherwise he might have kissed her. Or something. He wasn't quite sure what. For the first time in memory, Malik felt dazed and confused, and angry too. Had that extraordinary scene back at the hotel been a demonstration of Sorrel's newly discovered sexual power? he wondered. Or of control? She had played sexual games with *him*!

Because you played them with *her*? taunted the voice of his conscience?

The lift doors slid open and the bodyguard stepped out first, as protocol and safety dictated. Malik took the opportunity to bend his head to Sorrel's ear.

'You can wipe that triumphant smile off your sweet little mouth,' he grated. 'You may have won the temporary reprieve of a meal with Xavier and his wife—but I haven't forgotten what took place earlier.' Somehow he doubted that he would ever forget it—but that did not lessen his anger towards her. 'And we shall discuss it later. Alone.'

His words were coated with a dark danger which made Sorrel's heart pound uncomfortably, but she kept her voice light. 'You make that sound like a threat, Malik.'

The black eyes glittered her a silent challenge. 'Do I? It's all in your interpretation, surely?' he questioned, and then there was a small buzz as he walked into the restaurant, with Sorrel trailing behind him.

Had she done something she was now going to live to regret? she wondered, as she followed in his dazzling wake. Played games with a man who liked to be in total control?

She could see heads turning, even though tonight he had elected to wear one of his beautifully cut suits. In theory, the Western garb should have made him blend in with the expensive clientele more than his robes ever did—but somehow it didn't. His tall figure was striking no matter what he wore—his jet-dark hair and olive skin even more so—and the autocratic way with which he moved across the room told even the most casual onlooker that this was a man of power and authority.

Xavier and Laura were already seated, but they rose to their feet as Malik arrived, and the four of them greeted one another with the familiarity born out of the extraordinary circumstances in which they'd all met.

Sorrel had first encountered Xavier when he'd arrived at the Blue Palace—the first of the sons to be introduced to his father—and Laura had been the English lawyer who had accompanied him. Sorrel hadn't seen them for ages, and she thought how tired Laura looked.

She found herself looking closely at Xavier and comparing him to Malik to see if she could see any family resemblance—but in reality the two men were strikingly different. Malik's skin was darker than Xavier's, but then he was of pure Kharastani blood, and only their statuesque physique and glittering black eyes showed any real similarities between them.

Almost as if it were yesterday Sorrel remembered when Xavier and Laura's wedding had been announced to a country hungry for the continuity of its royal family—and to a world who wanted the inevitable glamour of a royal wedding.

The people of Kharastan had rejoiced in the marriage of the Frenchman to Laura 'with the sunset hair', and many had hoped that the newlyweds would choose to make their home there.

Instead, they had gone back to Xavier's native France, where they now lived in a cosmopolitan area of Paris—although they were in the process of building a beach-house in Kardal, on the shores of the Balsora

Sea because, as Laura said, they wanted to build ties with Kharastan.

'Why did you not come to our apartment this evening instead of this fancy restaurant, *mon frère*?' asked Xavier with the glimmer of a smile, as he looked around the immaculately formal room with its dazzling bird's-eye view of night-time Paris and the perfect dome of the Sacré Coeur gleaming with light. 'I could have cooked you *moules*, and Laura could have shown off how well she has mastered *tarte aux pommes*! She is proud of what a French housewife she has become—aren't you, *cherie*?'

'*Mais, bien sûr!*' said Laura, with the carefully correct accent of someone who has learnt a foreign language as an adult.

How comfortably *domestic* it sounded, thought Sorrel, unable to suppress a brief pang of envy—but she saw Malik give the faintest of frowns, and wondered if it was Xavier's easy familiarity with him which had caused such disquiet. Did his sheikhdom and the icy barrier he had erected around himself mean that he wouldn't even let himself get close to his brother? At least it isn't just around *me* that he keeps at an emotional distance, she thought bitterly.

Malik shrugged apologetically. 'That would have been wonderful,' he said smoothly. 'But unfortunately my security vetoed it in favour of this place.'

'Only because it justifies their salary and they love the whole red carpet bit whenever you go out anywhere in public,' said Sorrel, flashing her blue eyes at him.

Because she knew and he knew that he could have over-ridden their objections any time he'd wanted.

There was the tiniest of silences, and Malik saw a look being exchanged between Xavier and his wife. Were they surprised that the Sheikh should allow one of his aides to be so familiar with him? He certainly couldn't blame them if they were.

How dared Sorrel offer an implied criticism like that—against him and also against his staff? Who the *hell* did she think she was? Was that why she had out-rageously seduced him earlier, against his better judge-ment—thinking that sex gave a woman power over a man like Delilah chopping off Samson's hair? Well, she was going to get a short, sharp lesson in just who was master!

They glared at one another as the wine waiter ap-proached.

'So, what's it like accompanying Malik on his trip, Sorrel?' asked Laura, breaking the rather awkward silence and shaking her head as a bottle of chilled cham-pagne was held towards her glass. 'No, thanks. Just water for me. Is he an easy man to work for?'

Sorrel's lips twitched as the two women's eyes met in a moment of perfect understanding. 'Protocol dictates that I cannot answer that truthfully in front of the man in question,' she replied demurely, and Xavier and Laura both laughed.

Malik, on the other hand, did not. He just sat back in his chair, surveying her with a quietly brooding look that was making her feel more uncomfortable by the minute. Well, if he'd wanted her to sit there mutely he should have told her so at the beginning!

'And how is life in Kharastan?' asked Xavier, after they had eaten oysters with raspberry vinegar and then creamy scrambled eggs topped with shaved truffles, which was a speciality of the famous restaurant.

Malik smiled. 'The country continues to develop—culturally as well as financially,' he said thoughtfully. 'Everyone is naturally jubilant about the new oil-field—but there is an archaeological expedition over from the States which I'm particularly excited about. They've brought up some exquisite pots and bowls. We're hoping to open a new museum at the entrance to the site—but first, of course, we need to improve the access road.'

'Sounds like you've been working hard,' said Laura. 'And what's it like for women now? Any big changes since I was last there?'

Malik's gaze came to rest on Sorrel's pink and white face, and he felt a terrible jerk of sheer excitement as he remembered just where it had been positioned earlier. It was, he realised with a start, the only time in his life that he had ever been out on an occasion like this—with family, and also accompanied by a woman he was being intimate with. Or nearly intimate with.

Usually he compartmentalised. Women were for sex and relaxation. They were diversionary. He tried and failed to think of any other he would have brought along to an occasion like this.

'Sorrel would be better qualified to answer that than me,' he conceded.

Sorrel met his eyes, knowing that—despite the tensions between them which lay simmering beneath the surface—as ruler of his country, she admired him utterly and absolutely.

'We are introducing the driving test for women,' she said softly. 'Which is long overdue. Malik...well, Malik fought hard for that.' His black eyes mocked her stumbled compliment, but she meant every word of it—and she had to bite back a great wave of sadness as she watched Xavier place his hand over Laura's. They were so in love, she thought—and not afraid to show it.

Whereas they...

No. Stop it, she corrected herself—because that was all fantasy. There was no *they* with her and Malik—it was all *her. She. She* was in love with him and always had been, and *she* was the one who had walked arrogantly and gleefully into a situation which was now threatening to self-destruct. Like a tiny kitten challenging a fierce lion she had told him she wanted a lover, and he had called her bluff—but none of it had worked out. Why, they weren't even lovers!

She suspected that Malik had been holding back from full sex in order to give her time to retract her agreement and change her mind—because there was a part of him that always wanted her to remain sweet and pure Sorrel in his eyes.

He had held back with the kind of iron-hard restraint that she couldn't imagine in anyone else. But now she had probably blown it by seducing him. Such a proud and virile man would now surely take what he must consider to be his by rights. She could read it from the edgy and restless look in his black eyes when he looked at her—tonight he intended to finally take up her challenge and make love to her in the fullest sense.

But instead of feeling excited, and eager for it to happen, inside Sorrel was eaten up with nerves. Because deep down she suspected that the final intimacy would spell the end for them—once she had given him that, there would be nothing left to give. Her virginity would be signed, sealed and delivered, and her relationship with Malik—such as it was—would be over. Her mystique would be no more and she would become just another in the long line of his lovers.

'Sorrel?' A voice broke into her thoughts

'Mmm? Oh, sorry, Laura—I was miles away.'

'So are *les toilettes*!' Laura gave her a searching smile. 'Shall we go and find them together, and leave these men with an opportunity to talk to one another?'

Sorrel nodded, rising to her feet—aware of Malik's gaze burning into her and wondering if the simple sheath of black silk she wore which fell like a dark waterfall to the ground met with his approval.

Eyes followed the two women as they made their way across the restaurant, and Malik's were among them as he watched her go. In a room full of beautiful and expensively dressed women Sorrel stood out like the natural beauty she was—though he didn't like her dressed in that sombre colour.

He turned back to find Xavier watching him intently,

and suddenly he felt stricken with a pang of guilt, recognising that Sorrel had been right—his preferred option *had* been to try and get out of this meeting. To act as if he had no family at all. Yet a part of him bitterly regretted that he hadn't got to know his father until the last days of years of his life. Wouldn't he regret it even more if he didn't attempt to forge a better relationship with his two brothers? And the fact that he was here at all was Sorrel's doing, he reminded himself. *She* had battled to get him here.

He raised his glass. 'It is good to see you again, Xavier.' And to his surprise he found that he meant it.

'Et toi aussi, mon frère.' His half-brother sat back in his chair, his eyes full of question. 'How I long to ask you a question that protocol would frown on,' he murmured.

'Ask me what you will,' said Malik gruffly. 'For are we not brothers?'

For a split-second their eyes met in a moment of pure kinship, and Xavier nodded in silent and grateful acknowledgement of the bond. 'Is it serious?' he asked softly. 'With Sorrel?'

'Serious?' Malik was taken aback. 'How the hell can it be serious?'

Xavier shrugged. 'I just felt that there was something…between you.'

'But we've been snapping at each other all evening,' objected Malik.

'Precisely,' said Xavier dryly. He glanced towards the direction of the restroom and hesitated. 'You are lovers, perhaps?'

Malik sighed and shook his dark head. That depended on your definition of the word. 'No. For she is a virgin,' he said slowly, almost as if he had forgotten Xavier were there.

Xavier's black eyes narrowed as he looked at his half-brother. 'Ah! I see. Yes, I see,' he said slowly. He stared down at his hands for a moment—and when he looked up again his black eyes were clear and candid. 'Then you must leave her now,' he said. 'Or marry her.'

'I know that,' said Malik fiercely. 'Don't you think I don't know that?'

The women came back in time for dessert and coffee—though Laura refused the restaurant's famous chocolate mousse and just sipped at a cup of fruit tea instead.

In the lobby they said their farewells, and Malik agreed to visit them in Kardal, when their beach-house was completed. Amid the chatter of future plans Sorrel stood to one side—feeling left out and not knowing whether, if ever, she would see the couple again.

It didn't get any better once they were inside the limousine, because Malik seemed preoccupied and Sorrel sensed that some sea-change had occurred over the course of the evening. He did not touch her, nor even look at her—and there was none of the flirtation she had come to expect from him. Without knowing how—or why—she suspected that it was going to be over between them before it had even started.

But you do know why, she thought unhappily. *You have crossed over an invisible line. By seducing him you have discarded your pure and virginal identity and he will have lost respect for you.* And even though she tried to tell herself that she had been acting like an *equal*, instead of a submissive little yes-woman, it still hurt—and she still wished she could rewind the clock for it never to have happened.

Malik turned his head to stare out of the window, where tourists wandered the streets as happily as if it was daylight. The car sped down the Champs-Elysées and skated the edge of the Trocadero—all floodlit, like a giant film set, with the watchful frame of the Arc de Triomphe in the background—but Malik saw nothing of these.

His head was full of conflicting thoughts as he balanced dreams against reality, desire against morality. By playing sexual games with Sorrel he now found himself in deep and dark swirling waters—not knowing which way the land ahead lay. If he took her virginity, then he would have to marry her. He hadn't needed Xavier to voice it for in his heart he had always known this. And yet now—as then—the same question reared its head. Was the price too high?

Wouldn't it be better for all concerned if he did what most men in his position would do? If he forgot all about Sorrel? If he played the field for a few more years and then settled down with a meek Kharastani wife who would allow him rightful dominance in his home as well as in his country? Not a woman he knew almost too well to be comfortable with, who was in turn feisty and manipulative and, with her English boarding-school education sometimes just too independent for her own good.

She chose just that moment to cross one leg over the other—so that he could see its long and shapely definition through the silky caress of the black gown she wore. He wondered if she was wearing stockings underneath, and swallowed down the sudden thickness in his throat. Could he bear never to penetrate her? Never to know that unbearably sweet sensation of completion with her—their contrasting rhythms finding sweet communion in the coming together of their bodies? His tongue snaked out over suddenly dry lips.

'Laura's pregnant, you know,' she said, searching around desperately to fill in the yawning silence.

Malik stilled, erotic thoughts swept away like leaves from a path. He frowned. 'She told you that?'

'She didn't need to—not at first. Because I guessed—didn't you? She wouldn't drink wine, and she looked so tired. I asked her if she was okay when we were in the loo and she told me.' She wasn't going to tell him that she'd almost broken down and told Laura that she was in love with the Sheikh. 'They haven't said anything about the baby yet because they're terrified of jinxing it—she had a miscarriage last year. Did you know that?'

'No,' he said slowly. 'I didn't know that.'

'But she's past three months, so it looks fine,' she added, then saw the dawning of a new burden which shadowed his dark face and wondered how she could have been so dense. Because for Malik it was not just cheery news that his half-brother was about to become a father. When you were royal the repercussions of a new life were even more significant than usual.

Xavier's baby would become the first of a new generation of the Ak Atyn family. He—or she—was its future, and would continue its line even if Malik were never to produce a child of his own. Would that make him feel threatened, she wondered, or under some kind of subtle pressure to lay the foundation for creating his own dynasty?

She stole a glance at the hard and rugged profile, but he sat silently, as if carved from some dark and immutable stone, seemingly oblivious to her presence.

Malik's head was buzzing—his mind filled with all the repercussions of his half-brother producing an heir. Was this the wake-up call he had needed to stop avoiding the issue which had been hanging over him ever since the golden crown of Kharastan had been placed on his head at his coronation?

As they let themselves into the suite, leaving the bodyguard standing on guard outside the heavy-duty door, Malik thought how quickly the focus of what troubled you could change. Earlier this evening he had been caught up with nothing more far-reaching than a tussle with his pride and a battle with his conscience. Whether or not he would take Sorrel to his bed for the night had been the question looming large.

But now—with the news that his half-brother was to become a father—his own very existence had been brought into the equation. Malik took his Sheikhdom very seriously—he had not been born to power and did not wear its mantle lightly. He was aware of its honour, and all its responsibilities, and these were what absorbed him now.

Should his first consideration not be to his people, rather than to himself? Were they troubled by the fact that he had shown no signs of settling down—when in fact most of his energies had been spent adapting to his new role and bringing Kharastan into the twenty-first Century.

Sorrel turned to look at him, and as she did so he was aware of the contrast between hair and gown—moon-pale and sky-dark—both gleaming as softly as stars. Her eyes were large and blue and very beautiful, and the curve of her hips spoke instinctively of the dual role at the heart of every woman: lover and mother.

Suddenly he forgot all thoughts of home as his other dilemma took shape in his mind. Because Sorrel had become a problem, and he was a fool not to have anticipated that this would happen.

He wanted Sorrel more than he had ever wanted any other woman in his life, but if he took her virginity he would have to marry her.

Yet he needed a wife!

As never before—he needed a wife!

Was this fate, interceding as it had done so many times before? he wondered. Was practicality enough reason to align their futures?

Yet if he didn't act, then he would lose her. Someone else would swoop in and take her—for she was ripe and ready for love. Could he bear the thought that another man should know her intimately?

Seized with a certainty that this was the path he was meant to take, he caught her in the crossfire of his black gaze. 'Sorrel?'

She frowned, sensing something momentous shimmering in the air around them. 'Yes, Malik?'

There was a pause before he spoke. One of those pauses which seemed to go on for ever, like the moments before birth, or death. Life-changing moments. 'Will you marry me?'

It was the last thing in the world she had expected, and Sorrel was confused. She met his eyes, her own candid with question. 'Why?'

In a way he knew her too well to tell her anything but the truth. 'I need a wife.'

'Because of Laura's baby?' she questioned dully, wondering if the ache in her heart showed on her face.

'That's one of the reasons, yes.'

'And because of my virginity, presumably?' she asked him painfully.

He felt his body tense. 'That's another reason, yes. I cannot take it without offering you something in return—and I cannot contemplate the thought of another man being intimate with you.'

'Gosh, what a lot of reasons!' she said sarcastically. Jealousy, possession and expediency—they were what lay behind his proposal. He hadn't said a word about the way he felt—but maybe that shouldn't have surprised her. To Malik, she was a woman who had been prepared to barter her virginity—all he had done was offer the highest price.

Malik saw the cloud which had crossed over her delicate features, but now that the idea had taken shape in his mind he pursued it with the single-mindedness that he brought to everything. 'You told me how much you missed Kharastan, Sorrel—how did you describe it? Like there was a hole in your heart.'

Oh, the stupid man—didn't he realise that she had been missing *him* as much as her adopted homeland? 'I don't remember saying anything like that,' she said coolly.

'But you do miss Kharastan,' he said silkily. 'I can see it in your face whenever you talk about it. The dreamy look in your eyes.' His mouth hardened with resolve. 'I cannot think of a woman better qualified to help me rule—and just think what your father would say if he knew what I was asking you today, Sorrel, can you imagine?'

How clever and calculating he could be, she thought—he knew that those particular words would affect her in a way that few others could. Her father and mother's happiest years had been spent serving the country they had grown to love with a passion—a passion they had passed on to their only child. Malik had witnessed the close bond which had existed between her and her parents—indeed, at times he had seemed almost wistful about it, and Sorrel had said as much to her mother.

'That's because Malik has never known what it is to

have a family,' her mother had said. Had that been
another reason why Sorrel had always hung around
him? Always delighted when she could manage to put
a smile on that stern, handsome face of his? Was that
the reason why her father had taken the extraordinary
step of making Malik her guardian? Had such an
unusual union been one of his own dreams?

No. Now she was just getting fanciful—but it was
difficult to avoid it when that same Malik was standing
in front of her now, with a question on a face grown
harder and yet more beautiful over the years.

'I will ask you once more, Sorrel,' he said silkily.
'And then never again. Will you marry me?'

CHAPTER TEN

OF COURSE she said yes. What else could she say?

Sorrel had loved Malik since the year dot—long before he became his Serene Highness the Sheikh—and she loved him still. Despite his moods and his arrogance and his icy control, she couldn't just switch that love off like a tap—no matter how hard she might try.

Yet what could have seemed like a fairytale was most emphatically not. There was none of the romance or celebration or joy associated with such an occasion. They discussed it with the same kind of emotion with which they might have discussed the takeover of a business.

The first thing he did was kiss her—but it was a perfunctory kiss, like the rubber stamping of a contract—and the next thing he did was ring for Fariq, who bowed and congratulated him with a face so shadowed that Sorrel couldn't tell whether or not he was pleased.

'Sorrel must be assigned another room immediately,' Malik said, and Fariq bowed once more and went off to do the Sheikh's bidding.

'*Why?*' whispered Sorrel.

Malik's black eyes narrowed. 'Because there shall be no more temptation before the wedding.'

Sorrel laughed uneasily. What better night to consummate their relationship than this, and get properly close to him? This had to be some kind of joke, surely? Then she saw his look of determination and realised that it was nothing of the sort. 'But what difference does it make now?' she demanded. 'We're engaged!'

'It makes all the difference in the world, Sorrel,' he retorted. 'For it is custom and tradition that the Sheikh should marry a woman who is intact.' He saw her wince at his choice of word, but it was too late to take it back. Her eyes were big and blue and appealing, and the look in them had the power to make him ache...

'Malik—'

He halted her with a fierce look, remembering how defenceless he had felt beneath the merciless onslaught of her hands and her mouth when she had seduced him before dinner. And he resented that feeling—just as he resented her for having caused it—even while his body shivered with the erotic memory of it. 'Don't even think about it,' he warned softly. 'I know that you want to demonstrate your new-found sexual confidence, and you will have every opportunity to do so, but it will have to wait until afterwards. I want to do this properly.'

'And if I disobey you?' She flicked her blonde hair back. 'If I come over there and take you in my arms?'

His black gaze was steady. She must learn two lessons: that *his* wishes were paramount and that she must never, *ever* disobey him. 'Then there will be no marriage—for no such contract will take place unless I can present the betrothal to my people with a clear conscience.'

'No one will actually *know* if I'm a virgin, Malik!'

'You will know. And I will know. And that is what matters. You will come to me pure and unsullied on our wedding night.'

He saw her look of hurt disappointment and steeled his heart against it. Because suddenly events felt as if they were overtaking him—as if the order he had created in his newly made life was in danger of slipping into chaos if he did not take control. His senses felt raw—as if the layers with which he protected himself were slowly being peeled away to expose the man beneath.

Malik swallowed down his desire, and the anger that she could make him feel this way—but most of it he put down to frustration. At least it wouldn't be much longer. He intended to order that the wedding take place as quickly as possible. His mind skated ahead. There would have to a few changes made in the laws governing his choice of bride—but what the hell? He *was* the law!

'Trust me, Sorrel—the wait will be worth it,' he murmured. 'By the time I take you to my bed it will far surpass all our expectations.'

She had wanted comfort and reassurance as much as anything else—though Malik seemed to think this was simply about sex. And yet could she really blame him if he did? After all, hadn't she behaved in a way which deep down he must disapprove of? Kharastani women were not brought up to think of themselves as sexual equals—and, while Malik might desire her with an intensity which had banished all reason, would he have any genuine respect left for her? When desire dimmed what would be left to sustain a marriage?

But it was too late for doubts—and royal brides-to-be weren't allowed to have them anyway. She had given him her answer and she must honour that.

And by the time they arrived back in Kharastan preparations for the wedding and the deluge of interview requests from the world's press meant that she didn't have a minute to call her own, so her doubts were pushed away.

She quickly began to realise that her life was going to be very different from now on.

Someone from her schooldays had sold a very unflattering photo of her wearing a pair of shorts to the newspapers—and people that Sorrel hardly remembered were suddenly coming out with old 'quotes' which she didn't recognise as the kind of thing she'd ever said.

Then there was the added pressure of a leak to the press that Laura and Xavier were expecting a boy. The first Sorrel knew about it was when she was giving a rare, pre-wedding interview and was asked, "Will you be trying for a baby straight away?"

It seemed that no subject was deemed taboo. Now that she was seen as a piece of public property her life had changed for ever. And things within Kharastan itself had changed, too—something she hadn't anticipated.

For years Sorrel had had the run of the palace, and felt totally at ease there. She had always swum in the Olympic-sized pool and petted the Akal Teke horses in the stables, wandered in the beautiful gardens and generally felt that it was her home.

Now she was watched. She was no longer just Sorrel—the blonde Englishwoman who had worked her way into the affection of the Kharastani people by virtue of her long association with the royal family. Now she was to become the Queen, and people began to be guarded whenever she was around. Gone for ever was the spontaneity and freedom of her life, and with hindsight she could see how much she had taken those simple pleasures for granted.

But she had accepted Malik without any terms or conditions on her part. She had not asked for his love— probably because she knew he would not lie about it, or pretend to feel something he didn't. And the alternative—a life *without* Malik—was something she wasn't prepared to contemplate. Not now that she had tasted temptation in his arms…

Her face was icy with terror as she dressed for her wedding, and her isolation seemed to mock her once she had dismissed the maidservants, afraid that emotion might get the better of her and that she might break down in front of them—an unforgivable crime for a Queen-to-be.

The immense silence seemed to deafen her, and it had been a long time since Sorrel could remember feeling quite so lonely as she did at that moment—which was ironic, really, given that she would soon have a husband. But it was at times like this that you really noticed the lack of a family—and Malik's words came back to her. Through the sudden blur of tears she saw her golden and scarlet reflection looking back at her from the mirror—wishing above all else that her parents could have seen her today, in all her wedding finery.

And Malik was right—how proud her father would have been that she was marrying the Sheikh.

Yet would Sorrel's perceptive mother have noticed the faint sadness which clouded her daughter's blue eyes? Or observed the very real anxiety which was making her skin feel cold and clammy?

The fear that she had leapt too hastily at Malik's unexpected proposal and was now worried that she was going to live to regret it.

How she wished that she had had the courage to ask her husband-to-be about just what kind of marriage he was anticipating.

But she had not had the opportunity to ask him—and now it was too late. The guests were assembled and waiting, and in an hour she would no longer be Sorrel, who didn't know where in life she fitted in, but Queen, married to a man who didn't love her.

A rap at the door interrupted her thoughts, and Sorrel opened it to find her two sisters-in-law standing there,

carrying her bouquet which had been freshly gathere
from the palace gardens that morning.

The two women had arrived with Malik's half
brothers a week ago, and Sorrel had been showing then
the hidden treasures of the country while Malik locke
himself away in his office to deal with the borde
dispute with Maraban and the constitutional change
thrown up by their marriage. He had made sure tha
they were never alone—and even at the formal dinner
which had been held every night in the run-up to th
ceremony barely more than a few words had passe
between her and her fiancé.

Laura looked glowing—especially compared to th
night Sorrel had seen her in Paris. Her sunset-coloure
hair was woven with creamy stephanotis, and a jade sil
coat-dress disguised all signs of her pregnancy. Sorre
wondered how she must have felt about the hospita
leaking the result of her scan—but somehow it didn'
seem appropriate for her to ask.

'Look at these!' exclaimed Alexa, Giovanni's wife
as she put the bridal bouquet down on a carve
mulberry dresser. 'Aren't they the most beautiful rose
you ever did see?'

'Mmm!' Sorrel picked them up and sniffed at then
dutifully, but when she looked up it was to find Laur
staring at her, and she wondered if she had seen he
fingers trembling.

'Are these just normal pre-wedding nerves, Sorrel?
Laura asked softly.

'Well…' Sorrel flashed the smile she had been prac

ng in front of the mirror all week, hoping that it
would convince Laura as well as the rest of the waiting
world. 'Does the word "normal" ever apply where the
k Atyn family is concerned?'

Laura smiled back. 'I guess not!'

'Come on—we've come to walk with you to the
eremony,' Alexa said to Sorrel. 'Are you ready?'

Sorrel bit her lip. Was she?

Every woman dreamed of her wedding day, and
orrel had lived out this fantasy many times. Of moving
lowly towards Malik, her eyes downcast and her head
weighted by the circlet of flowers which surrounded a
iamond crown.

When she reached him, she looked up into his eyes—
er heart leaping with love as she issued one last small
rayer that he would be smiling the kind of smile that
is dream-like counterpart always had. But her prayers
emained unanswered, for his face was as serious as she
ad ever seen it—the black eyes flinty and cold.

Was he regretting it too? she wondered.

The *maulvi* began to read aloud the vows in the
lassic combination of the formal, the spiritual and the
egal which was at the heart of every marriage
eremony, no matter what religion. Deeply profound
words that Sorrel's shaky voice stumbled over once or
wice as she repeated them.

They each sipped from the goblet of life—a thick
nd sweet mixture of pomegranate flavoured with
omething no one could pronounce properly, but which
asted a bit like Turkish Delight.

She shivered as Malik tied the traditional double loop of silver and black beads around her neck— supposed to protect the marriage against evil—and then they were man and wife at last.

The guests dropped deep bows and curtsies as she and the Sheikh passed through the high-vaulted room to a courtyard decked with garlands, where traditional lute players sat strumming by one of the smaller fountains.

Outside, they stood in the bright sunshine, and Malik raised her fingers to his lips.

'So you are my Queen at last,' he murmured, his face shadowed by the flowing headdress he wore. 'And although you have just promised to obey, I see that already you have broken your promise to me.'

Sorrel's eyes widened, startled, her fingers flying to her throat—hurt that his first words as her husband should be those of reprimand. 'I have?'

Malik's mouth curved into an odd kind of smile. How brittle she looked—as if she might snap if he took her into his arms. 'I was teasing,' he said softly. 'You promised to always wear your hair down for your Sheikh, remember?' His eyes glittered with dark sexual promise. He was wishing that he could take her in his arms and kiss her properly—but propriety must be observed. At least until they were in their bedchamber. 'But I shall unpin it myself later—when we are alone.'

She stared up at him, scarcely able to believe that she was now his wife. Wanting to pinch herself to check that she was really alive and not still dreaming. Wanting

ome kind of reassurance that she hadn't just done the
most foolish thing. 'Malik, I'm terrified of doing the
wrong thing.'

'There is no need. I shall teach you—as I have taught
you everything else.' He thought how long she had been
forced to wait for the pleasure she craved, and sought
to put her mind at rest. 'You are a sensual and willing
pupil, Sorrel.'

Did he think that everything came back to *sex*? she
thought in despair. Or maybe this was the punishment
for young women who announced that they wanted a
lover—afterwards they would never be taken seriously.
'I meant...I'm scared that people won't accept me.'

He tipped her chin up with the tips of his fingers and
stared down into the beguiling blue shimmer of her
eyes. 'How can you be?' he asked simply, shaking his
head so that the flowers in his own headdress shimmered like butterflies in the bright sunshine. 'When
you look so perfect, and everyone is so happy about our
marriage.'

'Are they, Malik? Really?'

'*Yes*. Really. They have watched you grow and they
have seen how much you love our country. Why would
you know even a second of doubt about the ceremonies
today, when you could almost write a book about
Kharastani protocol?' He shrugged as he saw her still
needing to be convinced. 'Oh, there will always be
people who think that I should have married a woman
of pure blood—but it is up to you to win their hearts
and prove them wrong. You may look like a foreigner,

but you certainly don't act like one. You'll be fine Sorrel—but you must learn to disguise your doubts an to hide your true feelings *behind the patina of confi dence. That is what your people expect of you—indeed what I* expect of you. So, come, let us go and greet ou guests.'

She took his arm and they walked into the feast t the sound of fanfare and the flutter of rose petals—both Western touches which had been ordered by Malik fo his new bride. But for Sorrel the day proved to be some thing of an endurance test.

All those things he'd just said about having to hid her feelings—she'd known that was what she must do at least on an intellectual level. She was aware tha Malik did it all the time—certainly in public. But wa he going to carry on doing it in private, too? Were th two of them allowed to *have* feelings—or was every thing supposed to operate on some lofty, superficia level, where extremes of emotion weren't encouraged

But you've made your wedding bed—and now yo have to lie in it!

He had not forced her to marry him. He had askee her coolly and calmly and she had agreed. She ha walked into the marriage as an adult—so she had bette start behaving like one. No one got everything the wanted in life—maybe this was enough.

Their bedchamber was lit with candles and scentee with cedarwood and amber—both rich and earth notes, believed by Kharastani custom to enhance th fertility of every bride-to-be on her wedding night.

As Sorrel slipped the sheer cream organza gown over her head, she began to understand a little of some of these old rituals. Suddenly she understood the necessity behind Malik's insistence that she come to him untouched on this significant night. She was the wife of the King—of *course* she must be pure.

'Sorrel?'

She heard his soft, deep voice—rich as honey, with its distinctive accent which never failed to send shivers down her spine—and turned to see him standing there, shimmering as if lit from within, in his cloth of gold with his belt and his sword slung around the narrow line of his hips.

'Yes, Malik,' she whispered.

He walked over to her, cupping her face in his hands and then touching them to the intricate confection of her hair, still crowned with the diamond circlet. 'I want to unpin your hair,' he said, his voice unsteady.

Carefully, he lifted off the glittering crown and laid it down, and then he set about removing the pearl pins, one by one—so that her hair began to tumble down around her shoulders, strand by strand. It was slow and sexual and highly symbolic of what was about to come. It was like every fantasy come to life—Malik, her husband, his handsome face focussed entirely on the task in hand. When her hair was finally freed he ran his fingers through it greedily—like a man who had discovered treasure.

'I have dreamed of this moment,' he said softly.

So had she. But now that it was upon her Sorrel felt

stricken by a terrible shyness. This was no longer an erotic fight for equality in a Parisian bedroom, but an ancient submission of wife to master.

It was a union fuelled by convention, and by Malik's urgent need for an heir—but it would never be fanned by the flames of love. And yet surely that did not preclude a kind of tenderness between them—the kind that could never have existed during the cold-blooded arrangement of her sexual education? Did their long standing friendship not count for something in the bedroom?

'Malik,' she whispered.

'Ah, Sorrel,' he said, his voice roughened with the urgency of self-denial. He had wanted her so badly, and for so long, and yet he knew that he must make this memorable for her, since it would colour her opinion of sex for evermore. But, by the desert storm, he was aching!

'Do you know how I have hungered for this moment?' he demanded. 'How night after night I have thought of this—and you—naked and pale in my arms and in my bed? And you have thought of me in the same way,' he stated with satisfaction.

'Y-yes,' whispered Sorrel, but there was something fierce—almost savage—about his dark features which made him look almost like a stranger.

'I think you're wearing too much,' he murmured. 'I think we both are. Ah, the sweet pleasures of disrobing! Shall I take this off?' His finger brushed over the diaphanous material of her nightgown.

'Y-yes,' she said again—and wondered where that über-confident Sorrel had gone—the one who had seduced *him* with such panache. Had the magnitude of their wedding day somehow inhibited her?

Laying her on the bed, he peeled her nightgown off and then began to remove his ceremonial robes. He had seen most of her body before—though never completely bare, always insisting on some wispy little thong or a pair of French knickers being worn, as if to conform to some ancient idea of decorum. But—apart from that night in Paris—there had only ever been one occasion when Sorrel had seen Malik partially unclothed.

It had been when she was still a teenager, and she'd come across him sword-fighting in the courtyard, with one of the grooms. The sight of his bare, hard torso—sheened with sweat and grimy with dust—had imprinted itself on her mind and fuelled her fantasies for years to follow.

But now, as he removed his robes, nothing could have prepared her for the magnificence of his naked body—with all its daunting strength and latent power.

In the candlelight his honed flesh gleamed, all golden and shadow, and Sorrel's fears multiplied. She wanted to tell him that she had been acting out when she'd said she wanted a lover—and that the last thing she had expected was for him to call her bluff. She wanted to say something as corny as *Please be gentle with me*—but she didn't even know whether he'd hear. Because now his face looked as if it was a tight, hard mask—it was if he wasn't really there with her, or maybe that he just didn't see her.

'Malik!' she gasped, as he climbed onto the bed and their warm flesh met.

'Sorrel.' He began to stroke her body, holding himself in check as his fingers began to tiptoe over her soft flesh. 'Sorrel,' he said again, more fiercely this time.

As a lover he was textbook perfect. He knew when to incite and when to retreat. The first thrust hurt—but that seemed to please him, for he gave a low laugh of almost indulgent pleasure. And afterwards it didn't hurt at all—he made sure of that. How perfectly he built the wall of desire, brick by brick, his lips in her hair and over her breast and in her mouth. She felt his body hardening inside hers, and suddenly she could bear it no longer and tumbled over the edge, her body convulsing over and over again.

'Malik, oh, *Malik*,' she groaned.

Sorrel was no stranger to orgasm—Malik had made sure of that too—but this time was different. This time it felt as though she would never be the same person again afterwards. Perhaps because his own sharp release came almost immediately, and she heard the ragged groan which sounded as if it had been ripped from the very core of his being.

Afterwards he withdrew, and kissed her hair and stroked her damp brow, but it was the same kind of perfunctory kiss with which he'd sealed their engagement, and which told her his thoughts were elsewhere. As if *he* were elsewhere. He rolled away from her and onto

is back. Suddenly the space between them on the divan
might have been a million miles. Was this what
happened afterwards? thought Sorrel with a newly
rising tide of panic. Did the joining of their bodies
cease once they had been greedily fed with satisfaction—and why had it left her feeling *empty* inside?

Because he doesn't love you as you long to be loved,
as you love him. And being Malik—hard, precise and
perfectionist Malik—he wouldn't go through the pantomime of saying the words unless he really meant them.

Sharply, Sorrel bit her lip—tasting the sudden salt
taste of blood and blinking rapidly in an attempt to
keep her tears at bay, wondering if he could hear the tiny
shuttering sound her eyes made.

Malik lay staring up at the ceiling, but he saw
nothing of the dancing light show provided by the guttering candle flames. He thought of the long road which
had carried him to where he found himself now.
Brought to the palace by a white-faced midwife who
had heard rumours of his progeny, taken in by the
sheikh but brought up by servants, never acknowledged
as his heir until soon before his death.

For Malik, life had been a series of tests, of hoops
to jump through. For most he had been guided by
example—on others he'd relied on instinct. But relationships were the most tricky of all—and never more
so than with Sorrel. Yet just for now all those minutes
and months and years which had ticked by to bring him
to just this point culminated in a perfect moment of
peace. And he closed his eyes and fell asleep.

She lay, frozen with disbelief, until the soft and steady breathing of the man who lay beside her told her that she was not mistaken.

Malik was asleep!

The emotions which had been simmering away inside her for so long finally bubbled up to the surface and she felt tears beginning to slip from the corners of her closed eyes. She swallowed them down, but she could feel them rising again—like a rock pool when the tide started to pour in. In a minute she would wake him—and could she bear to have Malik find her crying on her wedding night, demanding to know why?

Sliding from the bed, she shivered a little as her bare feet touched the marble floor. Unaccustomed to her nakedness, nonetheless she did not dare risk pulling her discarded nightdress from the mattress and waking him.

But at least the night air was warm, and she blew out a couple of candles along the way, before going over to stand by the long windows. Their shutters were open to the beautiful palace gardens, and the moon was big and fat and full in the sky—but then, the wedding had been planned around the glory of its cycle, since a full moon was considered an auspicious omen in the Kharastani culture.

Honeymoon.

Oh, how the word mocked her! The tears rose in the back of her throat and she choked them back, but it was too late—for the dark figure on the bed stirred.

For a moment Malik experienced the split-second of disorientation which came between waking and sleep.

ing. His senses were keen and ever-alert—he had spent long nights of vigil in the desert as part of his passage from boy to man. But snakes and scorpions and the crackle of a larger predator in the distance were threats he could deal with.

His new wife crying on her wedding night was not.

In the half-light, he frowned before he spoke. 'I believe that many women cry after the first time. They say that orgasm is a little death.'

Sorrel didn't turn, just nodded her head so violently that her hair fell all over her face. Her shoulders were shaking. 'Yes, that must be it!' she sobbed. 'It *must* be a reaction to sex! Because *that's* what's important—isn't it, Malik?'

Malik was outraged. 'That is rich, coming from you!' He sat up, the rumpled sheet falling around his hips, to see Sorrel carved in moonlight, her womanly curves like a silvered violin and her hair streaming down her back like white gold. But he hardened his heart against the dip in her back, the way her bottom curved into such perfect symmetry.

He spoke quickly and asked the question—before she could turn round and bewitch him with those big blue eyes. Even though the room was dimly lit there seemed to be no known antidote to her particular brand of enchantment.

'You are unhappy?' he grated.

'Yes!'

'Perhaps you regret having married me?'

'Yes, Malik!' she cried again, and the words broke loose from the dam inside her. 'Yes, I do!'

CHAPTER ELEVEN

FOR minutes there was silence—broken only by the fading sounds of Sorrel's crying, gradually becoming more muffled as her sobs grew less. She could hear the flick of a match and see a sudden increase of light as he must have lit a candle behind her. And because she couldn't keep standing with her back to him she turned round, expecting the fury on his face but still recoiling from its dark ferocity.

'Wouldn't it have made more sense to have thought about this *before* the wedding?' he snapped.

Now Sorrel felt even more vulnerable—naked, and facing the contempt which radiated from the powerful frame in waves so strong that she could almost see them. Sucking in a breath which still shuddered from her tears, she walked over to one of the low divans, where the golden lace veil she had worn for her wedding lay, and she picked it up and tied it around herself, knotting it like a sarong.

'I thought... I thought...'

'No—that's just it!' he stormed. 'You *didn't* think!

If you had these kind of…*doubts*—' he fixed on the word exasperatedly, wanting to bang his fists in frustration against the wall '—then you should have shared them with me!'

She wanted to say that it had been difficult to share *anything* with him when they had been living on opposite sides of the palace and kept apart by convention. But even if they had been together would she have had the nerve to tell him how she really felt? Since when had Malik ever invited her confidences?

Malik's mind was racing. He had chosen Sorrel as his bride *despite* the fact that she was not native to his land—because part of him admired her adaptable character which her unique upbringing had helped forge. But when it came to the crunch she was *not* a Kharastani—and she was not constrained by the deeply-engrained values of that land.

Whereas a Kharastani would sooner walk barefoot over the burning desert sands than give up on her marriage—why, a Western woman would terminate such a sacred union as ruthlessly as the falcon swooped down to seize its bait.

As Sheikh—and as a relatively new and untested sheikh—it was his role to lead by example. What a fool he would look if his marriage was dissolved before the rose petals had been swept from the palace courtyard.

But Malik knew better than anyone that the only way to defeat fear was to confront it. Face your own worst nightmare and come through it and what else could possibly hurt you? At least, that was the theory.

'So you want to end the marriage?' he demanded.

Sorrel gasped. Was that how disposable an asset he saw her? 'Do you?'

'Of course I don't want to end the marriage!' he raged. 'My reputation will be in complete tatters if I do!'

The hope which had flared in her heart died a spectacular death, and Sorrel bit her lip. 'Well, we can't have *that*, can we?'

His instinct was to lash back at her verbally, to hide his hurt and his outrage that she should speak to him in such a way. But behind her sarcasm he heard the tremor of her own pain, and he stared at her—feeling as out of his depth as a non-swimmer who had just been hurled into the watery stew of the Balsora Sea in winter time.

Because Malik knew little about women—save for the very obvious stuff about how to please them in bed. The servants who had tended him during his growing-up years at the palace had wanted to adore him, but the proud little boy had always kept himself apart—had held something back. Perhaps it was being the product of a union about which there had always been whispers and rumours that had made Malik always feel as if he were floundering around in the dark. And when your mother died in childbirth people tended to pity you— and pity had been the last thing he'd wanted. Sorrel hadn't pitied him. She had been kind and she had been sweet—but somewhere along the way that sweetness and kindness had fled. He had taken them away, and left her with only hurt and anger.

His voice was sombre. 'What is it that you want, Sorrel?'

She could tell him that she wanted his love—but that would be like a child demanding a golden coach to travel around in, like the one Cinderella had. You should only ask for the achievable—and no one ever guaranteed that your heart's desire would be achievable.

'I'm afraid that we're going to have a marriage like your father's,' she admitted, giving voice to a concern she hadn't even known existed until now. 'With you travelling the world and making love to different women and siring babies by them.'

Had she alighted on that to wound him? Because wound him it did—but it was the pain of having a long-neglected and deep wound being hacked open before being cleansed by something harsh and antiseptic, allowing it the conditions in which to heal.

'My father did what his people wanted of him at the time,' he said simply. 'His wife, the Queen, was barren—and the country desperately needed an heir.'

'It still does.'

He didn't say *But we might have children of our own,* because somehow it seemed inappropriate—like a vision of a future that you might never have. 'Xavier is carrying on the next generation,' he said firmly.

'I thought that rivalry over *that* was one of the reasons you asked me to marry you.'

From anyone else this might have sounded like a criticism—but then, no one else would have said it, especially at a time like this, when their brand-new marriage hung precariously in the balance. This was Sorrel as he knew her best. Reminding him of what was real and what was not.

'It was,' he admitted. 'But maybe it wasn't enough. Like your virginity wasn't enough.'

And now Sorrel was properly scared. It was one thing for her to express her doubts—but quite another when Malik did it back to her. Because women verbalised while men *acted*, and it sounded as if….as if he really *did* want to finish it. A tight, cold dread clamped its way around her heart. 'What do you mean—it wasn't enough?'

For the first time in his life he felt helpless. Even when his suspicions about being the Sheikh's son had crystallised into fact he had not felt like this. As though he was being swept down a fast-raging torrent which used to be the trickle of a stream.

'I just wish we could have back what we used to have,' he said simply.

Sorrel stared at him. 'And what was that?' she whispered.

'It used to be so easy between us,' he said. 'I liked knowing you were there—only I didn't realise that until you'd gone.' He shrugged, like the little boy who had never been allowed to be just that. Who had always been told to behave like a man. It was the earliest lesson he had learnt—that men didn't show emotion—and there had been no loving mother around to tell him that they could.

'Maybe it was the sex that complicated our relationship,' he said slowly, when still she didn't speak, just continued to look at him with those big blue eyes, and in them an expression he didn't know. 'But I wanted you so much, Sorrel. When I walked into your flat and saw you looking like a tramp...' His voice was husky, his eyes opaque with remembered lust. 'I suddenly realised how much I wanted you.'

'Malik,' she said urgently—because she knew that she couldn't carry on holding back in case she got hurt. Because half-truths could hurt just as much. He might not feel the same way about her, but he needed to know what she felt for him—because surely it was churlish and unkind to hold back on emotions simply because you wanted something for yourself?

'I was crying because I love you,' she said quietly. 'Just the way I've always loved you. That's why I went away—because you seemed to look right through me and because I was projecting into an unbearable future, when you would take another woman as your wife. And I couldn't take it. I was crying because you will never love me back in the same way—and because I would never be able to tell you how I feel about you.'

His eyes narrowed suspiciously—like a wild horse the first time it was offered food from the bowl. 'So you don't want to leave me?'

'Of course I don't,' she whispered. How could he honestly believe that? she wondered. But in the same moment she recognised that Malik didn't know how to receive love—probably because he'd never had any experience of it before. 'Never, never, never,' she affirmed ardently.

A sigh escaped his lips and she touched her fingertips to them, her eyes searching his face. And written there she could see the glimmer of something she dared not put a name to—but it set off the distant clamour of hope deep in her heart. In a way they were very similar: two outsiders, who blended in wherever they needed to but had never made a place of their own.

She loved Malik, and she wanted him to love her back, but one wasn't dependent on the other. She suspected that most of the ingredients were in place—he just needed to work out his own particular recipe.

But in the meantime she could show him hers. Show him with all her heart how love could be. She would be his partner in every way that counted—if he would let her.

'I love you, my darling Malik,' she said. 'I love you so very much.'

And Malik felt the sting of tears as he recognised that she had humbled herself before him—had not been afraid to put her feelings on the line. It was as if a veil had been lifted from before his eyes, and everything suddenly became clear.

There was a word to describe the way he'd missed her, the way he'd wanted her, and the way he'd felt as if his heart would break into tiny pieces if she ever went away again.

The lump in his throat made speaking difficult, but

the word seemed determined to be spoken. 'I love you too, Sorrel,' he said, and then he repeated it. 'I *love* you.'

There was wonder in his voice as he let this brand-new emotion of love flood in—like sunlight streaming into a room which had always been dark before—and other emotions quickly came following in its wake. Joy. Comfort. Belonging. And longing. Oh, yes—there was longing.

But even the longing felt different as he cupped her face gently in the palms of his hands and looked down at her. 'Sorrel?' he said, almost brokenly.

'Malik?' she questioned, and the wonder she'd heard in his voice was now echoed in her own one-word question.

He bent his head so that their lips were almost brushing—their warm breath mingling, their gazes locked—and just in that moment before he kissed her his eyes gleamed with sheer delight, even as his body hardened as never before.

'I love you,' he said again. 'And now I'm going to show you just how much.'

He carried her over to the bed, and for the first time in his life he paid homage to a woman—his mouth deliciously brushing every centimetre of her soft, scented body. Suddenly, an act that he had performed countless times in his life—with predictable and pleasurable outcome—became something completely outside his experience. It felt as if he'd been catapulted into a brand-new dimension—like stepping into a place where colours were brighter and more intense, and everything somehow felt more *real*.

The joining together of their bodies felt so... *profound*...something so close to the spiritual that it almost defied description.

Afterwards, he felt the wetness of his tears mixed with hers. Only now he was discovering that you could cry for all kinds of reasons, and that these were tears of joy—and there was nothing wrong with *that*. Not in the sanctuary of the bedchamber, alone with this re-markable woman with whom he could be the man he could never be with anyone else.

He held her very tight and kissed her, and then bent his mouth to her ear. 'I never want to let you go, Sorrel,' he said fiercely. 'My Queen, my wife, my lover.'

And Sorrel kissed the top of his tangled black head and hugged him back just as tightly, her heart burning with love for him.

EPILOGUE

SORREL sat before the mirror, brushing her hair until it hung heavy and free in a shimmering blonde curtain. She yawned. It had been a long evening—but a successful one. An evening to celebrate the opening of the first part of the new road which stretched from the capital all the way round to the western side of the country. One day it would reach as far as the beautiful mountains which divided Kharastan from the neighbouring country of Maraban. It would bring with it life and tourism—and the new jobs which were so needed in Kharastan—though there were those who opposed it.

'People always oppose progress, Sorrel,' Malik had commented quietly, when she had relayed to him some of the rumblings of discontent she'd heard—mainly from visiting foreigners who wanted to keep the country to themselves, like a glorious undiscovered treasure.

'It's change they don't like,' she had replied thoughtfully.

'Well, that's always a stumbling block,' he agreed with a smile.

As a couple they'd had to cope with some big changes themselves—much more than the average newlyweds. The adjustment to married life. The getting used to living together. Sorrel's being thrown in at the deep end and learning how to be Queen. It was like being on a rollercoaster ride—dizzy and exciting and colourful, though occasionally exhausting.

To escape the exhaustion they had commissioned a leading Kharastani architect to build them a house on the Balsora Sea—a short distance away from where Xavier and Laura had their holiday home, and where Giovanni and Alexa were now looking to buy.

Their new house was full of the most amazing light, and the soothing sound of the nearby waves was better than a trip to any therapist! They were going there tomorrow, for the weekend, and Sorrel couldn't wait.

'Ah! You're still awake!'

Sorrel heard the satisfied voice of her husband, and Malik came to stand behind her, so that she saw his reflection in the mirror—his white robes shimmering—and leaned her head back against him.

'I always wait up for you,' she protested, and then murmured her pleasure as he began to massage her shoulders.

'I know you do, my angel.' He kissed the top of her head and then frowned. 'But I thought you looked tired tonight.'

How perceptive he had become, she thought lovingly. Yes, she *had* been tired, but there was a reason for that. 'A little.' She smiled, savouring the anticipa-

ion of telling him, and turned round, getting to her feet
and putting her arms around his neck, her eyes soft as
she looked at his beloved face. 'Remember you asked
me to find your cufflinks? The ones that Giovanni and
Alexa bought for your birthday last year?'

He lifted her hand and kissed the tips of her
fingers. 'Mmm?'

'Well, I did. I found them in the back of the drawer
in your dressing room.' She hesitated. 'And I found
something else, too.'

'Oh?' He laughed. 'A secret?'

'Sort of.' She reached down to the dressing table and
picked up a little box, held it up. It was a cheap little
thing—covered in shells, with the word *Brighton* written
on it. The kind of holiday souvenir that thousands of
small children bought with their saved-up pocket money.

He looked at it, and then smiled. 'Ah.'

'*I*...bought you this, didn't I?' she affirmed tremblingly.

'Yes, you did, my darling. I think you must have
been about ten.'

'And you kept it—all this time?'

Malik's eyes softened in a way he would once never
have allowed them to—but he had learnt that it was
okay to show his feelings to his wife, his beautiful and
precious Sorrel.

'Yes, I kept it. It was the first real present I ever
received.' He took it from her and turned it over
thoughtfully in his hands, and then he looked at her.
'How appropriate that it should have come from you.'

There was a pause, and her heart pounded. 'I have...
have another present to give you,' she said softly
'Something I think you might like even more.'

Malik's eyes narrowed as he stared at her blushing
cheeks. Already he knew her so well, but every day was
like a voyage of amazing discovery—and this soft, almost
luminous Sorrel was one he hadn't seen before. 'Sorrel?'

Feeling suddenly shy, Sorrel lowered her eyes, and
when she lifted them to meet his she felt the glow of
pride. 'I'm pregnant,' she whispered, meeting his in
credulous look with a nod.

'You're going to have a baby?'

'Yes!' she said, and then started laughing. *Yes!*

They had both hoped for a baby, but it had been one
of those wishes not really wished aloud—some primi
tive superstition making them think that would jinx it
Malik had never had a family of his own, and Sorrel'
had been lost overnight, and this meant more to both of
them than they would ever dare to admit.

'When?'

'I've only just found out...it's early days...but—'

He gave a whoop, and then a kind of proprietoria
growl, as he put the box down and gathered her into his
arms. 'You need to rest?' he demanded.

'No, darling.'

'You need to rest,' he said firmly, and picked her up
and carried her to the low divan beside the windows
which overlooked the palace gardens.

'Yes, darling.' Sorrel smiled, thinking that she would
let him have his way and then later she would give him

er book on pregnancy to read—giving special atten-
ion to the chapter which included notes on 'How Not
o Wrap the Pregnant Woman in Cotton Wool'. But just
or now she would allow him to fuss over her. Because
he could understand why he needed to.

This baby meant more to them than the continuance
of a noble bloodline. In the end they were just the same
as any other couple in love—and this baby was an expression of that love.

He sat at her feet and kissed her fingertips, and the
sunshine illuminated the gleaming little shell-covered
box—the only *real* present Malik had ever received,
until Sorrel had grown up and come back and given him
something more precious than the emeralds which were
mined on the farthest reaches of his kingdom, or even
than tiny shell boxes. The greatest gift of all.

The gift of love.

THE

Balfour
LEGACY

𝓔IGHT SISTERS, 𝓔IGHT SCANDALS

VOLUME 1 – JUNE 2010
Mia's Scandal
by Michelle Reid

VOLUME 2 – JULY 2010
Kat's Pride
by Sharon Kendrick

VOLUME 3 – AUGUST 2010
Emily's Innocence
by India Grey

VOLUME 4 – SEPTEMBER 2010
Sophie's Seduction
by Kim Lawrence

8 VOLUMES IN ALL TO COLLECT!

B290

Fill your summer with four volumes of red-hot Australians!

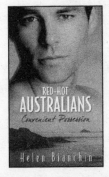

Convenient Possession
by Helen Bianchin

Available 4th June 2010

Billionaires' Marriages
by Emma Darcy

Available 2nd July 2010

Ruthless Seduction
by Miranda Lee

Available 6th August 2010

Outback Engagements
by Margaret Way

**Available 3rd September
2010**

www.millsandboon.co.uk

M&B

0510_10_MB282

A collection of three powerful, intense romances featuring sexy, wealthy Greek heroes

The Greek Millionaires' Seduction
Available 16th April 2010

The Greek Tycoons' Takeover
Available 21st May 2010

The Greeks' Bought Brides
Available 18th June 2010

www.millsandboon.co.uk

1B292

Three volumes of gorgeous, hot-blooded Italian heroes

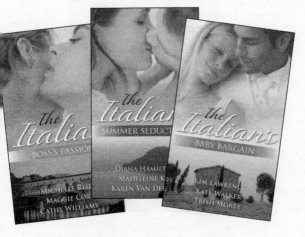

The Italian Boss's Passion
Available 16th July 2010

The Italian's Summer Seduction
Available 20th August 2010

The Italian's Baby Bargain
Available 17th September 2010

COLLECT ALL THREE!

www.millsandboon.co.uk

0610/25/MB288

Escape to exotic lands. . .

. . .with the perfect hero by your side

Three whirlwind weddings in dream destinations

A wedding in China...

An Indian affair...

Alone on a desert island...

Available 4th June 2010

www.millsandboon.co.uk

M&B

B296

Three gorgeous and sexy Mediterranean men

RAYE MORGAN
CAROL GRACE
DONNA ALWARD

MEDITERRANEAN
Men & Marriage

– but are they marriage material?

The Italian's Forgotten Baby
by Raye Morgan

The Sicilian's Bride by Carol Grace

Hired: The Italian's Bride by Donna Alward

Available 2nd July 2010

www.millsandboon.co.uk

M&B

GENERIC_01_10

MILLS & BOON®
MODERN™

...*International affairs, seduction and passion guaranteed*

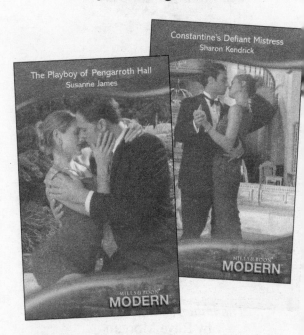

8 brand-new titles each month

4 available on the first Friday of every month and
4 available on the third Friday of every month from
WHSmith, ASDA, Tesco, Eason
and all good bookshops
Also available as eBooks
www.millsandboon.co.uk

MILLS & BOON®

MODERN *Heat*™

Sizzling, stylish, sensual –
the ultimate temptation

2 brand-new titles each month

1 available on the first Friday of every month and
1 available on the third Friday of every month from
WHSmith, ASDA, Tesco, Eason
and all good bookshops
Also available as eBooks
www.millsandboon.co.uk

WEB/M&B/RTL2

Discover Pure Reading Pleasure with

**Visit the Mills & Boon website for all
the latest in romance**

◉ **Buy** all the latest
releases, backlist
and eBooks

◉ **Find out** more
about our authors
and their books

◉ **Join** our community
and chat to authors
and other readers

◉ **Free** online reads
from your favourite
authors

◉ **Win** with our
fantastic online
competitions

◉ **Sign** up for our
free monthly
eNewsletter

◉ **Tell us** what you
think by signing up to
our reader panel

◉ **Rate** and review
books with our star
system

www.millsandboon.co.uk

 Follow us at twitter.com/millsandboonuk

 Become a fan at facebook.com/romancehq